Stay Safe, Buddy

A Story of Humor & Horror during the Korean War

J. Charles Cheek

Lee:
Enjoyed working for you at PP&L

John
9-8-03

PublishAmerica
Baltimore

© 2003 by J. Charles Cheek.
All rights reserved. No part of this book may be reproduced in any form without written permission from the publishers, except by a reviewer who may quote brief passages in a review to be printed in a newspaper or magazine.

First printing

ISBN: 1-59286-631-X
PUBLISHED BY PUBLISHAMERICA BOOK PUBLISHERS
www.publishamerica.com
Baltimore

Printed in the United States of America

*This novel is dedicated to the Army buddies
I served with during the Korean War.*

*It is also dedicated to the love of my life, Bev,
who waited for me at home, then waited on me ever since.
— Thanks, Sweetheart.*

Jackie Sofianos helped me turn the rough draft into a novel. Now she knows that accepting a signed copy as full payment for her editing prowess is perhaps the worst business deal she ever made. But friendship can't be given a price — Thanks, Jackie.

Many thanks also to my loving wife Bev who read the drafts many times and patiently put up with my long daily absences while writing this novel.

PREFACE

The Korean War ended at 10 a.m. on July 28, 1953. In the 37-month long war, total casualties from the 22 countries of the United Nations were over 555,000, including 95,000 deaths. The United States had almost 34,000 killed in action and 103,000 wounded. The U.S. Army alone had almost 28,000 dead and nearly 78,000 wounded. The U.S. Marines had about 4,500 killed and 30,000 wounded. The Chinese had some 900,000 casualties and North Korea had 600,000 casualties.

The last two months of the war were horrifying. The Communist artillery fired over 700,000 rounds at UN positions and the UN artillery fired back 4,700,000 rounds. Around 53,000 UN personnel and upwards of 100,000 Communist troops were wounded, killed or captured during that final 60 days.

There was no clear winner in the Korean War, but the United Nations, led by the United States of America, successfully prevented the Communists from conquering South Korea.

CHAPTER ONE

A strange feeling came over the passenger, Private Lefter, as Corporal Mewman drove the jeep through the dark and empty streets of the war-ravaged city. His eyes searched the outlines of the bombed out and jutted buildings that lined both sides of the narrow street. In a little over two years Seoul had been the scene of major battles and changed hands four times. The devastation was massive. The empty streets looked ghostly. The jeep's heater blew out warm air that contained the faint smell of sewage. The engine and rolling tires made the only noise. The streets were silent. *Spooky*, thought Lefter. Suddenly, a screaming, screeching sound rang out from an alleyway.

"Ohhhhh!" Lefter was startled, his body jerked and he sucked in a large breath. He gripped tightly on the carbine in his lap. A wild domestic cat darted through the beam of the headlights. Mewman laughed and said, "There's one they ain't caught and cooked. Good thing them fucking cats breed so fast or they'd all be in a kimchi barrel by now." Mewman let out a big belly laugh.

Lefter didn't respond. His wide eyes swept the area in the jeep's headlights and he impulsively gripped harder on his M-2 carbine. He tried to blank out the uneasiness welling up inside him. As a new arrival in Korea, he had already heard about the estimated 8,000 to 20,000 guerrillas and bandits operating behind the front lines. In an operation called RATKILLER, an entire division of 30,000 soldiers was searching for them. Their orders said round them up, dead or alive.

Lefter thought these empty streets of Seoul in the middle of the night would be ideal for an ambush. This was the first time that Lefter had felt totally insecure since arriving at ASAK yesterday afternoon. *OK*, he thought, *it's not insecurity. It's beginning to feel more like fear*. Then he was quickly annoyed as he asked himself, *What the hell are we doing out here in the black of night instead of driving north in the daylight?* It didn't make sense to Lefter. Why didn't they just stay overnight at ASAK and leave early the next morning?

ASAK, a.k.a. Army Security Agency Korea, and a.k.a. 501st Reconnaissance Group, was now the occupant of the former campus of Ewha College. Before the Korean War Ewha had been the largest women's college in Asia. Because of the war, the faculty and students abandoned the school, and now it was a fenced and guarded compound of the U.S. Army. Lefter had felt safe there during his short stay, but now he was on his way north toward the combat area. Up ahead, men were fighting for a cause few of them understood, or even cared to understand. Lefter could feel fear welling up in his chest.

"Hey, Lefter, wanna stop at a whore house on the way and check out some fucking pussy? My favorite, Dong's Place, is up ahead." Mewman let out another belly roar before Lefter could answer.

"Huh? Oh no, thanks." Lefter paused then added, "My new wife back home wouldn't think too highly of that. Besides, I don't want to catch any of those cock-rotting diseases they showed in the movies on the troop ship."

"OK, Lefter, you can have a raincheck. But I'm betting you'll change your mind after being in this fucking kimchi bowl for a while. Wet dreams ain't no fucking fun in a mummy bag." Again, the little man let out that big man belly laugh. If Mewman were as big as his laugh, he'd be a center in the NBA. Instead, he could barely see over the steering wheel of the jeep. "You'll change your fucking mind," said Mewman with finality in his voice.

"I doubt it," said Lefter, thinking of an analogy that might impress Mewman's filthy little mind. "The Korean women I've seen since getting here are uglier than the tits and noses on Halloween witches." Lefter chuckled at his own quick wit, then waited for a response from Mewman.

Mewman fell quiet for a few minutes as he tried to visualize Lefter's ugly witch analogy.

Meanwhile, Lefter's mind wandered back two days to the troop ship landing at Yokohama, and then the early evening train ride to a processing center in Tokyo. Painted in four foot high letters across the enormous block-long processing building was "THROUGH THESE PORTALS PASS THE BEST DAMN FIGHTING MEN ON EARTH."

Several hundred soldiers, including Lefter, were lined up on the cold, dark street. Just before midnight, a burly master sergeant addressed them from atop an empty ammo box. "Sorry, men, but replacements are needed right away in Korea so we're gonna process you tonight. In a couple of hours you'll be on your way to Korea."

Then they were herded inside the cavernous building and told to line up by last name. They were being issued their combat gear. Long underwear, parkas and mukluk boots were being handed out. Duffel bags were being traded in for packs already pre-loaded with a GI shovel, first aid packet, mummy bag, one additional pair of wool socks and underwear, field personal hygiene kit, and other items needed in the combat area. Each man was issued an M-1 rifle, cartridge belt and ten clips of ammunition. Other weapons would be issued when they arrived in Korea and received a combat assignment.

Lefter was standing in the line marked 'K – O', army lingo for the first letter in a man's last name. By the numbers, and by the letters, that's the way they trained new soldiers. "Now listen up, Cruts, sound off by the numbers. ONE, TWO, THREE … I CAN'T HEAR YOU, REPEAT — ONE, TWO, THREE. LINE UP IN ALPHABETICAL ORDER; *NOW*, MOVE IT!"

Then there was roll call after assembly each morning: "Allen."
"HERE."
"Abbott."
"YO."
"Brown."
"PRESENT."

Then on the drill field, "FIX BAYONETS—CHARGE!" Orders, orders, and more orders, everywhere and at all times. Don't question it, just DO IT is the mentality instilled in every soldier during boot camp. Never, never, NEVER, question the order of a superior. Just DO IT, and DO IT *NOW*!

How in the hell did I get into this mess? thought Lefter.

Then Lefter's mind jumped back seven months to his induction into the Army. The draft notice actually said, *Greetings: Your friends and neighbors have selected you for service in the Armed Forces of the United States of America.* Up until then he thought that phrase was just part of a Bob Hope joke opening. *Friends and neighbors, my ass*, he thought. *Harry Truman wants me to fight in his Korean War. My friends and neighbors didn't have a damn thing to do with it.* The letter instructed him to report to the Armed Forces Induction Center in Seattle for a pre-induction test and physical examination. "OK, Harry, since you asked so nicely, I'll be there."

A drizzling rain fell from the sky as he reported to the Armed Forces Induction Center in Seattle, Washington. The humid air smelled clean and fresh. *It's raining on my parade*, thought Lefter with a grin. Inside the building Lefter and a couple of hundred of his fellow inductees were assembled in a large room. "When I call your name, come forward and take the next available desk," said an Army Corporal. "Allen, Abbott, Brown..." And the list went on through Lefter to Zarkeski.

They took written tests all morning. Soon after starting, Lefter gazed around the room and notice that many of those taking the written test looked puzzled and just stared forward or looked out the windows. Their apparent lack of interest stimulated Lefter to concentrate intensely in an all-out effort to get a good score on the test. Instinctively, he knew that a good score would likely result in good things to follow. When he finished the test, Lefter was confident that he had done well. It was nearly noon, hunger and thirst gnawed at his stomach. He craved a cold beer, but there would be no alcoholic drinks today. A glass of cold milk and a hamburger would have to suffice for a victory celebration.

Right after lunch, they had another large dose of the military method of handling large groups of men. Dressed only in their underwear and carrying the rest of their clothes in a wire basket, they had physical examinations, military assembly line style. The room air felt chilly and Lefter shivered as he felt goose pimples forming on his exposed skin.

"Turn your head and cough," was the doctor's command while checking for a hernia. "Good, move on to the next check point."

Then moving on to the next check area, Lefter was given another command prior to the check for hemorrhoids, "Bend over and spread your cheeks," said the doctor as he aimed a flashlight beam on Lefter's anus. "Good tight bunghole," said the doctor. "Keep on moving, kid." Lefter was embarrassed and humiliated but followed the orders without comment. He felt vulnerable. Then he smiled as he thought, *What a terrible job, looking at anuses all day. Ugh!*

After the physical examinations were completed, the two hundred of them were herded together back into the large testing room. An Army Sergeant, with a chest full of medals, addressed the group. "The following seven men are to meet me in the hallway right now." He proceeded to call out the names. Lefter was not surprised when his name was called. He sensed a payoff was coming for doing well on the written test. He was right.

"You seven men have done especially well in the morning tests and I want to offer you a special opportunity." Then he gave them a sales pitch about all the advantages of voluntarily joining the Army Security Agency. "You won't be in the infantry," he pitched. "Only about one percent of ASA men get sent to Korea and even that one percent don't have to fight."

The jeep hit a large pothole and jarred Lefter back to the present. *Crap,* he thought. *I'm not only in the one-percent group, I was almost issued combat gear. What a crock, based on that recruiting sergeant's bullshit sales pitch I signed up for a 3-year enlistment instead of taking the 2-year draft.*

"Bastard," Lefter mumbled out loud without thinking.

"Huh?" said Mewman.

"Not you, sorry, I was just thinking out loud about the recruiting sergeant that fed me a line of bullshit about the ASA never having to fight and now here I am headed toward the front line in Korea. I damn near got shipped out with the infantry troops at the processing center in Tokyo. Fortunately, someone from ASA Pacific paged me over the loud speaker, pulled me out of the line, whisked me out the back door and drove me to our headquarters in Tokyo. What a relief that was. Thought I might get assigned to Tokyo, but no such luck. The next day they put me on a plane to K-19, then a deuce-and-a-half to ASAK in Seoul, and here I am headed toward the combat area of the Korean War."

"That's a sad fucking story, Lefter." Mewman belly laughed.

Lefter realized that he had just told Mewman "a whinny-ass story," so he changed the subject. "Where the hell are we anyway?"

"We are coming up on Dong's Place. Last chance to get laid tonight, Lefter. After that we head out through the fucking kimchi fields to Uijongbu."

Lefter didn't respond, so Mewman fell into a disappointed silence. A few minutes later, the jeep was bouncing along a two-lane gravel road known as a Main Supply Route. The road was full of icy potholes and an occasional sign along the edge read, SPEED 35. Some of the potholes were as big as bathtubs and Mewman swerved around most of them but hit enough of them to bounce the jeep violently up and down. Sometimes the jeep started to skid sideways and Mewman would jerk it back on a straight-ahead track. They seemed to be the only ones traveling on the road tonight. It felt very lonely. It was graveyard spooky.

As the jeep bounced and jerked along, Lefter held onto his carbine with one hand and the bottom of the jeep seat with the other hand. "This road is in terrible shape."

Mewman laughed. "You'd be in terrible shape yourself if you had them fucking ammo supply trucks running over your body all day."

Way up ahead, the night sky was filled with flashes of light that seemed to appear at random across the horizon. "What are all those flashes of light up ahead?" asked Lefter.

"Looks like a little shit being thrown around up on the front line tonight."

"What do you mean?" asked Lefter anxiously.

"Artillery firing, mortar firing, machine guns, hand grenades, flares and all the other fucking weapons of war."

Mewman seemed to Lefter to be the sort of fellow whose filthy mouth got him in a lot of trouble. At the time, Lefter didn't know that Mewman had already been busted in rank four times in his twelve-year Army career. Each time he was demoted and shipped out to another outfit. How he got into the ASA was a mystery. ASA was supposed to be a bunch of bright, intelligent people. Many had college degrees. Mewman was, in college talk, an anomaly, but referred to in the Army as an odd ball.

After almost an hour of driving, they still hadn't seen another vehicle. The flashes of light ahead were much brighter now and Lefter could hear the muffled sound of explosions. The jeep lights shined on a sign along the road that said BLACKOUT ZONE AHEAD. Mewman slowed the jeep to a crawl, reached forward and pushed in the main headlight switch on the dashboard then switched on the blackout lights. Only a small sliver of light still shone on the road ahead of each front fender. Now the spooky fearful feeling returned to Lefter's mind and he thought again of the ambush that could be awaiting them along the blackened roadway. *We must be getting close to the combat area*, Lefter thought. He again gripped the carbine tightly and strained to see into the darkness.

The jeep was barely moving so the half-mile or so to the entrance gate at I-Corps took a good six to ten minutes. It felt like an hour to Lefter.

"HALT!" Lefter jumped at the command of one of the gate guards. Mewman stopped the jeep and one of the guards inspected Mewman's trip pass briefly, leaned over and gazed at Lefter. "Is this a newbie?" asked the guard.

"Yeah," replied Mewman, "he's a real fucking tender ass just in from the States."

The guard laughed then said, "Welcome, buddy," then motioned them to drive on. Mewman drove slowly past the dim outline of some tents, Quonset huts and temporary metal buildings. Mewman laughed big again. "Bet you thought we was gonna drive right into the fucking fighting area, didn't ya?" Then he followed with the big belly laugh.

Lefter thought about saying, "That's not fucking funny," but he didn't say anything.

Mewman continued. "Our 303 ASA headquarters is inside I-Corps headquarters here. This is where General TT lives. He's got 50-caliber machine gun nests every 50 yards around the outside of the fence. Fucking gooks ain't gonna try sneaking in here."

"Who the hell is General TT?" said Lefter.

"He's a fucking career man like me. Only difference is he's a West Point gentleman and I'm just a fucking grunt. You'll probably see him tomorrow. His helicopter pad is next to our headquarters Quonset hut. He's a real Tall Turd and carries a long staff. Don't tell him I call him General TT, OK?" Then Mewman cracks up belly laughing at his behind-the-back put down of the I-Corps Commander, a two-star Army General.

"What's the general's real name?" asked Lefter.

"Name is Bruce Blark; his big brother, Mark Blark, is the big fucking mucky-muck Far East Commander with headquarters in Tokyo. TT reports to General something-or-other, the Eight Army Commander; can't remember his fucking name. Eight Army headquarters is in Seoul some fucking place."

"End of the line," said Mewman as he stopped the jeep and turned off the engine. "Let's get this fucking mail sack checked in and hit the rack."

Lefter could barely read the large red sign on the door that said RESTRICTED AREA.

Mewman knocked on the door of the metal building and the CQ on duty opened the door into a lighted room. The name sewn on the fatigue jacket of the CQ said *Crovelli*. He was only a Private First Class, but tonight he was in Charge of Quarters. In other words, he stayed awake and watched the office while everyone else slept.

"Crovelli, this is Lefter," said Mewman looking upward at the six-foot two-inch Crovelli. "Sign for this crap so Lefter and I can go hit the rack."

Crovelli and Lefter shook hands and exchanged greetings. Lefter had to look up two or three inches to meet his eyes. Crovelli inspected the combination lock on the mailbag before signing the release paper that Mewman had handed him, "OK, Mewman, you're clear. Hit the sack."

"Don't say that like a god damn order; I outrank you," said Mewman.

"Screw you," said Crovelli, "I'm the CQ tonight. That means I'm in Charge of Quarters, so don't piss me off, you nasty mouth little midget."

"Fuck you," said Mewman.

Crovelli held up his middle finger toward Mewman. Both men smiled.

Outside, Mewman said, "Grab your fucking duffel bag and follow me. Oh yeah, get your weapon and be sure to pack it everywhere you go around here. Wear the fucking cartridge belt also. They don't give us any fucking ammo to carry in the cartridge belt but they get all twisted out of shape if you don't wear the empty belt. That fifteen round clip in your carbine wouldn't last long." He threw both hands in the air, sighed and said, "Oh well, that's the fucking career Army I love."

"Where the hell is the other ammo if we need it?" asked Lefter, feeling vulnerable.

Mewman pointed westerly, "In the supply tent, ain't that a bunch of fucking shit?" Then the big belly laugh that Lefter was beginning to expect from Mewman.

The action up north had slowed with only an occasional flash of light. However, an occasional muffled explosive sound could be heard faintly in the distance. The flashes and muffled explosions didn't seem to be related which seemed weird to Lefter.

"How far are we from the combat area?" asked Lefter.

"Oh, maybe fifteen miles as the crow flies." Then Mewman said excitedly, "You wanna drive on up to the MLR tonight and shoot a fucking gook?"

Odd, thought Lefter, *Mewman didn't follow that statement with a belly laugh*. Lefter didn't respond because he had a notion that, if encouraged, Mewman might actually drive them off into the night looking for a gook to shoot.

Mewman led the way into a squad tent and used his flashlight beam to point out an empty cot. "That's your mummy bag on that cot, checked it out of supply earlier for you. Sweet dreams," said Mewman as he crossed the tent, undressed to his skivvies and crawled into his mummy bag.

Lefter undressed to his skivvies, crawled into the mummy sleeping bag, then shivered from the surreal feeling that overcome him. It all seemed so weird. It was cold in the tent although two GI stoves showed a sliver of flame through the fire sight hole. *No wonder it's cold*, thought Lefter. *What the hell, it's mid January*. With all the excitement of the ride north in the heated jeep, he had completely forgot about the bitter cold winter weather. The down-filled sleeping bag quickly became warm and cozy. Lefter drifted off to sleep despite the nagging worry about the occasional muffled sounds of explosions in the distance.

CHAPTER TWO

Suddenly, Lefter found himself sitting up in the mummy bag. A siren was howling and a couple of flashlights were shining beams of light around the squad tent. At first he thought it was a dream then he heard Mewman say, "Come on, Lefter, it's time for you to meet old Bed-check Charlie. Rip on some fucking clothes and follow me."

The mummy bag restricted his movement somewhat as Lefter fumbled around finding the zipper. He struggled and finally got out of the mummy bag. He quickly put on his shirt and pants, slipped on his GI boots without any socks, grabbed the winter parka and his carbine and followed Mewman out of the tent and across the compound. He led Lefter into a long trench that was about waist deep and four feet wide. The dirt of the trench was frozen hard. Several other soldiers showed up with flashlights and jumped into the trench.

Overhead and off to the north Lefter could hear what appeared to be a small plane engine penetrating the frigid air. As the sound got closer Lefter said to Mewman, "Sounds like a Piper Cub."

"Don't know," said Mewman, "Never seen old Bed-check Charlie since he only comes at night; after we are in bed of course, the bastard. I hear it's some kind of fucking bi-plane. Old BC goes down around Seoul and throws out a few grenades and mortar shells, then heads back to North Korea. Shit, it's probably a setup by General TT to get us to practice for an air raid without him getting the blame. Sneaky fucking bastards, them West Pointers you know."

That would be real clever tactic, thought Lefter. *Maybe Mewman does have some intelligence swimming around in that sewer mind of his.* After twenty minutes or so, the all clear sounded and everyone went back to bed.

"Hey, Lefter. LEFTER! Get the hell up, it's time to get some fucking chow," said Mewman, shaking the foot of Lefter's cot. Soldiers experienced in living together learn early to wake men by shaking some area outside of striking distance of the sleeping man's fists. Some come awake swinging, especially in combat areas.

Lefter opened his eyes, rolled onto his side, and looked around the tent. It was still dark outside, but a single light bulb was glowing in the middle of the tent. *I'll be damned*, thought Lefter, *they have an electric light in this tent*. Again, he fumbled around getting out of the mummy bag. Looking around the tent as he dressed quickly in the chill, Lefter counted ten cots, five down either side of the tent. All the cots had sleeping bags and personal gear around them except one. Then he noticed a hand-printed sign taped to the end of the empty cot, GUEST.

Mewman noticed Lefter looking at the guest bunk and said, "That one is for a girl from Madam Dong's Place. We share one every now and then." Then the belly laugh. "Just kidding, that bunk is for a stray detachment guy who needs to sleep off a big fucking drunk before going back to the MLR."

Lefter wondered about the acronym MLR but didn't ask and later found out that it meant Main Line of Resistance — the fighting area. After they dressed, Mewman led the way out through the wooden tent door. Nobody else in the squad tent seemed to be waking up and getting dressed, although the light bulb glowed brightly.

"Here, take this spare fucking mess gear," said Mewman.

Outside the tent, even dressed in a parka with the hood up over his fatigue cap, it still felt bitter cold to Lefter. A fine mist of snow was swirling around atop the frozen ground. Dawn was just peaking over the hills to the east and in the hazy light the forms of the ASA Compound began to take shape.

A fifty-gallon drum of heating oil was mounted horizontally on a wooden frame near the end of their squad tent. A small copper tube came out of the drum and disappeared under the tent wall. *Must be the line feeding the GI stoves inside the tent*, thought Lefter. Another squad tent was set up about fifty feet north and a larger tent was adjacent to the other side of the squad tent; a sign on the door said SUPPLY. Two hundred feet or so east across an open dirt area was the headquarters building where the jeep was still parked outside. Two bedroom-size officer tents were beyond the headquarters building.

"Damn, don't this fucking cold, fresh air smell good?" said Mewman as he sucked in a deep breath.

"Yeah, real good," replied Lefter as he took a long breath.

"Wait till the spring thaw, you won't be breathing deep when this whole fucking country starts smelling like a shit house. Speaking of shit houses, that's it over there." Mewman pointed to a small plywood shack about 50 yards north. "I see Shit House Charlie is already on duty over there; he keeps the place orderly. He looks to be about 12 years old but he's thirty-four and has three kids. Fuck, he ain't even tall enough to piss hard against the ground." Then the familiar belly laugh.

It was obvious that Mewman hadn't noticed that, at about five foot two inches, he was only a couple of inches taller than Shit House Charlie. Mewman and the Korean were build similarly, short legs and a husky upper body. Both probably weighed around 125 pounds.

"He's paid a dollar per week and all the shit he can sell to the honey wagon." Mewman let out another belly laugh.

"What's a honey wagon?"

"Fucking shit collection wagon pulled by oxen. They collect it all winter, then fertilize the fucking rice fields with it in the spring. That's why the whole fucking country starts smelling like a shit house."

"Yuck," replied Lefter.

"It's worse than yuck," said Mewman. "It's fucking putrid. You'll see. Come on, let's go over and make old Shit House Charlie happy by taking a morning piss in his fucking shit house." Another belly laugh.

As they walked toward the outhouse Lefter reached in a pocket and pulled out a cigarette. It dawned on him that he hadn't smoked a cigarette since leaving Seoul the night before. *Must have been too damn scared to think about smoking*, he thought. He lit up, took a deep puff and inhaled the smoke into his lungs. Almost immediately, the nicotine worked its wonders and Lefter felt a calming effect begin.

"Does he ever quit smiling?" asked Lefter, thinking that he and Mewman had that in common.

"Naw," said Mewman. "He smiles and bows all day long while standing outside the shit house, whistles when he's cleaning the fucking place. He must be the happiest shithead in Korea." Belly laugh!

Or you, Lefter thought. Mewman's filthy mouth and constant belly laughing were starting to get on Lefter's nerves. Fart-head would be a good nickname for Mewman, meaning someone in training for being a full-blown shithead. "Funny," said Lefter with a broad smile and a laugh.

"What's so damn funny?" said Mewman.

"Nothing, just letting my mind wander," said Lefter.

The walk to the mess hall wound along a frozen pathway through some spindly trees for about 200 yards. Mewman pointed out the sights along the way.

"That's the general's digs on the right. That big hut he's in could house a platoon of 36 men. Understand he's in there with some major who's his orderly and a houseboy. Tough duty, right! Gonna get me one of them fucking Or-der-lees when I make Master Sergeant someday." Belly laugh!

Mewman paused then said, "Oh yeah, me understands old TT entertains one of those white Red Cross cunts at his hut every few nights. Wouldn't you like to hide out in there and watch that fucking action? Wonder what old TT's Army wife would think of that?" Belly laugh! "They's three of them white cunts stationed here at I-Corps headquarters. The Army bakers here stay up all night making donuts so them fucking broads can hand 'em out from a Red Cross truck that goes up every afternoon to the rest areas behind the MLR. They have a doggy driving the truck so all they do is smile and hand out them cold donuts. But I been there and seen them grunts fresh off the MLR fall all over themselves grabbing them donuts. I'll tell ya though, they're a hell of a lot better tasting than them fucking C-rations they get fed up at the front."

Mewman paused, then continued his tirade against the Red Cross. "Them cultivated Red Cross ladies all eat at the Officers' Dining Room and party at the Officers' Club. The only time we see them is once a week on Fridays when they hand out donuts at the mess hall for a mid-morning coffee break. Ain't we a buncha lucky fucking enlisted men?" Belly laugh!

"That's a sad fucking story," said Lefter, surprised that he used the Mewman-like expression.

Inside the mess hall a dozen or so men were already going down the chow line. Koreans in civilian clothes were putting items in their mess container as the soldiers passed by. Today, the main course was biscuits and gravy, known affectionately by servicemen worldwide as SOS. Not very appetizing to think of it that way, but Lefter put it aside in his brain and accepted the hot food that also included some reconstituted eggs and a large helping of applesauce. He filled his canteen cup with coffee from the spigot of a very large field thermos container.

Lefter looked around at the few men already seated and noticed that they had slung their rifle or carbine over the back of their wooden chair. He put his mess gear on the table, sat down, then took the carbine and hung the sling over the back of the chair. He shook pepper and salt onto everything except the applesauce and began to eat. The food didn't look all that good, but it was hot and tasted good.

"Don't know about you, Lefter, but I like this Shit on a Shingle meal. SOS tastes real fucking good to me." Belly laugh.

Lefter ignored the remark. Looking across the table, he noticed for the first time that Mewman wasn't carrying a carbine. He had a 45 pistol hanging from his cartridge belt.

"How do you get away with carrying a pistol instead of a carbine?" said Lefter.

Mewman shrugged his shoulders and said, "I'm carrying a weapon, ain't I? Nobody says jack-shit as long as you carry a weapon and a cartridge belt. Got this forty-five off a Marine Sergeant a couple of months ago. Bought him a couple of beers here at the EM Club and he sold me this fucking forty-five for twenty bucks. Said it belonged to his platoon leader, a smart-ass greenhorn second lieutenant that never made it back from his first time up a hill called Vegas." Lefter quit listening and just nodded occasionally as Mewman kept on talking about something or other.

Lefter finished eating and waited for Mewman to quit talking and finish eating. Finally, Mewman took his last bite and said, "Let's get the fuck out of here," and rose from his chair.

Lefter stood up. The carbine pulled his chair over backwards and both fell to the wooden floor making a very loud noise. By now, there were fifty or so men eating breakfast and they all started laughing and applauding. Lefter's face turned red with embarrassment as he bent and retrieved the carbine from the floor then stood up the chair. Mewman was having another belly laugh. He held out both arms toward Lefter as if to introduce him to the still applauding and laughing men.

"You've just been welcomed as a fucking newbie here," said Mewman as he patted Lefter on the back. "It happens to everyone the first time so don't get all jacked out of shape over it." After washing their mess gear, they walked back up the path to the 303 CRB Compound. Lefter noticed for the first time that the large sign saying RESTRICTED AREA was below a smaller sign stenciled *303 Communication Reconnaissance Battalion.*

Back at the squad tent the other men were rising and starting to get dressed. Mewman introduced Lefter around. "Crovelli, this is Lefter. Crovelli runs the message center and mailroom; he was the CQ last night when we came in. Stay on his good side cause he hands out the fucking magazines when they come in." Then Mewman introduced the others and each man waved acknowledgment, "This is Bob Sichie who runs the motor pool, over there is clerk typist Charles Nissing, next to him is Bill Quigley our mechanic, Bob

Bednell hides out in Operations. And that's it except for our First Sergeant Noitra who's on R&R in Tokyo this week chasing them cute, little, slant-eyed cunts."

Crovelli walked over to Lefter and said, "I see Mewman conned you into going to breakfast with him. He is the only one in here that would rather eat than sleep. Too bad he don't have to eat some of that crap that spews out of his mouth all the time."

Lefter nodded agreement.

"Bullshit," said Mewman. "I just calls 'em as I sees 'em; don't beat around the bush like you fucking college boys."

"Yeah, yeah, yeah," said Crovelli and showed Mewman the middle finger of his right hand.

"Fuck you," said Mewman.

"Screw you," said Crovelli.

Both men smiled.

"Come with me," said Crovelli. "I'll introduce you to Colonel O'Hara over at the Operations Hut. He'll tell you what your assignment is here. Hope you get assigned to help me in the Message Center, been running it all by myself since Hill rotated over a month ago."

Inside the 303 CRB Operations Hut, Crovelli led Lefter to a plywood-walled office adjacent to and just beyond the caged area. Crovelli leaned on the open door and said, "Colonel, this is — what's your name again?"

"Lefter, John Lefter," said Lefter as he saluted the colonel.

"Don't do much saluting around here," said the colonel as he rose from his chair and extended his hand. "We're all pros here so we're pretty loose on the military stuff. Sit down, Lefter, you too Crovelli; let's talk a bit."

With his old-timer style glasses and thin gray hair, Colonel O'Hara seemed real old to Lefter. *What's an old guy like him doing here? He must be going on fifty*, thought Lefter. He was smoking a pipe and the smoke smelled sweet. He looked more like a kind old grandfather than a military commander.

"Tell me about yourself," said the colonel. "What were you doing before getting into the Army?"

"I worked on a survey crew for the Bureau of Reclamation on the Columbia Basin Project."

"Oh yeah," said the colonel, "that's a massive irrigation project to take water from the reservoir behind Grand Coulee Dam, isn't it?"

"That's it," said Lefter. He seemed genuinely interested and asked about Lefter's family, where he went to school, and other personal questions.

Then the colonel turned to business. "Well, John, your personnel file arrived about three weeks ago and we've been expecting you ever since." He picked up a file folder on his desk. "You must have come over by boat."

"Yes, sir," said Lefter. "My orders said FAT and unfortunately the boat was the first available transportation, or at least that's what they told me."

"That happens a lot. Says here you got trained as a Cryptosecurity Specialist; is that right?"

"Yes, sir," said Lefter as he noticed a smile forming across the face of Crovelli.

"Well, Crovelli, your help has finally arrived," said the colonel. "Take him into the Message Center and show him the ropes."

Crovelli stood up and Lefter followed him out of the office and into the adjacent caged area. The caged area had a wide wire door which split in half about waist high. The bottom half had a foot-wide shelf mounted at the waist level. Both halves of the door swung independently and each had a combination lock hanging open in the locking hasp.

"You, me, Colonel O'Hara, and Captain Eten are the only ones allowed in here and we're the only ones who get the combination of that safe," said Crovelli. Pointing at the large, refrigerator-size safe, Crovelli said, "All our classified material gets locked up in there every day after work. We have to keep real good track of that stuff; expect they taught you all that stuff in Crypto School, right?"

"Yeah," said Lefter.

Crovelli dropped his voice to a whisper, "The safe combination is 36R, 38L, 40R. Memorize it, then eat the paper I didn't write it on."

"Yeah sure," responded Lefter to the dry wit of Crovelli.

Crovelli smiled and continued, "We'll have to change the combo in another two or three months when Colonel O'Hara rotates and a new CO comes on board. Go ahead and practice opening it, and while you're in there, take out the log book and sign the page that shows you've been given the combo."

Crovelli explained how the caged area was also used as the mailroom. "The best part of this job is that we get the 303's magazines first, so we get to hand them out. Good trading stuff, know what I mean?"

"Yeah," responded Lefter, although he didn't yet appreciate the trading power of a new magazine.

"Right after lunch each day, one of us drives to the I-Corps Post Office and picks up the mail for the 303 CRB. It's regular mail from home like letters, packages, and magazines. We bring it back to the mailroom, sort it into the appropriate mailbox. Got it?"

"Got it," replied Lefter.

"Every day, a man from each detachment on the MLR drives down, drops off their report for the previous 24 hours, then picks up their mail and returns to the detachment. Got it?"

"Got it," mimicked Lefter.

"That's it. For this, I went to college — ha!"

"Well," said Lefter, "I haven't been to college but I think I can handle the mail duties."

"When the new batch of magazines come in, I'll teach you the distribution rules."

"There are magazine distribution rules?" questioned Lefter. "Where do those come from?"

"Right here," said Crovelli as he pointed to his head.

"Oh," said Lefter. "Seems like everyone in the Army is working a deal, except me."

Crovelli just shrugged, picked up a magazine and started reading.

Soon some other guys came in and disappeared through a door beyond the colonel's office. A sign on the door they were going through said RESTRICTED AREA. Lefter noticed a captain come in and go into an office across from the colonel's door. The sign on the door said CAPTAIN ETEN, EXECUTIVE OFFICER — Army lingo for second in the chain of command.

"What's going on in that back room?" asked Lefter.

"Analysis Group," said Crovelli without looking up from his magazine. "Secret stuff, they try to figure out if all this info we collect on the MLR means anything."

"What information?" said Lefter.

"We have bunkers on the MLR and listen to the front line radio communication of the enemy. It's called LLVI, Low Level Voice Intercept."

"How many of these bunkers do we have?"

"Twenty or so all total, but the 303 is responsible for the seven in I-Corps."

"Do they live in these bunkers?"

"Not really, they have a staging area a few miles behind the line where they sleep and rest up after standing twenty-four hour watches in the bunker."

"Do these guys understand Chinese and Korean?" said Lefter.

"Hell no," said Crovelli. "They just oversee the operation. Native Chinese and Korean guys do all the listening. They were all born in the Far East but they all have college degrees and speak English. Some of them have Master's Degrees from prestigious colleges such as Harvard, Yale, Columbia, and so on."

"Are they in the Army?" said Lefter.

"Nope, most of them are not even U.S. citizens. They're called DACs, meaning Department of the Army Civilians. A couple of weeks ago they predicted an attack on the 1st Marine Division. Nailed it right down to the time and location so the Marines had a couple of days to get ready for it. Consequently, they really creamed the Chinks when they attacked. Guy named Sergeant Campbell figured it out. Understand he may get a Bronze Star for it. White guy, but he does speak Chinese. He's the man in charge of our Detachment #1 in the 1st Marines. As far as I know, he's the only one of our guys that actually speaks and understands Chinese. You're very curious, aren't you? You're wearing me out with questions, Lefter. Save a few for later."

Crovelli picked up a large, loose-leaf notebook and handed it to Lefter. "Our Cryptosecurity rulebook, study it for the rest of day, then eat it." Lefter looked up with mild surprise and saw Crovelli grinning.

"Just kidding, about the eating it that is," said Crovelli. "Wouldn't ask you to do that without mustard and catsup."

Lefter decided he was going to enjoy working with Crovelli and his dry sense of humor.

Lefter quickly settled into the daily routine duties. He had even come to like Mewman, whose only meaningful work seemed to be making out the morning report. Each morning Mewman ran around with his clipboard checking off names, then typed up a report on a form and gave it to the colonel. Then he would plop his dirty boots on his desktop and read magazines — mostly girlie magazines.

Mewman's desk faced the door and he was always the first one to greet anyone entering the Quonset. It was his duty to make sure the visitor had the necessary security clearance to enter the 303 CRB's building. His standard greeting for someone he knew was, "Welcome to my domain, good friend, do you have clearance to enter?" He must have heard that line in a movie.

"Screw you, Mewman!" was a typical answer from a known visitor.

"Fuck you," Mewman always answered.

"Up yours," was the standard reply.

Lefter got used to getting up several times per week at two or three in the morning for a Bed-check Charlie air raid exercise. While standing in the trench Captain Eten taught him how to spot the bi-plane's location by watching for the stars being blocked out as it flew southward. The captain had learned this during an assignment with an anti-aircraft battery during WWII.

Several times each week, after dinner, some of the 303 men go to the EM Club. The club opens at six o'clock and closes at midnight. Beer costs five cents a can. Nearly every night, long before closing time, Mewman gets drunk, runs off at the mouth, and then gets kicked out. He doesn't have a lick of sense when drinking and mouths off to anyone within earshot. The ever-present belly laugh is probably what saves him from getting killed.

Sometimes combat men traveling through stop at the EM Club for a few beers. Their dirty clothes, mud-caked boots, and overall rumpled looks make them easy to recognize. They usually down their first beer in three or four swigs. They keep to themselves, don't say much and nobody, but NOBODY, gives them even a tiny bit of crap, except for Mewman of course.

Tonight, Lefter, Crovelli and Mewman are the only 303 men at the club. "What the hell are them fucking gooks doing in here?" Mewman said loudly, pointing toward six men at the table next to him.

Crovelli grabbed Mewman arm and said, "Shut up, stupid, those aren't gooks, they're Turkish soldiers."

Mewman jerked his arm loose and said, "Hey, I hear them fucking Turks each have a special knife." Then he quickly turned and said to the table of Turks, "Can we look at one of them special knives?"

One of the Turkish soldiers, an officer, answered with an English accent, "I will ask of my men." As he spoke to his men in their native language, they all turned and looked with poker faces at Mewman. One of the soldiers pulled his knife from its sheath and, handle first, offered it to Mewman.

Mewman stared at the knife, then reached out slowly and took the knife. He turned to Lefter and Crovelli with a big smile, "Look at this fancy fucking knife." The knife had a curved blade about eight inches long, and a pearl inlaid handle. The blade was sharpened on both sides. Mewman looked closely at the knife then offered to hand it to Lefter and Crovelli.

"No, no," said Lefter, holding up his hands with palms out.

Crovelli shook his head and said, "Give it back to the man." Mewman slowly and carefully handed it back to the Turkish soldier who immediately stuck the pointed end of the blade through the skin between his thumb and first finger. Blood oozed out of the wound as the soldier returned the knife to its sheath. The Turkish officer quickly said, "We believe that a knife taken from its sheath must draw blood before returning to the sheath; its part of our culture."

Mewman's face turned chalky and his lips clamped up tight, sealing up his filthy mouth. Although he's still drunk, he appeared to have sobered up instantly. He looked at Lefter, then Crovelli, and then at the Turkish soldier's bloody hand. Shaking his head from side to side, and without saying a word, he got up, staggered outside, stumbled back to the squad tent and passed out on top of his mummy bag.

"That was spooky," said Lefter.

"First time I've ever seen Mewman clam up," said Crovelli.

"And he left without being kicked out," said Lefter. "That may be a first also." Then he imitated Mewman's belly laugh.

Crovelli echoed the belly laugh, "Must have scared the crap out of him. Word is that the Turks have never turned in a prisoner during the entire Korean War. They captured many but never turned one in. Our radio intercepts of the Chinese and North Koreans hear them referring to the Turks as Red Devils."

This was all news to Lefter. He had not heard anything about the Turks. "So, what happens to the prisoners the Turks capture?"

"The Turks take prisoners in pairs to an interrogation tent, then hold one outside while the other one is questioned inside the tent. Typically, the first one, knowing the other prisoner can hear him, won't say anything. Then, back outside, they cut his throat in front of the waiting prisoner. As you can imagine, the second prisoner sings like a birdie, then they kill him also."

"Holy crap, that is cruel," said Lefter.

"Yeah, well, it's the way they operate. They love hand to hand combat with their knives and they believe there is no greater honor than to die on the field of battle."

"Holy crap!" said Lefter again.

"A Battalion of the Red Devils is attached to the right flank of 1st Marine Division."

"So the Turks are the toughest fighters here?" asked Lefter. "These Turks at the table don't look to be any bigger than Mewman."

"Yeah, they're all little guys. I didn't say they are the toughest, but they're damn sure the meanest."

"Any other mean-ass outfits?" asked Lefter.

"You're wearing me out sucking information out of me. Maybe if I had another beer it would revive me."

"Yeah, hang on," said Lefter as he went for another two beers.

"There, that's better," said Crovelli as he took a swig of the beer. "OK, the other group of fighters the Chinese and North Koreans are deathly afraid of is a battalion of giant black men. Each man is over six and a half feet tall with coal black skin. The gooks call them Black Devils. A regiment of them is attached to the British Commonwealth Division."

"So what do the gooks do about the Red Devils and the Black Devils?" asked Lefter.

"Whenever a probe occurs on the MLR, the gooks try to avoid the areas occupied by the Red Devils and the Black Devils.

"How do they avoid them?" asked Lefter.

"You're wearing me out, Lefter. Save some questions for later. Drink up and let's get the hell out of here before Mewman comes back and gets us both killed."

They finished their beer, then walked silently back to their sleeping tent and went to bed.

CHAPTER THREE

Sergeant Noitra decided that the men of 303 should have their own private clubhouse. So with the help of Sichie, Quigley and Bednell, they scrounged materials and built a day room inside an unused squad tent. They built a bar out of plywood complete with a large, double-wall wooden cooler. The top-opening hinged door, the floor, and the walls were filled with sawdust insulation obtained from the I-Corps carpenter shop. Everyone in the 303 headquarters donated to a fund that Noitra used to pay a Korean in Uijonjbu to build a stuffed couch and four stuffed chairs. He found several 60-watt wall lamps, mounted them on the false plywood walls and wired them into the I-Corps electrical system. Sergeant Noitra even built a special padded box for Smoky, his German Shepherd dog and the 303 mascot.

Although beer was only five cents per can at the EM Club, it cost ten cents in the Day Room Tent. Soft drinks, at the same price, were also kept on ice for those few that didn't drink alcohol. Noitra used the profits to buy hard liquor to trade to the mess hall sergeant for ice and snacks.

The men used the Day Room Tent for writing letters home and bull sessions over a cold beer or soft drink. Colonel O'Hara had authorized building the Day Room with the understanding that the men would behave themselves, and they did. Rarely did anyone get drunk here; except for Mewman of course. Mewman got drunk nearly every night, either in the Day Room or the EM Club. While drinking in the Day Room, everyone made sure that Mewman didn't do anything worse than shoot off his filthy mouth.

Noitra scheduled a going away party for April 21 in honor of Colonel O'Hara, who was leaving the next day for home. April 21 was also the first day of Operation Little Switch, the exchange of sick and wounded prisoners. The exchange was agreed to during the truce talks at Panmunjom on April 11.

Lefter and Mewman, along with many others, stood along the MSR in the village of Uijongbu and waved to the sick and wounded being transported south by a caravan of ambulances and open trucks. It was a moving and joyous occasion. After the last vehicle passed, Lefter pulled out his olive drab handkerchief, wiped his eyes then blew his nose.

"Are you crying, Lefter?" asked Mewman seriously.

"Shut up, you little prick," responded Lefter. "I just got some dirt in my eyes from all this damn dust."

"Fuck you," said Mewman.

"Screw you," responded Lefter.

"Up yours," said Mewman.

Lefter held up his middle finger to Mewman. "Come on, let's get back to work."

"Don't order me the fuck around, I outrank you," said Mewman defiantly.

Lefter climbed in the driver's seat of the jeep then said, "You coming?"

"Fuck you," said Mewman with his hands on his hips.

Lefter put the jeep in gear and started moving slowly away. Mewman ran and jumped into the passenger seat.

"I ought to have your fucking ass court-martialed," said Mewman.

"Yeah, yeah, yeah," taunted Lefter. "Why don't you go tell Grandpa O'Hara on me."

"Fuck you," mumbled Mewman.

"Huh?" said Lefter just as they approached the I-Corps guard station.

Mewman raised his voice, "I said FUCK YOU."

Just as Lefter braked to a stop at the guard station, he leaned over and said softly to Mewman, "I can't hear you."

Mewman yelled out, "FUCK YOU!"

"Oh yeah!" said the guard. "Are you looking to get run off to the brig, soldier?"

"I didn't mean you," said Mewman. He pointed at Lefter, "I meant this fucker. Damn you, Lefter. You set me up, didn't you?"

Lefter just smiled, shrugged his shoulders and raised his hands with palms up.

"Get the hell out of here," said the guard as he waved them on through the gate.

Colonel O'Hara's replacement, Major John Soss, had been staying at the I-Corps Transient Officer Quarters for three weeks. He was eager to become the Commanding Officer of the 303 CRB. Major Soss had already been introduced around the 303 headquarters and the enlisted men were not looking forward to having him as their CO. He was one of those little guys, built like

Mewman and Shit House Charlie. He had a giant ego. He walked with a pompous strut. He made it clear that, as a West Point graduate, he was Superior with a capital S. He fiddled with his West Point ring as if to draw attention to it. The men were already referring to him as Shit-Don't-Stink Soss. Later they would think up many more colorful names for him. When Sergeant Noitra invited him to the party, Soss just said, "I don't think so," then turned and strutted away.

Captain Eten was also invited to the party. He had obtained a battlefield commission during WWII after his company CO was killed in action during the Normandy invasion. He treated all the enlisted men with respect and dignity. He took a personal interest in each man and they respected him highly. Often he would ignore the military's rule preventing officers from 'fraternizing' with enlisted men and drink a beer or two with them.

The honored guest, Colonel O'Hara, brought a bottle of Scotch to the party although he had specified, with the wink of one eye, that no hard liquor was to be stored and served in the Day Room. Officers could buy hard liquor at their Officers' Club but no hard liquor was served at the Enlisted Men's Club.

Enlisted men were not supposed to have access to hard liquor anywhere in Korea. However, the ASA enlisted men were an exception. ASA did not report to Eight Army. They reported to their own command in Tokyo. Known as ASAPAC, a.k.a. ASA Pacific, the Tokyo command reported directly to its headquarters in Washington, DC, rather than to the Far East Commander, General Mark Blark.

Enlisted men of the 303 ordered a supply of hard liquor every two weeks and it was shipped directly from ASA in Tokyo to ASA in Seoul, thus avoiding the normal supply route. The cost was $10 per case for any brand. Guys in the detachments sold it to the troops for $10 per bottle, or $90 per case, or used it for trade. Every two weeks a deuce-and-a-half truck was sent to Seoul to pick up a load of hard liquor that had been ordered by enlisted men of 303. Each Detachment would have a ¾ ton truck waiting at the 303 headquarters. Within 15 minutes after the return of the deuce-and-a-half, each detachment's booze order was transferred to their ¾ ton truck, then they headed back to their detachment where the next transfer put most of the hard liquor in the hands of the fighting men at the front line positions.

Noitra had traded two bottles of whiskey to the I-Corps mess hall sergeant for enough canned ham, cheese and crackers to feed a platoon.

It was a great party. There were many toasts of good wishes for Colonel

STAY SAFE, BUDDY

O'Hara. Colonel O'Hara offered a toast to the UN prisoners being released that day and those being released in the future. "If we're lucky this will lead to an armistice for ending the war," said the colonel.

With all the toasting and celebrating, nearly everyone got a buzz on. Smoky, the German Shepherd mascot, got drunk. He had a bowl placed next to his box, which the men kept full of beer. Poor Smoky, he was a worse drinker than Mewman and soon went outside the tent and started throwing up. The next day Smoky had a worse hangover than Mewman and walked around very slowly with his head hanging low and a sad look in his eyes. His tail didn't wag much that day. In just a few months, Smoky had become an alcoholic dog. He would be waiting at the Day Room door each evening for his nightly beer. For meals, the men also brought him scraps from the mess hall.

Everyone from the 303 headquarters turned out the next morning after the party to say goodbye to Colonel O'Hara. Additionally, each detachment sent at least one representative. The colonel was well liked by both officers and enlisted men. Even General Blark made a surprise visit to wish him well and to personally formalize the change of command. The colonel was on the verge of tears as he waved and saluted from the passenger seat of the departing jeep.

Mewman was driving the colonel to a busy military airfield located just a few miles south of Seoul. From there, the colonel would fly by military transport to Tokyo where he would board a commercial airliner bound for his hometown of Seattle, Washington. Fort Lewis, located about some 25 miles south of Seattle, would be his discharge point. The colonel had entered active duty there, having been called up from US Military Reserve status.

Lefter was on CQ duty that night. He had a slight headache from drinking several beers at the colonel's going away party. He was getting worried about Mewman. It was three in the morning and he wasn't back yet. Finally, after another twenty minutes, Lefter decided to do something. He was thinking about it and imagining an accident, or worse yet, Mewman killed or captured by the North Korean gorillas. Potentially deadly situations were to be reported immediately to the unit commander. Also, Mewman was carrying classified material. Lefter decided to report it.

Reluctantly, Lefter knocked on the wooden door of Major Soss' tent. "Major, this is Lefter. I'm on CQ duty, sorry to wake you, sir, but I think it's very important."

After a minute or so the door opened and Major Soss said, "What is it, soldier?"

Lefter hesitated then said, "Mewman's not back with the courier run from Seoul and it's after 3 a.m."

The major responded immediately and sounded pleased to have the crisis occur. "Call the CQ at ASAK and see if he's still there, and if he's not, find out from the gate guard when he checked out. Get back to me right away with their answers."

As Lefter trotted back to the headquarters building and unlocked the door, his mood changed from worry to aggravation. Hopefully, that idiot didn't get drunk and stop at Madam Dong's Place. Lefter liked Mewman, in spite of his filthy mouth, and was concerned about his safety.

"ASAK CQ, Corporal Staid speaking."

"This is Private Lefter, CQ at the 303. Is our courier, Corporal Mewman still there?"

"Don't know him. I'll transfer you to the gate guard and he can check the log."

The guard checked the logbook and reported that Mewman had left at 0035 and he was alone. Lefter's mood swung back to worried as he thought about the recent warnings regarding possible guerrilla action by North Korean Infiltrators.

Usually Charles Nissing rode shotgun every night on the courier run. Charles was studying the Korean language. While waiting for the mail to be sorted and sacked, Charles would practice the language by talking with the Koreans that worked at ASAK. However, Colonel O'Hara had acted as shotgun for the ride south, and Nissing, who was returning from R&R, was to ride shotgun for the trip back north.

Lefter still had the phone to his ear when the door opened and in walked Mewman. "Never mind," said Lefter to the ASAK guard, "he just walked through the door."

Lefter looked down at his watch then glared at Mewman, "You asshole, it's three-thirty. I just reported you to Major Soss as missing; where the hell have you been?"

Mewman threw up both hands and said, "You fucking snitch, I ran out of gas and had to wait for someone to come by and help."

Lefter wasn't buying it. "Bullshit, that courier jeep is filled with gas every afternoon by one of the motor pool guys; standard procedure."

Mewman hesitated then in a low voice said, "OK, OK, I got horny watching those porno flicks at ASAK and stopped off at Madam Dong's Place; big fucking deal."

"You dumb shit, Mewman, you know that courier run carries classified material, you could get your ass court-martialed. Where the hell is Nissing? He was supposed to be riding shotgun."

Just as Mewman said, "His plane was delayed," the door opened behind Mewman and Major Soss walked in. Mewman turned, faced the major and wisely kept his mouth shut and saluted. Lefter didn't salute but the major didn't notice.

"He just came in thirty seconds ago," said Lefter. "Everything is OK now."

"NO, it is not OK now!" The major stared Mewman in the eyes. "Where is the mailbag, Corporal?"

Pointing toward the door Mewman said, "In the jeep, sir. I'll get it pronto." He whirled around and hustled out the door. Lefter and the major followed him. There was no mailbag in the jeep.

Back inside the major ordered, "Lefter, call the MP station and tell them to send a patrol up here immediately," then he turned to Mewman and said, "Corporal Mewman, you are under arrest, do not leave the building." Again, Mewman wisely kept his mouth shut. A few minutes later two military policemen arrived and knocked on the door.

The major glared at Mewman and said to him, "Open the door, stupid."

Mewman cracked. "Open the fucking door yourself, you asshole."

Oh crap, thought Lefter, *he just jumped from the frying pan into the fire.*

The major opened the door, jammed his finger into Mewman's chest and said, "I want this man arrested for dereliction of duty and insulting an officer."

Mewman was pushed off balance and took a step backward. "Ouch!" said Mewman as he pointed his hand close to the major's face. "You all are witnesses, this fucking major just struck me."

Major Soss knocked Mewman's hand aside and said, "Get this idiot out of here."

One MP handcuffed Mewman then they led him outside and hauled him away in their jeep.

CHAPTER FOUR

As he passed the artillery captain's tent, Mighty Joe's pace slowed to a crawl. He cocked his ears and eavesdropped on the ass chewing being received by one of his fellow searchlight operators.

"You were careless to turn it up too high and burn out the expensive filament," said the captain. "If it happens again, I will have no alternative but to ship you out of my outfit."

"Yes, sir," said the operator. "I just got flustered with all that incoming artillery last night."

Amen to that, thought Mighty Joe. *It scared the hell out of me too*.

"It flusters us all," said the captain, "but we are the best damn searchlight battery in the Army and we can't make expensive mistakes like that."

"Yes, sir. I know we're the best and we have all the awards to prove it. I won't let it happen again."

"OK, but keep in mind that if you screw up again, I'll ship you out.

Listen to all that esprit de corps shit, thought Mighty Joe. *I was just happy to have survived my first night of duty in this outfit*.

Now Mighty Joe wished he hadn't partied so much, flunked out of law school and got drafted into the Army. True, his first Army assignment was a soft job in the adjutant's office at Fort Benning, Georgia, and he would have never been sent to Korea had he not lost an argument regarding an Army regulation.

He had shown the colonel in charge of the adjutant's office a regulation that seemed to bar the Army from shipping anyone overseas if they had less that a year left in the two years of mandatory service. The colonel did not agree. An argument resulted and the colonel proved his point by shipping Mighty Joe off to Korea although he had just eleven months left in his hitch.

Moving on to his cot in the sleeping tent, Mighty Joe thought about his current situation and devised a deceitful plan for the following night. Then he slept well.

The next night Mighty Joe was shaking with fear as the Chinese started targeting the searchlights again. However, the rounds stopped hitting near him soon after he burned out the filament on his light. *Ah ha*, thought Mighty Joe proudly, *the bastards think they blew up my searchlight*. He felt relatively safe for the rest of the night.

Although he pretended to be hurt, Mighty Joe was delighted to receive the early morning tongue lashing from the captain. He couldn't sleep much that day. He was in a hurry to go out the next night and burn out another filament.

The next night Mighty Joe "accidentally" burned out another filament. The captain was aghast and furious. He never expected such ineptness and suspected it might have something to do with Mighty Joe's legal background as a pre-law college student and a clerk in the AG Office at Fort Benning.

"You word merchants are all clumsy and careless. Damn legal-minded people are all thumbs." He never suspected for a moment that Mighty Joe might have deliberately burned out the filaments.

Mighty Joe looked at his boots and said with all the sincerity he could muster, "I'm really sorry, Captain, but I just can't seem to get the hang of operating the light. Guess I don't have the aptitude and skills necessary to be a good searchlight operator."

The captain had to carry through on his threat and arranged for Mighty Joe to be transferred to the adjutant's office of I-Corps headquarters as a legal clerk. He hated the weekly reports he had to make out and file back at I-Corps headquarters so he, in searchlight parlance, "hit two targets with one beam." He sent Mighty Joe to I-Corps headquarters to act as his personal clerk, and prepare all the required reports and have them ready each week for his approval signature. Mighty Joe would get his instructions by telephone or handwritten notes delivered by courier.

All went well and Mighty Joe had the weekly reports neatly typed and ready for signature when the captain made his weekly trip to I-Corps headquarters. "You're doing a good job," said the captain. "I only have to spend a few minutes signing all this paperwork crap."

At the end of Mighty Joe's first month at I-Corps headquarters the captain came down to sign his weekly and month end reports. One of the documents was a list of soldiers in the Searchlight Battery that were being recommended for promotion to Private First-Class. Mighty Joe typed his own name in the lower third of the list. Sure enough, the captain never noticed and signed the document. In a couple of weeks Mighty Joe received notice of his promotion to PFC.

The following month Mighty Joe buried his name in the list of men being promoted to Corporal. All went well, the captain never noticed the additional name, and in a couple of weeks Mighty Joe again received notice of his promotion to Corporal.

The third month, he was afraid to type his name on the list of men being promoted to Sergeant because it was only three men and the captain would surely notice the addition of Mighty Joe's name. However, the master schemer had a plan.

"How are the wife and kids doing?" asked Mighty Joe

"Great," said the captain. "I'm looking forward to being back in the States with them in a couple of months."

Shaking his head from side to side, Mighty Joe said, "Too bad about Corporal Mavin, he was getting close to rotating wasn't he?"

"Yeah, like me, he only had a couple of months to go before returning to the States. I really hate writing those death notice letters to the loved ones back home."

"Don't blame you," said Mighty Joe. "It bothered me just typing up that letter for you. It's really weird how so many guys get hit when their combat tour is almost over."

"Yeah," said the captain. "I'm getting the short-timer jitters myself."

"Don't blame you, I hate typing them for you," said Mighty Joe again. "However, I think you are mistaken about the amount of time you have left before rotating home."

"What?"

"You're due to rotate at the end of the month. Look, here's the latest report I just typed up regarding total rotation points. I show you as having thirty-six points as of the end of this month."

"Really!" commented the captain. "Thirty-six is all the points anyone needs to rotate."

"Yeah, and if there's a mistake in there, the monkey's on my back, not yours."

"Not if I sign it," said the captain.

"I already signed it and sent it out. The rules don't say you have to sign that report personally. Did I do wrong?"

"No, no, that's OK. Are the other reports ready for my signature?"

"You bet, here they are." Mighty Joe pointed to the signature spot on several reports. The captain started signing each report. When he came to the promotion report, he hesitated, looked up at Might Joe, smiled and then signed the document.

Mighty Joe's "mistake" that added two months to the written record of the captain's total time served in Korea was not discovered. The captain left for the States a few days later and Mighty Joe received notice of his promotion to Sergeant. Score another one for clever and cunning Mighty Joe. Mighty Joe never had stripes of any of the ranks sewn onto his uniforms, so nobody knew of the promotions from Private to Sergeant over the three months duration. Of course, he received the pay assigned to the rank.

When Mighty Joe first met the ASA beer drinkers at the EM Club, he quickly became the nightly table leader. He presided over a drinking game he called Mumblejon. Each game began with Mighty Joe acting as the Priest. The Priest would make up some silly story that had some sort of "who done it" mystery. The Priest gave each person a name. One person at the table must always be named Mumblejon. All the people in the game are collectively known as The Court. Mighty Joe gave the following example.

The Priest says, *There is a rumor going around I-Corps headquarters that someone sneaked into General TT's place, hid out in a closet, and watched Madam Dong instructing the naked Red Cross ladies in the art of entertaining a West Point Gentleman. Now some say the sneaky person who hid out there was, either Mumblejon, Red Cap, White Cap, Blue Cap, Hub Cap, Stocking Cap, or even the Priest.* The Priest points at each person being named Red Cap, White Cap, etc. Then, after each person has received a name, the Priest repeats the naming process. If he fails to remember a name, or even hesitates too long before recalling a person's name, any person at the table may ask the Court for a vote; Guilty — two thumbs down, not guilty — two thumbs up.

After the Priest has twice named each person without error or guilty vote of the Court, he then states, *I say that sneaky bastard that hid out in General TT's place was White Cap.* The person named White Cap must answer without hesitation with only two words, *Who, me?* The Priest answers: *Yeah, you!* White Cap replies: *You lie!* Priest says: *Who then?* White Cap then names another person, say *Mumblejon.* The person named Mumblejon then says: *Who, me?* White Cap says: *Yeah, you!* Mumblejon answers: *You lie!* White Cap says: *Who then?* The banter continues until someone screws up and answers wrong, or hesitates too long and gets challenged, then the Court votes.

The vote is usually a unanimous "thumbs down." A thumbs-down vote means the person must chugalug from a can of beer while the Court sings, *Here's to Charlie* (real name of the person), *he's true blue, he's a drunkard through and through, so drink chugalug, drink chugalug, drink chugalug.* As long as the Court continues to sing the penalized person must keep drinking until his can is empty. If a person quits drinking before his can of beer is empty or before the Court quits singing he may be declared DEAD by another vote of the Court.

If declared DEAD, nobody is allowed to speak to that person for the rest of the evening. They must act as if that person is dead and gone. Right after a person is declared dead, each person at the table may offer some final words as a toast to the deceased. For example, Red Cap might say while raising his can of beer, *Here's to Charlie. He was a damn good typist but a sissy beer drinker. We will miss his typing.* After the laughter and frivolity stop, the game continues and the dead person is completely ignored.

Lefter and the others would soon learn that the game always began with Mighty Joe as Priest and he remained Priest until declared DEAD by the Court. Mighty Joe was so good at playing the Mumblejon game that he was never declared DEAD. Furthermore, it was wise to not annoy him because he would then attack that person in the game and they would surely end up DEAD.

"OK, let's play a round," instructed Mighty Joe. "By the way, I got the first round of beer so one of you guys pony up to the bar and bring back a round before we begin."

CHAPTER FIVE

The day after Colonel O'Hara left, Major Soss displayed the tyrannical authority he would use as the Commanding Officer. He ordered Sergeant Noitra to assemble all the men, at 0800 hours, in a military formation just outside the headquarters building. Then the major deliberately kept them waiting in formation for fifteen minutes before he appeared. Finally, he strode pompously out the door.

Sergeant Noitra called out, "Ten HUT!" saluted the major and said, "The men are assembled as you ordered, sir."

Major Soss flipped a return salute then promptly ignored Sergeant Noitra. He scanned the group of men standing at attention in front of him and said with a scowl on his face, "You men are sloppy and undisciplined. That is going to change. Do you hear me?" Nobody responded so the major yelled, "DO YOU HEAR ME?"

"Yes, sir. We hear you," answered Sergeant Noitra.

"Shut up, Sergeant. I'm not talking to you!" He pointed to the formation of men and growled, "I am talking to this shabby bunch of pretend-to-be soldiers." He pointed in a sweeping motion to the group and said, "Military kindergarten lesson number one; when I ask you a question, you answer YES SIR or NO SIR. You men are going to shape up. Shape up and shape up NOW." Then he raised both arms as if directing an orchestra and said, "DO YOU HEAR ME?"

The men mumbled, "Yes, sir."

"LOUDER!" commanded the major.

"YES, SIR," yelled the men in unison.

"That's better. Now that you understand your role, I will continue." He raised his arms and orchestrated again, "Would you like to hear what I have to say?"

Lefter was tempted to yell, "HELL NO!" but instead he responded in unison with the other men, "YES, SIR."

The major stood up extra straight, extended his chest and barked, "Last night, Corporal Mewman was on courier run to Seoul and left the mailbag in a whorehouse. He is currently under arrest and will be court-martialed for his stupid action and dereliction of duty."

Lefter could feel his face flushing. *You son-of-a-bitch*, he thought. *We are still standing at attention. He doesn't even have the courtesy of letting us stand at ease while he runs off at the mouth.* He could hardly restrain himself from spewing out what Mewman might have been thinking had he been there with them. *Correction*, he thought, *Mewman would have done more than just think it. Mewman would have said it, FUCK YOU, ASSHOLE SOSS.* Lefter thought briefly about mumbling the words out loud but didn't succumb. *Don't do something stupid*, he kept thinking. *Don't do something stupid. Don't do something stupid.*

The major took a piece of paper from his pocket, unfolded it and started reading loudly:

"Beginning immediately, you will salute all officers you meet anywhere and address them as SIR.

You will address each other by rank and last name.

You will dress in clean and pressed uniforms at all times.

Your living area will be inspected at least once each week.

There will be no smoking or drinking inside the tents, the headquarters building or any vehicles.

There will be no liquor kept in this compound anywhere and that includes the sleeping tents and the Day Room Tent."

Captain Eten had quietly come out the door behind Major Soss and listened in silence.

Major Soss made a dramatic pause as he strode back and forth in front of the men. Then he continued, "Men, we are in a war zone and I would advise you to obtain and read the Army regulations referred to as the Articles of War. I expect every man to abide strictly by those regulations. I will have a copy placed in the mailroom that you can check out and study."

Captain Eten shook his head, shrugged and went back into the building. Major Soss didn't know that the captain had heard him reading off what the enlisted men would later refer to by the acronym, ASS Rules — Asshole Soss' Shitty Rules.

The major made another long dramatic pause as his eyes swept across the men's faces, threw his chest out and barked, "Now get back to work. DISMISSED!"

Back in the cage room, Crovelli and Lefter took turns whispering almost voiceless words to each other while pointing toward the major's office.

"Asshole."

"Son-of-a-bitch."

"Fucker."

"Cocksucker."

"Bastard."

Suddenly the tension burst and they both started laughing. They held their mouths, bent over in their chairs and laughed until tears formed. Each time they would raise up and look at each other one of them would mouth a dirty name and the gut-wrenching laughter would start again. This went on for a good ten minutes and seemed to have no stopping point.

Now the mouthed words and pointing were no longer necessary. All they had to do is look at each other and the uncontrollable laughter would erupt. They became concerned the major would hear them through the thin wall to his office.

Finally, Crovelli had the presence of mind to leave the building for a few minutes. However, when he came back they both started laughing immediately upon seeing each other.

Then Lefter stood up and left the building. Outside smoking a cigarette, he was still having outbursts of laughter. He was laughing out loud when the door opened and out strode Major Soss. *Oh crap*, thought Lefter as he noticed that the major had on his combat helmet, *where the hell did I put my helmet and liner?* That asshole is probably going to ask.

The major stopped and glared at Lefter. Suddenly, Lefter remembered the ASS salute rule and saluted. Returning the salute, the major said, "What is so humorous, soldier?"

"Nothing, sir," said Lefter. "I was just thinking of a joke I heard recently."

"Oh really," said Major Soss. "Perhaps you should tell it to me and see if I agree that it is humorous."

"No, sir. I wouldn't be comfortable telling this joke to an officer and gentleman such as you, SIR."

"All right, soldier, as you were." And he swaggered off toward his tent.

Mewman's court-martial proceeding was held on April 25 and lasted just three hours. Major Soss provided testimony for the prosecution. In cross examination, Mewman's Army lawyer tried to divert the military court's attention to Major Soss and his caustic personality. If he could get the court's sympathy, they might not punish Mewman on the charge of disrespecting an officer.

"Major Soss, did you call Corporal Mewman an idiot?"

"I don't recall exactly," said the major.

"The MP report says they heard someone say, 'Open the door, stupid.' Now you, Corporal Mewman and Private Lefter were the only ones there. One of you said, 'Open the door, stupid.'"

"OK, OK," said the major. "I may have said that."

"You stuck your hand hard into his chest and pushed him didn't you, Major?"

"I just meant to tap him lightly on the chest," said the major.

"Well, it wasn't a light tap, Major. The MP report says you, and I quote, *appeared angry as you pushed hard on Corporal Mewman's chest causing him to lose balance and take one step back,* end quote. Were you angry, Major?"

"Maybe a little bit."

"This is rather irrelevant to the central issue that is dereliction of duty," said the bird colonel who headed the three-man court. "Lieutenant, under the circumstance I doubt very much that this court will find the corporal guilty of disrespecting the major. In fact, it might be wise for the prosecution to drop that charge and concentrate on the central issue. Now get on with your defense to the serious charge of dereliction of duty, the facts of which the defense has already stipulated to. Major, you may step down. Let's hear your summary argument, Lieutenant."

"Yes, sir," said the lieutenant. "The responsibility of each man who makes this courier run is to guard and protect the mailbag. Corporal Mewman did just that. He did not abandon his duty to guard and protect the mailbag. He took it with him into Madam Dong's Place. At most, he is guilty of forgetfulness in that, upon leaving, he forgot to put the mailbag back into the jeep. However, the mailbag was still guarded and protected from falling into the hands of anyone who would use it to harm our cause here in Korea. Aside from what Madam Dong does to survive in this war-ravaged country, she is a patriot of South Korea. She flies the South Korean flag and the flag of the United States side by side on her building. Before the Korean War, she was the head mistress of the largest women's college in Asia, the Ewha College. That college campus is now the headquarters of the Army Security Agency's operations in Korea. The military police will testify that Madam Dong had the locked mailbag inside a locked footlocker. She fully expected Corporal

Mewman to return that night and retrieve the mailbag. Meanwhile, the information inside that locked mailbag was doubly secure because it was under double lock. Corporal Mewman would have returned immediately and retrieved the mailbag had the major not lost his temper and turned the situation into a personal confrontation."

The prosecution didn't put up much of a counter argument. After all, no actual harm had occurred as a result of Mewman's handling of the mailbag. With the begrudging permission of Major Soss, the disrespecting an officer charge was withdrawn.

On the charge of dereliction of duty, Mewman was busted to Private E-1, the lowest rank of enlisted man, and fined seventy-five percent of his pay for the next six months. The fact that no classified material was lost probably saved Mewman from getting a dishonorable discharge and being sentenced to a couple of years at Leavenworth, the Army prison in Kansas. The lieutenant's impassioned argument may have helped.

Additionally, Mewman's military records file was "red tagged" with a restriction that prevented him from ever again handling classified material. Never again could Mewman make out, or even see, a morning report because those reports were classified CONFIDENTIAL. Mewman was transferred to a combat company in the 25th Infantry Division. Now his earlier words spoken to Lefter rang crystal clear, "I'm just a fucking grunt!" Now he really was JUST A FUCKING GRUNT.

The day after Mewman's court-martial Sergeant Noitra was again ordered to assemble the enlisted men at 0800 hours for an address by the major.

Again, the major made them wait fifteen minutes after being assembled, but this time the speech was short — still caustic but at least short.

"Men, we are leaving at 1500 hours today on an overnight maneuver. Have your gear packed and ready to leave immediately after dinner. I have already instructed Sergeant Noitra on the details of the maneuver. That is all. Carry on, Sergeant Noitra."

As the major strutted away, Sergeant Noitra said, "At ease, men.

"Now here's the basic plan. Supply Sergeant Thomas, Private Quigley and Private Lefter will stay here and guard the compound while we are away. The rest of us are going on the major's little camping trip. I will post this list on the bulletin board of the items you are to bring along. Have it all packed up and meet me at the motor pool at 1430 hours."

Later, Lefter went to Sergeant Thomas and said, "What the hell is going on here?"

"The only thing I know is that we are to walk guard from dusk till dawn while they are away. Meet me at my supply tent at 1500 hours and we will develop a plan for walking guard during the night."

"This is absolutely stupid," said Lefter. "We are inside I-Corps headquarters which is fenced, and 50-caliber machine gun nests are located every 50 yards or so outside the fence. Who the hell are we guarding against, our own troops?"

"Ease up, Lefter," said the career sergeant. "It's just one of those shit details that happens every now and then. It happens."

"Yeah, I guess so," said Lefter.

Lefter and Quigley met Sergeant Thomas in front of the supply tent. Major Soss was just leading his convoy of 303 CRB vehicles out of the compound. He was wearing a winter parka and his steel helmet. He, of course, had the top and windshield down on his jeep. It was a humorous sight.

As they watched the procession leave, Lefter said to Quigley and Thomas, "Just look at that, a bunch of candy-ass administrative folks being lead to the battleground by their fearless leader." They saluted as the major drove by. Then, as each remaining vehicle drove by, Lefter yelled out, "Have fun at camp." Quigley yelled, "You all come back and see us now, you hear." In reply, they got lots of one-finger waves accompanied by a variety of filthy expressions.

"Where the hell are they going anyway?" Lefter asked Thomas.

"Who gives a shit," said Thomas. "OK, here's the plan. You and Quigley will take two-hour shifts walking guard around the compound. I will stay in the supply tent and man the phone."

Lefter threw up his hands up and said, "That figures, you sit on your ass all night in a heated tent and nap while we take turns walking guard in the cold and black of night."

Quigley added, "Yeah, there may not be any gooks but the spooks will be out in the black of night."

"Rank has its privilege. Quit pissing and moaning and let's get started. Which one of you wants the first shift?"

"I'll take it," said Quigley.

"OK, Quigley, get out there and start walking. It's not dark yet but you can practice while it is still light out." Then the supply sergeant laughed heartily and slapped Lefter on the back. "Lefter, come on inside, we'll play some cards."

"OK, Sarg, might as well make the best of it. As you say, Shit Happens."

Lefter thought for a moment then added, "I have a brilliant idea, give me a marking pen and a piece of typing paper."

"What the hell for?"

"You'll see."

Lefter made a sign and hung it above the supply sergeant's desk. The sign read: SHIT HAPPENS! "That's hilarious, Lefter. I like it," said Sergeant Thomas. "It should explain to you troops why I don't have any socks to hand out."

"Yeah, yeah, I know," replied Lefter. "You keep giving me underwear every time I ask for socks. Here, I'll show you all the repairs the mama sans have done to my socks."

"Don't you pull off them boots and expose your stinking feet. I'll take your word for it."

"Well, when in the hell are you going to get some socks?"

"Don't know. How about some underwear? I got plenty of them." Then he followed with a hearty laugh and pointed to the sign. "You said it Lefter, Shit Happens."

"Crap, Sergeant, I already have a couple of dozen pairs of underwear. I have only two pair of socks and they are both rags."

"Sad, sad story, Lefter." Again, Sergeant Thomas pointed to the sign and said, "SHIT HAPPENS!"

This time Lefter broke down and laughed with him, "OK, I see the humor in it."

"Good, let's play cards," replied Sergeant Thomas.

As they played gin, Lefter would occasionally look at his sign and chuckle. It made him smile every time he looked at it. Later, he and Thomas started using the expression in conversations with other enlisted men and it spread like wildfire among the enlisted men across all of Korea, then worked its way to military men everywhere. It became a morale booster and Lefter was proud of getting it started. One of the drivers of the 444th Transportation Corps named his ammo truck *SHIT HAPPENS!*

When Lefter began the midnight to 0200 shift, it was bone-chilling cold and a light breeze was blowing from the north. He could hear the muffled sound of artillery firing along the fighting line. It was foggy so he couldn't see the flashes in the distance. A faint smell of human feces was riding in on the fog. The Korean farmers had begun to spread the human wastes in the rice fields. It was very still around the compound and he found himself getting spooked. He removed his hands from the warm parka pockets, took the carbine that was slung from his shoulder, slid a round into the chamber, and began carrying the carbine at the ready position. *Should I take off the safety?* he thought. *Yes, no, yes, no.* He kept changing his mind and sliding the safety back and forth from on to off and back on again.

He continued walking around the compound with the carbine in the ready position. Near the end of his shift, he heard a noise over by the motor pool and walked slowly and quietly over there. With pulse pounding in his chest, he sneaked up to an open maintenance bay and peeked in. Something came running toward him in the dark. "Shit!" Impulsively, he threw the carbine to his shoulder and pulled the trigger. Nothing happened. The safety was on. A cat came running by him. "Holy crap," he said out loud. His pulse was pounding. *Sure glad that safety was on*, he thought. *That would have been embarrassing.*

Then he heard another noise coming from the maintenance bay. Taking off the safety lock, he peeked into the bay again with the carbine up and ready to fire. There stood the desperado. "Smoky, get the hell out here; I damn near shot you." He reached down and petted the dog. "Here, boy. Come on, Smoky. You can walk guard with me for the rest of this shift."

Quigley took over the guard duty at 2 a.m. but Smoky wouldn't stay with him. He followed Lefter to the warmth of the supply tent and curled up by the stove. Lefter didn't tell Quigley and Thomas about the encounters in the maintenance bay. They would have teased him and told the story to everyone when they returned from the maneuvers. Worse yet, if he had shot Smoky, the guys would have hung him by the testicles in the maintenance bay.

"Hey, Sarg, look at this. The Stars & Stripes Newspaper has an article on Operation Little Switch. It says the Communist side repatriated 684 UN sick and wounded troops of which 149 were US troops. The UN Command returned 1,030 Chinese and 5,194 Koreans, together with 446 civilians."

"Only 149 were US troops," said Thomas. "Those bastards gotta be holding more than that. They must have captured more than 149 wounded US troops. Pisses me off."

"Me too," said Lefter, "but I don't want to think about it. Deal the cards."

At 4 a.m., when Lefter again started walking guard, Smoky still wouldn't leave the warmth of the supply tent. "Smart dog," said Sergeant Thomas. Lefter reluctantly agreed.

It was getting daylight as Lefter finished the four to six a.m. guard shift. Sergeant Thomas told him to go to the mess hall and pick up coffee and donuts for them. "Just tell the mess hall sergeant that I sent you."

STAY SAFE, BUDDY

"Are you trading him socks for this?" teased Lefter.

"Hell no," retorted the wary supply sergeant. "But I may trade your new socks off if they ever come in, and right now it looks like they will be a long time coming."

"Hey, I was just kidding, Sarg. Don't declare me DEAD."

"Don't beg, Lefter, just go get the coffee and donuts."

Lefter took a large thermos, went to the mess hall and came back with a full thermos and a dozen fresh donuts. The three of them were sitting in the supply tent drinking coffee and eating donuts when the tent door flew open.

Major Soss, red faced and angry, had kicked open the door and came storming in. He yelled, "I LEFT ORDERS FOR YOU MEN TO WALK GUARD WHILE WE WERE AWAY AND NOBODY IS ON DUTY. ALL OF YOU DUNCES REPORT TO MY OFFICE IMMEDIATELY." Then he stomped out. He was so mad and out of control that he forgot to chew them out for not saluting him.

"What the hell is going on?" said Lefter.

"Don't know, but we are sure as hell going to find out," said Thomas. "Come on, let's get over to his office."

The major called each one of them separately into his office, handed them a book titled *Uniform Code of Military Justice*, pointed to words he had underlined and ordered them to read it aloud:

> *Any sentinel or look-out who is found drunk or sleeping upon his post, or leaves it before he is regularly relieved, shall be punished, if the offense is committed in time of war, by death or such other punishment as a court-martial may direct, if the offense is committed at any other time, by such punishment other than death as court-martial may direct.*

After each of them read the rule, he said, "You are going to face a court-martial for abandoning your post in time of war. Meanwhile you are restricted to quarters. Dismissed!"

Sergeant Thomas went to Captain Eten and told him of the major's actions. "Captain, you reminded me just before leaving on the maneuver that a guard was to walk the compound from *dusk until dawn*." Captain Eten agreed that he had said just that because the major had ordered him to remind the men of that specific duty assignment. He said he had a handwritten note from the major saying, "remind the men that they are to walk guard from dusk till dawn." He assured the sergeant that they would not be court-martialed.

The major got very upset when Captain Eten showed him the handwritten note. He was especially upset when Captain Eten told him he would submit the note in evidence for the men's defense if court-martial proceedings were started.

Red faced, enraged and putting a heavy emphasis on the "I" word, he barked, "Captain, *I* order you to tell the men that *I* have decided to be compassionate and just restrict them to quarters for one week of punishment."

When the captain passed the major's decision to the three men, he offered some fatherly advice. "Since the major will probably be just waiting to nail you with something, you may want to ask for a transfer to a detachment. That way, you'll be out of sight and out of his mind."

Lefter and Quigley readily agreed and the captain said, "You don't need to do anything, I'll take care of it." Later that day he informed them that their transfers had been approved. They left the next day, Quigley to the Commonwealth Detachment and Lefter to the detachment in the 1st Marine Division.

They never knew that the captain went back to the major and threatened to reveal several embarrassing incidents in which the major participated that were unbecoming for an officer and gentleman. "I don't give a shit what you try and do to me," said the captain. "I will see that your ass goes down the tube with me. I'll tell them about all your stupid and silly decisions, including going on an overnight camping trip like a Boy Scout."

Major Soss was fuming mad but kept his temper from erupting.

Captain Eten continued, "Now here is what I want from you, I want Lefter and Quigley transferred to a detachment immediately. You won't screw around with Sergeant Thomas because even you know that a supply sergeant is one of the most influential positions in the US Army. Screw around with him and you're dead meat for sure."

"That's blackmail," blurted out the red-faced major.

"Call it what you will, Major, but take it or leave it."

"OK, and good riddance. Brief Lefter and Quigley and get them out of my sight tomorrow."

Early the next morning Captain Eten called Lefter and Quigley separately into his office and briefed them on their overall duties in a detachment. He spent what seemed to Lefter to be an inordinate amount of time describing in detail the various tortures the gooks would use on the Department of Army Civilians if they were captured. "Then, after the gooks are satisfied that they've got all the information possible, the DACs will be killed anyway, or left to die from their torture wounds." He said several times that "they would be better off dead." It appeared to Lefter that he was supposed to kill the DACs if the enemy overran the bunker. At least it was clear to him that the captain believed they would be better off if they didn't get taken alive. Lefter hoped to God that he never had to make that decision. The briefing ended with Captain Eten saying, "Your detachment commander will brief you on the details of your duties there. Good luck."

CHAPTER SIX

"You ready to go?" asked Sergeant Campbell.

"More than ready," replied Lefter. "I'm raring to leave the 303 headquarters area."

Sergeant Campbell was in charge of Detachment #1, the ASA Detachment in the 1st Marine Division. Campbell was a six-foot, square jawed, and husky fellow with the raw look of a fighting man. The look was authentic. He had been a Marine during World War II, then was voluntarily transferred to the Army Security Agency during the Korean War. Lefter remembered Crovelli saying that Sergeant Campbell spoke Chinese.

Ordinarily, a lieutenant would be the CO of a detachment but the Commanding General of the 1st Marines insisted that the detachment assigned to his division be commanded by a high-ranking career enlisted man with combat experience. General Stoney, like Captain Eten, had progressed up the ranks beginning as an enlisted man in WW II. Now he was a two-star General and highly respected by his officers and enlisted men. He made it clear that "no greenhorn Army lieutenant is to be assigned to any area of my command." His superior, General Bruce Blark, had assured him that his wishes would be respected.

On the drive north to Detachment #1, Lefter filled in Sergeant Campbell on all of the recent actions of Major Soss including the threatened court-martial of Quigley, Sergeant Thomas and himself.

"Be patient," said Campbell. "I've been in the military long enough to know that assholes don't get away with it forever. I understand that the major is not respected by his fellow officers either."

"Man, I hope I am around to see it when he gets his mean, arrogant face stuffed up his own cocky ass," said Lefter.

"Me too," said Campbell as he chuckled at Lefter's wit.

The rest of the ride to the base camp of Detachment #1 was filled with small talk about back home and learning of each other's background. Master

Sergeant Campbell was a career man who enlisted in 1942 and spent WW II in the South Pacific Command. Lefter later found out that General Stoney, who also spend WW II in the South Pacific, came by occasionally to visit with Campbell at the ASA bunker or at the base camp. The general spent at least several days each week visiting his front line troops.

"I hear you speak Chinese, how did you learn it?" asked Lefter.

"Spent a year at the ASA Language School in Monterey, California."

Lefter was impressed. "Wow, you learned the language in just one year of schooling?"

"Had to, we lived at the school and weren't allowed to speak English there, so I dealt with the Chinese language twenty-four hours a day, seven days per week."

"You never talked English for a year?"

"Oh yes, we could use English when we were on leave and outside the school compound but we usually didn't unless someone spoke to us in English."

"Why not?"

"It was fun seeing and hearing the reaction of folks as they heard us white guys talking to each other in Chinese."

The drive north started out stinky but now the odor of human feces was fading. The land up near the MLR was not being farmed so the air didn't have the putrid smell that was inescapable elsewhere in Korea. The air smelled so good that Lefter hardly noticed the dust off the road. It was a beautiful sunny day.

They passed through an artillery emplacement a couple of miles before reaching the Detachment #1 base camp. Campbell pointed out a BLACKOUT AREA sign along the road just before reaching the artillery emplacement "If you're coming through here at night be sure to use the blackout lights only," said Campbell. "MPs check this area regularly."

The detachment base camp was composed of just two squad tents. The Army enlisted men used one tent and the other housed the DACs. Other detachments had a separate smaller tent for their CO, but Sergeant Campbell stayed with the enlisted men in his command.

As they drove up, Lefter noticed that another jeep, a three-quarter ton truck and a deuce-and-a-half truck were parked in front of the tents. "How many ASA guys are assigned here?" he asked.

"Four of us counting you," said Campbell. "You are replacing Jackenson who just rotated two days ago. You must have met him."

Lefter nodded yes.

"You and I are the only ones here today. Hillman is on R&R and Jolcomb is on duty in the bunker now." He pointed to the most easterly tent and said, "We have six DACs that stay in that squad tent over there."

He turned off the jeep engine and they sat and talked. He went on to explain that each 24-hour shift in the bunker involved one ASA man and two DACs, one Chinese and the other Korean. When not in the bunker the ASA guys maintained the base camp and vehicles. The DACs kept up their own tent but do nothing else except bunker duty. Each DAC is paid six hundred dollars for the first month then ten more for each month thereafter. So for the tenth month they get seven hundred. It keeps going up ten bucks per month for as long as they are willing to stay. They are also furnished food and other supplies. "They save up a lot of money," said Campbell.

"Crap," said Lefter. "I am getting paid just a hundred and fifteen bucks per month and that includes the eighty-five dollar marriage allowance that is sent to my wife."

"Well, you just got a good raise, buddy," said Campbell. "Up here you get an additional fifty dollars per month for combat pay. Also, you get four points per month toward rotation back to the States."

"That's great," said Lefter. "It takes a total of thirty-six points to rotate, right?"

"Yeah, you got two points per month for the duty at I-Corps headquarters. The poor guys in Japan only get one point per month, so it is a three-year assignment there or until their enlistment is up, whichever comes first."

"That's a crock of crap," said Lefter.

"I'll take you up the hill tomorrow for your first 24-hour shift. I'll stay up there with you for a couple of hours to brief you on bunker duties. Now, let's get some chores done around here then go over to our friendly Marine battalion next door for dinner."

Lefter spent the rest of the day on regular chores such as checking and fueling the vehicles, hauling water, and tidying up the sleeping tent and outside area. He found time to write a long letter home and tell his wife of his good fortune of being transferred to an area that allowed twice as many points towards rotation home. He also mentioned the combat pay but assured her that he would be safe in a bunker that could not be destroyed by artillery fire of the enemy. After finishing the letter he sealed it in an envelope, addressed it and wrote "free" in the upper right hand corner. He put the letter in a box on the table marked COURIER.

After he had completed all the chores that Sergeant Campbell had assigned him, he decided to rest for a while. He crossed the rock hard dirt floor of the tent, flopped down on his cot, fell asleep immediately and started having pleasant dreams. He woke up with Campbell tugging on his foot as he said, "Come on, Lefter, it's time for dinner. Grab your mess gear."

Crap, thought Lefter. *That reminds me of Mewman waking me up the first morning at the 303 headquarters.* He smiled as he rose from the cot. He was thinking of his embarrassment when his carbine crashed to the floor in the mess hall there. He resolved to not make that rookie mistake again.

They walked the 200 yards to the mess tent of the Marine Battalion Headquarters. Campbell explained, "This is the First Battalion of the Seventh Regiment of the First Marine Division. Men from the MLR come to the 1st Bat 7th every couple of weeks for a shower, clean clothes and a couple of hot meals."

Inside the mess tent, they went through a short food line. Dinner was corned beef and cabbage, corn, peas and crackers. It smelled good. Everything except the crackers got piled in together. At the end of the line, each man was given a can of beer. The can was opened just before it was handed to them.

"Nice service," said Lefter. "They even open the beer for us."

Campbell laughed. "Orders from General Stoney. He's been there and knows they would save them up for a big drunk if they weren't opened."

Lefter noticed that a few guys were giving their opened can of beer to someone else. "Apparently, some of these guys don't drink because they are giving away their beer," said Lefter.

"Don't bet on it," said Campbell. "They may be selling it or trading it for a shot of hard liquor later on. Very few just give it away. Booze is too hard to come by up here."

Two young Marines sat down at the table with Campbell and Lefter. They had obviously just arrived as replacements because their uniforms were tidy and clean. They wore their fatigue caps at a cocky angle. Each had a single medal pinned on their shirt, a sharpshooter badge. Demonstrating skill on the rifle range is the only medal that could be earned in boot camp. These two guys had to be right out of boot camp from the States.

"Hey, look here, Freddie," said one of the young Marines in an arrogant manner. "We have a couple of fucking doggies here."

"Knock it off," said a Marine Sergeant who was already sitting at the table. "These guys are on our side." Then he ordered, "Take off your cap when you're eating inside." He turned to Campbell and Lefter and said,

"They'll lose that smart-ass attitude after they've been up the hill a time or two." Then he added as he turned and glared at the young Marines. "That is assuming they make it back down the hill."

The two young Marines took off their caps, looked at one another, then laughed and began eating their food.

Again, the Marine Sergeant glared at the two newbies. "When you get out there in gooneyland and ol' Joe Chink gets on your ass, you won't be laughing."

A loudspeaker outside somewhere blared out, "ATTENTION: ALL MARINES. ATTENTION: ALL MARINES. GET YOUR COMBAT GEAR AND FALL OUT IN THE YARD IN 15 MINUTES. THIS INCLUDES ALL SUPPORT PERSONNEL, COOKS, CLERKS, TRUCK DRIVERS, EVERYONE. I REPEAT. GET YOUR COMBAT GEAR AND FALL OUT IN THE YARD IN 15 MINUTES. THIS INCLUDES ALL SUPPORT PERSONNEL."

The Marine Sergeant stood up and said to Lefter and Campbell, "Looks like it's time to go duel with 'ol Joe Chink, see ya." Then he turned to the two young Marines and said, "Come on, hot shots, it's time for your first lesson in MLR humility, compliments of the gooks."

The young Marines shoveled their mouths full of food, washed it down with beer, then stood up and followed the Marine Sergeant outside.

"What's going on?" said Lefter.

"Getting ready to fend off a big attack I suspect. We've been getting some data that indicates the gooks may be mobilizing for an attack on the 1st Marines. I stuck out my neck and predicted a possible attack tonight. Appears that General Stoney is getting ready with all he's got, including the support personnel." Campbell didn't tell Lefter that General Stoney had called him on the land-line early in the morning and discussed the situation with him.

That night, around ten o'clock, the shelling began and Lefter was awakened from a pleasant sleep. Inside the base-camp tent, Lefter could see flashes of light through the tent canvas. It reminded him of a massive lightening storm. Loud explosions occurred in rapid succession. Boom, boom-boom, boom-boom-boom! Far off he could hear what sounded like machine guns firing. The tent seemed to shake occasionally. He started getting concerned.

That must be my imagination, thought Lefter, because he could not hear anything landing nearby. Lefter wondered when it would end. *They must be shooting hundreds and hundreds of rounds of artillery.*

Lefter could hear a whirring, whispering, whooshing sounds penetrating the air above the tent. "Outgoing," said Campbell from his cot. "Our artillery is hitting back." The artillery rounds going overhead sounded a little like a steam train chugging up a hill.

The air was filled with the sound of outgoing artillery rounds. Again he could hear the boom, boom, boom of shells landing in the distance but the explosions seemed much farther away. Some time later the outgoing quit flying overhead and muffled thuds could be heard along with a lot more machine gun fire.

"Mortars and machine guns," said Campbell. "The troops on the ground are getting into the fight big time now."

Lefter was now wide eyed and excited. He thought of the two young Marines at the mess tent. They were probably right in the middle of this battle. Now he sure was glad he joined the ASA rather that getting drafted into the infantry. He also thought of Mewman and wondered what he was doing right now. Then it dawned on him that tomorrow night he would be in a bunker on the MLR. What would that be like? Would another battle like the one tonight occur? He shivered.

"Lefter! Wake up! It's time to go relieve Jolcomb."

Lefter opened his eyes and looked around. At first, he didn't know where he was. He briefly thought it was his dad waking him to get ready for work on the survey crew. Then it rapidly came back to his mind. *Holy crap*, he thought, *I actually fell asleep during that battle last night.*

As he was getting dressed, Lefter said to Campbell, "When did the big battle end?"

"Don't know," said Campbell. "I fell asleep. The mess tent over at 1st Bat 7th won't be open so we'll grab a C-ration up at the bunker."

Campbell drove the ¾ ton truck to the staging site on the back of the hill. A Chinese and Korean DAC were riding in the back of the truck. In the passenger seat Lefter was wide-eyed and looking for shell craters. He didn't see any obvious new shell craters until they got near the MLR. It was quiet and they didn't pass any other vehicles on the road. The land there was potmarked with the jeep-size holes that had been blasted in the ground by artillery rounds. The only shell craters he had seen before were on the infiltration practice range during boot camp.

Lefter was keenly alert as he carried a five gallon jerry-can of water up the hill along with his pack containing C-Rations and a couple of packs of cigarettes. Campbell carried up a gallon container of lamp kerosene. The

DACs each had a pack with C-rations and personal gear.

After a few rest stops along the way, they finally reached the bunker. Lefter was sweating profusely. A trench angled at 45 degrees to the east-west direction led to a wooden bunker door. Lefter would later find out that most bunkers had only a blanket or pieces of canvas covering the door. Nailed to the door was a horizontal wood plank with the stenciled words RESTRICTED AREA. Campbell knocked on the bunker door and said, "Jolcomb, it's Campbell."

Jolcomb opened the bunker door and said with a North Carolina accent, "You missed one hell of a show up here last night. Whoee! It was downright fright'en, I was sweatin' like a dog pooping a peach seed."

"I know," said Campbell. "We could hear it down at the base camp. Jolcomb, this is Lefter, you know him from the 303 Mail Room."

"Yeah, right," said Jolcomb. "Welcome to the MLR, Lefter. Hear you had a run in with Asshole Soss."

"Yeah, but not sure which is more dangerous, Asshole Soss or this bunker duty. Sounded like you really caught hell last night."

"You'll get used to it," said Jolcomb. "Thank God we don't have to go out there in No-Man's-Land with them Marines. Well, I'm outta' here, see ya."

Jolcomb and the two DACs going off duty left the bunker, hurried down the back of the hill and returned to the base camp.

The Chinese DAC sat down facing away from the bunker door and put on a set of headsets. He reached out and began slowly turning a knob on the large radio in front of him. The Korean DAC lay down on a cot nearby.

Campbell explained that each DAC worked a two-hour shift before being relieved. "If the Chinese DAC comes across a conversation in Chinese he will take it down verbatim in Chinese then translate it to English immediately after the conversation is finished. Then you and the DACs must decide if it seems important enough to report right away over the land-line or wait and bring it back at the end of your shift. You must make the final decision and personally phone in the report. In any event, we report all the conversations in a written report going back each day by courier to the 303 CRB."

"What happens if the Chinese guy picks up a communication in Korean?"

"Then the Korean puts on the headsets and does the same routine. They will wake up the other if he's sleeping at the time."

"Makes sense," said Lefter.

The bunker was larger than Lefter had imagined. It was about the size of

STAY SAFE, BUDDY

a medium-size bedroom, maybe 12 feet by 12 feet. A kerosene lantern hanging from the ceiling dimly lighted the area. A kerosene stove about the size of a gallon bucket was near the back wall of sandbags. It had a small chimney pipe that disappeared into the wooden ceiling. The dirt floor was as hard as concrete. A makeshift wood table and four ammo box seats occupied the center of the bunker. The bunker contained two sleeping cots. One cot was near the radios and the other cot was at the far end of the bunker.

"That's your cot over there," said Campbell as he pointed to the one on the far end. "Technically, we are supposed to stay awake for the 24-hour shift but if you just can't, set that alarm clock over there for 15 or 20 minutes and take a nap. The DACs will wake you if they start picking up anything while you're asleep."

"How sturdy is this bunker?" asked Lefter.

"As you can see the ceiling right above you is solid twelve by twelve timbers. Above the timbers are six layers of sandbags, then lots of canvas for waterproofing covered by about a foot of dirt. I don't think the gooks have anything that can penetrate it."

Campbell stayed around for a couple of hours chatting with Lefter then said, "I'll be on the courier run today but Jolcomb will answer the land-line if anything important happens. See you tomorrow morning."

The bunker door opened shortly after Campbell left and he again appeared. "Forgot to tell you something important," he said. "Don't go loitering around outside the bunker. We've only had one ASA guy killed so far and it was his own fault. Over in Ten Corps, he was trying to repair the land-line outside the bunker when the artillery round came in and got him with shell fragments. So, don't play hero, Lefter. Stay in the bunker during a shelling."

"Right, Sarg," replied Lefter.

"There is a piss tube about 20 feet back of the bunker. The crapper is a 100 feet or so down the back slope. OK, I'm gone for sure this time. Stay safe, buddy."

"OK," said Lefter. He had never heard the expression, "stay safe, buddy," but it sounded sincere and comforting.

Lefter felt alone in the bunker although the two DACs were there. *What the hell am I going to do for 24 hours?* he thought. *I'll be bored to death by the end of my shift.*

The day passed slowly. The DACs didn't pick up anything of consequence. They changed shifts every two hours and the one going off duty would lie down on the cot and read or go to sleep. Lefter found a deck of worn cards and started playing solitaire. Other than playing solitaire and eating a couple of cans of the C-rations, he hadn't done anything all day except sneak out behind the bunker once to take a piss into the piss tube. He smoked more cigarettes than usual. *Crap*, he thought again, *This is boring, boring, boring!*

The front left side of the bunker had a small area enclosed with canvas. He investigated and found a narrow viewing slit looking north. He would later learn that it was called a firing aperture. He surmised correctly that this enclosed area must be to protect against the bunker light being seen glowing through the slit at night. Lefter stood looking out toward No-Man's-Land and could not see movement of any kind. Some fifty yards out from the base of the hill, he could see a bunker on the south side of three lines of coiled barbed wire. The three lines of barbed wire continued as far west and east as he could see. He wondered why the bunker was down there. He thought about the greenhorn Marines in the mess tent and wondered if they had survived the previous night's battle. What would be their attitude now? Lefter went back to the table and smoked another cigarette.

Later he made another visit to the viewing slit and noticed that it was getting dark outside. Off to the far left he could see what appeared to be balloons flying high in the air. *What could that be?* Then he remembered having heard that barrage balloons and a vertical searchlight beam marked the no-fire zone at the Panmunjom peace talk site.

He went out back of the bunker to urinate before it got completely dark outside. He didn't want to be out there after dark. The sky was cloudy but there was a beautiful sunset in the westerly sky. *Hard to believe there is a war up here*, he thought when looking at a beautiful sunset. Now, it was peaceful and serene. The air smelled fresh. *Boring*, he thought, *but peaceful and quiet.*

Back inside the bunker, he went back to playing solitaire and occasionally glancing at the back of the DAC at the radio or the other DAC lying on the cot.

Somewhere around one in the morning, he was standing at the narrow slit for the umpteenth time. The night was without light except for the searchlight shining straight up in the northwest sky over Panmunjon. He was looking out into the blackness yawning and thinking, *boring, boring, boring.*

Suddenly, he jumped back startled as something exploded down the hill in front of him. It was a very loud thud. Almost instantly, the night was filled with flashes and the thud, thud, thud of incoming mortar rounds. This time he didn't hear the chugging sound of outgoing artillery. Instead, he heard the whooshing sound of outgoing mortar rounds going overhead. He had no way of knowing that the gooks had taken part of the Nevada Complex during the previous night's battle and were now using it as a staging area for attacking the MLR. The Nevada Complex was made up of three strategic outposts — hills known as Reno, Carson and Vegas that lay between the Marine MLR and the enemy MLR. Whoever held these hills could use them as a staging area to attack the other's main forces on their MLR.

Hundreds of explosions and their accompanying flashes were occurring all across his field of view. Sometimes the bunker shook and dirt fell from the ceiling. Ten or fifteen minutes later the incoming explosions stopped and he saw several phosphorous parachute flares dangling in the sky. The eerie light from the flares lit up the area like broad daylight as they floated very slowly downward. Other flares went off in the sky. Lefter thought he heard the sound of whistles and bugles. Then machine gun fire erupted from seemingly everywhere along the Marine MLR and Lefter could see hundreds of phosphorous tracer bullets flying horizontally as they burned their way northward. The tracers flew in the overlapping firing pattern that he had learned in boot camp. That pattern was used to make sure no area was left uncovered from the deadly 50-caliber bullets. He knew from basic training that only every fifth round was a tracer bullet. *Surely*, he thought, *the Chinese can't possibly get through that intense machine gun fire, not to mention the hundreds of outgoing mortar rounds exploding almost constantly.*

More phosphorous flares went off lighting up the area just beyond the bottom of the hill. Tracer bullets started flying northward from a position near the bottom of the hill. Lefter wondered if that firing was coming from the Marine bunker he had seen just back of the barbwire lines. He thought he could see figures moving out beyond the barbwire lines. Then the flash of an explosion at the point of origin of the machine gun fire and the tracers quit leaving that area. *What the hell was that? Did the gooks just blow up the Marine machine gun nest down there by the barbwire entanglements?*

He went back to the table and sat down. He took a cigarette from his fatigue pocket and lit it with a shaking hand. *Holy crap, holy crap*, he thought, *it's sure as hell not boring now*. Then, in spite of his fear, Lefter's sense of humor kicked into his thoughts. *What I need right now is a searchlight on the top of this bunker with the beam pointed straight up.* He laughed nervously, took long drags off the cigarette then lit another from the still-glowing butt. "Stupid sense of humor," he said out loud.

He noticed that the Chinese DAC was taking notes. "What's going on?"

Lefter said to the Korean DAC who was sitting up on his bunk.

"Chinese battle talk," said the Korean DAC.

"What are they saying?" said Lefter.

"He will translate soon," said the Korean DAC.

The Korean leaned over and tapped the Chinese DAC on the shoulder. The Chinese DAC turned around and said loudly, "Only attack talk."

"What the hell does that mean?" said Lefter to the Korean.

"Words like, move up squad two on our right flank, or keep moving ahead. Nothing we can use. I write down anyway."

Lefter would later learn by experience that the Chinese gave most of their immediate battle orders to field troops using whistles and bugles.

The battle lasted for several hours. He thought he heard small arms fire and the small explosive sound of hand grenades. *Oh shit, I hope not*, he thought. *It scared the hell out of me handling those grenades in boot camp training.*

Lefter never went back to the firing aperture. He sat at the table with one hand on his carbine and smoked cigarettes almost one after the other until his throat was sore. He thought about his new wife back home and wondered if he would ever see her again. *Crap, I am an only child and my line may end right here before I have any children of my own.* That thought preyed on his mind.

He looked up to see the Chinese DAC taking off the headset and handing it to the Korean. The Chinese DAC looked up at Lefter and said, "I translate now."

That stunned Lefter into realizing that the firing had stopped. The battle was apparently over, at least for tonight he hoped. He was happy to be alive.

As the Chinese DAC translated each sheet of his note, he handed it to Lefter. The notes were on lined paper and below the line written in Chinese was the translated line written in English. Lefter looked at the notes and agreed with the earlier statement that is was all immediate battle talk of the Chinese attack. At least, that was what it was to his inexperienced eye.

The rest of the night was silent although Lefter realized that his ears were ringing from all the sounds of the earlier battle. When it got light outside Lefter couldn't resist going outside the bunker and taking a quick look. He was shocked.

Down at the base of the hill on the south side of the barbwire line, a deuce-and-a-half Marine truck with sideboards moved slowly along. It stopped briefly ever 20 feet or so while four men tossed dead Chinese soldiers into the back of the truck. They were policing up the immediate battlefield. Lefter noticed that the bunker near the nearest barbwire line had been blown up. That must have happened when he saw the machine gun stop firing from down there last night. *What in the world do they do with all those Chinese bodies?* he wondered. He never found out and he never asked anyone. He just hoped to hell that he could keep it from preying on his mind in the future.

He went back into the bunker and got his backpack ready to go. Soon, Jolcomb knocked and came in smiling. "Relief is here," he said. "How was your first day of bunker duty?"

"Started out boring," said Lefter, "then an hour or so after midnight, all hell broke loose. Scared the living hell out of me."

"I know what you mean," said Jolcomb. "Fortunately, the big battles don't occur too often. We could hear the action hot and heavy from the base camp. Looks like you damn near got overrun last night though. I see the Choggi boys are picking up gook bodies down on the front of the hill."

"What's a Choggi boy?" asked Lefter.

"Korean civilian volunteers," answered Jolcomb.

"I have a lot to learn," said Lefter.

"You'll catch on quick. See you tomorrow."

"Yeah, stay safe, buddy," replied Lefter.

Back at the base camp Campbell looked at the notes and said to Lefter, "You take the courier run today. Hillman should be back from R&R and waiting for you there at the 303. After you get back, you can catch up on sack time. You should be back by noon."

"OK, it will be great to see Asshole Soss again," he said sarcastically.

"Just get in and out, avoid him and don't take any chances," replied Campbell.

"OK, Boss," said Lefter with a smile and a snappy salute. He liked Sergeant Campbell and meant the comment respectively. Campbell must have taken it that way because he smiled back and said, "Stay safe, buddy."

Lefter drove to the 303 and managed to avoid seeing Major Soss who had already left to visit the ASA detachment in the Commonwealth Division. He told Crovelli about his night in the bunker.

Crovelli said, "You lucky bastard, on top of getting combat pay and four points a month you get to have all that excitement."

Lefter couldn't decide if Crovelli was serious or not so he just responded, "Screw you, Crovelli."

"Up yours," said Crovelli as both men smiled.

"Here's your mail," said Crovelli as he handed Lefter a duffel bag. "Jolcomb has a large package from home. Maybe he'll share his goodies with you. Hillman is waiting for you over in the Day Room Tent."

"Thanks, buddy, see ya," said Lefter.

"Stay safe, buddy," said Crovelli seriously and held out his hand.

Lefter shook his hand and left without saying anything. He almost got choked up.

Lefter went to the Day Room Tent and told Hillman he was now assigned to Detachment #1 and was on courier run from there. The two men already knew each other.

As Lefter drove back to the base camp, Hillman told him about all the fun things he had done while on R&R in Tokyo for a week. "It was a great I & I," said Hillman.

"Yeah, well you single guys can call it intercourse and intoxication but married guys like me are just going to call it intoxication and intoxication." They both laughed.

Back at the base camp Lefter collapsed on his cot and fell into a nervous sleep. Campbell woke him up at five o'clock and the three of them went next door to the Marine Company for dinner. The mess tent was open but all they had to eat was vegetable soup and crackers. They did have the beer though and this time each man was getting two cans — opened of course.

"What's the deal on the extra can?" said Lefter to the Marine handing out the beer.

"Extra reward for those who survived the last two nights on the hill," said the Marine.

"Got ya," said Lefter. "Thanks."

A Marine Sergeant at the next table picked up his beers and mess kit of soup then joined the three ASA men at their table. He was the same Marine Sergeant they had met earlier.

"Sergeant Papatrana, they call me Pappy, nice to see you again," he said as he held out his hand.

All three ASA men shook his hand and introduced themselves.

"Thought you might like to know that those two smart-ass, greenhorn Marines survived the last two nights. They won't be such smart asses anymore now that they've had a chance to be heroes. They both decided that imitating a rock was better than playing Superman." He chuckled and added, "Now they know that they're not the only lean, mean, fighting machine. Them little gooks are pretty damn tough also."

"Thanks, Pappy," said Campbell. "It don't take them long to get wise up here, does it?"

"Where are you guys located on the MLR?" asked Pappy.

Campbell hesitated then said, "Don't take this wrong but we are not allowed to tell anyone the location of our bunker. However, I will say that if you walk west from any Marine position on the MLR, you can't miss us. On our bunker door is a sign that says RESTRICTED AREA. Come by and visit anytime."

As Pappy downed his last beer and picked up his empty mess gear he said, "I just may do that. You must be right on the western edge. Well, gotta run. The grapevine says that the 25th Army Division is relieving us later today. See you later."

Campbell, Hillman and Lefter got up, washed and rinsed their mess gear, then went back to their base camp. Campbell assigned Hillman to the next bunker watch and told Lefter he could have the day off.

"Thanks, think I'll just stick around and help out with the base camp chores." Truth was he was still tired and wanted to rest up. He could hardly keep his eyes open for the after-dinner bull session with Campbell and Hillman. He spent most of the time just listening and nodding off. He crawled into his mummy bag as soon as it got dark.

He woke up in a cold sweat several times from dreaming he was in the bunker during an attack. Each time he awakened, he would think of the Chinese bodies being thrown on the deuce-and-a-half truck. He wanted to know what happened to the Marines in the machine gun nest down by the barbwire lines. On the other hand, he thought, *maybe it would be better to not know.*

The next morning, Lefter, Hillman, and Campbell were sitting at the table having a C-ration breakfast when the phone buzzed. Campbell answered and said "yes sir" a couple of times, then hung up. Returning to the table he said, "The First Marine Division is being relieved today by the Twenty-fifth Infantry Division."

"That's the outfit that Mewman was transferred to," said Lefter. "Maybe we'll run into him up on the MLR."

"Could happen," said Campbell as he returned to eating a can of apricots.

CHAPTER SEVEN

Major Soss strutted quickly to the CO's jeep, lowered the windshield, and sat erect in the driver's seat as he drove away.

Standing in the cloud of dust stirred up by the passing jeep, Sitchie and Crovelli saluted.

"The transportation guys from the 444th are going to have fun meeting him on the MSR today," said Sitchie. "They drive them ammo trucks like maniacs up and down the main supply routes. Asshole Soss is going to eat a lot of their dust today."

"Agreed, I hear the men of the 444th are ninety-nine point nine percent wild party animals."

"You got that right," replied Sitchie. "They ain't even human, they're Neanderthal men."

"Why is that?" asked Crovelli.

"Most of them are from the slum areas of the big northern cities. A few of them are rednecks from the Deep South. They're very poorly educated. Most of them don't know shit from corned beef hash."

"I don't like corned beef hash," replied Crovelli.

Ignoring the Crovelli comment, Sitchie continued. "Their Operations Center is just a few miles south of us. The drivers are real proud of their trucks. They name the truck they drive and paint the name on the side of it. I saw one named *Gook Buster*, another named *Death Hauler*. Oh yeah, one was named *Shit Happens*."

"How do you know all this?" quizzed Crovelli.

"Me and Quigley went down there one day. We looked the place over then hung around and went to their EM Club that night. We was damn lucky to get out alive."

"You never mentioned that before," replied Crovelli.

"Well, I guess it scared me speechless. We saw a buncha fights — one with knives. Scared the corn beef hash outta me."

"No shit," said Crovelli smiling.

"Funny," said Sitchie.

"They sure seem to enjoy driving those ammo trucks," said Crovelli.

"Yeah," replied Sitchie, "they really do seem to enjoy their work and they appear to be dedicated to supporting the fighting men on the front line too."

Crovelli laughed. "I hear that if you called the 444th at night the CQ will answer the phone and say, 'This is Private Jones of the four-four-four transportation corps, you call we haul you all. We got two-bys, four-bys, six-bys, eight-bys and them great big mother fuckers that bend in the middle and go choo choo.'"

"No shit, really?"

"Yeah, really," said Crovelli. "Call them the next time you're on CQ duty and see."

"Think I will," said Sitchie as they entered the 303 headquarters building.

Captain Eten was on the land-line warning Campbell that Asshole Soss was on his way to up to the MLR.

As the major drove past the guard shack at the entrance to I-Corps headquarters, the MP gave Major Soss a friendly wave. The major braked the jeep to a stop, backed up, stopped beside the MP and said, "Soldier, don't you know you should salute an officer?"

The startled MP said, "Yes, sir," and saluted.

"Remember that from now on," said the major as he returned the salute and drove on.

The MP jotted down the identifying marks stenciled on the jeep bumper, then got on the telephone in the guard shack and laughingly reported the incident to his first sergeant.

"Would you believe it, some asshole major from the 303 CRB just chewed my ass for not saluting him as he drove by? He's not happy with our standard friendly wave."

"Well, shit happens," replied the sergeant. "Don't dirty your drawers over it."

Along the MSR through the small town of Uijongbu, the major stopped to study his map. A small Korean boy about nine or ten years old ran up to the driver side of the jeep. The little boy was being paid to pimp for a prostitute. He said in broken English a phrase that some soldier had taught him, "Eh GI, you wanna fucky me mother; she never been fucked before."

"Get out of here," said the major as he reached out with his left boot and pushed the boy hard to the ground.

"Fucky you, GI," said the boy as he held up his middle finger.

"You impertinent little brat," said the major as he spun the jeep tires and threw dirt and dust onto the little boy.

The little boy spread the word around the small town that he was kicked by an Army Major driving a jeep from the 303 CRB. From now on Major Soss would be seen in the eyes of the people of this small town as an Ugly American.

Before arriving at the 25th Division's position on the MLR, the major pulled off the main road and into a battery of 105mm artillery pieces. Stopping near two soldiers dressed in mismatched and dirty fatigue uniforms, the major motioned them to come to his jeep.

As they approached the jeep one of the soldiers said, "What can we do for you, Major?"

"To begin with, you can salute. I am an officer, you know."

"Yesss, sirrrr!" snapped one of the soldiers as they both saluted and stood at rigid attention.

"At ease," commanded the major as he flipped a return salute. Then he put his finger on the map where an X marked the position of the ASA bunker and said, "I'm headed for this position, what is the best way to get there?"

Tracing his dirty finger along the map, one of the enlisted men said, "Sir, it is a steep, sweaty climb by foot if you go up the trail on the back side of the hill here. I think you can probably drive right up to that bunker from the front side of the hill though. Just drive along this trail until you get near the barbed wire entanglement then turn back and work your way up the hill in four wheel drive."

As the major turned around and drove off without saying anything, the artillerymen looked at each other and smiled mischievously.

Up on the hill, Corporal Haiser looked out the firing aperture of his fighting bunker and couldn't believe what he was seeing. "Hey, Happy, come over here and check this out; some idiot is driving a jeep out toward the barbed wire line."

As the two men watched, the jeep turned southeasterly and started climbing diagonally up the steep slope in front of them. Sergeant Happy picked up his binoculars, focused on the driver and said, "It's some major with the I-Corps black asshole patch on his shoulder."

Haiser replied, "That new rapid-fire volunteer we got today has that black asshole patch, what's his name?"

"Name's Mewman, go find 'em and bring 'em up here," replied Happy.

Haiser left the bunker on the run and within a couple of minutes came back with Private Mewman. Happy handed Mewman the binoculars and said, "Here take a look and see if you know that idiot in the jeep coming up the hill toward us."

Mewman looked through the binoculars just in time to see the jeep switch back and start climbing in a southwesterly direction. "Holy shit, it's that fucking major that court-martialed me."

"He's in deep shit now," said Happy as the shrill sound of an incoming artillery shell penetrated the sunny morning and exploded midway between the jeep and their bunker. "A gook spotter is zeroing in on that jeep."

Major Soss jumped out, crouched down behind the jeep, pulled his 45 pistol and fired several rounds northward.

"Unbelievable, that asshole is shooting back with his pistol. He should be running like hell toward us. He's dead meat for sure if he stays with that jeep," said Happy.

"I'll go get the dumb fucker," said Mewman.

Sergeant Happy said, "Go ahead if you want too but if I was you I'd let the dumb shit figure it out himself or perish."

Mewman ran out of the bunker and scrambled down the hill to the jeep. Just as he got to the jeep, another round hit about 100 yards downhill from the jeep. He grabbed the speechless and frightened Major Soss by the arm and led him back up the hill to the bunker. Just as they scrambled into the bunker a third round blew the jeep apart and it started to burn.

The major's eyes were wild looking. He tried to speak but was shaking so hard that he just mumbled and stuttered. He was waving the pistol around as he tried to speak so Happy pulled it from his grip and handed it to Haiser.

"Come with me, Major. I'll take you to our CP." Happy led the still speechless and shaking major outside and along the trench to Charlie Company's Command Post. "Found this major on the front slope," Happy said to his CO, Captain Knuckleman. Then he added with a big grin, "He was coming up the front side of the hill in a jeep."

"Up the front side in a jeep?" questioned the captain in an unbelieving tone.

Happy shrugged his shoulders and held out his hands with the palms up. "My new guy, Mewman, went down and led him up to my bunker just before the jeep took a direct hit. He was Mewman's CO back at I-Corps headquarters."

Captain Knuckleman patted Happy on the shoulder and said, "OK, Happy,

I'll see that he gets back to his outfit. Thanks." Happy chuckled and shook his head all the way back to his bunker.

The still-speechless major sat down at the captain's makeshift desk and, with his right hand palm up, started tapping his West Point ring on the plywood desktop.

In a few minutes, Captain Knuckleman got word back to the 303CRB that their CO had a breakdown of his jeep and needed a ride back. Crovelli took the message and relayed it immediately to Captain Eten. "Major Soss is at the CP bunker of a Charlie Company in the 25th Division and wants someone to come and get him, seems his jeep broke down. They gave me the coordinates; it's not our bunker, it's one of the infantry bunkers."

"That's weird," said Captain Eten. "Wonder why the hell he's at an infantry bunker instead of our bunker?" As Captain Eten picked up the phone he said, "Thanks, Crovelli, I'll have someone from the detachment go get him."

Sergeant Campbell answered the phone at the rear sleeping area of the detachment. He listened for a minute then said, "Yeah, Captain, that CP bunker is east of our bunker about 500 yards. I'll go up there and get the major and bring him back to I-Corps."

It was mid-afternoon when Campbell drove into the 303 CRB with Major Soss. The major stomped into the building, went directly to his office and slammed the door shut. Crovelli noticed that the major's pistol holster was empty.

Campbell motioned Crovelli to follow him outside. He led Crovelli over by his jeep, lit a cigarette and said, "I think the major has cracked up; he babbled all the way down here and I didn't understand a damn thing he said."

"He's nuts all right," said Crovelli.

"Oh yeah, something else. You won't believe it; Mewman's in that outfit."

"No shit, did you get to talk to him?"

"Nope, I was already a ways down the back of the hill with the major when Mewman yelled my name. When I turned around he yelled out, 'tell my fucking buddies in the 303 hello,' and then he did that big belly laugh of his."

"I'll be damned," said Crovelli.

Campbell climbed into his jeep, started the engine and said, "The major's your problem now, buddy. I'm outta here. Sayounara!"

When the CQ duty started at 1700 hours, the major had not yet come out of his office. Crovelli could hear his voice every now and then but couldn't understand what he was saying. They also heard sounds like something being thrown or kicked around.

That night after dinner a group of ASA guys were at Mighty Joe's table at the EM Club. Mighty Joe always got the same table because he always skipped dinner to be the first one in line when the Club opened at 1800 hours. The ASA guys at the table were Crovelli, Nissing, Quigley, Bednell, Noitra and a Sergeant Nay.

Sergeant Nay had just arrived late that afternoon from the States. He had been at Officers Candidate School and broke his arm playing touch football with only a week of training left before getting commissioned a 2nd Lieutenant. Rather than go back and start all over after the arm healed, he elected to finish his two-year draft hitch as an enlisted man.

Ironically, Nay knew Mighty Joe from their college days. They had both graduated from an elite and prestigious private college in the State of New York. Mighty Joe was a year ahead of Nay and was nearly through his first year at Harvard Law School when he flunked out, lost his deferment and got drafted. Nay was drafted immediately upon graduation.

Mighty Joe had already heard about the major's ASS Rules.

"How the hell did you find out about that so quick?" Crovelli responded.

"Never reveal my sources but I checked up on the man's background and it's real juicy." Mighty Joe had connections that would make a FBI agent envious.

"Not till I get a beer. I got the first round."

"Hell yes, you were the only one here at the time. Right?"

"Do you want to hear the juice or what?"

"All right," said Crovelli as he rose from the table, "I'll get the first round — excuse me, the second round."

Soon Crovelli returned with eight beers and said, "OK, now tell us the skinny on Asshole Soss."

"Hang on, need to get my whistle greased first with a cool one." Mighty Joe could see he had everyone hooked, except maybe Nay, and he was deliberately stringing out the story.

"What the hell are you guys talking about?" said Nay.

Crovelli jumped in and said, "Suffice it to say that the CO you haven't met yet is a real space case; he's nuttier than a fruit cake."

"Great," said Nay sarcastically. "Now I have a reason to look forward to tomorrow."

Mighty Joe decided to go for a little more payoffs, "I've decided my information on Soss is worth at least two rounds of beer, now who's going to buy the next round?"

"OK, I'll get it," said Sitchie. "Now let's hear the dirt."

"This is really good stuff, how about a third round?"

Groaning started up around the table and Nay said, "Spit it out, asshole, can't you see two beers is the ransom limit on this?"

Mighty Joe gave up the play for more ransom and said, "OK, here's the deal. He's a West Point boy. He's been a staff man his whole career specializing in setting up dinner parties, cocktail parties, conferences and all that stuff. You lucky bastards are his first command."

"Well, that's just great! No wonder he's so gung-ho," said Crovelli. "It's his first chance to play leader and we're the guinea pigs. How are we gonna' get rid of the yo-yo?"

"The SOB probably came in dead last in his class at West Point," said Sitchie. "Maybe we can build him an observation command chair, put it on top of a detachment bunker and let him sit up there and lecture the gooks." Everyone laughed and had a drink of beer.

"Good idea," said Crovelli, "and if we're lucky a gook sniper will pick him off." Everybody laughed and had another drink of from their beer.

"We need to get rid of that asshole some way," said Crovelli.

Sichie, Nissing and Bednell were the quiet type and didn't talk much but they could be counted on to participate in any plan to get Major Soss. Nothing was said around the table for a half-minute or so. They were swallowing beer and trying to think of a way to get the major out of their life.

Finally Sergeant Noitra spoke up, "You guys can do what you want but don't count me in. I'll be shipping out to the States as soon as I get Nay trained. I don't want anything to screw that up."

Everyone looked at Noitra but didn't say anything. They liked Noitra and wouldn't do anything to cause him harm. They also knew that he was a very intelligent man. He had to be smart to be the head of the analysis group.

"If I were you," said Noitra as he stood up to leave, "I wouldn't do anything out of line. Just follow the dumb shit's rules and wait for him to hang himself."

"That's a good strategy," said Mighty Joe. "Fits right in with the other dirt I dug up on him."

"What else?" said Crovelli.

"Oh no, not so fast. You've already got your two beers worth of information. This final stuff is really juicy, but it's worth another two beers."

Lots of groaning and mumbling could be heard around the table.

"Bullshit!" "Horseshit!" "Robber!" "Screw you!" "Up yours!"

"I see you're still a real prick of a negotiator," said Nay.

"Got that right," said Mighty Joe. "Oh the hell with it, let's get a game of Mumblejon started."

"OK, I got you covered for one beer," said Nissing, speaking his first words at the table tonight.

"I'll cover the second one," said Quigley. "Now spill it!"

"What I am about to tell you now is worth another couple of beers but I am letting you have it cheap because you're buddies."

"Cut the crap and get on with it," said Crovelli. "You've already conned us out of four beers."

"Sure you won't pay just one more?" said Mighty Joe as he smiled and held up his hands in a defensive position. "OK, just kidding."

"The asshole major was kicked out of Headquarters Far East Command by General Mark Blark himself. Soss got real drunk at a big cocktail and dinner party he arranged for the general and his staff. He was sitting next to the general's wife when he got sick and started puking. As he got up and whirled around to make a run to the Men's Room some of that puke got on the general's wife."

The table broke out in laughter. They all laughed until they choked and wiped tears from their eyes.

"Crap, you could have got a whole case for that info," said Crovelli. Heads nodded agreement as they laughed and held their beer up toward Mighty Joe.

"You haven't heard the best part yet," said Mighty Joe.

"I would have to shoot off my mouth early," said Crovelli. "Go ahead and spill it, I'll buy you that fifth beer."

"General Mark Blark's little brother Bruce found out about the puking incident and kidded the hell out of him, so guess how Mark got back at his little brother Bruce?"

"Well, I'll be a god damn monkey's uncle," said Quigley. "Bruce Blark is our I-Corps commander, ain't he?"

"Got that right," said Mighty Joe. "You guys are just pawns in Mark Blark's practical joke on his little brother Bruce."

Suddenly, a solemn mood fell over the table. Finally, Nay said, "I'm buying a round for the table, let's get a game of Mumblejon going."

Mighty Joe said, "There is rumor going around that somebody spread kimchi all over Major Soss' tent. Now some say it was our new man here

Nay Boy, some say it was Lefter Boy, some say it was Crovelli Boy…" and the game was on.

Nissing lost almost every game and must have chugged down a dozen beers. He was, in GI language, "shit faced." He tried to stay in the game by lapping spilled beer off the table but Mighty Joe was uncompromising and had him declared DEAD. The game went on until Mighty Joe had consumed his six free beers. Then the party broke up and everyone went back to their tents. Nissing had to be half carried back.

"See you tomorrow," said Mighty Joe. "Remember, first one here gets a free beer."

First thing the next day Noitra briefed Nay on Major Soss' chicken shit rules. Next, he introduced Nay to Captain Eten. Nay saluted and the captain told him not to bother with saluting unless Major Soss was present. "I assume you have been briefed on the major's special rules?"

Nay nodded yes.

"As you know, Captain, Sergeant Nay is my replacement and I'll be leaving as soon as he knows the ropes in the Analysis Group; it shouldn't take more than a week or so."

"OK, Noitra, might as well get started on it then. The major is still in a bit of shock so don't bother him today. You can introduce Nay to him later."

Back in the Analysis Group, Noitra led Nay to each man's desk for a briefing on his individual responsibilities. Noitra could tell from Nay's questions and comments that he was catching on quick. "I can see you are a quick learner, Nay. I may get out of here in less than a week."

"I'll let you know when I'm ready," said Nay.

Again, Major Soss spent the entire day in his office with the door closed. Everyone wondered what he was doing in there. It made them nervous.

Again after dinner, the previous night's beer drinking group assembled at Mighty Joe's table in the EM Club. Each man bought his own first beer. Nay came back from the bar with two and set one down in front of Mighty Joe. "Here," said Nay, "is your free beer for being the first one here. Also prepayment for any additional information you have on the major." Nay turned to the others at the table and said, "He didn't even come out for lunch, did he?"

"If he came out I didn't see it," said Crovelli.

"What in the cat hair is he up to?" said Quigley.

Sitchie made an attempt at humor, "Hope he's not planning World War Three with us as the pawns." No one laughed.

"I'm rotating any day now so I don't have to sweat it but you guys better stay alert and protect your ass," said Sergeant Noitra. "That bastard is dangerous. He's a West Point boy with his first command and he wants to play soldier real bad."

"We've got to come up with a plan to get rid of the ol' boy," said Quigley. "That dog won't hunt, so we might just as well get rid of him."

"What the hell does that mean?" asked Crovelli.

"Just a down home expression," answered Quigley.

"Charlie," said Lefter to Nissing, "put your head in high gear. With all that stuff you've memorized there must be something in there that can help us start a rebellion." Again, no one laughed. Nissing just raised his shoulders and held both hands out palms up.

"I'm ready for another beer," said Mighty Joe, trying to gain control of the table conversation by changing the subject.

"What the hell did you do with the one I just brought you, pour it on the floor?" said Nay. "Mine is still full. Buy yourself a beer, Prick!"

"Sticks and stones may break my bones and cause me *not* to tell you today's intelligence on your loving major," said Mighty Joe in a mocking tone.

"Screw you," said Nay.

"Up yours," replied Mighty Joe.

Crovelli got up, left the table and returned with a beer. Setting it down in front of Mighty Joe, he said, "OK, let's hear it."

Mighty Joe smiled. He was back in control of the table. "I have confirmed that the major had a jeep breakdown for sure. It was blown up and burned. Took a direct hit from a gook artillery round." He fell silent and looked intently from one man to another.

Finally, Noitra said, "Did you say it was blown up by a gook artillery round?"

"Yep, that's it," said Might Joe and fell silent.

"What the hell do you mean, 'that's it'? I just bought you the beer, now keep talking," said Crovelli. "Where was he and how come he got out without a scratch?"

Mighty Joe was back in his element, keeping the table occupants under his firm control and awaiting his next words. "This will cost you big time. You thought what I told you last night was a big laugh, wait till you hear this."

Nay said, "Cut all the preliminary crap and spill it. If what you say is worth it we'll each buy you one. Right, guys?" Each man around the table nodded yes.

"Like I said, it's worth more than last night's news."

"Well, forget it then," replied Nay. "Whatever it is will be in the grapevine in a couple of days anyway."

Mighty Joe caved in, "OK, hardass, you've got a deal." He proceeded to explain what had happened to the major in the 25th Division. When he told them about the major firing back toward No-Man's-Land with his 45 pistol, the table broke out in uproarious laughter. Each time the laughter would die down someone would make a comment and the laughing would break out again.

"My hero, wheeeeeee!" said Nissing. More laughter erupted.

"He's a regular fucking John Wayne," said Crovelli surprising himself at using a Mewman-type expression. More laughter again.

"No wonder the asshole won't come out of his office. He's probably writing himself up for the Medal of Honor," said Quigley. Nobody laughed at his comment because they each knew what a heroic act was required to get the Medal of Honor. It wasn't something to be used in humor, at least for this situation.

Quigley looked at the somber faces around the table and said, "Sorry, shouldn't have said that. The major shouldn't be in any conversation that mentions the Medal of Honor; it's insulting."

"OK, now how did he come out of it alive?" asked Crovelli.

"This is the best part. He was rescued by an Army grunt that went down and led him back up the hill to a bunker." Making a dramatic pause as he looked around the table from one man to the next, "The grunt's name that rescued him is…"

Crovelli jumped in before Mighty Joe finished his sentence and said, "Mewman! It was Mewman, wasn't it?" A stunned silence fell over the table.

"You got it," said Mighty Joe. "It was Mewman."

"I knew it," said Crovelli. "Campbell told me he saw Mewman up there when he picked up the major."

"That dumb shit Mewman," said Quigley. "His big dream is to kill a gook but he woulda got more points with us by letting the major get hit with artillery fire while he was fighting them off with his 45." Laughter erupted at the table.

"How do you find out all this stuff?" said Sitchie.

"Never reveal my sources, but I will tell you one more thing. Your loving major is providing a lot of laughs among the officer corps around here. They are laughing their asses off."

"Well, why not?" said Nay. "Somebody once said, 'humor is the truth turned upside down' and this sure is upside down stuff."

"Here's to upside down stuff," said Quigley as he raised his beer in toast. Everyone joined in.

"OK, are you ready for some Mumblejon? It's time to start some serious intoxicating."

"Intoxicating! Intoxicating? You been studying a dictionary today?" said Nay.

"Screw you," said Mighty Joe.

"Up yours," said Nay.

"Let the contest begin," said Nissing as he picked up his beer and emptied the can. "I'll go get another round."

As soon as Nissing returned with a beer for everyone Mighty Joe held up his hand palms out and said, "Shhhhhh! There is a rumor going around..." and the game was on.

CHAPTER EIGHT

The next morning, Major Soss came in, went directly into his office and slammed the door. Shortly after the lunch hour, Sitchie came through the front door, leaned into the cage room and whispered to Crovelli while pointing toward the major's office, "He's going on the road again; just phoned and ordered me to bring a jeep up here."

"Good, maybe some dumb shit like Mewman won't rescue him this time," Crovelli whispered back.

Sitchie smiled and nodded yes, then walked over and knocked on the major's door, "Sir, your jeep is out front and ready to go; I put down the top and windshield for you."

The door opened and out walked the major without saying a word. He was wearing a flak jacket and his steel helmet. He stormed past Sitchie, out the door, climbed into the jeep and drove away.

"Crap, I didn't even have time to give the asshole a big salute," said Sitchie. "I'm really torn up over that."

"What's going on anyway?" said Crovelli.

"Major Asshole is on the road again; didn't you see him stomp out of here?"

"Hell no, I was busy reading the intellectual article in this girlie magazine."

"Yeah right, you're real scholar!" Sitchie said sarcastically.

"Screw you," said Crovelli.

"Up yours," retorted Sitchie.

"I hear you flunked out of Cal State even though you were a starter on their basketball team."

Crovelli took the bait, "I didn't flunk out, dipshit. My grades got down a little and the damn Army drafted me out of college. What the hell are you getting at?"

"I'm saving the answer for a Court session," said Sitchie. "It's gotta be worth a beer from someone."

"Screw you," said Crovelli.

"Up yours," said Sitchie.

Captain Eten came out of his office, walked to the cage and said, "The major's door is open and he's not there, where did he go?"

"Don't know," said Sitchie. "He had me bring up a jeep for him; he just took it and left. He was wearing his steel helmet and a flak jacket."

Captain Eten shook his head from side to side, went into the major's office and came back with a sheet of paper in his hand. "He left a note saying he'd be visiting the MLR today, and that's all it says." He threw both hands up, shrugged his shoulders and returned to his office.

Major Soss drove north through a fog of yellowish-red dust. Convoys of ammo trucks were on the move in both directions, loaded ones going north and empties headed south. Some drivers of southbound trucks honked their horns when they saw the helmeted Major Soss approaching in his jeep with the top and windshield down. Many of them were laughing as they drove by.

Covered with a thick layer of dust, Major Soss drove into the artillery battery. He was looking for the two soldiers he talked to on his previous visit to the MLR. Not surprisingly, they were at their duty station of a 105mm-artillery piece.

They spotted the major and recognized him. "Here comes John Wayne," said one of the soldiers. "Let's give 'em the palms-out salute."

As the major drove up to their position, both soldiers slowly raised their hands to their foreheads with palms facing toward the major.

Major Soss ignored the insulting salute and flipped a return salute. "You men deliberately gave me incorrect instructions the other day and it almost got me killed driving up to that bunker."

"Sorry 'bout that, major," the other man said grinning. "As I recall we just told you how to get there by foot or by jeep. You made the decision. We heard the story 'bout your close call up there." Both men were grinning widely and on the verge of laughing.

The major knew he'd been had so he put the jeep in gear, spun the jeep around and left without saying another word. He could hear the soldiers laughing behind him. He looked back and saw them bent over leaning on their knees. Perhaps he would return another day and report them to their CO but it was not a priority for today.

Soon he reached the 303 parking area on the back face of the hill. He pulled into an open area just off the road and parked beside a jeep that had 303 CRB stenciled on the bumper. After checking on his map he got out of the jeep and, carrying a briefcase, started climbing up the hill on the trail. It was obvious the trail was used a lot. Steps were built into the trail at its steepest locations. After several rest stops, panting and dripping sweat, he finally reached the bunker at the crest of the hill. He stood outside the bunker door for a couple of minutes getting his breath back, then knocked on the door.

"Who is it?" said someone inside the bunker.

"Major Soss, open the door, soldier," he ordered.

Corporal Jolcomb opened the bunker door, and fortunately, recognized the major. Had he not recognized him security rules would have required Jolcomb to not allow entrance regardless of rank; even if it had been a general. Major Soss had previously sent an eight by ten photo of himself to each detachment. Jolcomb saluted and said, "Come in, sir."

While flipping back a John Wayne-type salute the major said, "I don't have time right now, Corporal. Take me to the bunker where Mewman is stationed."

"Where is it, sir?"

"Right here," said Major Soss pointing to a position he had circled on a map.

"There is nobody here except me and the DACs, sir. Do you want me to leave them alone?"

"No, no, no, that would be a violation of security," said the major. "Just tell me how to get there."

Jolcomb wondered how Soss graduated from West Point without learning how to read a map. Maybe he was just showing off his command position. Jolcomb pointed east. "Just follow this trench. It's about 500 yards from here."

"Very well," said the major as he turned and started strutting swiftly down the trench. His arms swung back and forth in an exaggerated manner.

Jolcomb had heard all the stories about Major Soss but this was their first meeting. He was glad it didn't last long. From what he had heard, the major was a real weirdo and he felt lucky to be rid of him so soon. Jolcomb's good luck didn't last long.

Ten minutes later the major reappeared and this time he came inside the bunker and announced, "Mewman is out on a detail but should be back in a few hours. I'll wait here and go back later."

Damn! thought Jolcomb. *How long is he going to hang around here?*

"By the way, Corporal, what are those things reflecting in the sun down the hill out back?"

"Don't know, sir; guess I didn't notice."

"Come outside and I'll show you," said the major.

Outside he pointed down the back of the hill 30 or 40 yards and said, "See that, what is it?"

"Don't know, sir; first time I noticed it."

Major Soss went down the steep hill sideways and came back up with a beer can. Breathing hard he said, "Corporal, there are a lot more beer cans down there. Get a bag and go down there and police the area."

Jolcomb's face flushed. "Yes, sir. I have a duffel bag in the bunker."

Jolcomb went into the bunker. He briefly thought about getting the hand grenade he had in his pack. *I could push the bastard down the hill, hit him with the grenade and claim it was an incoming mortar round. No one would know the difference.* Shaking the thoughts from his head he picked up the empty duffel bag and went back outside.

"Well, get on with it!" ordered the major as he pointed down the hill toward the cans.

Jolcomb went down the hill and picked up 50 or more beer cans. Jolcomb whispered under his breath, "That asshole doesn't know how close he came to getting a grenade bath."

The major stood up by the bunker, hands on his hips and whistled the West Point fight song softly through his teeth.

After lugging the duffel bag of beer cans up to the hill, he led the major into the bunker and introduced him to the Chinese civilian who was sitting nearby. The Chinese DAC had a Master's Degree from Harvard but pretended to not speak much English. The Korean civilian sat at the monitoring radio with earphones over his ears and slowly turned the frequency control knob. Jolcomb didn't introduce him.

Jolcomb didn't know what to say so he reverted to his southern upbringing and offered food, "Are you hungry, Major? I have some C-rations."

"Very good," said the major.

Jolcomb brought over a new package of C-rations and said, "Have a seat there, Major, and I'll get you some eating tools."

The major sat down on an ammo box at the rough wood table that was made from the crating lumber. A chessboard with the pieces was sitting on the table.

"Sit down, soldier," ordered the major. "We will play a game of chess while I eat. Open this corn beef hash for me."

It figures, thought Jolcomb. *That's proof that he's a weirdo, nobody else likes that damn corn beef hash. How can I salt this hash with rat poison?* He took out his GI can opener, opened the can and handed it over together with a spoon. *Yuck, he's eating the damn stuff cold.*

The major was an excellent chess player and beat Jolcomb three games in a row. Jolcomb was a little taken back and had to admit that the major was no dummy when it came to playing chess. But he sure was a stupid ass when it came to having common sense. He could end up being a casualty of friendly fire. Also, that damn soft whistling through his teeth bugged the hell out of Jolcomb. He had whistled that damn tune all during their chess games. *Worse yet*, thought Jolcomb, *he seemed to really enjoy that cold corned beef hash — Yuck!*

"Do you play chess?" the major said to the Chinese DAC.

"Iie," meaning, "no," said the DAC in Japanese.

The word "Iie" went over the major's head, "OK, let's see what you can do," he said assertively. "Jolcomb isn't even a challenge."

Jolcomb relinquished his seat to the Department of Army Civilian. *Now he's in deep kimchi*, thought Jolcomb. The Chinese DAC was the best chess player in the detachment.

The first game went on for over an hour. The major was holding up well but the DAC finally won. "One more," said the major as he reset his chess pieces.

It was getting late in the day and Jolcomb was more than ready to get rid of Major Soss. "Sir, would you like me to run down to Mewman's bunker and see if he's back yet?"

"No, no. I'll go down there myself as soon as we finish this game."

Disappointed, Jolcomb decided to refill the three kerosene lanterns in the bunker. As he switched the lantern over the table with a newly-filled one, he noticed that the major appeared to have the advantage in the game. He was also doing that damn soft whistle. A few minutes later the major said, "Checkmate," and the game was over. Rising from the table he said, "I shall return another day."

Jolcomb thought, *What is this 'I shall return' shit! Who the hell does he think he is, General Douglas MacArthur?*

Jolcomb walked outside with the major. "If you don't mind me asking, sir, couldn't help noticing that your pistol holster is empty?"

"Forgot it up at Mewman's bunker. The sergeant there said he asked a Marine headed home to stop off at I-Corps and return it to me. I never got it.

Now I'll have to buy one to replace it."

Chuckling silently, Jolcomb thought, *Appears the sergeant has himself a 45 pistol now.* He watched the major strut east along the trench then went back into the bunker and finished his 24-hour shift without hearing from the major again that day.

It was after eight that night when Major Soss got back to his tent at the 303. He was covered with dust and he was cold and hungry. He was looking forward to heating some tea water and C-rations on the GI stove. He discovered the stove's firebox was full of burnt paper and trash. Infuriated, he immediately concluded that the enlisted men had clogged up his stove as a prank.

He went to Captain Eten's tent and accused him of fraternizing with the enlisted men and encouraging them to be rebellious. "You caused this, so you can clean out my stove. Now get over to my tent and get it done immediately."

Stunned and mad as hell, the captain held his temper, got dressed and complied with the major's order then went directly to the office and typed out his resignation as an officer. He sealed his resignation in an envelope, addressed it to 'Commander, ASAK' and dropped it into the outgoing mail container at the cage room.

Captain Eten was up and waiting for early morning arrival of the houseboy responsible for cleaning his tent and the major's tent. The houseboy admitted that he had burned the paper and trash in the major's stove rather than take it to a burn barrel. The enlisted men later found out that the officers' houseboy was the big brother of the little boy in Uijonbu that the major had mistreated.

When his relief, Hillman, came up the hill the next morning Jolcomb told him of the major's visit. "He never said why he came up here to see Mewman, but surely it was to thank him for saving his sorry ass," said Jolcomb.

Before driving back to the detachment sleeping area, Jolcomb walked down to Mewman's bunker. Mewman was pleasantly surprised. "Did he come up here to thank you?" said Jolcomb.

"Fuck no, he offered me a deal and I signed up."

"What deal?" said Jolcomb.

"Fuck you, just wait and see."

"Come on, Mewman," said a corporal standing nearby. "Time to go get briefed on tonight's patrol."

"Sorry, candy ass, gotta go get ready to kill some fucking gooks. Say hello to my 'ol fucking buddies in the 303."

Jolcomb was a little miffed that Mewman called him a candy ass. It was a term normally used for the administrative support troops behind the lines. Granted, Jolcomb didn't have to go out on patrols and encounter the enemy in firefights but it was no picnic in the ASA bunker during a barrage of mortar and artillery fire either. He had learned that incoming mortar and artillery rounds sounded different and were easy to identify. Knowing that the gooks were much closer when firing the mortars made it especially frightening, for it meant that a ground assault might follow.

Jolcomb often worried about what he would do if overrun by the Chinese. Would he put up a fight with his puny carbine or just give up? He would be killed for sure if he fought because the Chinese would have the bunker surrounded. If he gave up they might kill him anyway. On the other hand, if he fought he might get one or two of them. Academic, he usually concluded, the gooks would probably just blow the door with a planted explosive then lob in a fragmentation grenade. End of Jolcomb, but what if one or both DACs survived or surrendered? He didn't even want to think about the torture they would suffer before being killed. Colonel O'Hara, when briefing Jolcomb for the detachment duty, had described in detail the various tortures the gooks would use on the DACs if they were captured. "They would be better off dead," the colonel had said several times during the briefing.

Jolcomb returned to the ASA bunker, took one empty beer can out of the duffel bag and threw it down the hill. "That felt good," he said loudly. "Yeah!" He picked up the duffel bag and set it back down. "Oh, what the hell," he said out loud as he took another can and threw it down the hill. *Must be the North Carolina rebel in me*, he thought as he picked up the duffel bag containing the remaining cans. He carried it down the hill and handed it to one of the DACs from his shift. "Here, present from Major Soss Ass," he said while bowing. "Major want clean and tidy war." Both DACs laughed and climbed into the vehicle for the ride back to the base camp.

CHAPTER NINE

"I'll take the courier run to the 303 today," said Lefter. "Got a tentative lunch date with Crovelli."

"Good," said Campbell. "I was not looking forward to going down there. I hear the major is a little miffed that I didn't give him a personal briefing regarding my prediction of the attacks."

Lefter said, "You report to Captain Eten, don't you?"

"Hell yes, and I told him what we were hearing up here. Noitra and Nay in Analysis looked at the data and agreed with me. I don't know why in the hell the major didn't know about it. It's not up to me to keep him informed of their results."

Lefter arrived at the 303 just in time for having lunch with Crovelli. "Hey, Lefter, did you know we have a new executive officer, Lieutenant Landa?"

"No, what happened to Captain Eten?" asked Lefter.

"He transferred to ASA in Japan. Noitra has also left for home. Things are changing fast around here."

"When is Asshole Soss leaving?" replied Lefter.

"Soon. He's sure to end up at the loony farm any day."

After lunch, Crovelli introduced Lefter to the new EO. *Older fellow, close to forty*, thought Lefter.

"This job is all new to me so bear with me while I learn the ropes," said the lieutenant.

"Yes, sir, I sure will," replied Lefter as he turned and headed for lunch with Crovelli.

"Landa's record jacket shows he has a degree in Electrical Engineering from Washington State College," said Crovelli. "He was called into the service from an active reserve unit at Moses Lake, Washington."

"I know where that is," said Lefter. "I'm from the little town of Warden just 15 or 20 miles south of Moses Lake."

"So the new lieutenant is a shit kicker just like you, eh Lefter!"

"Screw you, San Francisco Boy," said Lefter as he grabbed the carbine before getting out of the chair.

"Up yours," replied Crovelli. "Got time to stay for dinner and a couple of beers after dinner; I'll buy?"

"Well maybe, Campbell did say I could have today off. I'll get on the land-line in the cage and double check with him."

After talking to Campbell on the phone, Lefter turned to Crovelli and said, "You're on, buddy. I'll go screw off in the Day Tent until time for dinner. Now, I gotta get out of here before Soss catches me."

Just the mention of Soss annoyed Lefter. He was still "highly pissed" about the way he had been treated by Asshole Soss and didn't want anything to do with him. *Hope the bastard doesn't come up to the 1st Marines when I'm on duty in the bunker*, he thought. *I might loose my cool and kill the son-of-a-bitch.*

Crovelli came to the Day Room Tent just after five and said, "Let's hit the chow line, buddy."

Lefter got a set of mess gear from behind the bar and went with Crovelli to the mess hall. It occurred to Lefter that the place looked like a fancy restaurant compared to the mess tent at the Marine Company. They ate their dinner at a leisurely pace and finished up at about ten to six. Just before they got up, there was a loud noise nearby as a rifle went crashing to the floor, then loud applause broke out.

"Another rookie getting his greeting," said Crovelli laughing.

"Yeah," said Lefter as he smiled. *Crap*, thought Lefter, *if that hadn't happened I might have forgot to sling my carbine before getting up. Damn near forgot it at lunch; been there, done that.* He smiled again as he recalled Mewman using the hand gestures to introduce him at the mess hall on the day he arrived in January.

Nothing had changed at the EM Club. When they arrived at about five minutes before the Club opened at six, there stood Mighty Joe at the head of a line of fifteen or twenty soldiers. The door was unlocked from the inside precisely at six and the line of soldiers moved forward to the beer dispensing area.

"This is your lucky day, guys, I got the first round," said Mighty Joe as they walked up to the table where he sat alone. Crovelli shook his head in mock disgust, turned and headed for the bar to get three beers.

Lefter sat down and said, "How you doing, Mighty?"

"Doing good," said Mighty Joe. "You up to a game of Mumblejon tonight?"

"Naw," said Lefter. "Gotta go back to the detachment tonight so I gotta leave after a couple of beers."

Crovelli came back with three cans of beer and sat them in the middle of the table. Mighty Joe finished his first beer, reached out and pulled one of the three cans up in front of him.

"Hear 'ol Soss was going to court-martial you," said Mighty Joe to Lefter.

"Where did you hear that?" said Lefter.

"Never reveal my —"

Before he could finish the statement Crovelli said, "Bullshit, I told him about it and it cost him two beers too."

"OK, so you got me a little bit once," said Mighty Joe. "But tonight I have some stuff that will blow your socks off."

"Might as well spill it now," said Crovelli. "Looks like we are the only ones here. I told Lefter I would buy him a couple of beers. I'll include you in the deal if you promise to lay off the arm twisting tonight."

"You're on," said Mighty Joe. "Go get the other beer."

Crovelli left and came back with three more cans of beer. "OK turkey, gobble!"

"This is the straight skinny. Your hero major has been issued a medal and you won't believe which one." He paused and looked intently into the eyes of each Lefter and Crovelli.

"I'll shoot myself if you tell me it is a Good Conduct Medal," said Crovelli.

Lefter laughed. "It's probably a Purple Heart for a hangnail he got shooting that 45 pistol across No-Man's-Land."

"That's close, Lefter. It's a combat medal," said Mighty Joe.

A silly thought jumped into Lefter's head. "Oh no, don't tell me he got a Combat Infantryman Badge."

Mighty Joe raised both thumbs skyward. "Bingo!"

Lefter and Crovelli were stunned. Their mouths fell open and they both picked up their can of beer and took a couple of large gulps.

"You got proof of this?" Crovelli asked.

"Hell yes, I absolutely guarantee it as fact. He went to the Officers' Club last night with it pinned on his chest."

"Holy crap," said Lefter. "How in the hell did he qualify for that?"

"Surely he didn't get it for getting his jeep blown up," said Crovelli.

"Must be, I looked up the qualifications in the manual and typed out the appropriate rules. Here look at this," said Mighty Joe as took a paper from his pocket and unfolded it. Lefter and Crovelli read the rules intently.

> *A soldier must be an Army infantry or special forces Officer (SSI 11 or 18) in the grade of colonel or below, or an Army enlisted soldier or warrant officer with an infantry or special forces MOS, who subsequent to 6 December 1941 has satisfactorily performed duty while assigned or attached as a member of an infantry, ranger or special forces unit of brigade, regimental, or smaller size during any period such unit was engaged in active ground combat.*
>
> *A recipient must be personally present and under hostile fire while serving in an assigned infantry or special forces primary duty, in a unit actively engaged in ground combat with the enemy. The unit in question can be of any size smaller than brigade. For example, personnel possessing an infantry MOS in a rifle squad of a cavalry platoon in a cavalry troop would be eligible for award of the CIB. Battle or campaign participation credit alone is not sufficient; the unit must have been in active ground combat with the enemy during the period.*

"Note the loopholes," said Mighty Joe. He took out a pencil and underlined some words. "Although the medal is probably intended only for those in close combat on a regular basis it doesn't actually say that. It can be awarded to someone who is attached and was personally present and under hostile fire in a unit engaged in ground combat with the enemy."

"OK, but who awarded it to him? Wouldn't he need a witness?" said Crovelli.

"Yeah, it must have been some other asshole like himself," said Crovelli laughingly.

"Oh no, you don't suppose Mewman is in on this, do you?" said Lefter. "Jolcomb said Mewman made some sort of deal with Asshole Soss but wouldn't say what it was. Mewman just said to, 'Wait and see.'"

Mighty Joe put his hand on his chin and said, "Hum, I don't think an enlisted man could recommend an officer for the medal. It would have to be the other way around." Then he added sarcastically with heavy emphasis on some words, "BUT, an OFFICER AND GENTLEMAN could write up his own EXPERIENCE and have an enlisted man sign as a witness."

Lefter added while overly emphasizing certain words, "On top of that, if he is a shit-don't-stink West Point man, his word is golden, right?"

The other two men nodded agreement.

"Holy crap," said Lefter. "It's damn near eight-thirty. I have got to get going. I told Campbell I would be back before dark."

"He'll forgive you when he hears the news I gave you," said Mighty Joe.

"I'll go get the mail for you," said Crovelli.

"Think I'll stay and have another beer or two," said Mighty Joe. "Get some of the boys down here tomorrow night, Crovelli, and we'll gang up on them in Mumblejon," said Mighty Joe.

"I'll give it some thought," said Crovelli.

"Do that," replied Mighty Joe.

"Will do," said Crovelli.

"OK," said Mighty Joe.

Crovelli gave up on getting the last word with Mighty Joe. It was an impossible task. The guy was always going to have the last word no matter what.

Back at the cage Lefter called Campbell and told him he was going to be leaving in five minutes. Campbell asked if he had a package for him. Lefter said yes and apologized for not returning earlier and added, "I do have some very interesting news to tell you when I get there."

"Stay safe, buddy," said Campbell.

It was pitch black out by the time Lefter got to the blackout zone. He turned out the headlights and drove the jeep along slowly. It had begun to rain heavy and he could only see a couple of feet in front of the jeep fenders. Several times the jeep wandered and he felt it beginning to go off the shoulder of the road toward the ditch. He jerked it back swiftly and kept it from leaving the road. Luckily, there was no other traffic on the road.

Suddenly the blackness was split wide open with flashes of light and three very loud explosions. Boom, boom, boom! His heart rate immediately doubled as he hit the brakes and involuntarily jumped violently up out of the seat. He hit his head on a bar supporting the canvas jeep top.

Sitting there with his heart pounding, he reached up, rubbed his head and felt wetness. *Crap, I got hit! What the hell is going on here anyway?* Then it dawned on him. He was adjacent to the artillery emplacement. He took out his handkerchief and wiped the blood from his forehead as he drove slowly on toward the ASA base camp.

As he walked into the squad tent carrying the mailbag Campbell said, "What the hell happened to you. Is that blood on your face?"

"Yeah, I had a fight with Major Soss; I killed the son-of-a-bitch!"

The face of Campbell took on a stunned look of disbelief.

Lefter quickly added, "Just kidding, I hit my head on the crossbar of the jeep top. I was in the blackout zone and feeling my way along in this damn rain and those artillery guys shot off a triple while I was right in the middle of them."

Campbell laughed and Lefter just smiled weakly.

"Do I get a Purple Heart for it?" Lefter asked.

"I'll put you in for it as soon as I get my Medal of Honor," replied Campbell. "Tell you what I will do though, I'll buy you a drink." He pulled an open fifth of whiskey from under his cot and handed it to Lefter. "Furthermore, if there are some goodies in that package of mine I'll share some with you."

"Thanks, Camp," said Lefter as he handed the mailbag to Campbell. Campbell opened his package and sorted through the contents. "How about a can of smoked baby oysters? That should go good with whiskey."

"Never tasted an oyster but I'm game," said Lefter.

The two men sat at the table in the middle of the tent taking sips from the whiskey bottle and picking the baby oysters out of the can with their mess kit forks.

While Campbell and Lefter ate oysters and drank the whiskey, Jolcomb lay in his cot snoring softly.

The whiskey must have helped Lefter relax as he awoke the next morning having slept all night without a nightmare. His head throbbed a little though.

"What the hell happened to your face?" said Jolcomb.

"Oh crap, I forgot to wash my face last night," said Lefter as he headed for the water can. He poured some water into his steel helmet and washed his face with his hands. "Bumped my head last night. Camp says he will put me in for the Purple Heart."

Campbell jumped in. "He forgot my qualification. I told him I'd recommend him right after I get the Medal of Honor."

All three men laughed.

Lefter had the next bunker duty and soon had the supplies and the two DACs loaded up. Campbell was outside seeing them off. "Stay safe, buddy," he said as Lefter climbed into the ¾ ton truck.

"You too. See you in twenty-four," replied Lefter.

Up at the bunker Hillman said it had been a quiet night with only one page of notes by the DACs that contained nothing of consequence. "Well I'm outta here. Stay safe, buddy," said Hillman as he headed down the hill.

STAY SAFE, BUDDY

This time in the bunker Lefter hoped for a boring night. Never again would he think a quiet night in the bunker was boring. It was a warm and sunny day. Lefter was sitting on an old ammo box out back of the bunker enjoying the sun and eating a can of C-rations when to his surprise Mewman came walking down the trench from the east. His uniform was very dirty and torn in a couple of spots. His face and hands were dirty. As he got close Lefter said to him, "Hello, buddy. Welcome to my home. Can I get you a C-ration?"

"No fucking way. I get plenty of those. Just checking out where the fuck you live. My sleeping bunker is just east a few hundred yards. We're neighbors. Ain't that a fucking hoot?"

Lefter waited for Mewman to finish his big belly laugh, which didn't annoy him as it had in the past. This time the belly laugh appeared warm. "Be damned. Couldn't ask for a better neighbor from what I've seen so far," said Lefter. "Have a seat." He took out his package of cigarettes and handed it to Mewman. "Have a smoke."

Mewman took a cigarette from the pack and lit up. "How long you been here, Lef?" asked Mewman.

As Lefter lit himself a cigarette, he noted that Mewman had called him Lef and took that to mean he considered him a good friend. "Appears I got on the MLR just a few days before you came up here with the 25th Infantry. In fact, that big battle the other night was my first to sit through."

"You're fucking lucky to just sit through it," said Mewman. "My squad was out there in all that shit. We were out on a fucking recon patrol so when all the shit hit the fan we just got the fuck out of there and hustled back to the MLR."

"So you didn't get a chance to kill a gook?" said Lefter with a grin.

"Nope, not yet. We was just learning the lay of the land from a couple of Marine escorts. It is so fucking dark out there I don't know how to tell when I get one anyway."

"Can't you see them in the light of the flares?" asked Lefter.

Mewman whooped and belly laughed, "Good point, Lef, maybe I had my fucking eyes closed."

Lefter didn't know what to say. Neither man said anything for a couple of minutes. A feeling of close comradeship was stirring in their hearts. They just puffed on their cigarettes and looked at the ground. For some reason, Lefter thought of a Chinese proverb he had heard somewhere: "War does not determine who is right, war determines who is left."

Finally, Mewman broke the silence and said, "Well, I better get the fuck back. I'll drop by and see you again."

"I'll look forward to it," replied Lefter.

Mewman turned and started walking east.

"Stay safe, buddy," Lefter called after him.

Mewman didn't say anything and didn't turn around. He just raised his right hand and waved slightly.

The rest of the day passed slowly but Lefter enjoyed every minute of the quiet. He made occasional trips to the firing aperture to look out over No-Man's-Land. Even with field glasses, he couldn't see any movement in No-Man's-Land or on the higher hills farther north on the Chinese MLR. There was some activity down by the barbwire lines. It appeared Korean civilians were rebuilding the Marine machine gun bunker. *Bet they are sweating their asses off*, Lefter thought.

The DACs were not hearing anything of consequence. Lefter played solitaire and wrote a letter to his wife and another to his father. *It's good to have the time to leisurely compose a letter*, he thought.

Night fell and it was still quiet. In fact, it was so quiet that it made him nervous. As the time approached midnight, he started to get a little on edge. Still it was totally silent both in the bunker and outside. One DAC was on duty at the radio and the other was sleeping. Occasionally Lefter got up and peered out the firing aperture into the blackness. He couldn't see a thing. Not a star was showing, so there must be a cloud cover. He wondered if Mewman was out there crawling around in the darkness. That must be a real spooky feeling. He shivered.

Sitting at the table around 0100, he heard a scratching noise outside the bunker door. Immediately, he thought that it might be a Chinese infiltrator planting an explosive to blow the door down. He got his carbine, pointed it at the door and slowly inserted a cartridge into the chamber from the 15 round clip. Then he eased off the safety and sat with the carbine in the ready position. *Maybe I can get at least one of the bastards*, he thought. How would he do that? His mind raced. If they blew the door and followed immediately with a grenade, he wouldn't have a chance. *What the hell should I do?* he thought. *In basic training, they never taught me anything about this kind of situation.* Maybe when the door came down he could charge and catch them before they threw a grenade. On the other hand, he could go open the door right now and force the confrontation. The scratching ceased and he found himself saying out loud, "Oh shit, here it comes!" Nothing happened. The door didn't blow and Lefter didn't go open it to investigate. Then it dawned on him!

Holy crap, he thought, *I've been carrying this carbine around for months now and never fired it. Shit, the damn thing may not even work.* Then he remembered the guard duty at the 303 when he tried to fire the carbine but it was on the safety position. Firing at the cat would have been embarrassing but not deadly. Now, he could die because he hadn't test fired the carbine.

For the rest of the night Lefter sat at the table saying under his breath now and then, "Dumb Shit, dumb shit." He could hardly keep from pointing the carbine at the door and pulling the trigger. *Damn, it's tempting. I could just tell the DACs it went off while I was cleaning it.*

Time passed very slowly as Lefter waited for dawn. He spent most of his time sitting and looking at the bunker door and whispering, "Dumb shit, dumb shit!"

Finally, after what seemed like days to Lefter, dawn arrived. With the carbine in the ready position he walked over and jerked open the bunker door. To his great relief, nothing was there. "Holy crap," he whispered. "You survived another one, you lucky dumb ass."

He walked out a few feet behind the bunker, raised the carbine and fired the full clip into a nearby bush. "YAHHH-HOOOOO!" he yelled at the top of his voice. "Take that, you bastards," he mumbled. Two wide-eyed DACs came running out of the bunker. "Just checking out my weapon," said Lefter calmly as he turned and walked back into the bunker. He got the spare 15-round clip out of his pack and locked it into the carbine. "God damn, that felt good," he said out loud as he clinched his fist and threw a body punch into thin air.

When Hillman and his DACs arrived for the next shift, Lefter told him about shooting a full 15-round clip into the bush out back. If I don't tell him the DACs will, was his reasoning. Hillman cracked up laughing when Lefter told him that was the first time he had fired the carbine since drawing it in mid-January. "I'm laughing with you, buddy," said Hillman. "Almost the same thing happened to me. Dawned on me one night up here when the some Marines were having a firefight somewhere out in No-Man's-Land. Suddenly, it dawned on me that I had never fired my carbine. Sat there the rest of the night worrying about it then did the same thing you did; shot the hell out of a bush the next morning."

Both men laughed heartily.

Lefter stuck out his hand and said, "Stay safe, buddy."

"I will. You too," said Hillman as he shook hands with Lefter. "By the way, I'm leaving on R&R late tomorrow. That's why I'm pulling this shift instead of Jolcomb. It gives him a little extra rest. You and Jolcomb will have to hold down the fort for a week. Is there anything I can get for you in Tokyo?"

"Can't think of anything right now," said Lefter. "Thanks for asking though."

"No problem," said Hillman.

"Stay safe, buddy," Lefter said again then turned and started walking down the hill.

On the drive back to the base camp Lefter got to thinking about the relationships he had developed with the men he had met in Korea. He had known the men back at 303 headquarters for several months and he considered each of them as friends. However, Crovelli was the only one there who had become a good friend. No one at 303 knew any of Lefter's personal background except Crovelli. The rest were working friends and beer drinking friends. Up here in the detachment, it was different.

With the exception of Crovelli, Lefter felt closer to the three men in his detachment than he did with anyone at 303 headquarters. He admired Campbell for his intelligence, his caring attitude, his modesty and his overall leadership ability. Lefter knew that Campbell spoke Chinese fluently but had not heard him do so. Maybe he spoke Chinese to the DACs when he visited them in their tent for a few minutes every day.

First thing each morning Campbell spent an hour or more sitting at the table studying the notes and translations of the Chinese DACs. Lefter felt honored to report to Campbell. Campbell was an outstanding NCO. *If he could have attended West Point he would have been a general by the time he was forty years old. It's just not fair*, thought Lefter. *That damn Major Soss shouldn't be in a leadership position.* He hoped Campbell was right when he said, "Be patient, assholes in this Army don't get away with it forever."

CHAPTER TEN

Campbell was sitting in the squad tent talking on the telephone when Lefter returned from the bunker. "Yes sir, I understand, day after tomorrow at 0845 hours. I'll see to it that the bunker is in tip-top shape." Campbell hung up, turned to Lefter and said, "Chicken Shit Soss is honoring us with a bunker inspection day after tomorrow; says he'll be at the bunker at precisely 0845."

"What?" said Lefter.

"You heard me right, a bunker inspection. I have never heard of such a thing. He told me it better be clean and tidy."

"Hey, Camp, maybe he would like to drive up the front of the hill and we could tip off the gooks ahead of time?"

"Wouldn't that be a blast?" said Campbell. Neither man laughed. "You take the courier run tomorrow and I'll go up and help Jolcomb tidy up the place and get ready for the honored event."

Lefter thought for a few seconds then said, "It just dawned on me that I'm going to be on duty when he comes up there. Hillman will be on R&R, right?"

"Sorry, Lef, can't do much about that other than holding back Hillman from R&R or having Jolcomb pull a double shift."

"Don't do either," said Lefter. "I can survive it."

"Your damn right you will," said Campbell. "I'll be up there with you. We'll kill the son-of-a-bitch if it comes down to that."

Campbell wasn't laughing when Lefter looked at him. "Really?" said Lefter.

"Maybe," said Campbell with a wink. "Think I may have just thought of a better plan though."

"What?" said Lefter.

"Tell you later, maybe. Go check the vehicles and haul a can of water before you hit the sack. I have a couple of calls to make." He went over and picked up the handset.

As Lefter exited the tent he heard Campbell say, "Please ask General Stoney to call me when he gets a chance. Tell him Sergeant Campbell called from the ASA Detachment."

Lefter smiled as he thought of what Major Soss would probably think of Campbell's close friendship with General Stoney. *That suck ass Soss would be green with envy.*

Jolcomb was out in the yard and had just completed checking out the vehicles. He was just getting ready to leave on the water run so Lefter joined him and they hauled back ten gallons of water from the water truck parked in the Marine area. Lefter didn't mention the bunker inspection coming up. He didn't want to one-up Campbell. Besides, he didn't want to take a chance of betraying what could be a confidential matter with Campbell.

Right after the water run, Lefter was prone on his cot and just starting to doze off when he heard Campbell answer the phone and say, "Thank you for calling back, sir. I was just wondering if you would be visiting on the MLR tomorrow, say around eight-thirty? I am having a powerful urge to talk to a former grunt that made it to the big time." Campbell listened and then said, "0830 would be great, sir. See you there."

Holy crap, thought Lefter. *Imagine talking to a general like that.* He was mulling that around in his mind when he fell sleep.

Lefter slept nearly all day. He didn't like to do that for fear that he couldn't sleep through the coming night. The night seemed to go on forever when he was lying wide-eyed in the darkness of the tent. He woke up in time to go with Campbell and Jolcomb to the Marine mess tent for dinner. Corned beef and cabbage again with just one beer.

Two dirty-faced Marines came over and sat down at the table. The one nearest to Lefter said, "How you doing today, buddy?"

At first, Lefter didn't recognize them, and then it came to him. It was the two smart-ass newbies that had started to give him a bad time. "Not too bad," said Lefter as he half expected to get a smart-ass reply.

"Look, buddy, we owe you an apology for the stupid-ass attitude we displaced to you the other day."

"No problem," said Lefter. Campbell and Jolcomb didn't say anything.

"Here. Have one on me," said the Marine as he placed his full can of beer in front of Lefter. The other Marine picked up his can and set it in front of Campbell. "Me too," he said.

Lefter, Campbell and Jolcomb starred into the eyes of the Marines. They were not being smart asses. They were dead serious. Campbell and Lefter

STAY SAFE, BUDDY

each picked up the beer can in front of them and put it back in front of the Marines. "Thanks, but that's not necessary," said Campbell as he smiled.

"Same for me," said Lefter and he smiled also.

"Thanks," said each Marine in turn as they began eating the corn beef and cabbage. "Stay safe, man," said one of the Marines as the three ASA men left the table.

"You too," they each said back.

Lefter stayed up until ten hours composing a letter to his wife.

> *The last couple of days have been peaceful and quiet. The weather is so beautiful here it is hard to realize that a war is going on. The early mornings are especially beautiful. Easy to see why Korea is known as the Land of the Morning Calm.*
>
> *I had a scare at the bunker the other night. A rat or some kind of animal was scratching around at the door in the wee hours. It gave me the willies. It was so quiet you could have heard a pin drop. The next morning I went outside looking for the rat but couldn't find him, so I shot the hell out of a nearby bush. Ha, Ha. Ain't I a regular John Wayne? Your hero, right?*
>
> *I am on courier run to Uijonbu tomorrow so I'll see some of the guys I worked with down there then. Other than that, not much happening here. How are you doing?*
>
> *Oh yes, thanks for the package of goodies. It got here a couple of days ago. I shared it with the guys in the detachment. They said to tell you that the cookies are delicious. I think so also. It sure is a special treat when we get a package from home.*
>
> *Well, that's five for now.*
>
> *Love you, John*

Lefter went to sleep thinking about his wife and wondering if he would ever see her again. Again, he selfishly wished that he had got her pregnant before shipping out. Then at least his genealogical line would not end with him.

The next morning Campbell and Jolcomb were preparing to leave for the bunker as Lefter was getting dressed.

"I'll check over Hillman's report up at the bunker," said Campbell. "Hillman will be riding down with you, so he can put the report with the other stuff in the mail pouch that you are to deliver to the cage at 303. I have already asked the DACs to keep a sharp eye out around here and call me at the bunker if need be."

"Yeah, I know," said Lefter. "This time I'll be back early also. I'll start back right after they sort the noon mail."

"OK," said Campbell. "I should be back from the bunker by the time you get back."

"Stay safe, you guys," said Lefter.

"Will do," they each answered as they got into the ¾ ton. The two DACs riding in the canvas-topped bed of the truck waved as the truck pulled away. Lefter waved back, then returned to the tent and got ready for the courier run to the 303. He wanted to be ready to go when Hillman showed up.

Within the hour, Hillman showed up, packed up a few things and they left for the drive south to the 303 at I-Corps headquarters. "Campbell tells me Chicken Shit Soss is on the prowl again," said Hillman.

"Yeah, we gotta shape up and have a spic-and-span bunker," said Lefter sarcastically. "Just had a great thought; think I'll find some flowers and arrange a bouquet in the middle of the bunker table. Wouldn't that be a nice touch for the major's visit?"

"Damn I'd like to see that," said Hillman. "You haven't got a hair in your ass if you don't. Take me a picture of that bouquet, will ya?

"You got it," said Lefter. "Wonder if I could find a tablecloth somewhere?"

"Yeah," said Hillman. "One of those frilly ones."

Both men laughed and spent the rest of the drive entertaining each other by coming up with a variety of ways the bunker could be fixed up with a homey atmosphere.

Arriving at the 303 Lefter could hardly wait to start collecting the homey stuff. He went to the supply tent and told Sergeant Thomas about the coming bunker inspection and the homey atmosphere that he intended to create. Thomas cracked up and laughed until he was coughing and choking.

"That's the best goddamn idea you ever came up with, Lefter. I'll get on the land-line and round up some homey and frilly stuff for you. Come back in a couple of hours and pick it up."

"Thanks, Sarg," said Lefter. He knew that Thomas had the connections to get anything he wanted.

Lefter went to the Day Tent and joined Hillman who was killing time reading magazines until the courier run would leave for Seoul after dinner. Lefter and Hillman joined Crovelli for lunch at the mess hall. Then Lefter went back to the supply tent. Sergeant Thomas had two large cardboard boxes containing a variety of homey things. He had a 6' x 8' frilly tablecloth, three large red candles, 3 lace curtains about the size of a small window, three throw pillows with knitted covers, and a flower vase with a dozen silk roses.

"I want a photograph of that bunker after it's decorated," said Thomas.

"You got it," said Lefter excitedly.

"Think you can get a photo of Major Soss in the homey bunker?"

"I'll give it a try," said Lefter.

Lefter loaded the boxes, picked up the detachment mailbag and drove excitedly all the way back to base camp smiling and chuckling out loud. Occasionally he would hit the steering wheel with the heel of both hands and say out loud, "Damn, this is going to be fun, fun, fun!" Normally, he was nervous and up tight when passing through the artillery emplacement but this trip he waved excitedly to the artillerymen and yelled out several times, "HAPPY DAYS ARE HERE AGAIN!" They must have thought he was cracking up.

Campbell laughed heartily as Lefter showed him the homey things. "This is going to be great," said Campbell. He was almost as excited as Lefter was. "We'll get up there early and decorate the bunker up real pretty."

"I can hardly wait," said Lefter.

They celebrated by having a few drinks and going to bed early.

Both men were up a first light. Campbell went to the DAC tent and told them it was necessary to leave for the bunker an hour early. The DACs complained but Campbell assured them that he would do them a special favor to make up for the additional hour of bunker duty.

Up at the bunker Jolcomb reported that it had been a quiet night with only one intercept. An Officer of the Chinese Peoples Army wanted to know the location of the Red Devils. "Didn't call it down because the gooks are always wanting to know the whereabouts of the Turks," said Jolcomb.

"Yeah, hard to tell if it means anything of consequence," said Campbell. "The CPA has a fearsome respect for the Turks. It's understandable, those little Turks are ferocious fighters."

Lefter patted Jolcomb on the back and said, "Sorry you're going to miss our white hanky inspection."

"If I didn't have to haul these DACs back to base camp, I'd stay up here another few hours just to see the fun," said Jolcomb. "I am going to help you decorate the place though. Them DACs can just sit on their asses and wait."

The three men went about decorating the bunker with the homey things Lefter had obtained. The table looked real pretty with the frilly tablecloth and the vase containing the dozen roses. They hung one lace window curtain on the inside of the bunker door and another on the outside of the door. The third lace curtain was hung over the viewing slit. Campbell had told the DACs that the bunker was to be decorated with a homey atmosphere. One DAC produced a tea set from his pack. Another had three silver-plated candleholders. Although the DACs didn't know why the bunker was being decorated, they laughed along with the GIs as the bunker took on a real homey look.

After it was finished, Lefter took several pictures for himself and Sergeant Thomas. "Crap, this is real pretty," said Lefter.

"Well, I'm outta here," said Jolcomb. "You prissy boys stay safe now, you hear."

"Yeah, stay safe, buddy," said Lefter as he waved a loosed-wrist goodbye and belly laughed. *A little bit of Mewman's personality is rubbing off on me*, he thought.

After Jolcomb left, Campbell and Lefter were making a few final adjustments of the decorations when there was a knock at the bunker door. "Who is it?" said Campbell.

"General Stoney."

"Come in, General," said Campbell.

Campbell and Lefter saluted as General Stoney entered the bunker. General Stoney threw back a casual salute, looked around the bunker and started laughing. He bent over, rested a hand on each knee and kept on laughing. Campbell and Lefter started laughing also. The DACs looked at them with broad smiles as if they were all nuts.

"This is the best goddamn tension reliever I've had since…well, never mind," said General Stoney.

"Have a seat, sir, and we'll fix you a tea," said Campbell.

The general cracked up laughing again and finally said through wet eyes, "If you say so, Sergeant," as he sat down at the table, took another look around and busted out laughing again.

Now Lefter knew why Campbell had been heating water on the sterno stove. Campbell took a couple tea bags from his pocket, put them in the teapot and poured in the hot water. He placed one of the teacups in front of the general. Just as the general broke out laughing again, the bunker door flew open and Major Soss said, "What the hell is going on in here?"

"Come right in and join the party," said General Stoney.

As the major's eyes adjusted to the dim lighting of the bunker he saw the Marine General and gave him a brisk salute. "At ease, sit down and join us for tea," said General Stoney, as he didn't return the salute.

Even in the dim light of the bunker, Lefter could see the crimson red face of Major Soss as he sat down at the table opposite the general.

Campbell put a teacup in front of the major and one on either side for himself and Lefter. "The tea will be ready in a couple of minutes," said Campbell.

"This is the best goddamn morale booster I have seen in a long time," said the general. "I want some photographs of this. I'm going to have it written up in the Stars and Stripes. Does anyone here have a camera?"

"I do, sir," said Lefter.

"OK, soldier, take a photo of me and the major here having tea," said the general. "Goddamn, this is hilarious, don't you think, Major?"

Major Soss, looking like a whipped puppy, nodded agreement.

"You've got some good men here, Major, innovators and morale boosters. See that they get rewarded for this innovative morale booster, will you?"

"Yes, sir," said the major.

Campbell poured the tea in order of rank; General, Major, himself, and Lefter. General Stoney raised the delicate teacup toward his mouth with his little finger extended and said, "Here's to our sense of humor, may we never lose it." Lefter snapped a picture of the general and the major with their teacups raised in toast. The general took a small sip, put down the cup and started laughing. Campbell and Lefter joined in. Major Soss just stared at them with his red face and a small pathetic grin.

"Well, I better be going," said the general. "Major, I'd like you to walk back down the hill with me."

Campbell and Lefter went outside the bunker with the two officers. "You go ahead of me so an ambush gets you first," said the general with a laugh. As they started down the hill, the general said in a stern tone, "Major, you're in my area of command here so in the future when you decide to visit my area you'll need my prior permission. Savvy?"

"Yes, sir," said Major Soss.

"One more thing," said the general. "If you want to bring up a special lunch for these guys sometime, I could meet you at their base camp and participate."

"Yes, sir," said Major Soss.

"You sure have some good soldiers up here."

"Yes, sir," said Major Soss.

"Are they getting promoted as soon as they're eligible?"

"Yes, sir," said Major Soss.

"Well, if there is any hold up in their promotions I'd be happy to recommend them."

"Yes, sir," said Major Soss.

"I'll look forward to attending the lunch you'll be setting up for them."

"Yes, sir," said Major Soss.

"By the way, Major, I was just kidding about putting the story in the Stars and Stripes newspaper. I know your operation is hush-hush stuff even though we all know that the gooks know we listen to them and we know they are listening to us."

"Yes, sir," said Major Soss.

The general laughed heartily again. "I'm damn sure going to treasure those pictures though. Fresh hot tea in a line bunker on a lace tablecloth, with candles, roses and frilly curtains. My staff is going to crack up when they see the photographs."

Back at the bunker, Campbell and Lefter were hysterical with laughter. The DACs were sure they had flipped out. Campbell poured a tea for each of the DACs. The Korean DAC was on duty at the radio and was served his tea there but the Chinese DAC joined them at the table. Although the DACs didn't understand the significance of the event, it nevertheless resulted in a togetherness and camaraderie that had not previously existed between them.

Lefter took a few more photos around the bunker and handed the camera to Campbell. "Take this back to base camp for me. If we're overrun up here tonight I don't want this important information captured."

Campbell took the camera and headed out the door laughing. "You've got your priorities right there. Keep the place spotless." Then he added seriously, "Stay safe, buddy."

Lefter walked outside the bunker with Campbell. They both started laughing again. "I hope this stupid idea of mine doesn't screw up your career," said Lefter.

"Not a chance," said Campbell. "If it does I'll kill the son-of-a-bitch." He didn't laugh.

The rest of the day and night passed quietly without one single intercept. Lefter made the only noise. Alone in the bunker with the DACs he would periodically think about the inspection by Major Soss and break out snickering. Then the snickering would erupt into loud laughter. Soon the DACs would be laughing also.

Jolcomb showed up early the next morning with his camera and, after his laughing subsided, snapped several photos around the bunker. As Lefter picked up his pack and went outside, Jolcomb followed. Something brushed across the top of Lefter's head as he left the bunker. Looking back, he saw a pair of women's panties and a brassiere attached to a wire strung above the bunker door.

Lefter started laughing. He pointed at Jolcomb and said, "I hope some Marine passing by doesn't think those belong to you."

"Never thought of that," said Jolcomb. "If anyone asks I'll just tell them they belong to you."

Both men laughed and Lefter headed down the hill to catch up with the DACs going off duty.

The next few days passed peacefully with no intercepts of consequence and no word from Major Soss. Lefter had the film developed and gave prints to Campbell for transmittal to General Stoney.

Lefter had avoided Major Soss when on the courier run to the 303 CRB. Crovelli said Soss went out every day in his jeep and stayed out until after dark. He came back after dark, parked in front of his tent, and didn't come out until the next morning. Each morning he went straight to his office for about an hour of signing paperwork then left for the day. No one knew where he went each day. Actually, no one seemed to give a damn where he was, so long as he was gone. Most wished he would disappear completely. Fortunately, Lieutenant Landa ran the show well considering he was a short timer in the 303. However, they all wanted to find out where Soss went every day.

CHAPTER ELEVEN

Hillman came back from R&R talking about Japanese bathhouses and drinking in little bars on the Ginza Strip where he picked up a different Japanese girl for each night in a hotel. "Great I & I," said Hillman.

Lefter was a little envious of Hillman's reckless abandon and sometimes wished he could act that way. "Glad you had fun. I hope you don't come down with one of those Asian pecker-rotting diseases and spoil your great memories."

"Bad thought, Lef," replied Hillman. Then he changed the subject and said, "Hear the daily courier run has been eliminated."

"Yeah," replied Lefter. "Campbell and the other detachment leaders made a deal with Lieutenant Landa. We only make a run when the intercept records indicated a need for Nay and his boys to use our data for a quick analysis. Otherwise, it's up to each detachment leader to determine when to make a run."

Now that Hillman was back, Lefter only had bunker duty every third day. One of the days off was occupied with chores around the detachment but the second day was completely open. Each man had a permanent trip ticket and could use one of the jeeps at will. Lefter decided to drive to Seoul, spend the day sightseeing around the area and taking pictures, then, drive back for dinner at the I-Corps mess hall followed by a few beers at the EM Club. Then he would spend the night on the guest cot, get up early and get the hell out of the 303 before Asshole Soss saw him. Ordinarily he would have to be on duty early the next day but Hillman and his DACs had offered to stay late in the bunker provided they were relieved by noon.

Lefter stopped briefly at the 303 to shoot the bull with Crovelli for a few minutes. Quigley was just coming out when Lefter parked in front of the building. "What's up, my man?" said Quigley.

"Just dropping in for a few minutes before heading out on a sightseeing trip down by Seoul," said Lefter.

"Want some company? I have the day off with nothing to do but bum around," said Quigley.

"Glad to have you join me. My jeep or yours?" responded Lefter.

"Let's take mine," said Quigley. "I shot a pheasant on the way down here. It's in my jeep. We'll get some mama san in Seoul to clean and cook it for us. Damn thing fell in a minefield after I shot it so I just tiptoed softly over and picked it up. Do you think I'm crazy?"

"Did you say you walked into a minefield to get a pheasant?"

"No, I said I *tiptoed* into a minefield to get the pheasant," replied Quigley with a broad smile.

"Yeah, you're nuts but then you're not known as the Mississippi Maniac for nothing," responded Lefter with a laugh.

Quigley laughed also and led the way to his jeep.

On the way to Seoul Lefter told Quigley about the inspection of the specially-decorated bunker. Quigley responded with was an astonished, "No shit! And you call me crazy. You better hide out from AssHole Soss. He'll be laying for you."

"I fully intend to avoid him like the plague," responded Lefter. "I made sure he wasn't going to be around before I stopped to see Crovelli."

Quigley chuckled, "That's funny stuff though. Where in the world do you get these ideas from?"

"Weird sense of humor," replied Lefter.

"Wish I could embarrass the bastard too."

"Be patient, buddy, your turn will come," said Lefter.

As they entered the outskirts of Seoul Quigley said, "Let's stop at Madam Dong's Place and ask where to get the pheasant cooked." Soon Quigley stopped the jeep in front of Madam Dong's building.

"I'll wait in the jeep," said Lefter.

Quigley was only gone for a few minutes. "Madam Dong says one of her girls is an expert cook and will make us a fancy meal for five dollars if I furnish the bird.

"What else is involved in the deal?" said Lefter suspiciously.

"Nothing, for two-fifty each we can have a fine meal. Madam Dong says to park the jeep in the back alley and bring in the bird."

"OK," said Lefter, "but I'm not interested in anything else."

"Yeah, right!" responded Quigley.

"I'm serious, buddy. No hanky-panky for me."

"Well, it ain't going to hurt nothing to take a look at the merchandise in the store," said Quigley with a broad smile.

"No deal," said Lefter.

After parking the jeep in the alley they took their carbines and the pheasant and went to the back door. Madam Dong opened the door, took the pheasant and handed it to a young Korean woman. "This is Wachimo," said Madam Dong. "She will cook and serve the meal." Lefter took out his wallet but Madam Dong raised her hand and said, "You pay later, maybe you decide to have something else after good meal."

"Yeah, maybe," said Quigley with a broad smile.

"Not me," said Lefter. He thought of his first trip through Seoul when he turned down Mewman's offer to stop at the Madam Dong Whore House. "You'll change you mind after being in this fucking kimchi bowl for a while," Mewman had said.

Lefter thought Madam Dong appeared to be around 40 to 45 years old. *Hard to tell*, he thought, *they all get homely as they age.* Her smile appeared friendly and sincere.

Wachimo, even without any Western makeup, was a striking woman with beautiful, clear, golden-brown skin. She appeared to be around 20 years old. She was wearing a robe-like dress resembling the Japanese kimono. Her coal black hair was in a shoulder length braid. Her dark brown eyes sparkled as she grinned broadly, bowed gracefully and said, "I go fix meal now."

"Change your mind yet, buddy?" asked Quigley.

"No way!" He was tempted though.

"Come to eating room and sit down," said Madam Dong as she led the way into another room. The room had several low tables with cushions for seats. None of the tables were occupied. Quigley and Lefter sat down at the nearest table just as Wachimo came in with a tray containing a teapot and teacups. "Wachimo helper cleaning bird," she said while bowing and pouring tea.

"Madam Dong, please join us," Lefter said as he motioned toward a cushion.

"Yes, please do," said Quigley.

Madam Dong seemed taken back and flustered by the invitation. "I am honored by your invitation," she said while taking a seat next to Lefter. "Why do you invite me to join you?" she asked.

"Because you are doing us a favor by preparing the pheasant for only five dollars," said Quigley. "We will share the meal with you and Wachimo. Is that OK with you?"

Again, Madam Dong was surprised by the invitation to share the meal. She hesitated for a few seconds then said, "Wachimo and me pleased to eat with you."

"Where did you learn to speak such good English?" asked Lefter.

"I run girls school before war and teach English-speaking class," said Madam Dong.

"Was the school located in Seoul?" asked Quigley.

"Yes, school called Etwa College."

"Holy moly," said Quigley, "Isn't that the buildings where ASA is now located?"

"Yes, we happy to loan area to U.S. Army for as long as they need. They save South Korea in war. Etwa College best girl college in all Asia," she added proudly. "You like Japanese sake?" she asked.

"How much will it cost?" asked Lefter.

"Nothing, on house," replied Madam Dong as she clapped her hands together twice. Another young Korean woman came into the room and bowed deeply. Madam Dong spoke to her in Korean, the only word understood by Quigley and Lefter was sake.

Madam Dong was a charming woman. She asked each of them about their families in America and seemed genuinely interested in their responses. She had heard about Washington state and Mississippi. She asked Lefter how far he lived from Seattle. "Someday, maybe I visit America but as scholar, not as whorehouse madam," she said with a small giggle.

Lefter and Quigley were really enjoying the sake. Madam Dong had refilled their cups several times and they were getting a little tipsy.

Wachimo entered the room with a tray containing a large bowl of steaming rice and four individual rice bowls. After placing the items on the table she left and soon returned with a large platter containing the meat of the pheasant. The meat had been removed from the bones and cooked in a candied solution. It was, as Quigley said, "mouth-watering good."

Lefter and Quigley were having a difficult time eating the rice with chopsticks so Wachimo left the table and returned with a forks and spoons. The meal of rice, candied pheasant and sake lingered on for over an hour. "Now for the entertainment," said Madam Dong then she spoke to Wachimo in Korean.

Wachimo rose from the table and began dancing close to each man with a swaying motion. Her body moved gently back and forth as she hummed a tune. Then she began to sing the melody in Korean. Her voice was soft and clear. Lefter and Quigley had no idea what she was saying but they were each mesmerized.

"Wachimo was number one music student at Etwa," whispered Madam Dong.

"Is she one of your girls for hire?" asked Quigley.

"Only if she decide it special occasion. She regular cook for my place."

"Knock it off, Quigley. I told you no hanky panky," said Lefter.

"Hey, buddy, just because you no hanky panky, not mean me go without," responded Quigley with a big grin.

Madam Dong said something in Korean and Wachimo bent down and took Quigley by the hand. He stood up and she led him from the room.

Lefter drank some more sake and told Madam Dong about his new wife back in Washington state. He fought off the urge to tell her that he, too, would like to be privately entertained by Wachimo. Mewman's words kept popping into his head: "You'll change your mind after you've been in this fucking kimchi bowl for a while."

In about fifteen minutes, Quigley came back in the room. "Hot damn, that is some kind of woman."

"Knock it off and let's cutta chogi," said Lefter. "I don't need any more temptation tonight."

"Yeah, I know, leave quickly, right?" responded Quigley.

"That's what I said, cutta chogi," answered Lefter.

Quigley turned and said to Madam Dong, "How much do we owe you?"

"Five dollars," replied Madam Dong. "Deal was five dollars."

Quigley took out five dollars and handed it to her. Lefter took out five dollars and held it out to her. "No, deal was five dollars," said Madam Dong refusing to take the money from Lefter. "Wachimo and me enjoy your company. Come back again and we make new deal, OK?"

"Sure will," said Quigley. Lefter nodded agreement.

Madam Dong followed them out to the jeep. "Damn," said Quigley as he removed an MP ticket from the windshield. "How the hell am I going to explain this?"

"No worry," said Madam Dong as she took the ticket from Quigley. "I handle."

"Don't know how you will do that but thank you," said Quigley.

"I handle; no sweat," said Madam Dong.

Madam Dong hugged each man and said softly, "Thank you for saving Korea."

STAY SAFE, BUDDY

Quigley drove on to ASAK while Lefter kept dozing off. At ASAK they both found a cot in the transient room and took a long nap. They spend the rest of the day driving around the outskirts of Seoul and taking pictures of monuments, shrines and a grand finale photo of the palace occupied by South Korea's first president, Syngman Rhee. Rhee had been president since 1945 and claimed to be the president of all of Korea. Obviously, North Korea didn't agree or Quigley and Lefter wouldn't be here, not to mention the rest of the UN troops.

Just before heading back north, they stopped at the military PX in Seoul. Lefter and Quigley each bought a carton of Chesterfield cigarettes for one dollar per carton. Quigley didn't smoke so they stopped on the way out of town and Quigley gave his carton of cigarettes to Madam Dong. She seemed overcome with emotion and hugged Quigley tightly.

They arrived back at I-Corps just barely in time for dinner at the mess hall. "Wouldn't you just know it?" said Quigley. "Chicken and dumplings!"

"Yeah," said Lefter laughing. "Want me to do a slow dance for you after chow?"

"Up yours," said Quigley while smiling broadly.

"Yours too," replied Lefter as he returned an exaggerated smile.

After dinner they went to the EM Club and spotted Mighty Joe, Nay and Crovelli already seated. As they walked toward the table Mighty Joe said as they walked up, "I got the first round."

"Have a seat and take one of these beers," said Nay pointing to dozen or so full cans in the center of the table. "Mighty Joe got a couple of quick promotions so the beer is on him tonight, right Joe?"

"OK, you guys are having a unique treat. It's not often that the Priest treats the Court."

"I'm beholding, here's to you," said Quigley holding up a beer in toast.

Everyone took a drink from his can of beer.

"I'm beholding too," said Lefter as he raised his can.

Again, everyone drank from his can of beer.

"What's new?" said Mighty Joe.

"Tell 'em about Asshole Soss' white-hanky bunker inspection, Lefter," said Quigley.

"Well," said Lefter, "I was hoping to nail Mighty Joe for a couple of beers to hear that story but since he's buying for the whole evening anyway, why not!" Lefter told them every detail and the table almost turned over from men slapping it. They howled with laughter. Even Mighty Joe had tears running down his cheeks.

"Now if I could figure a way to get the SOB to police up the empty cans behind my bunker, that would be a whooping coup," said Quigley. "Any chance of getting General Stoney to transfer to my outfit?"

"A Marine transferring to an Army Unit? Are you out of your mind?" said Lefter. "Mixing Jarheads and Doggies is like mixing baking soda with battery acid, it causes a violent boiling action." Everybody laughed heartily.

Lefter told them about the young smart-ass Marines straight from boot camp and their change of attitude after surviving their first battle. "When we first met they were swaggering around showing off their sharp shooter badges and shooting off their mouths. Then them Chinks made believers out of them."

"Well, I've about had it for tonight," said Nay. "You guys are sending nothing down but boring stuff. Nothing to analyze there."

"That's the way we like it, peaceful and quiet," said Lefter.

"Ditto on that," said Quigley. "Where are we going to sleep tonight?"

"The guest bunk is available but one of you will have to use the couch in the Day Room," said Nay.

"I'll take the couch," said Lefter. "Less chance that Soss will see me there. Besides, I want to take Smoky a beer."

Upon entering the Day Room, Smoky greeted Lefter with a wagging tail and sniffed at the open beer. Lefter poured the can of beer into the dog's bowl and Smoky began to lap it up with gusto. Sitchie was sitting in one of the stuffed chairs writing a letter. "Gonna flake out on the couch for the night if you don't mind," said Lefter.

"Be my guest," said Sitchie. "I'll be out of here in a few minutes. It's damn near midnight and I need my beauty sleep."

"Ugly sleep is more like it," said Lefter.

"Screw you," said Sitchie.

"Up yours," replied Lefter.

Both smiled.

Smoky finished his can of beer and started burping. "How many beers did Smoky have before I got here?" asked Lefter.

"You're lucky, Lefter. When Smoky burps it's a sure sign that he's not going to get sick. However, if he starts gagging, let him out of the tent pronto or you'll have a stinky cleanup job to do."

"I forgot to ask if he had been drinking before I got here. Not too bright of me," said Lefter.

In a few minutes Sitchie left and Lefter turned out the light, took off his boots, lay down on the couch and fell asleep immediately.

Soon, mortar rounds started exploding all around and shrapnel tore through the tent canvas in all directions. Lefter ran to the bar, opened the cooler, climbed in and pulled the door down tight over him. It was frigid in there with the ice and soft drinks. At least that damn Soss had still allowed the men to keep soft drinks in the cooler. Outside the mortar rounds kept coming in and the sound of shrapnel ripping though the tent accelerated. He started shivering and it was getting hard to breathe. All the air was being used up in the cooler. He had to make a decision, shiver and die from lack of air or jump out of the cooler and take shrapnel. He threw open the cooler's door, climbed out and started gulping in air.

Suddenly, he was sitting up on the couch, shaking, sweating profusely and gasping. *Another damn nightmare*, he thought. A siren was wailing outside. At first, he didn't know where he was but then he heard Smoky gagging over by of the door. *It must be an air raid alert. The hell with it, I'm staying right here. Bed-check Charlie never dumps out anything here anyway. Better let that damn dog out before he makes a mess I'll have to clean up.* He went to the door and opened it. Smoky ran out into a moon lit night and started vomiting.

He had just sat back down on the couch when a large explosion occurred nearby. Something started hitting the tent with a thumping sound. Thump, thump, thump. It sounded like mud hitting the tent. Smoky was barking and scratching at the door. He went over and opened the door. Smoky ran in, stopped and shook himself like dogs do after they come out of water. Something splattered all over Lefter. "Holy crap," said Lefter out loud, "you stink like shit." Then it dawned on him. Bed-check Charlie had just bombed the shit house. That was shit falling onto the tent. The stench was horrific. "Damn you," he said to Smoky, "you shook shit all over me." He started gagging and ran out the door.

He could hear men yelling and cursing nearby. That must have been some shit fallout to hit them in the air raid trench, which was about fifty yards away. Then it occurred to him that the wind was blowing from the north. That big explosion threw several hundred gallons of shit up high in the air and the wind carried it over the compound. The smell was putrid. He walked toward the main EM tent, gagging every few feet.

Nay and Crovelli were just returning from the air raid trench. "Did you get any of that shit fallout?" said Lefter as he approached them.

"Got crap all over my shoulders," said Nay. "Damn good thing I put on the steel pot or my head would be covered."

"Same here," said Crovelli. "Where were you, Lefter?"

"Stayed in the Day Tent but that damn dog was outside and when I let him in he shook shit all over me. Would one of you loan me a set of clothes?

"I've got a spare set you can use," said Crovelli.

Other men started returning to the tent. Nay took charge. "Don't anyone go in the tent with their clothes and shoes on. Undress outside and leave your shitty gear out here until tomorrow when it gets daylight."

"Good plan," said Crovelli. "No wonder they had you slated for OCS."

"Screw you," said Nay.

"Up yours," replied Crovelli.

"Will you guys knock off the lovey-dovey talk and get me a clean outfit? I'll spend the rest of the night on the floor in your tent. I'm not going back in there tonight with that stinking dog."

"OK," said Nay, "but you get cleanup duty on the Day Tent tomorrow morning."

"Fair enough, but that damn dog is gonna help," said Lefter laughing.

"This is the first literally shitty situation I have ever been in," said Nay, laughing.

"Who would ever think shit would be falling from the sky?" said Crovelli.

"Well, SHIT HAPPENS," yelled Lefter.

Lefter, Nay, Crovelli and the other men milling around started laughing. "All together now," said Lefter, "say SHIT HAPPENS."

"One, two, three," and they all said in unison, "SHIT HAPPENS!"

"Louder," ordered Nay.

"SHIT HAPPENS," they yelled at the top of their voices.

"Three more in quick time," ordered Nay, "Sound Off."

"SHIT HAPPENS, SHIT HAPPENS, SHIT HAPPENS," they yelled in the marching quick time tempo.

"One, two, three, four — SOUND OFF," said Crovelli.

"SHIT HAPPENS," they all said again in unison.

"OK, smoke 'em if you got 'em," said Nay.

The group of men broke out laughing while taking off their boots and clothes.

"What is going on over here and what is that awful smell?" said Major Soss as he strode up. "What is all the yelling and why does it stink around here?"

Lefter eased in behind Crovelli and hoped the major wouldn't recognize him in the moonlight.

"Bed-check Charlie blew up the shit house, sir," said Nay. "Shit flew into the sky and dropped on us in the air raid trench."

"Well, get the place cleaned up and quiet down around here," said the major as he turned and marched off.

"That turkey didn't leave his tent or he would have shit on him like the rest of us," Nay whispered. "The asshole will track it into his tent on his shoes though."

Lefter spent the rest of the night sleeping on the wooden floor of the tent covered only with a wool army blanket. The air in the tent still smelled like shit to Lefter.

At first light everyone got up and headed for the I-Corps shower area. It wasn't open yet but Nay bribed the operators with the promise of a bottle of whiskey and they fired up the water heaters. After soaping up and rinsing off several times Lefter said, "This is the best damn shower I have ever had."

"Amen to that," said Crovelli.

"You guys owe me a few beers for setting this up," said Nay.

"You got it," said Lefter and Crovelli in unison.

Upon returning to the 303 CRB area, Lefter remembered that Quigley was supposed to be sleeping on the guest cot. "Where the hell is Quigley?" asked Lefter as he walked over to the guest cot and picked up a note lying on top of the sleeping bag. Lefter read the note out loud: *Can't sleep, returning to my detachment tonight – Quigley.*

"Lucky timing," said Nay. "He missed the shit storm."

"The guy is lucky," said Lefter. "He walked into a minefield on the way down to get a pheasant he'd shot."

"What?" Crovelli answered in astonishment.

"You heard me," said Lefter. "He told me he tiptoed into a minefield to get the pheasant. We took it to Seoul yesterday and had it cooked for lunch."

"No shit?" queried Nay.

"Ha, ha, funny," said Lefter. "Guess I better start working on getting the Day Room cleaned up."

Shit-house Charlie showed up for work and was standing staring at the remains of his "place of employment." Lefter gave him a dollar to clean up the Day Tent and give Smoky a bath. The fire truck washed down the outside of the tents but the stench was still putrid. Lefter had his jeep washed out with the fire truck hose then he picked up the mail and headed back to his detachment.

As he walked into the detachment tent, Campbell looked up from his papers at the table and said with a big grin, "Here you had a stinking good time at the 303 last night."

"Shitty news travels fast," said Lefter, smiling back.

Still grinning, Campbell said, "Other than the shit storm, how was the rest of your day off?"

"Great. Ran into Quigley at the 303 and I joined him for a vacation trip to Seoul and vicinity. We stopped in at Madam Dong's Place and had a pheasant lunch with steamed rice, tea and a few cups of good sake. Quigley furnished the pheasant that he shot on the way to 303 from his detachment."

"Spent the whole month's pay already, huh?" said Campbell.

"You won't believe it but she only charged us five dollars total for the whole works. Seems she took a liking to us after we asked her to join us for the meal. Guess it was our lucky day."

"Appears your luck ended when darkness set in," said Campbell with a grin.

"Yeah, that reminds me. I borrowed some clothes from Crovelli; better change into my own before going to the bunker." He told Campbell about the shit falling on the Day Tent and Smoky coming inside and shaking shit everywhere. Campbell started howling with laughter. Jolcomb was still in his sleeping bag but started laughing hard also.

"You turkey, Jolcomb, you've been playing possum and eavesdropping," said Lefter.

"How do you get into these cotton-picking messes, Lefter?" said Jolcomb.

"Just damn lucky, I guess," responded Lefter.

"Don't rub any of that kind of luck off on me," said Jolcomb.

"Screw you," said Lefter grinning as he flicked the finger toward Jolcomb.

"Up yours," responded Jolcomb, smiling as he returned the finger.

"I don't have to stay around here and take all this shit. I'm headed for the hill right now."

Hillman was smiling broadly as he opened the bunker door to let Lefter in.

"I see you already heard the odoriferous news," said Lefter, acting proud.

Still grinning and with a little snickering laugh Hillman said, "Whatever could you mean by that?"

"You asshole, you know what," said Lefter.

"OK, so Campbell mentioned something about it raining shit at the 303 last night but that is about all I know." Then with a little curtsy he continued, "or was it raining odoriferous excreta?"

Lefter spilled out the whole sordid details while Hillman made a feeble attempt to be sympathetic. Even the DACs were laughing heartily.

"It was absolutely disgusting," said Lefter as he shivered and made a gurgling sound. "A once-in-a-lifetime experience I could have done without."

"Just another war story to tell your kids someday," said Hillman with another big grin. "Stay safe, buddy," said Hillman as he turned and joined the waiting DACs for the trek down the back of the hill.

"You, too, hope to see you in twenty-four," replied Lefter.

CHAPTER TWELVE

"Damn it!" said Lefter as he jumped and spilled cherry juice on himself. He was sitting at the table eating a can of C-Ration cherries when someone pounded loudly on the bunker door.

"Get the fuck out here ASA boy before I shoot the fucking door down." Then a big belly laugh.

The DACs were looking worried as Lefter opened the door. "Relax, I know this asshole," said Lefter to the DACs. He recognized the voice and the charming manner of speaking and knew it was Mewman. "Well hello, Mew, what's up?"

"Was over here earlier and that fucking Hillman told me you were coming up today. Got a smoke?"

Lefter pulled out his pack of cigarettes and handed it to Mewman. "Keep the pack if you need some. I have another pack in the bunker."

"Naw," said Mewman, "I'm trying to quit the fucking things; bad for your health, you know." Then Mewman let out the familiar belly laugh.

"Sorry I can't invite you in the bunker, but you know the rules," said Lefter.

"It's a nice fucking day so let's just sit out here on one of these ammo boxes," replied Mewman. "I'm telling you, Lef, this stuff I do now is real fucking fun.

"What stuff?"

"Went out on an ambush patrol last night and it was a fucking hoot. Left the MLR around ten o'clock and spent over an hour sneaking out across that fucking No-Man's-Land. Then we set up an ambush along a popular trail used by the gooks. Laid out there in the dark for two hours before a gook patrol showed up then we shot the fucking shit out of them."

"Didn't they fight back?" asked Lefter.

"Hell yes, that is what made it so much fun." Mewman held up his weapon and said, "I was using this BAR; it's a fucking blast to shoot." He kissed the

BAR and said, "She sure is sweet."

Mewman's eyes were sparkling and it was obvious to Lefter that he had enjoyed the encounter. "Them fucking chicken shit gooks pulled back and called in mortar fire on us so we had to pull back in a hurry. Then we called in our mortars on them."

"My regular assignment is with a machine gun on the MLR but I volunteered for the fucking patrol. I'm telling you, Lef, it is real damn exciting and fun, fun, fun. That fucking major did me a favor by kicking me out of the ASA."

"Did you hit any of them?" asked Lefter.

"Must have, they were only fifteen or twenty yards away when we opened up on them. Think I shot my first fucking gook. Hot damn!"

"Sounds like you have the right duty," said Lefter.

"Like I said, that fucking major did me a favor by kicking me out of the ASA. Think I'll kiss his ass the next time I see him."

"Word is out that you already kissed his ass," said Lefter, baiting Mewman.

"I ain't never kissed nobody's fucking ass," responded Mewman with indignity.

"What about the deal I hear you made with Asshole Soss?" said Lefter.

"Making a fucking deal ain't kissing ass," said Mewman.

"What was the deal you made?" asked Lefter.

"OK, I'll tell you," said Mewman. "I saved his sorry ass from that artillery attack and he wanted me to be a witness that he was in combat. He offered to put me in for a Silver Star if I would be his witness, so I signed on the fucking dotted line."

"So that's it," said Lefter.

"Damn right," said Mewman. "I wouldn't give that fucking asshole the sweat off my balls unless I got something real good in return." Big belly laugh.

Lefter laughed along with Mewman and offered him another cigarette.

"No, thanks, gotta get back and get some sleep. I volunteered for a combat patrol that's going out tonight. We're going out there and pick a fight. That should be more fucking fun than the ambush patrol."

"Glad you're having a good time," said Lefter.

"It's a fucking hoot," said Mewman as he stood up and picked up the BAR.

"Stay safe, buddy," said Lefter as he stuck out his right hand.

Mewman shook Lefter's hand vigorously and said, "Thanks, Lef. I'll come down early tomorrow morning and see you."

"I'll look forward to seeing you," said Lefter.

Mewman turned and started walking east along the MLR trench.

Lefter called after him, "Stay safe now, you hear."

Mewman waved but didn't turn around.

Lefter spent a lot of time during the day thinking about Mewman. He sure made it sound exciting to be involved directly in combat. Hunkering down in the ASA bunker during an attack was not only frightening, it was frustrating. It might be easier to take if he could fight back with more effort than shooting a bush. In a way, he admired Mewman and his simple mentality: "Kill the fuckers, they ain't even human anyway."

Looking out through the viewing slit Lefter studied the terrain in No-Man's-Land and tried to figure out where Mewman's patrol might be headed tonight. He intended to keep a sharp lookout tonight after dark and maybe see them as they went through the barbwire lines. The gate through the wire must be near the machine gun nest that the Marines had manned down by the barbwire lines. Surely, the Army guys were manning the same bunker now.

Lefter took a close look at topographic map on the table. Looking directly north from the ASA bunker, Outpost Elko was located about 700 yards out and slightly to the east. Outpost Carson was about the same distance but off to the northwest about 30 degrees. Outpost Vegas was about 300 yards northeast of Outpost Elko. Outpost Reno was 300 yards north and slightly east of Outpost Carson. Someone had penciled an oblong circle around the four Outposts and labeled it "Nevada Complex." West of Outposts Carson and Reno, a dirt road ran northerly.

Directly north of Outpost Vegas about 300 yards was one labeled Outpost Berlin. Outpost East Berlin appeared to be about 1000 yards east of Outpost Berlin. Outpost Detroit was located about 400 years north of Outpost East Berlin.

Chances are, Lefter reasoned, Mewman's platoon is probably responsible for the area directly in front of them. That would be the land area between the MLR and Outposts Elko and Vegas and maybe Berlin. He took the map to the viewing slit and, studying the terrain decided where Elko, Vegas and Berlin were located. That would be the target area he would watch tonight. Now how would he locate that area in the dark of night? He put three matches on the firing aperture and lined them up with the three outposts.

Lefter had been so busy studying the map and the actual terrain that he was surprised when the light of day began to fade into dusk. Just toward the end of dusk, machine guns began firing in small bursts all along the MLR. Chinese mortars began firing toward the machine gun positions and U.S. mortars returned fire. The mortar exchanges went on for ten or fifteen minutes then died down and the battlefront fell quiet.

Under cover of the mortar fire, Mewman's combat patrol had slipped down the front slope of the MLR and out through the barbwire lines. Moving slowly, they reached Outpost Carson in about an hour. Using tonight's password "Cobra," they were recognized by the men manning Outpost Carson.

Passing directly in front of Outpost Carson, they veered left and crept along a ridge for some 200 yards. Then down on their bellies they crawled forward another 100 yards. Ahead they could hear the sounds of digging. The Chinese must be reinforcing their outpost on Hill 101.

Back in the ASA bunker, Lefter stared intently through the viewing slit into the darkness and toward what he believed to be the area of Outpost Elko, Vegas and Berlin. There was no moon and it was pitch black. The only light anywhere was the vertical searchlight beam from Panmunjom far off to the west. He was getting nervous and was tempted to light a cigarette, but recalled reading recently that a burning match could be seen from seven miles in the dark. He couldn't remember for sure but thought he might have been guilty of previously striking a match at the viewing slit. Another rookie mistake he thought. *Should have known better. Dumb shit!*

Just as he was about to go sit at the table and smoke, he heard the sound of outgoing mortar rounds. Then, as the rounds began landing, orange flashes started appearing over toward Outpost Carson. Within two or three seconds the muffled sounds traveled back to Lefter's ears. That's about right, he thought, at about 700 feet per second it would take about three seconds for the sound to travel back to his position on the MLR. Then the muzzle blasts of small arms started showing up on the south side of the mortar flashes. Among all the small arms fire, Lefter thought he recognized the sharp sound of a BAR. *Could that be Mewman?*

Flares burst in the sky above the area of the firefight. The small arms firing slacked off briefly then seemed to pick up speed. Lefter couldn't tell for sure because the outgoing mortar barrage had increased considerably. It sounded like a constant stream of them going over the bunker. Dozens of mortar rounds seem to be exploding every second. Thud, thud, thud — thud — thud. Lefter mumbled under his breath, "Mewman must be having a fucking good time out there right now."

Lefter ducked back from the viewing slit, turned his back and lit a cigarette.

He glanced over toward the DACs and they were in their usual positions. The DACs were so used to hearing firefights in the distance that they paid little attention to it. Back at the viewing slit with the cigarette cupped in his hand he watched as the firefight slowly decreased and then ceased entirely. "That was one hell of a show. Hope you survived it, buddy," Lefter said out loud.

Suddenly, Lefter realized he was all tensed up. He sat down at the table and tried to relax. His heart was pounding and he was shaking. It was the kind of shaking that is closely akin to shivering from cold. He was also sweating although it was a cool night. "Mewman is certainly right that firefights are exciting, even at distance of 700 yards. It must be gut wrenching to actually be in a close up firefight."

An inordinate amount of intercepts were coming in on the radios but neither the DACs nor Lefter could make any sense of what was being said so they had decided to not call in anything during the night.

Just before dawn, Mewman pounded at the door of the ASA bunker and said, "Hey, candy ass, get the hell out here before I shoot in the fucking door."

After being startled by Mewman's pounding, Lefter was not impressed with Mewman calling him a candy ass. Lefter jerked open the bunker door and glared at Mewman. "Look, John Wayne, don't call me candy ass and I won't call you shit head, deal?"

Mewman was surprised by the aggressive response and just stared at Lefter.

Lefter continued, "And another thing, quit pounding on my door or I just might answer it with a burst from my carbine."

Mewman regained his composure and started belly laughing then said with sincerity, "OK, Lef, you got it. I don't want to fuck up a good buddy."

Lefter stepped outside, took out his cigarettes and offered one to Mewman. "Don't mind if I do," said Mewman as he took one and waited for a light from Lefter.

Lefter struck a match, lit his own cigarette then shook out the match. Mewman looked shocked and said, "What the fu—" and stopped as Lefter held out his own cigarette fire end toward Mewman.

"If three on a match is unlucky, maybe two is also," said Lefter. "I don't want to fuck up a good buddy."

They both laughed. Then Mewman took Lefter's cigarette and lit his own cigarette.

"Pull up an ammo box and sit a spell," said Lefter.

Mewman lowered himself to an ammo box and said, "Got any booze?"

"Not in the bunker," lied Lefter. "Got some back at the detachment base camp if you can visit me there."

"Maybe in a couple of days," said Mewman. "They let us go back to the fucking battalion headquarters every week or two for a shower and clean clothes."

"Well, Mew, as you probably know, the ASA base camp is adjacent to the battalion headquarters."

"How about bringing a few bottles of booze up here and I'll buy the fucking stuff from you for the going rate. I'll pay you the full bore; it's still $90 bucks a case, ain't it?"

"I'll see if something can be worked out," said Lefter nervously. He knew from experience that Mewman lost total control when drinking the hard stuff. Lefter quickly added, "On another subject, I watched a firefight from the bunker last night. Were you in it?"

Mewman's eyes lit up and he smiled. "Damn right and I think I got me another fucking gook last night too. Me and this BAR are good fucking buddies."

"What happened?" said Lefter. "It looked like the fight was over by Outpost Carson."

"Yeah, it was actually west of Carson near a fucking gook outpost called Ungook. Don't ask me why they call the fucking thing Ungook, I don't know and it don't make a shit anyway."

"Well, what happened?" asked Lefter again.

"We sneaked up on the bastards and somehow they knew we was coming. They hit us with a bunch of mortar fire then launched some fucking flares and came at us head on. They was screaming and yelling and blowing bugles and whistles. Must have been a platoon of them and we only had nine guys."

Mewman was really getting excited and it showed in his eyes and facial expressions. "My BAR buddy here fired something like three hundred rounds at the fuckers. I threw four grenades at the fuckers also. That was fun. My patrol leader called in our mortars in a box so we could get the hell out of there."

"What do you mean by a box?" asked Lefter.

"Mortar barrage in front of us and on both sides with the open end toward the MLR so we could get the fuck out. See?"

"Yeah," said Lefter as he pondered the situation. "Anybody hurt? That's a stupid question, isn't it?"

"Yeah," said Mewman. "Our point man is MIA and two guys got hit by fragments from the mortar barrage but we brought 'em back and Doc says they will live to fight another day. We must have killed or wounded eight or ten of them fucking gooks though. I think I got two of them fucking gooks myself. I saw them fall about ten yards in front of me."

"You seem to have finally found your niche in this man's Army," said Lefter.

Mewman smiled broadly and said, "Yeah, I tell you, Lef, it's better than sex. Gives me a fucking hard-on just telling you about it." Then the familiar belly laugh.

"You do make it sound exciting," said Lefter.

An Army Sergeant came walking down the trench line toward Mewman and Lefter.

"Here comes my boss man now," said Mewman. "Hey, Happy, come on down here and meet my good fucking buddy from the ASA."

As the Army Sergeant walked up to them Mewman said, "Happy, this is Lefter from the ASA. We've been negotiating for some booze. Like I told you these fucking ASA guys can get the hard stuff by the case."

"Good, we could use a little booze every now and then," said Happy as he shook hands with Lefter.

Now that Lefter knew that Mewman's immediate leader wanted the hard liquor he felt more comfortable with the situation. "I will try and line up some hard stuff for you," said Lefter. "How much do you want?"

"A case," responded Mewman.

"Naw, just a couple of bottles for starters," said Happy, "then maybe more later."

"I'll try and bring up a couple of bottles on my next shift, which should be the third day from now."

"How's that for a soft fucking assignment," said Mewman. "He works one day and then gets two off." Then the belly laugh. "Too goddamn boring for me though," he added.

"Good meeting you, Lefter," said Happy. "Come on, Gung-ho, it's time for us to get some beauty sleep after playing games all night."

Mewman stood up and said, "They started calling me Gung-ho because I'm so fucking enthusiastic. Can't help it if I just love killing them fucking gooks."

"OK, stay safe, guys," said Lefter.

"Will do, see you in three days," said Happy.

"Hope so," said Lefter. He stood and watched Happy and Mewman walk east down the MLR trench. Lefter briefly wished he could experience going out into No-Man's-Land on a patrol. Then he shook his head and said out loud, "Lefter, you dumb shit, what kind of stupid thinking is that!"

A while later, Lefter was at the viewing slit and thought he heard music. Yes, there was some kind of eerie music coming across No-Man's-Land. The Chinese must have a loud speaker set up out there. Then a man's voice said over the speaker, "*Men of the 25th infante, come to oul side or you die. Come to oul side or die. Come to oul side or die.*" It sounded like a stuck record. *Maybe it is*, thought Lefter. In any event, it was damn annoying. It was Lefter's first encounter with the Chinese front line propaganda. With cupped hands around his mouth, Lefter yelled northward at the top of his lungs, "FUUUUCK YOUUUUU!" Then he started getting ready to be relieved by Jolcomb.

Twenty minutes later when Jolcomb showed up the gooks were still using the loud speaker system to broadcast threatening messages. "*GI you die tonight. Come to oul side and you not die. Le-mem-beh pletty gill back home da lait flo you, come to oul side and you live.*"

A 50-caliber machine gun began firing from a location somewhere east of the ASA bunker.

"Maybe that's Mewman firing," said Lefter to Jolcomb "You wouldn't believe how much he is enjoying the combat stuff. He was over here earlier telling me about a combat patrol he was on last night. He was all fired up and excited just telling me about it. He said it was better than sex, and I think he was serious."

"Different things for different folks," replied Jolcomb as he shrugged his shoulders and held his hands out palms up.

"Those damn gooks been bombarding us with that loud speaker for the last half hour and it's getting on my nerves," said Lefter.

Just as Lefter said the last couple of words, they heard the sound of three outgoing mortar rounds.

"Appears you're not the only one annoyed," said Jolcomb as he pointed upward.

"Well," replied Lefter jokingly, "I hope they have the bastard zeroed in. Otherwise I may volunteer to go out on patrol with Mewman tonight and get the bastard myself." Then he hastily added, "Just kidding."

The loud speaker ceased operating and Jolcomb said, "Those mortar shots must have got him or at least come close. If he survived the mortars that gook with the loud speaker is probably running like hell right now to get out of the way of the next barrage."

Overhead they heard the sound of another three outgoing mortar rounds. East on the MLR, at about Mewman's location, the machine gun sounded again; tat-tat-tat, tat-tat, tat-tat-tat. Other machine guns echoed the same shot pattern and tempo all along the MLR.

"We win," said Jolcomb. "Our guys are just having fun with the propaganda now."

"Good," said Lefter, "the bastards were getting to me."

Jolcomb smiled and patted Lefter on the shoulder, "Ease up, Lef. According to many of our politicians it's only a little 'ol police action."

"Yeah, right," responded Lefter. "Wonder how he would describe it if these damn mortar rounds were falling around their place."

Jolcomb touched his temple and said, "Think you've got something, Lef. Now how do we arrange for these gooks to drop a barrage in on their Command Post in Washington, DC?"

Poking a finger toward Jolcomb, Lefter said, "Good idea. Maybe they would come to the MLR if we wrote them a nice letter of invitation. Or maybe we could get up a petition and pass it up and down the MLR to be signed by the POLICE."

Jolcomb laughed, "You're a natural troublemaker, Lef. Get the hell out of here and start writing that petition."

"OK, I'm gone. Stay safe, buddy."

"Will do, you too," replied Jolcomb.

Driving back to the base camp, Lefter kept thinking about the politics back in the States. Chances were that most of the politicians had no concept of the brutal reality of this war. They would be puking up their guts at the savage horror, the ferocity and the carnage on the battlefront.

President Dwight Eisenhower, as a General of the Army during World War II, knew the blood and guts of war, but he had inherited the Korean War from Harry Truman. Lefter knew that Truman had ordered the atomic bomb dropped on Hiroshima and Nagasaki at the end of WWII and Japan had surrendered unconditionally thereafter. That Truman decision was given credit for saving thousands of lives that would have been lost in a ground invasion of Japan. Now thousands of American soldiers were dying in Korea. Why? Lefter didn't have any idea why.

Sitting down at the table across from Campbell he handed him the intercept notes and said, "Hey, Camp, do you know why we are over here fighting this goddamn war?"

Campbell hesitated and decided that Lefter was serious. "For me, I am a career man so it's my job. Why are you here, Lef?"

Looking down at his dirty boots Lefter said, "Well, I guess the bottom line is, I was told to." Then he added, "I got this letter from an outfit that said it was my Selective Service Board and inside was my obituary. It said: Greetings, Your friends and neighbors have selected you to learn to kill people and maybe die for your country or at least get your ass wounded."

Lefter paused and looked at Campbell. Campbell looked down at his own boots and didn't respond.

Lefter continued, "I got lucky and was offered the chance to join the Army Security Agency. That was the best decision I've made so far in my entire life."

"What other big decisions have you made in your life?" said Campbell seriously.

Lefter got up, went to his cot, pulled a photo from beneath the head of his sleeping bag and held it up toward Campbell. "Well, I married this pretty little girl and that was a really big decision but I think time will prove that it was a good decision."

"Let's hope so," replied Campbell.

"Made one really stupid decision at the end of my senior year of high school," said Lefter. "Pacific Lutheran College offered me a full scholarship to play baseball and I turned it down. Now that was stupid, right?"

"Maybe so, maybe not," said Campbell.

Lefter continued, "Then Hub Kettle, the manager of the Yakima Bears double A baseball team, offered me a pitching job. Said he'd give me a hundred and fifty a month plus five dollars a day while on the road. Turned that down too."

"Why?" said Campbell.

"Knew I could make more money working in a fruit warehouse. I just wanted to get a job, buy a car, drink beer and chase girls. Come to think of it that kind of thinking is what makes a good soldier, right?"

"What do you mean?" said Campbell as he deliberately encouraged Lefter to get his frustration off his chest.

Lefter was really letting it out now. "Train, kill, drink booze, sleep, and chase girls; ain't that the life of a typical soldier?"

"It sure seems like it a lot of the time," replied Campbell.

It dawned on Lefter that he was whining to Campbell. "Sorry to unload on you, Camp. Like you're a chaplain or a shrink."

"No problem, anytime," replied Campbell.

Then changing the subject Lefter said, "I told Mewman and his sergeant that I would bring them a couple of bottles of booze and I don't have any right now. Would you loan me two bottles until I can order a case?"

Campbell went over and pulled out a cardboard box from underneath his cot. Removing two bottles of Canadian Club whiskey, he held it out toward Lefter. "Here, stick it in your pack now and you won't forget to take it up on your next shift."

"Thanks, Camp. I'll pay you back when the next shipment comes in." Lefter took the whiskey, put it into his pack and shoved it under his cot. "Guess I better try and get some sleep."

"I'll wake you up for chow tonight if you're still snoozing," said Campbell.

"Thanks, Camp," said Lefter as he sat down on his cot and started undressing. As he climbed into his sleeping bag, he tried to think of his wife, baseball, drinking beer with the guys; anything except the damn war. He wanted to avoid a nightmare.

The loud speaker announced to the several thousand people in the ballpark, *Coming into the game in relief for the Yakima Bears, Lefty Lefter*. Lefter walked to the mound and manager Hub Kettle handed him the ball and said, "Knock 'em dead, kid." After a few warm-up pitches the batter took his position and the catcher flashed Lefter the sign for throwing a fastball. Lefter threw the baseball straight down the gut for an obvious strike-one. As the ball hit the catcher's glove, it exploded violently. Bloody body parts flew out from the batting box area and a masked head fell at Lefter's feet.

"Ahhhhhhhh!" Lefter sat up straight in the sleeping bag. "Oh shit! Oh shit!" His pulse was racing and he was sweating profusely. He struggled out of the mummy bag and sat on the edge of the cot. It was hot inside the tent. "Feels like I'm in an oven." He looked at his watch that showed nearly 1600 hours. Trembling slightly he found a cigarette and lit it. "Holy crap," he said out loud then let out a large breath of air. "Damn nightmares."

He slipped on a pair of worn leather house slippers and walked across the dirt floor, opened the tent entrance flap and took a few steps away from the tent. The sun was shining but the air was cool and felt good on his sweaty body. Dressed only in his army shorts and a sweat-soaked tee shirt, he sat on an empty ammo box, inhaled deep drags from the cigarette and tried to erase the nightmare from his mind. He briefly thought about opening one of the bottles of Canadian Club and having a few sips. Instead he opened up a new pack of cigarettes and lit one from the still-burning butt.

Half startled, Lefter looked up as Campbell said, "Hey, Lef, what's up?"

"Just having a smoke and cooling off," replied Lefter as he looked at his watch. The watch showed 1645 hours. Beyond his wrist, Lefter could see six or seven cigarette butts at his feet. He didn't remember smoking them. He pulled out his pack of cigarettes and squeezed it. Sure enough, there were six or seven cigarettes missing from the pack.

"You OK, Lef?" questioned Campbell.

"Yeah, I am just recovering from another one of those goddamn nightmares. Do you get them? he asked Campbell.

"Sometimes," said Campbell. "Let's head over to the chow tent. Hillman is already over there." It was obvious to Lefter that Campbell didn't want to discuss nightmares.

After the three men returned from the dinner of roast beef and cabbage washed down with one beer, Lefter sat down at the table and began writing a letter.

> Dear Congressman:
>
> I am an enlisted man in the United States Armed Forces currently assigned to the front lines in Korea. I want to cordially invite you to be my guest for a few days enjoying the facilities here on the MLR.
>
> I understand that some political leaders in our country refer to our involvement here as a "Police Action." If you accept this invitation, my buddies and me will be pleased to take you along on some of our "police patrols" into the neighborhoods where the bad guys are located. We call the police stations in these neighborhoods Outposts. For example, we have four police stations in the Nevada Cities neighborhood. These stations are named OP Vegas, OP Reno, OP Carson and OP Elko. We have "cops" manning each of these stations most of the time. I say "most of the time" because on occasion the bad guys chase us out of them. We always take them back though because we know how important it is to you, our friends, and our loved ones back home.
>
> I hope you can accept this invitation and come spend a few days with us, or as some might say, walk a mile or so in our shoes.
>
> Please RSVP before the end of this "Police Action."
>
> Sincerely,
>
> Pfc. John Lefter, U.S. Army

"Damn! That makes me feel better even if I never do anything with it," said Lefter.

Campbell looked up from a book he was reading and said, "What makes you feel better?"

"Here, read this letter to my Congressman and tell me what you think of it," replied Lefter as he handed the letter to Campbell.

Campbell chuckled as he read Lefter's letter. "I like it. Do you know who your Congressman is?"

"Hell no," Lefter replied indignantly. "I won't be old enough to vote until July, so why should I know?"

"Easy, buddy," said Campbell. "I didn't mean to raise your ire. Good letter though. You ought to send it to one of those politicians."

"Ah ha, how about this," said Lefter. "Suppose I send it to the Stars and Stripes Newspaper. Do you think they would publish it?"

Campbell laughed, "Buddy, if they did publish it your ass would be mud with a capital M for jumping rank on all the officers in the Army."

"OK, suppose I just sign it GI Joe instead of putting my name on it?"

Campbell raised a hand to his chin and said, "That just might work if you could keep the brass from knowing that you wrote it."

"Well, you are the only one who knows so don't tell anyone, OK?"

"I won't tell," said Campbell. "How are you going to do it?"

"Never mind," said Lefter. "Let's just see what happens, OK?"

"OK, you got it," replied Campbell.

Lefter hand made several copies of the letter and signed each one as being from GI Joe. "Hey, Camp, any chance of me getting the day off tomorrow?"

"No problem, I'll do your chores tomorrow but you owe me a favor," replied Campbell.

"You got it," replied Lefter.

Hillman came back from getting water for the base camp and Lefter deliberately changed the subject. He didn't want anyone but Campbell to know anything about the letter.

It was the wee hours of the morning before Lefter could go to sleep. He was excited about the letter and the prospect of getting it published in the Stars and Stripes. He woke up at first light and left a note for Campbell saying he was going to Seoul and would pick up the mail on the way back in late afternoon.

Approaching Madam Dong's Place, Lefter was singing softly, *"Ten thousand chinks coming over the pass playing burp-gun boogie of the GI's ass and I'm a moving on."* The words of the song sounded humorous but were in fact a haunting reminder of the Eight Army's retreat to Inchon after the Chinese came storming into the Korean War. Pappy had told Lefter of his involvement in that retreat, or as Pappy said, "We're just advancing in a different direction." Leave it to the Marines to never admit retreating. The Marines were different from the other Armed Services. The Marine Corps was almost like a religion to its members.

During that retreat, Pappy was a forward artillery observer hunkered down on a high ridge overlooking a wide pass through a mountainous area. A column of two dozen or so friendly half-tracks with quad fifty machine guns mounted on them were moving slowly south along a road through the pass. Suddenly bugles started blaring and hundreds of Chinese foot soldiers poured over a low ridge and attacked the half-tracks.

The half-tracks pulled up bumper to bumper and their quad fifties cut down the Chinese by the dozens. Finally the column of half-tracks were overrun when their guns were firing point blank into stacks of dead and dying Chinese soldiers.

Realizing the Americans were being overwhelmed and killed in hand to hand combat by hoards of Chinese, Pappy called in an artillery barrage on the site in the hopes that a few Americans would survive the onslaught. Although severely wounded, one man did survive by playing dead and was rescued after a counter attack by the Marines.

Lefter wondered if Tennessee Ernie Ford had heard the version of "Moving On" being sung by the troops in Korea. Maybe Ford could be persuaded to record the GI version. *There's that warped sense of humor again,* he thought. Lefter was tempted to stop and say hello to Madam Dong but decided that it could lead to more than conversation. "Stay on course Lefter," he said out loud then went back to singing the tune. *"Ten thousand Chinks coming over the pass...."*

Inside the small library and reading room at ASAK Lefter found copies of the Wall Street Journal, The New York Times, The San Francisco Chronicle, and of course The Stars and Stripes. He copied the mailing address of each newspaper onto a separate envelope, inserted a copy of his letter, sealed it and wrote *FREE* on the upper right-hand corner. For a return address in the upper left-hand corner he wrote, *GI Joe, Korean Police Action, APO San Francisco.*

At the ASAK mail room Lefter asked and received directions to the main

U.S. Post Office in Seoul. He didn't want to mail the letters from ASAK for fear that they might be traced to someone at ASA. He drove to the main office and dropped the letters in a slot marked OUTGOING MAIL. Then he got back behind the wheel of his jeep and drove off while singing: *"When the politicians come marching in. When the politicians come marching in. Oh Lord I want to be there on the MLR when those politicians come marching in."*

Entering the 303 Compound Lefter drove immediately to the motor pool area. Still sitting in the jeep, Lefter yelled out, "Hey, Sitchie!"

Sitchie came out from behind a deuce-and-a-half in the service bay and said, "Be damned if it ain't one of my front line heroes. Hello, Lefter, what's up?"

"Well, I ain't here to kiss your candy ass," replied Lefter. "Where's that asshole Soss?"

Sitchie put his index finger to his lips just as Major Soss walked out of the service bay and demanded, "What did you say, soldier?"

Lefter saluted and said, "Sir, I said where is the apple sauce? Corporal Sitchie was going to get me some apple sauce to take back to the detachment."

Turning to Sitchie the major demanded, "Is that right, Corporal?"

"Yes, sir," replied Sitchie.

"Stupid," said the major as he turned and went back behind the truck in the service bay.

"Yes, sir," replied Lefter as he exchanged smirks with Sitchie. Both men fell silent and just waited to see what would happen.

Out from behind the big truck emerged a jeep driven by the major. He had on a flack jacket and steel helmet. The jeeps canvas top and its windshield were down. Sitchie and Lefter saluted as he drove by and the major flipped them a John Wayne type of salute in return.

They watched the jeep leave the 303 Compound then Sitchie said, "He drives out of here every day before noon and doesn't return until after dinner."

"Where the hell does he go?"

"Nobody seems to know," replied Sitchie.

Lefter looked at his watch. It read nearly 1000 hours. Starting the jeep engine he said, "I've got to run an errand right now but I'll see you at the chow hall for lunch."

Sitchie waved OK and returned to the service bay.

Lefter drove toward the guard gate and arrived just in time to see the Soss driving away. As Lefter showed his trip ticket to the guard he said, "Where does that major drive to every day when he leaves here?"

"Beats the hell out of me but he leaves every day before noon and comes back in around 1900. Why do you ask?" replied the guard.

"Just curious," said Lefter.

"You and everyone else," replied the guard.

"Have a nice day," said Lefter as he drove off.

Lefter followed far enough back that the major wouldn't be able to recognize him or his jeep with the telltale 303 CRB stenciled on the bumper. At the main north south MSR, the major turned south. Oncoming conveys of supply trucks from the 444th Transportation Corps honked and waved at the major. Apparently, they recognized him. Major Soss flipped salutes to them. He assumed the honking was a form of their recognizing him as an officer. A few miles down the road at the entrance to the 444th two MPs stopped north-south traffic while the supply trucks went both ways from the major supply staging area. Lefter pulled over, pretended to have a flat tire and waited until the northbound and southbound traffic resumed. Again, Lefter followed at a safe distance.

They passed Madam Dong's Place and proceeded south past the turnoff for going to ASAK. This area of Seoul was not familiar to Lefter. A couple of miles later the major turned off on a side street and after driving several blocks stopped in front of a very large building with a large red cross painted over the front entrance. It was a hospital. Major Soss parked out front and, carrying his briefcase, walked into the hospital. Lefter turned around immediately and drove back north.

Arriving back to I-Corps headquarters at 1210 hours, Lefter went immediately to the mess hall. Carrying his mess kit he entered the mess hall and went through the line. He spotted Crovelli, Nay and Sitchie and sat down at their table. "I followed Asshole Soss today and found out where he goes," said Lefter.

They quit eating and stared at Lefter. "Where," they each said almost in unison.

Lefter grinned broadly, "If I was going to be here tonight I'd charge several beers for this information but I'll tell you guys and you can get a few on me from Mighty Joe."

"Spill it," said Nay. "If it's worth it I'll owe you a couple."

"He goes to the main military hospital on the south side of Seoul, at least that is where he went today. Why he goes there, I don't know," said Lefter. "I was afraid to follow him into the hospital."

"Good work," said Nay. "I'll put Mighty Joe to work on it right after we use your information to con him out of a couple of beers tonight."

After lunch Lefter picked up the mail and headed back to his detachment. His parting words were, "I'll look forward to hearing why Soss goes to that hospital."

"I'll let you know," said Nay. Crovelli and Sitchie nodded agreement.

"Stay safe, buddy," they called after Lefter as he drove away.

CHAPTER THIRTEEN

Two days later, Mewman was waiting when Lefter arrived at the ASA bunker. "Where the fuck have you been, it's been daylight for over an hour," complained Mewman.

"I've been lounging around the pool down at base camp," replied Lefter sarcastically.

"Yeah, well I've got your fucking pool right here," replied Mewman as he grabbed his crotch.

"Knock it off, tough guy, we both know you ain't big enough to piss hard against the ground," growled Lefter.

Picking up his BAR Mewman said, "That's why I carry Barrie here, makes me the size of any fucking man." He let out his big belly laugh.

Lefter reached out and lifted the BAR, "That's a heavy weapon for a little fellow like you. How much does it weigh?"

"Sixteen fucking pounds," said Mewman, "but by the time I pack up three hundred rounds of ammo it's up around thirty or forty pounds. She don't feel heavy though, she's my buddy." He took the BAR from Lefter and stroked the barrel as if it was his mistress.

It was obvious to Lefter that the little fellow was obsessed with that weapon. "How is she in bed?" asked Lefter.

"A lot more useful than that fucking toy carbine of yours."

Lefter changed the subject. "Got something for you, buddy." He reached in his pack and pulled out the two bottles of whiskey. "Do you have anything to carry them in?"

"Oh, fuck no!" said Mewman.

"Mewman, sometimes I think you're twenty-four beers short of a case."

"What the fuck does that mean?" replied Mewman.

"I mean, it's hard to believe you beat out a million other sperm. I'll empty the other stuff out of my pack and you can borrow it to carry the booze."

"Thanks," said Mewman quietly. "What the fuck does that sperm crack mean?"

"Forget it," said Lefter as he went into the bunker and emptied the stuff in his pack out on the table. Returning outside he handed the pack containing the two bottles to Mewman. "Don't get wild ass drunk and get yourself in trouble," cautioned Lefter.

"I'll be real fucking careful, Mother," replied Mewman.

"Screw you, Mew!"

"Fuck you, Lef!"

"Up yours," said Lefter getting the last insult in while Mewman was belly laughing.

"Been gook hunting lately?" said Lefter as he held out his pack of cigarettes.

Mewman's eyes lit up. He took a cigarette and accepted a light from Lefter. "Went out on a fucking listening patrol last night and it was damn frustrating. We just laid out there in the dark and listened to the gooks digging and talking in that fuckety sing-song gibberish. Pissed me off just hearing them talking, I wanted to blow their fucking heads off but Happy held me back."

"What were you listening for?" asked Lefter.

Mewman threw both hands in the air and said, "Beats the hell out of me. None of us know what the fuck they're saying. Happy figured they was about six of them fuckers digging a trench about 200 yards in front of OP Vegas. Fuck, they was nine of us and we could have creamed their asses. I don't get it, do we kill them fucking gooks or don't we?"

"You got me," replied Lefter. "I don't get involved in any of that John Wayne stuff. As you know I'm just involved in listening, and like you I don't understand the language."

"Yeah, well, you don't have to listen to that fuckety sing-song crap either," said Mewman.

"Got that right, buddy, " said Lefter with a big grin as he pointed toward the bunker. "Got me a couple of DAC grunts to do that."

"They're in deep shit if them fucking gooks ever get hold of them," replied Mewman seriously.

"Got that right, Mew," replied Lefter. "I don't like to think about that happening. Let's talk about something else."

"OK, what's the latest on my fucking asshole buddy Soss?" asked Mewman.

"He spends most of every day at the big hospital in Seoul and nobody knows why. Come to think of it maybe he's in the psycho ward. He's crazier than you are."

"Fuck you, Lef."

"Up yours, Mew. How come you saved his sorry ass anyway?"

"He's just one of them helpless fuckers like you that I have to take care of," Mewman said in a serious tone.

Lefter started to make a caustic response but decided to let it go. "Have it your way, buddy. I know you can be counted on in a dire situation."

"Fucking A," said Mewman. "Well, I better get the fuck back, Happy is waiting for the booze."

"OK, stay safe, buddy, and stay out of trouble with that booze," said Lefter as they shook hands.

"Yeah, thanks, Ma," said Mewman sarcastically, then added seriously, "I'll be back to see you in a few days, good buddy."

Lefter noted that Mewman had made that last statement without either a belly laugh or use of the F word. He watched Mewman swaggering east along the trench line. *I hope that cocky little bastard can stay alive. I'd miss him*, he thought to himself.

There was the usual exchange of firing by mortars and artillery just after dark. Then, for the next few hours, it settled down to just an occasional nervous machine gunner letting go for a short burst or two.

Somewhere around one in the morning it sounded like a firefight going on out in No-Man's-Land so Lefter went to the viewing slit for a peek. Flares were lighting up the terrain in the vicinity of Outposts Elko or Vegas. He heard the now familiar sound of outgoing mortar rounds and could see the orange bursts of light at their landing area. After a few minutes the firing slowed and the mortar barrage stopped. Lefter sat down at the table, lit up a cigarette and thanked his lucky stars to be in the ASA rather than the infantry.

It was just beginning to get light when Mewman knocked lightly on the ASA bunker door. "Hey, Lef, it's, it's, it's yo 'ol, 'ol, 'ol fucking buddy Me — Me — Mewman."

Before he opened the bunker door Lefter already knew that Mewman was drunk. He opened the door and Mewman fell into him. "You dumb shit, Mewman, I asked you not to get shit faced."

"Just cela — cela — brating. Killed me 'nother fu — fu — king gook las nite."

Lefter half carried Mewman out and sat him down on an ammo box in the trench. "Sit right there and I'll go make you some instant coffee," said Lefter.

"OKeee, danks good 'ol fr — fr — friend," slurred Mewman.

Lefter went back in the bunker, poured some powdered coffee into a canteen cup and stirred in some unheated water. When he went back outside with the cold coffee Mewman was passed out in the trench. Lefter stood there looking down and wondering what the hell to do with Mewman when a voice said, "We'll take that drunk off your hands." Lefter looked up in the early morning light and recognized Mewman's squad leader Happy. He had a medic with him that was carrying a stretcher. They rolled Mewman onto the stretcher and carried him off down the trench line to the east.

Here comes another court-martial for Mewman, Lefter thought.

Mewman didn't show up on either Jolcomb's shift or Hillman's shift the next day. As Lefter climbed the hill for his next shift he was thinking of Mewman and hoping that he would be waiting at the bunker. He wasn't. Mewman didn't show up the next morning either but Happy was waiting outside when Lefter went out for his first trip of the day to the piss tube.

"Just thought you'd like to know that Mewman is in the hospital. He's being treated for combat shock. It was either that or a court-martial so I shipped him off to the hospital. He should be back in a few days though."

"Thanks, Happy," said Lefter. "I'm glad to hear he didn't get court-martialed."

"Oh yeah," said Happy, "do me a favor and don't sell any more booze to Mewman. I'll dole it out to him in small doses from my supply."

"You got it," said Lefter. "I was thinking the same thing myself recently. He has a history of getting in big trouble when he gets drunk."

"OK, I'll be seeing you," said Happy. "By the way, I could use another couple of bottles."

"You got it," replied Lefter. "I'll bring them up here on my next shift."

"Stay safe, buddy," said Happy as he extended his right hand.

"You too," said Lefter as he firmly gripped the hand of Happy.

Happy slung his M-1 rifle on his shoulder and walked east along the trench line. Lefter noticed that he was also armed with a 45 pistol. Lefter laughed out loud. *Must be that fucking major's pistol.*

The next time Lefter had bunker duty Mewman was waiting for him. "Where the fuck have you been, buddy? I been sitting here an hour waiting for you."

"Good to see you again, Mew," said Lefter. "How was the vacation at the hospital?"

"Boring. Hung around that fucking hospital with nothing to do but talk to them psycho doctors and the nuts that had cracked up in combat. They took all my clothes and gave me a set of them fucking flannel jamas like we had as kids. That way nobody can pull rank on anybody or run away."

"Oh yeah, see anyone you know?" said Lefter just making conversation.

"Fucking A," replied Mewman. "Asshole Soss was in one of the discussion groups. There he was, in his jamas, looking like a fucking whipped puppy."

Lefter ears perked up, "What did you just say?"

"I said he looked like a fucking whipped puppy."

"No, no, no," said Lefter. "Did you say it was Major Soss?"

"Yeah," said Mewman. "Guess I should have conned you out of some booze for that info like that fucking hustler Mighty Joe does."

"Did he recognize you?"

"Fucking A, he came up to me after the meeting and said he had put me in for a Silver Star award for saving his life. Also said he was just MONITORING the meeting." Mewman belly laughed.

"Yeah right, we believe that, don't we?" commented a smiling Lefter.

"You wouldn't believe it, Lef," said Mewman, "some of them guys is really fucked up in the head."

"I believe it," said Lefter, "and Soss is one of them. Only difference is he is still in a position to cause harm to people on our side of the MLR."

Mewman pointed at Lefter and said, "What the fuck do you mean by that? I don't harm nobody on our side."

"Right on," said Lefter.

Mewman scratched under his helmet and said quizzically, "OK!"

Mewman held out his hand to Lefter and said, "Well, I better get the fuck back. Happy tells me I got to go through him to get booze now. I'm beholding to him. The captain might have court-martialed my drunken ass except for Happy claiming I had that fucking combat shock thing."

Lefter nodded yes, shook Mewman's hand and said, "Stay safe, buddy."

"Fucking A, you too, buddy," said Mewman as he turned and walked east along the MLR trench line.

Fifty yards down the trench Mewman turned and yelled back to Lefter, "Keep a sharp lookout tonight. I'm going out to get me another fucking gook." Belly laughing he turned and swaggered east along the trench.

Lefter didn't tell Mewman that he had two bottles of booze for Happy. He didn't even trust Mewman to carry the booze back to Happy although it was only five hundred yards away. However, within the hour Happy showed up to claim the booze.

During the night, Lefter would rush to the viewing slit when he heard firing, an explosion or any outgoing mortar but each time it appeared to be random actions. Although firefights occurred farther east along No-Man's-Land, no firefights developed in the location of Nevada Cities or thereabouts.

At the dim light of dawn, Lefter was standing at the piss tube out back of the bunker when out of the corner of his eye something moved nearby. Immediately his stream stopped and his heart started racing. Mewman slid down from the side of the bunker and landed on his feet in the trench.

"Damn you, Mewman, you scared the piss out of me."

"Looks like it dried you the fuck up," replied Mewman with his belly laugh following immediately.

Lefter looked down and realized he was still holding onto his penis. Putting it back inside his trousers, he said to Mewman, "Up yours!"

"Fuck you," replied Mewman.

"Mewman, what the hell were you doing on the ground beside my bunker?"

"Been cat napping there for a couple of hours waiting for you to come the fuck outside. You said you didn't want me pounding on the fucking door."

"Thanks, Mew, I appreciate that but you could knock softly," said Lefter. "What's up?"

"Got me another fucking gook," said Mewman proudly.

Surprised, Lefter said, "How did you do that, I didn't see any firefights out in front of us last night?"

Mewman made a slashing motion across his neck with his right hand, "Cut his fucking throat!"

Stunned, Lefter could only respond with, "What?"

"Yeah," said Mewman, "had to throw away my clothes when we got back. They was soaked in blood."

"Holy crap! How the hell did that happen?" asked Lefter.

"Got a fucking smoke?" asked Mewman.

Lefter handed Mewman his pack of cigarettes and matches. Mewman lit one up and inhaled a couple of deep drags. Lefter realized his heart was racing with excitement so he lit up a cigarette also.

Mewman reached into a sheath attached to his cartridge belt and pulled out a curved handle knife with an ivory blade. The knife looked like one of those carried by the Turks.

Lefter pointed to the knife and said, "Where the hell did you get that?"

"Bought it from a fucking medic at the hospital in Seoul," said Mewman. "He said it had belonged to a Turk that died there."

STAY SAFE, BUDDY

"So how the hell did you come to cut a gook's throat with it?"

Mewman smiled a devilish grin. "We was on what they call an exploratory patrol last night. Not supposed to start anything, just find out what the fuck's going on out there."

"So?" asked Lefter, eager to hear the gory details.

"We was out there in front of Vegas where them gooks was digging a couple of weeks ago. It was so fucking dark I couldn't see but a couple of feet. Somebody coughed and then whispered something in Chinese. I could smell his garlic breath so I knew it was a fucking gook. The fucker was right in front of me so I slowly took out my knife and waited. He must have been sick because in a few minutes he started coughing hard. That's when I sprung forward, grabbed the son-of-a-bitch and cut his fucking throat." Mewman made a quick crouching move toward Lefter and a slashing motion with his right hand.

"Holy crap, that makes me about half sick hearing you tell about it," said Lefter.

"Well, I didn't feel too damn good for a few minutes with his fucking warm stinking blood all over me. Squirted all over me, including my face."

Lefter was still stunned and said again, "Holy crap!"

Mewman field stripped his cigarette and threw the remains in the trench. Lefter did the same.

"Holy crap," said Lefter again. He paused and said it again, "Holy crap!"

"Your fucking mouth stuck?" asked Mewman.

"Guess so," replied Lefter. He couldn't think of anything else to say.

"I got more talk if you got another cigarette," said Mewman.

"Here, take the whole pack, I have more in the bunker," said Lefter.

After lighting another cigarette, Mewman went on. "You know how them Ethiopians is said to creep into a gook trench in the black of night, slit one of the fucker's throats and then crawl back to our MLR?"

"Yeah," replied Lefter.

"Well, I'd like to do that sometime," said Mewman without using the F word and without laughing.

"You're serious, aren't you?" said Lefter.

"Fucking A," replied Mewman. "Wonder if them fucking gooks have a psycho ward for the one that didn't get his throat cut." Mewman let out his belly laugh.

Lefter didn't laugh or even smile. "Sometimes you scare the hell out of me, Mew."

"Don't sweat it, I ain't going to hurt you, buddy," said Mewman.

"That's not it, I'm scared you're going to get your little ass killed doing all this John Wayne stuff."

"Don't call me a little ass," said Mewman.

"OK, BIG ass," responded Lefter.

"Fuck you," said Mewman.

"Up yours," Lefter said back. "How about some chow?"

"What you got," asked Mewman.

"All the gourmet entrees, name one," replied Lefter.

"Corned beef hash," said Mewman.

Lefter made a lemon-tasting face, "Yuck, not sure I have one, but you could sure as hell have it if I did. The DACs like corned beef hash also. So does Asshole Soss."

"Then I'm not eating that fucking stuff anymore," smiled Mewman.

"How about beanie weenies?" asked Lefter.

"No fucking way," said Mewman. "Do you think I want to fart out there on patrol in No-Man's-Land and give away my position to some fucking gook?"

"Sorry, never thought of that; guess that could be a DEAD giveaway considering how bad your farts stink," said Lefter smiling.

"Fuck you," said Mewman, smiling.

"Up yours," replied Lefter, smiling back.

"Oh fuck, never mind," said Mewman, "I just remembered that Happy said we were going back to battalion later today to rest up, take a shower, get some clean clothes and a few hot meals."

"How long are you going to be there?" asked Lefter.

"Two or three days," said Mewman.

"Good, I'll look for you there," said Lefter.

"OK, I'm outta here," said Mewman.

"Stay safe, buddy," said Lefter.

"Fucking A, you too, friend," said Mewman as he picked up his BAR and walked easterly along the MLR trench. Lefter noticed that Mewman's swaggering walk was less pronounced.

Back at the ASA base camp, Lefter told Campbell about the early morning conversation with Mewman. First, he told of Mewman's encounter with Major Soss at the hospital in Seoul. "I could use that information to get a dozen beers from the guys at the 303 headquarters," said Lefter.

"Agree," said Campbell. "Don't you kind of feel a little sorry for the major though?"

"Well, let me think about it for a few seconds," said Lefter. He paused and then said with a smile, "Hmmm! No, no, I don't get that feeling at all."

Lefter then told Campbell about Mewman cutting the throat of a Chinese soldier. "Gave me a real queasy feeling. I thought I was going to throw up when he was talking about the gook's warm blood squirting all over him."

"Understandable," said Campbell. "With that kind of cold-blooded guts it sounds like Mewman ought to be a Marine. Fits the good Marine profile perfectly; he's arrogant, tough, ignorant and loyal."

"I agree," said Lefter, "but he'd make a good Turk also. He's about their size and I think he can be just as fierce. You should see the fire in his eyes when he talks about combat things. Come to think of it, maybe you can. He says his squad is coming down here to battalion for two or three days of rest. Maybe we can look him up at the mess tent."

"Good plan, get some rest and we'll go over there later," said Campbell.

"OK, but don't tell anyone about the major, would you? I want to use that information to get free beer the next time I'm at 303."

"You got it," replied Campbell. "You better get some sleep now."

CHAPTER FOURTEEN

Lefter woke up kicking violently and swinging his arms. "Shit, shit, shit. Damn it! I knew that was going to happen," said Lefter underneath his breath as he woke up in mid-afternoon. He had a nightmare in which he went on a night patrol with Mewman. The Chinese sent up flares and several of them charged the American patrol. When Lefter's carbine wouldn't fire, a Chinese soldier was about to bayonet him. Mewman came out of nowhere and slit his throat with a curved blade ivory handled knife. The Chinese soldier fell into Lefter and his blood squirted all over Lefter. The blood felt warm and it had a sickly sweet smell.

As usual with a nightmare, he was sweating profusely and trembling. Calming his nerves with a cigarette, he decided to write a letter home before going to the battalion mess tent. He sat down at the table with his writing tablet and composed a letter to his wife:

Hi Honey:

It's mid-afternoon here in the land of the morning calm. No big actions on the MLR recently. Well I take that back. My nutty friend Mewman has now killed four Chinese soldiers and he is so proud of it. He slit the throat of the latest one while out on a patrol last night. He came down to my bunker early this morning to tell me all about it. Then I had a nightmare about it while getting some sleep today. That's why my writing is kind of shaky. Not much fun.

In case you don't remember, Mewman is the guy who got transferred from ASA to the 25th Infantry Division. He is dumber than a Brussel sprout and talks with a sewer mouth but I like the guy. He has become my best buddy. I have decided to share my next goodie package from home with him (hint, hint). He has never mentioned any family and never gets any mail from anyone. I'll ask him why sometime when the situation is right.

Speaking of nuts, Major Soss is getting treated in the psycho ward at the military hospital in Seoul. He's still our CO and doesn't know we found out where he goes for most of every day. Actually, Mewman, Campbell and me are the only ones who know about it right now.

I should get to go on R & R (Rest and Recuperation) leave to Tokyo soon as I have been in Korea almost six months now. We get a week R & R every six months. We go in pairs and two of us can request that we go together. Don't know who is eligible at the same time I am. Jolcomb has been here about the same as me but an unlikely pairing since we are in the same detachment where there are only four of us. Oops! If that last line ends up blacked out, you'll know it didn't make it through the censors. (We are not supposed to talk about the number of men in our outfits.) Actually there are more than four but I definitely can't talk about that. I'll change the subject before I get in trouble.

Now I can't think of anything else to say right now so that's five for now.

Love you lots, John

Lefter decided he better not mail that letter right away. All that stuff about throat cutting might be upsetting to his wife. He folded up the letter and put it in his shirt pocket.

Lefter and Campbell couldn't find Mewman at the mess tent. Campbell went ahead and ate, then went back to the ASA base camp. Lefter didn't eat and waited around the mess tent for over almost an hour. Finally, he went to the headquarters tent where the CQ looked on a list and said Mewman was assigned to tent fourteen.

Laughter and smoke were coming from tent fourteen as Lefter approached. He looked through the open flap of the tent and there sat Mewman playing cards with four other soldiers. Mewman looked up and saw Lefter in the entrance. "Hey, Lef, get the fuck over here and join us in some drinking and poker."

It was obvious to Lefter that Mewman was already drunk, but not yet at the point of slurring his speech. "Naw, you know I don't gamble," said Lefter. "Just came over to join you for dinner; can you get away for a while?"

"What and leave as a big fucking winner?" said Mewman.

"You can always come back after dinner and lose it all like you always do," replied Lefter.

"Fuck you," said Mewman.

"Up yours. Have it your way, buddy, but I'm headed for the mess tent right now," said Lefter.

Mewman scooped up his money and stuffed it in his pocket. "OK, I'm coming, hold your fucking horses." Groans emerged around the table as Mewman stood up. "I'll be back later on to get the rest of your money," he said just before letting go with the big belly laugh.

Sitting at a table in the mess tent with their chow and one issued beer, Lefter said to Mewman, "This is the first time I know of that you have ever left a poker game as a winner. Would you like me to send some of that money back home for you? I'll be going on R&R in a week or so."

"Who the fuck would I send it to? I don't have any family. I'm a fucking orphan, didn't you know that?"

"No, you never said anything to me about your life back in the States," replied Lefter. "Who raised you?"

"Raised my fucking self. Started riding the rails when I was twelve and got a number fucking one education from them hobos."

Not knowing what else to say about family and growing up Lefter said, "You could always open a bank account and save up money for buying a car when you get back to the States."

Mewman stared Lefter in the eyes and said with finality, "I'll never leave this fucking country alive, Lef, but tell you what, I'll give you a hundred bucks of this money. Keep it for me and if I make it back I'll look you up and we'll have a big fucking party." He dug in his pocket and counted out one hundred dollars in military script. "If I don't make it back have a big fucking party anyway." He didn't laugh and neither did Lefter.

Lefter put the money in his pocket and said, "You got to make it back, buddy. I don't have enough capacity to drink a hundred bucks worth of booze. I'll need you there to drink ninety dollars of it and I'll drink the rest." They both laughed.

After dinner, they shook hands and Mewman headed back to his poker game. "Good luck, buddy," said Lefter knowing full well that Mewman wouldn't leave the table until he had lost all his money. He was kind of spooked by Mewman's serious statement about never leaving Korea alive. He hoped he was wrong. It would be good to have a party with Mewman back in the States and even introduce him to a nice girl. Well, anyway, some girl that would put up with his filthy mouth enough to find out that he had a big heart.

Back at the base camp, Campbell told Lefter that he had permission to leave on R&R anytime during the next week. "Am I paired up with anyone yet?" asked Lefter.

"Don't know, do you have someone in mind?"

"Not really. Quigley and I got to Korea about the same time and we seem to get along well together."

"We'll see," said Campbell.

Lefter was nervous about going to sleep and sat up at the table until after midnight. He was afraid of having another frightening nightmare. He took the letter out of his pocket and burned it in the butt can. "No sense laying all that killing crap on my wife," he whispered. Finally getting so tired he couldn't hold his eyes open, he went to the cot and fell asleep immediately.

Lefter woke up to someone whispering loudly, "Campbell, Campbell, wake up. I think there is a gook in here."

Heart pounding, Lefter carefully unzipped the mummy sleeping bag and tried to get out of it without making a sound. Finally, with his lower half still in the bag he found his carbine that was leaning against the head of his cot. Sitting up with the lower half of his body still in the mummy bag, he slowly eased a round into the chamber of the carbine, switched off the safety and pointed it toward a sound in front of him. It was pitch black in the tent.

Suddenly, Campbell lit up the tent with a battery-operated floodlight. Hillman was standing there with a 45 pistol pointed directly at Lefter. He was close enough that they could have reached out and touched each other. The 45 pistol was cocked and ready to fire and so was Lefter's carbine. Each man was shaking perceptively. Their eyes turned swiftly and watched as Campbell swept the tent with the floodlight. There was no bad guy in the tent.

"Damn you, Hillman, we almost shot each other," said Lefter.

"Sorry," said Hillman. "I've been on edge ever since my boots disappeared the other night."

"What?" said Lefter.

Campbell jumped in, "That's right, we have been having some things disappear out of the tent every few days." Campbell went to the table and lit the kerosene lantern.

"I haven't missed anything," said Lefter. "Who is the thief?" Then he quickly added, "I hope to hell we don't have infiltrators getting in here."

"I don't think so," said Campbell. "It's probably one of the ROK troops from down the road a couple of miles. They have been training there for the last two weeks."

"What happened to your boots?" said Lefter to Hillman.

"Don't know, they were gone when I got up in the morning," said Hillman.

"You mean somebody came in and took them while you were sleeping?" said Lefter with surprise.

"Must have," said Hillman.

"Holy crap!" exclaimed Lefter. "There goes the rest of my night's sleep."

"Let's have a drink," said Hillman.

"Good idea," responded Lefter.

"Go ahead," said Campbell. "You two stand watch while I sleep," and he lay back down on his cot.

"See, Hillman, that's why he's the leader and we're the peons. He just lets us outsmart ourselves. We voluntarily stand watch while he sleeps."

"Who gives a shit, let's have a drink," said Hillman.

"You're on," said Lefter as he finally freed himself of the mummy bag and went to the table dressed only in shorts and tee shirt.

"By the way," said Campbell. "We're being issued new sleeping bags to replace the mummy bags. Last month over in Ten Corps, while still in their sleeping bags, a whole squad of Army guys was bayoneted by North Korean Infintrators. The new bags are supposed to pop open immediately by just pushing hard on them with an outward movement."

"Now you've really screwed up my sleep," said Lefter.

"Mine too," said Hillman. "When do we get the new ones?"

"Any day now," said Campbell. "Got to get my beauty sleep now. Goodnight."

Shaking their heads sideways, Lefter and Hillman began passing the bottle back and forth and taking small sips. Soon the sips were getting larger as they acclimated to the whiskey. Finally, cold and in a stupor, they went back to bed.

Lefter woke up cold and shivering. It was daylight. He was lying on top of his mummy bag. He had a headache and felt kind of nauseous. "Oh crap," he said out loud as he jumped up and ran outside. "Oh crap," he said out loud again and began throwing up in the dirt. Then he heard someone gag and start throwing up nearby. It was Hillman.

"Damn you, Lefter," said Hillman as he gagged and threw up again. "I was holding it back until you ran out here and started chucking up your toe nails."

"It was your stupid idea to drink booze last night," said Lefter.

They took turns gagging and throwing up for a few minutes then Lefter said, "Crap, I have a horrible headache."

"Me too," said Hillman. "Shit, one of us has got to go up on the hill and relieve Jolcomb."

Campbell came out of the tent and said, "I ought to send both of you drunks up the hill today."

Lefter and Hillman just groaned.

"Someday I am going to learn not to be such a soft ass," said Campbell. "I'll go up and relieve Jolcomb and one of you come up when you recover, but be there before noon. OK?"

Lefter and Hillman nodded agreement and, holding their heads, went back into the tent and collapsed on their cots.

Lefter groaned and said, "Dumb shit, dumb shit, dumb shit."

"Fuck you," groaned Hillman.

"I was talking to myself not you," said Lefter, "but up yours anyway."

After a few minutes Lefter got up, took two aspirins from the First Aid Kit and washed them down with some warm water. "Ah yuck," he said struggling to keep the aspirins down.

"What?" said Hillman.

"Shut the hell up, I was talking to me again," said Lefter.

Hillman just groaned and rolled over on his cot.

Lefter got dressed slowly and, holding his head, went outside the tent and looked toward the battalion area. He walked slowly to the jeep, eased himself into the driver's seat and put his head on the steering wheel. "Dumb shit," he said under his breath as he sat up slowly and started the jeep engine.

He drove carefully over and parked in front of the shower tent. Walking gingerly into the tent, he took a wire basket from the Army attendant and started putting his personal gear into it. He pulled off his boots and put them in the basket.

"You look like you tied on a real dandy," said the attendant with a big smile.

"Yeah, sure did," said Lefter as he handed the basket back to the attendant. He took off his clothes and threw them in one of the large laundry hampers. He handed the basket back to the attendant who closed its wire top and snapped a padlock on it. He handed the padlock key to Lefter. The key was on a long shoestring tied in a loop. Lefter put the string around his neck and went to the shower area.

In the shower, Lefter stood in the warm water for a long time. Finally a voice said, "How long you gonna soak, buddy? Save some hot water for the rest of us."

"Sorry," said Lefter as he stepped out of the shower stream and headed for the drying-off area. The attendant tossed a towel to Lefter and said, "What size are you, buddy?

"Thirty-four waist, thirty length pants and medium shirt," replied Lefter. The attendant turned around and searched through a stack of pants and shirts, "Here, these should be close," he said. "Did you get a basket?"

"Oh yeah," said Lefter as he removed the shoestring with the key from around his neck and handed it to the attendant. The attendant again turned and looked through the baskets behind him, selected the correct one, sat it on the counter, unlocked and removed the padlock. He sat down on one of the wooden benches and dried himself. Lefter wondered how the attendant knew which basket was his. Just before he asked it dawned on him that the lock and key must have matching numbers. Simple, but tough for Lefter to figure out with a big hangover.

After dressing, Lefter returned to the base camp and slowly packed up. Jolcomb had already returned and was asleep on his cot. Hillman was also asleep and snoring loudly. Leaving a note on the table for Hillman, he drove to the parking area behind the hill and parked beside the other ASA jeep. While climbing the hill he would stop every ten steps or so and hold his head for a few seconds then take a deep breath and start climbing again.

He was nearing the top of the hill when it dawned on him that he had left his carbine in the jeep. "Dumb shit, dumb shit, dumb shit," he said as he sat down and buried his head in his hands. Then he went back down the hill and retrieved the carbine from the jeep. "Anything else," he said out loud, as he looked around the jeep. Just then, it dawned on him that he had carried his pack back down the hill. Shaking his head slowly he said, "You dumb shit, Lefter, why didn't you leave the pack up there along the trail?"

Slowly climbing the hill again in short stages he finally reached the top and entered the main MLR trench from an entrance trench near the ASA bunker. Leaning on the side of the entrance trench outside the ASA bunker door, Lefter took several deep breaths before knocking and saying, "It's Lefter." He was surprised at how weak his voice sounded.

Campbell opened the door and said, "I'm surprised you recovered so quickly."

Lefter looked at him through his bloodshot eyes and said weakly, "Well,

I'm feeling a lot better. I've quit wishing I would die."

"Really," said Campbell.

"Yeah, now I'm just wishing I was already dead," replied Lefter with a half-hearted laugh. *My stupid sense of humor won't even go away when I'm dying.*

Campbell didn't respond. He just packed up and left.

Lefter sat with his elbows on the table and his head in his hands. He was thinking that Campbell hadn't said, "Stay safe, buddy." He hoped that wasn't a bad omen.

All day he kept falling asleep at the table but would wake up in a few minutes when he leaned and started to fall sideways. The DACs ignored him. Stubbornly, he refused to retreat to the bunk and give in completely. The day seemed exceptionally long to Lefter. Occasionally he would lower one hand from his face, look at his watch and be surprised that only ten minutes had passed since he last looked.

In addition to fighting off nausea, he was feeling guilty and embarrassed. He was lucky to have Campbell as a leader. Others might have had him court-martialed. *Down deep*, he thought, *I'm a lot like Mewman but with a less filthy mouth and a little more education.* Lefter smiled inside his cupped hands and thought, *but I'm also prettier than Mewman.* He laughed causing his head to hurt. "Ouch! You dumb shit," he mumbled softly.

It was quiet in the bunker and the Korean DAC overhead his mumble. "Lew say som-sing te me?" asked the DAC.

"No, no, I was just mumbling to myself," said Lefter softly.

"Sound likey lew sai dumb slit; why lew sai dumb slit?" said the DAC.

"I am the dumb shit," said Lefter pointing to his chest. "I'm not feeling good." Patting his stomach then head, "Upset stomach and head ache."

"Oooooh," smiled the DAC, "da lew goling chucky-chucky by tent dis moling?"

Lefter thought the DAC might be deliberately exaggerating his accent but it was hard to know. Maybe he was just trying to be funny, or make fun of Lefter. He had to choose words carefully when talking with the DACs as the Department of the Army had promised them that they would be treated with the same courtesy and respect given officers. He and the other ASA guys just didn't talk to them much because they seemed to be easily offended. They often misunderstood American humor and would complain to an ASA officer or non-commissioned officer.

Lefter was tempted to say, "Chucky-chucky up lo ass," but he restrained himself. "Yeah, must have been something I ate. Hillman was sick also."

"Lew bof chucky-chucky?" asked the DAC.

Lefter was getting pissed. These DACs never said boo socially and now this one wants to shoot the shit. Bad timing. Now, Lefter couldn't even remember his name — the name of the DAC that is. Right now, he had enough challenge just remembering his own name.

The Korean DAC fell silent and Lefter went back to cradling his head in his hands and trying not to go "chucky-chucky."

The Korean DAC dug around in his pack, took out a small bottle, and carried it over to Lefter at the table. He handed the bottle to Lefter and said, "Blethe in." He put the fingers of one hand up to his nostrils and sniffed then stared at Lefter and nodded yes.

"What the hell, anything is worth a try at this point," said Lefter. He opened the lid on the small bottle and gently smelled the contents. "That smells odd," he said to the DAC.

"Blethe mol," said the DAC again taking a deep breath while pretending to hold something under his nostrils.

Lefter breathed in and out hard several times. "Holy crap, my head is feeling better. Thank you," he said to the DAC.

"No ploblem," said the DAC and returned to his bunk.

Lefter sat at the table and breathed in the aroma from the small bottle for several minutes. "This is great. What is it?" he said to the DAC.

"Ol Kolean lemedi," said the DAC. "Lew klep, I get mol."

"Thank you very much. Dometi gotto. Oh crap, that's Japanese isn't it? Sorry."

"OK, no ploblem," said the DAC.

Lefter's headache was almost gone and he was elated. He felt like running over and hugging the Korean DAC. *Yeah right*, he thought, *and then hug him and call him honey. There's my stupid sense of humor again.*

Lefter sat at the table and took periodic sniffs from the bottle for the next hour. Finally, he felt good enough to have a smoke. He took the pack of cigarettes from his fatigue shirt pocket and held it out toward the Korean DAC. "Smoke?" The DAC came to the table and took a cigarette. Lefter lit a match and held it out while the DAC started his cigarette. Lefter lit one for himself and said, "Thank you again. My headache is gone."

"No ploblem," said the DAC.

Lefter didn't know how to make conversation with the DAC. He didn't want to say anything that could be misinterpreted. The Korean apparently was having the same "ploblem," Lefter thought mockingly. *Don't try to be humorous*, he thought, *just have a friendly conversation. What to say, what to say*, he kept thinking as he looked at the DAC and smiled.

The DAC smiled back and kept looking at Lefter.

They each took a drag on their cigarette, inhaled and smiled at each other again.

"Oh crap," Lefter said out loud and burst out laughing.

The DAC started laughing also. "Lew clap now!"

"No, no, it's just an expression," said Lefter while laughing. "You've got my sense of humor."

"Lew clap now!" repeated the DAC while laughing.

They stared at each other while their laughter increased and tears started welling up in their eyes. Each of them tried to take a drag on their cigarette but couldn't stop laughing long enough. Finally, they each put out their cigarette in the old C-ration can ashtray on the table. They were getting worn out from the laughing.

Finally the Korean DAC went over to the radio area and tapped the Chinese DAC on the shoulder. The Chinese DAC took off the earphones, stood up and handed them to the Korean DAC. Still laughing the Korean DAC sat down, put on the earphones and began slowing turning the frequency selection knob. The Chinese DAC looked at Lefter who was also laughing and put out his hands in a position that Lefter interpreted as asking, "What the hell is going on?"

Lefter picked up his pack of cigarettes and held it out toward the Chinese DAC. The Chinese DAC bowed slightly, took the few steps to the table, removed a cigarette and sat down. Lefter lit a match and held it while the Chinese DAC lit his cigarette. Then he lit one for himself. *Now what*, Lefter thought, realizing he didn't know how to make conversation with the Chinese DAC either. *Dumb shit, you never learn*, he thought.

"What was so fucking funny?" said the Chinese DAC with only a slight accent.

Oh crap, how in hell do I explain it, thought Lefter. Then he decided that it would be easier to just make up a good lie. "I told him a joke," said Lefter.

"OK, tell me," said the Chinese DAC.

Lefter's sense of humor was about to get him in trouble if he wasn't careful because he thought about saying, "This Chink decided to go ice fishing." Grinning widely, he shook the thought out of his head and said, "Do you like Polish jokes?"

"Maybe, you try," said the DAC.

Lefter decided to give it a try. "A Polish guy decides to try ice fishing so he buys the fishing gear and stops by the bait shop on the way to the frozen lake." He says to the bait shop clerk, 'how much is your bait' and the clerk says, 'I can let you have all you want for a dollar.' So the Polish guy says, 'give me two dollars worth.'"

The Chinese DAC just stared at Lefter with a blank expression.

Oh crap, bad idea, he doesn't get it, thought Lefter and stared back at the DAC.

Lefter raised his hands in a palm up expression and shrugged his shoulders.

The Chinese DAC returned the shrugged shoulders and palms up sign and smiled broadly.

Lefter picked up the bottle containing the Korean DAC's headache remedy, removed the lid and took a big sniff. He smiled and handed the bottle to the Chinese DAC.

The Chinese DAC took a big sniff from the bottle and handed it back to Lefter. Then he laughed softly.

Lefter took a big sniff from the bottle, handed it back to the Chinese DAC and laughed.

"Sniffing bottle is punch line," said the Chinese DAC chuckling.

"Stinking good punch line," replied Lefter with a laugh.

"OK, I go rest," said the Chinese DAC as he put out the cigarette butt and went to his bunk.

"Good idea," said Lefter who put out his cigarette butt also and went to his bunk.

Lefter woke up with a start. Someone was knocking on the bunker door. "Hey Lefter, it's Hillman, open the door."

Lefter raised up out of the cot, looked at his watch and marveled at how fast the night had went by. No nightmare and he had not heard any firefights or outgoing mortar or artillery rounds. He felt guilty. He had taken small naps before but never slept through the entire night. *Entire night, hell*, he thought, *it was late afternoon when I laid down.*

"Open the door, Lefter," said Hillman again.

Lefter opened the door and Hillman said, "Thought you were dead in there. I've been knocking my damn knuckles off."

"Sorry, took a short nap," lied Lefter as he looked toward the DACs. Both DACs smiled and didn't say anything.

"I damn near died," said Hillman. "My head still throbs."

"I'm feeling great," said Lefter truthfully.
"How the hell did you manage to recover so well?" said Hillman.
"Used a secret fragrance," said Lefter as he smiled knowingly.
Hillman said quizzically, "What the hell are you talking about?"
Lefter picked up the small bottle from the table, sniffed at the lid and said, "Herein lies the secret to curing a massive hangover headache."
"Yeah, right," responded Hillman skeptically. "Just a little sniff will do you," he said mocking the radio ad for Brilcream hair tonic.
"OK skeptic, suffer then," said Lefter as he put the bottle in his pocket.
"I will," said Hillman. "Get the hell out of here so I can take a little nap."
"OK, stay safe, buddy," said Lefter.
"Will do," said Hillman.

After returning to the ASA base camp, Lefter did something that he had not done before. He looked carefully at the name of the DACs who signed each page of the handwritten intercept log. Kim Song Lu was the name of the Korean DAC and Tarcy Fong was the name of the Chinese DAC.

Contrary to the usual end-of-shift feelings, Lefter was not sleepy and felt quite rested. Feeling guilty, he volunteered to do chores around the detachment.

Campbell gave him a skeptical look and said, "If you weren't leaving on R&R I'd assign you a whole raft of chores around here."

"No kidding, when do I leave?" said Lefter.

"Officially starts tomorrow but if you're all perky, I'll drop you off at the 303 today then tomorrow Quigley will join you for the R&R trip to Tokyo. Sound OK?" asked Campbell.

"Great," said Lefter. "I'll pick up on those chores as soon as I get back."

Campbell completed his review of the logs and filled out his one-page daily report. Handing it to Lefter he said, "Take a good look at this report in case you ever have to make it out."

"Why would I be doing that?" asked Lefter.

"Who knows, I could get sick or something," replied Campbell.

Sensing something was wrong Lefter said, "What the hell is going on here, Camp?"

"Nothing, nothing." Campbell paused then said, "It's just that I'll be rotating in a couple of months and I'm getting the short-timer fever."

"I didn't know you were headed back to the States that soon. What is the short-timer fever?" asked Lefter.

"Fear of getting killed just before rotating out," replied Campbell.

Lefter stared at Campbell and could see a look of concern but not fear. "You don't look scared to me," said Lefter. "I'm betting you make it without any problem."

"Thanks," said Campbell. "Get your gear together and let's hit the road."

CHAPTER FIFTEEN

As they pulled into the 303 Compound and stopped, Lefter said to Campbell, "Do me a favor, would you, Camp? Tell Mewman I left on R&R and said for him to keep his nose down and not end up as a dead hero."

"Will do," said Campbell.

"Thanks, Camp, see you in a week," said Lefter as he took his pack and headed toward the Day Tent.

Except for going to lunch with Crovelli and Nay, Lefter stayed in the Day Tent reading magazines and writing two letters, one to his wife and another to his father. He went to dinner with Crovelli, Nay and Nissing then they all went to the EM Club and sat down at Mighty Joe's table.

"I got the first one," said Mighty Joe pointing at the single can of beer in front of him. "Who's buying the second round?"

"You are," said Lefter.

"The hell I am, the rule is…"

Lefter interrupted and said, "Hear you can't figure out where Asshole Soss goes every day."

"Been working on it but hit a brick wall so far," said Mighty Joe.

"Would you like to know where he goes?" asked Lefter looking intently at Mighty Joe.

"Well, yeah, OK," said Mighty Joe.

"OK," said Lefter, "pony up to the bar and bring us back a round and I'll tell you the straight skinny."

Crovelli, Nay and Nissing each looked surprised but pleased to see someone getting one up on Mighty Joe. At dinner, Lefter had asked if anyone had found out yet where Soss went each day but didn't tell them that he knew.

"How the hell did you find out?" said Mighty Joe.

"Never reveal my sources," replied Lefter. Mighty Joe grinned and the others laughed.

"OK, you win this round," said Mighty Joe. He left and returned shortly with five cans of beer on a tray. He placed the cans of beer on the table and said, "OK, spill it, Sherlock."

Lefter picked up a can of beer and took a sip. The others just stared at him with a look of anticipation. "Well, here's the story," said Lefter then paused to take another sip of beer. Mighty Joe and the others leaned slightly forward and remained silent. "Every week day the major drives south for..."

Mighty Joe interrupted and said, "Cut the crap and get to the point, Lefter."

"What's the matter, don't you like the tit for tat?" said Lefter.

"Come on, Lef," said Nay. "You've cut him up enough."

"OK," said Lefter, "he goes to the psycho ward at the hospital in Seoul."

Mouths around the table dropped open involuntarily and nobody, including Mighty Joe, said anything. "Yep, that's the story," said Lefter who then leaned back and slowly drank from his can of beer. Again, the others at the table just stared at him open mouthed. Lefter knew he had them hooked and wondered what was racing through their minds. It was special fun to have Mighty Joe on the hook.

"Go on," said Mighty Joe.

Lefter finished drinking his can of beer and said, "Think I'll need another beer to wet my whistle before I proceed."

Recognizing that Lefter was after Mighty Joe, the others at the table kept quiet although they were dying to hear more and would have gladly bought the next round of beer.

Lefter lit up a cigarette and leaned back in his chair, waiting.

"You're getting under my skin," complained Mighty Joe as he stood up and headed for the bar. Returning with another round of beer for those at the table, he smiled and said, "I do appreciate a good con job, Lefter, even if I am not the one doing it; now sing."

Lefter told them of Mewman's getting blind drunk and being sent to the psycho ward where he had the chance encounter with Major Soss.

"That's why I couldn't find out where he went," said Mighty Joe. "It's cloaked in that doctor/client confidentially stuff."

"Yeah," said Nay, "not to mention that his fellow officers don't want anyone to know that one of theirs is a psychopathic CO."

"They don't mind making fun of him though," said Crovelli.

"Well, he is a good Scoutmaster and took you all on a camping trip," said Lefter.

"Up yours," said Crovelli.

"Don't be so damn sensitive, I'm the one that damn near got court-martialed over your camping trip," said Lefter.

"Right, but now you've transferred out of the Scout Troop," said Crovelli smiling.

"Not only that but I'm going on R&R tomorrow," bragged Lefter.

"Rub it in," said Nay.

For the first time since dinner Nissing spoke, "I'm going on R&R tomorrow also."

"Be damned, are you paired up with anyone?" asked Lefter.

"Nope," replied Nissing.

"You're welcome to join up with Quigley and me if you want to," said Lefter.

"Thanks for the invite," said Nissing.

"How about a game of Mumblejon?" said Mighty Joe.

"Count me out," said Lefter, "I don't want to start my R&R with a hangover."

"Yeah, but you'll probably end it with one," quipped Nay.

Smiling back at Nay, Lefter said, "Maybe Charlie here, but not saintly me."

" Not me," said Nissing, "I am going to spend seven days soaking in a Japanese bath tended by two pretty maidens with toxon cheche."

"You're dreaming," said Mighty Joe. "None of them Japanese bath house girls have big tits."

"How would you know?" said Nay. "You've never spent any time in Japan."

"Been studying the culture," said Mighty Joe.

"Yeah, right," said Crovelli, "you've got all your culture between your legs."

"Screw you," said Mighty Joe.

"Up yours," replied Crovelli.

"Sounds like a swan song," said Lefter as he stood up. "Sayounara and goodnight."

"Hang on," said Nissing. "I'll walk back with you."

"Have fun," said Nay. Crovelli and Mighty Joe nodded agreement and waved goodbye.

Walking back to the 303 Compound, Lefter said, "It's early yet, got time for a nightcap? I have a bottle in my pack."

"Maybe one," said Nissing, "but I don't want to get loaded."

"Agreed," said Lefter. "My pack is in the Day Tent."

Nobody else was in the Day Tent. Lefter found a can of 7-Up in the cooler, opened it and motioned toward the couch and chair. "Have a seat and I'll get my bottle." He took a ten-cent piece of military script from his pocket and put it in the gallon can on the bar. Then, retrieving the whiskey from his pack, he joined Nissing on the couch. Lefter took the cap from the whiskey and handed it and the can of 7-Up to Nissing.

Nissing took a swig of the whiskey and then followed it with a swallow of 7-Up. Lefter took the bottle and 7-Up and did the same.

"Never had the chance to shoot the bull with you before, Charlie," said Lefter. "Where is home?"

"Phoenix, Arizona — land of the morning hot," replied Nissing. "How about you?"

"Warden, Washington — land of the morning cold, at least in the winter. The weather there is a lot like it is here; hot in the summer and frigid in the winter. I hear you have a photographic memory, Charlie."

"Well," said Nissing with a chuckle, "everyone has a photographic memory, some just don't have film." Then he added, "I work at it and keep practicing. It's something to do and keeps my mind occupied."

"Interesting, how do you practice?" asked Lefter as he handed the bottle back to Nissing.

"Well, one thing I do," said Nissing, "is memorize Modern Photography Magazine each month, just for the hell of it." Nissing took another drink of whiskey and 7-Up and handed them back to Lefter.

"No kidding, the entire magazine?" asked Lefter.

While Lefter had another drink, Nissing got up, walked across the tent and came back with a Modern Photography Magazine. "Here's last month's edition, ask me something about it," he said while handing the magazine to Lefter.

Lefter handed the bottle and 7-Up to Nissing and thumbed through the magazine as Nissing had another drink and handed the bottle back to Lefter.

Lefter took another drink of whiskey and skipped the 7-Up chaser. "OK, what is the article about that starts on page 39?"

"That's too damn general a question and easy to answer," said Nissing as he took the bottle from Lefter and, like Lefter, had a drink without the 7-Up chaser. Nissing leaned back, closed his eyes and said, "It's about the new Minolta thirty-five millimeter camera. The first paragraph reads — Photography buffs will be delighted with the myriad of features on this new

Minolta camera."

"That's amazing," said Lefter and took another swig of whiskey. As they each had a few more drinks, Lefter tested him several more times by asking for the specific words from a specific page number and paragraph. Each time Nissing quoted the words exactly as written in the magazine.

Smoky barked outside the door of the Day Tent. "Oh, fit! I mean shit. I forgot to bu-bu-bring a bu-bu-beer for Smoky."

"No pro-pro-problem," said Nissing. "I got sa-sa some hi-hi hidden. Be ri-ri right back." Nissing stood up and staggered out of the tent letting Smoky through the door in the process.

Smoky ran over and looked in his empty dish, then with drooping ears, looked over at Lefter. "So solly, Smoky," said Lefter. With his tail wagging, Smoky walked over to Lefter and put his head in Lefter's lap. Lefter patted the dog's head and felt guilty. "All I got is wh-wh whiskey," said Lefter to the dog. Lefter struggled to his feet, walked across the tent and poured about a half-cup of whiskey into the dog bowl. Smoky followed sniffed the bowl, took one lap and lay down in his bed. He looked at Lefter with sad eyes.

Nissing came staggering back with three cans of beer, went to the bar and opened all three. He took one can and poured it into the dog bowl. Smoky got out of his bed and had a few laps from the bowl then lay back down.

Nissing sat back down on the couch and gave one of the remaining beers to Lefter. They had a drink of whiskey, chased it with the beer, and toasted their good fortune of leaving on R&R the next day. They had a few more slurring toasts of whiskey chased a sip of beer.

Across the tent, Smoky would periodically take another few laps from the dog bowl. Then he started whining at the tent door. "Damn do-do dog wa-wa wants out," slurred Lefter as he staggered over and opened the door. Smoky ran out of the tent and started throwing up.

"Oh crap," said Lefter as he suddenly sobered up briefly, ran out the door and started throwing up beside Smoky. Then Nissing ran out and took the throw-up position on the other side of Smoky. Lefter's stupid sense of humor clicked in and he thought, *What a picture, two men and their dog throwing up together – now that's true companionship.*

Flash! Someone took a picture. Temporarily blinded by the flash bulb, neither Lefter nor Nissing saw who took the picture. At the time, they didn't much care as they continued to take turns vomiting. Lefter's sense of humor kicked in again and he thought, *This sounds like we are each calling for some fellow named Ralph. Even Smoky can call his name.* Lefter started to laugh out loud but it turned into another call for Ralph. Finally the gagging and heaving subsided and the three of them went back inside the Day Tent.

"Oh shit," said Nissing.

"Oh crap," said Lefter.

Smoky just whined softly and looked at them with sad eyes and droopy ears. Now he had his tail tucked low between his rear legs. Lefter patted him on the head and said, "Bad boy, stupid boy, just like me."

A bulb went off in Lefter's head. He went to his pack and took out the small bottle of Korean headache remedy. *It's worth a try*, he thought as he took off the lid and inhaled a deep breath. He took another deep inhalation then held it under Nissing's nose and said, "Smell this."

Nissing took a whiff off the bottle and said, "I know what that is. I have some also. It's called Kisoto — a blend of various plant oils to treat headaches."

"Right on," said Lefter, "it works great for a hangover headache so maybe it will work as a sort of 'hangover condom.'"

"Worth a try," said Nissing.

Nissing went to his sleeping tent and came back with his bottle of Kisoto and some snacks. The three of them sat on the couch and sniffed from their bottle of Kisoto. Lefter let Smoky smell his bottle but Smoky didn't seem to like it and soon went to his bed, lay down and moaned occasionally.

Soon Lefter and Nissing were feeling well enough to begin eating some snacks. "This is a fantastic potion," said Lefter, "we could make a fortune selling this."

"Just one problem," said Nissing, "only one family in Korea knows how to make it and they won't tell anyone the formula. It's very expensive; how did you get some?"

"A DAC gave it to me," said Lefter.

"He must really like you," said Nissing, "that little bottle probably cost him twenty dollars American money. The family won't take military script."

"Sometimes we don't know who our friends really are, do we?" said Lefter.

"How did you get your bottle?" asked Lefter.

"I know someone in the family," said Nissing.

"Really, how did that happen?" asked Lefter.

"Maybe I'll tell you sometime, but not now," said Nissing. "I'm going to go to bed."

"OK, me too," said Lefter.

They walked together to the sleeping tent and Lefter took the guest cot.

STAY SAFE, BUDDY

The last thing he remembered thinking after he got into the sleeping bag was, *I sure hope Bed-check Charlie stays home tonight.*

Suddenly, the tent was lit up bright with the Eire light of a prosperous flare. As Lefter sat up in his sleeping bag, he saw Chinese soldiers come storming into the tent. They had bayonets fixed on their rifles and started stabbing the ASA guys in their sleeping bags. Lefter struggled to get out of the bag but couldn't free himself. A Chinese soldier rushed up to him and stabbed downward with his bayonet. "Ahhhhhhhhhhhh!" Lefter woke up shaking and sweating profusely. His pulse was pounding in his neck. "Another damn nightmare," he said softly.

Moonlight filtered into the tent through the crack around the wooden door. The only sound was that of several men snoring softly. As he swung his feet and legs out over the edge of the cot, it dawned on him that the sleeping bag zipper was open. He ran his hand down the zipper until it reached the bottom of the sleeping bag. The zipper was open the entire length. *How the hell did that happen?* he thought. *I must have forgot to zip up the damn thing.* As his eyes adjusted, he could see the outline of the cots, stoves and other large items in the tent. He quietly slipped on his pants, shirt and boots, and made his way out of the tent. Outside he lit up a cigarette and sucked in the fresh air combined with the tobacco smoke. Soon, the nicotine began to calm his nerves.

Lefter tried to read his watch. He wasn't sure but it appeared to be somewhere around three a.m. Although it was mid June, the night air was cool and crisp. It was starting to feel cold. The night air was penetrating through to his sweat-soaked tee shirt and underwear. Shivering, he went back into the tent and quietly returned to the guest cot. Sitting on the cot he stripped naked, then removed a set of clean underclothes from his pack and put them on. The dry underclothes felt good but he was still shivering. He turned the damp sleeping bag inside out and tried, without success, to find the zipper pull. Finally, giving up on getting the bag zipped up, he just held the open area together and went to sleep.

Lefter woke up several more times during the rest of the night because he was cold. Without the zipper working the sleeping bag would be laying wide open. Finally, he woke up to daylight outside and a light bulb illuminating the tent. He sat up and inspected the sleeping bag in detail. It was not a mummy bag. It was wider and did not appear to be reversible. Even in the light, he couldn't find the zipper pull. *Maybe this is the new bag Campbell mentioned,* Lefter thought.

"Let's get some breakfast," called Nissing from across the tent.

"Yeah, OK," replied Lefter. Getting dressed it occurred to him that he didn't have a hangover. "Do you have a hangover?" he said to Nissing as they walked toward the mess hall.

"None," said Nissing.

"I got to find out the formula for that potion," said Lefter.

"Forget it," said Nissing, "before they would give up that formula, they would kill you, feed your carcass to the dogs, and then eat the dogs."

I like this guy's sense of humor, thought Lefter, *or was it humor? Nissing wasn't laughing.*

After they were sitting at a table with their reconstituted eggs, toast and greasy sausage, Lefter said, "What's the deal on those new sleeping bags?"

"Well," said Nissing, "the Army's had them made in a big hurry after those guys over in Ten Corps got bayoneted in their mummy bags awhile back."

"That may be the fastest the Army ever got something done," said Lefter.

"Of course, know why?"

Lefter thought a moment then said, "No, why?"

"Well, those guys that got killed were bayoneted by Infiltrators." Nissing paused and waited for Lefter to catch on.

Lefter thought briefly then said, "So?"

"*Infiltrators, behind* the MLR," said Nissing putting emphasis on the words infiltrator and behind.

Lefter thought, "infiltrator" and "behind the MLR" and came up with nothing. "Give me one more hint."

Nissing said, "Officers and commanders."

"Oh, I get it now. They moved fast because *their* ass was on the line. *Infiltrators* put them in jeopardy because *they* use the same mummy bags that we do up on the MLR."

"Now you got it," said Nissing. "They're protecting their fat-cat brass asses."

"Fat-cat brass asses," mimicked Lefter, "that's funny."

"The best thing about the new bag is that it pops open if you give it a big outward push with your arms and hands. Simple design, they just leave off the stop for the zipper pull so it just runs off the end when tensioned hard."

"Ah ha, that's what happened to my bag last night," said Lefter. "It popped open and then I couldn't get the damn zipper to work after that. When do we get the new bags up in the detachments?"

Nissing downed his coffee and said, "Truck loads of them coming in every day so it shouldn't be more than a couple of days."

"Figures," said Lefter. "You non-brass candy asses back here get the new bags first."

"Rank has its privileges. You ready to get out of here?"

"Yeah, but I want to take these eggs to Smoky. Wait a minute while I get some paper to wrap it in."

"Here," said Nissing, "use this copy of Stars and Stripes that I picked up on the way in. I'll get another one when we leave."

Lefter took the newspaper, opened it up and started to scrap the eggs onto it. "Whoa, look at this," he said pointing to the byline of an article in the paper that read: *GI INVITES POLITICIANS TO MLR*. Lefter read the article while Nissing waited. "Verbatim, just like I wr…" He barely stopped short of telling Nissing that he had wrote the letter. "Right on, couldn't have written it better myself," said Lefter as he passed the page containing the article to Nissing. While Nissing read the article, Lefter wrapped up the eggs in the remaining pages.

Nissing finished reading the article and said, "Great letter, what did you mean when you said verbatim?"

"Exactly as I would have written it, or nearly so," said Lefter evasively. "Let's get out of here. I want to feed this to Smoky."

Lefter and Nissing shouldered their carbines as they stood up, then walked back to the 303 compound. Lefter went to the Day Room and peered through the door he had left ajar last night for Smoky to get in and out during the night. Smoky was asleep in his bed. "Here, Smoky. Here, Smoky. Come on, boy," he called out. Smoky raised his head but didn't get up. Lefter went in, opened the paper containing the eggs and put it on the wood floor in front of Smoky. Smoky looked up at Lefter with sad eyes and his ears laid back. "Here, boy," said Lefter as he tapped on the eggs with his fingers. Smoky rose slowly, head hanging low, stepped slowly out of his bed and ate a little of the eggs. Then he trotted out the door and started throwing up. Lefter went outside, patted Smoky on the head and said, "Sorry, buddy, see you in a week."

By mid-morning Quigley showed up and they obtained their travel orders from Crovelli at the cage. The orders had been cut the previous day and signed by the executive officer. Crovelli drove the three of them to K-2, the Air Force Base just south of Seoul and left them at the building with a sign outside that said simply ALL PASSENGERS CHECK IN HERE. Inside they handed their orders to an Air Force enlisted man who handed back the papers and said, "Hurry up and get out to the plane. It's being loaded right now."

Lefter, Nissing and Quigley hurried out and got in the line of men loading onto the C-23 transport plane. An Air Force Sergeant was checking the written orders before allowing each man to board the plane. Lefter was the last in line just behind Nissing. After Nissing was cleared the sergeant held up his hand in front of Lefter and said, "Sorry, buddy, there is no more room on board. You'll have to take the next available flight."

"I'm going on R&R with those two guys in front of me," said Lefter pointing toward Nissing and Quigley who were climbing the boarding ladder.

"You're with them? Let me see your orders," said the sergeant. He looked at Lefter's orders and said, "Wait right here." The sergeant climbed aboard and came back in several minutes. "You owe me big time," said the sergeant. "I've got one pissed off major that you're bumping with your special orders." An irate Army Major came down the boarding steps and stormed off the boarding area. "OK, buddy, get on board and find the empty seat," said the sergeant.

The folding canvas seats were side by side along each side of the cabin. Lefter found the empty seat that was located across the isle from Nissing. "What the hell happened to you?" said Nissing across the isle.

"Beats me," replied Lefter holding out his hands and shrugging his shoulders, "the sergeant said I was bumping the major with my *special* orders."

An Army Colonel sitting next to Nissing said, "The major has *standard* orders. Your *special* orders give you priority over his *general* orders, so he gets bumped, it's that simple."

"Oh," said Lefter nodding his head up and down slowly to signify that he understood. Lefter smiled and thought, *This is a damn fun way to start my seven days of R&R.* Lefter knew that all ASA men traveled on special orders, but thought that only meant that they didn't travel with large numbers of people in what were commonly called troop movements. Now he had another reason to be glad he enlisted in the ASA.

It was a clear and sunny day as the DC-4 flew across the Sea of Japan and landed smoothly at Takakawa airport, about thirty miles from Tokyo. A corporal from ASA Pacific met them at the gate; he was holding a sign reading ASA REPORT HERE. He introduced himself as the R&R coordinator and drove them to the ASAPAC Tokyo headquarters in an Army six passenger automobile. At ASAPAC, they traded in their fatigue uniform for a summer dress uniform that actually fit good. The corporal said, "Anytime you want clean clothes, just show your orders to the Japanese shower attendant and he will give you clean clothes in exchange for your dirty ones. Also, you can get food in the dining room anytime by showing your orders to the dining room attendant. He'll find something for you no matter what time it is."

They were assigned a bed in a room identified by a sign on the door as VISITORS. The large room contained ten beds but it appeared that Lefter, Nissing and Quigley were the only occupants. "I'll leave you guys here but you can reach me anytime in the colonel's office area; I'm one of his clerks. Let me know if I can help you on anything. We want you guys to enjoy your stay. The packet I gave you should answer a lot of things like train schedules, good restaurants, how to buy things at the Ginza Strip and so on. Remember that there is a midnight curfew for military personnel, meaning you must not be on the streets from midnight to six a.m. Change your military script for Japanese yen at our little PX here at ASAPAC. Have fun."

Lefter was impressed. He had a real bed with a mattress. Instead of the olive drab color, the pillowcase was white. The bed had white sheets. "Look at this, white sheets!" Instead of the familiar olive drab blanket, each bed had a blanket with a different design. "Look at this," Lefter said to Nissing and Quigley, "sheets — we've died and gone to heaven." Nissing and Quigley nodded agreement and inspected their assigned space.

"I'm putting in for a transfer to this outfit," said Nissing.

A metal closet stood at the head of each bed. It had drawers below the hanging area. "Look at this," said Quigley as he pulled out one of the drawers. "What are these called? I can't remember," he said jokingly.

"Cotton picking boxes," said Lefter slowly in his best Southern drawl, "ain't that what you-all call them down south?"

"Or apple knocker boxes back where ya-all live," replied Quigley laughing.

"Don't matter anyway, we don't have anything to put in them no matter what you call them," said Nissing.

"Oh yeah," said Lefter, "I'm putting my tooth brush in the top one, the toothpaste in the middle one, and my razor in the bottom one."

All three laughed and placed their small bag of personal items in the top drawer. "Let's check out this place," said Nissing, "it's almost two o'clock and we've missed lunch; maybe we can find a candy machine somewhere."

Looking around the ASAPAC Compound they came across the PX and exchanged their military script for Japanese yen. The PX clerk, an ASA Corporal, said, "Be sure to convert any yen you have left back to script before going back to Korea." Then, smiling, he added, "Of course, most guys don't have any left by the end of their R&R."

They found the dining room entrance and stared in through the double entrance door. "This can't be the Army." said Lefter. "Curtains on the windows, table clothes, and place settings!"

"Holy moly, look at them fancy chairs with padded seats," said Quigley.

"I'm putting in for a transfer to this place," said Nissing. "Look at this." Nissing pointed to a sheet of typewritten paper attached to a small bulletin board:

WEDNESDAY DINNER
Italian Meat Balls in Tomato Sauce
Green Bean Salad with Sliced Tomatoes
Baked Potato w Butter, Sour Cream, Chives
Garlic Bread
Apple Pie with Ice Cream
Milk, Coffee, Tea, Fruit Juice

A Japanese man wearing a white smock came up to them and said, "You flom Kolea?"

Lefter, Nissing and Quigley nodded yes.

"You hunglee?" he asked.

Lefter, Nissing and Quigley nodded yes. Soldiers are always hungry.

"Sit plese, I bling food."

The three of them sat down at one of the tables, felt the tablecloth, felt the cloth napkins, fiddled with the silverware, and gawked around the room. The walls had large framed paintings of landscape scenes. There was a piano in one corner of the room.

"Holy crap, just look at this fancy place," said Lefter.

Soon, the Japanese attendant returned with a large tray containing sandwiches and placed it on the table, "Lew picke plese, I getee dlinks." Each of the six sandwiches was on a separate plate.

Lefter, Nissing and Quigley were still staring at the sandwiches with indecision when the attendant returned with another tray containing glasses, a quart of milk and a pitcher of orange juice. "You wan mole, cal me," said the attendant and walked to the kitchen entrance, turned and stood watching Lefter, Nissing and Quigley.

"Have we died and come back as generals?" asked Lefter.

"Them look like good vitals," said Quigley as he picked up a plate containing a tuna salad sandwich and smelled it. "Yummy, yummy, smells like pussy." He took a large bite, closed his eyes and chewed slowly.

"I'm not touching that one," said Lefter and picked up a turkey sandwich. He resisted the urge to smell it and give Quigley the opening to say what he knew he would say if Lefter smelled his sandwich. He took a bite and it was delicious. "Good turkey," he said.

"I'm asking for a transfer to this place," said Nissing.

"Snap out of it, Nissing, and eat up," said Lefter as he poured himself a glass of the cold milk and took a sip. "Wow, that tastes good; first real milk I've had since the first few days on the ship coming over here."

They ate all six sandwiches, drank all the milk and the orange juice. Lefter took out his army handkerchief and wiped his mouth. He didn't want to dirty the cloth napkin. Quigley used his handkerchief also but Nissing unfolded the cloth napkin and wiped his mouth. "What the hell are you dirtying up that pretty napkin for?" said Quigley.

"Getting used to it," said Nissing. "I told you, I'm transferring to this place."

"Yeah, right," said Lefter sarcastically, "then you better start practicing saying 'Lew hunglee,' cause that's the job they'll probably give you here."

"We'll see," said Nissing. "No harm in trying."

"Let's go to town," said Quigley.

"Not me," said Lefter. "I want some of that dinner that's listed on the sheet by the door."

"Me too," said Nissing. "Besides I want to check this place out more." Then he grinned and added, "Did I mention that I'm going to transfer here?"

"I think you mentioned it, maybe once or was it ten times," said Lefter.

"OK, I'll see you guys tonight," said Quigley and he got up from the table. "Be back before the midnight curfew."

The Japanese dining room attendant hurried over to the table, bowed and said, "Yew flew?"

Lefter and Nissing nodded yes. The attendant began cleaning off the table. "Wonder if we're supposed to tip him?" said Lefter.

"No tippy," said the attendant, as he shook his head no.

"I'm transferring to this place," said Nissing.

"No kidding," said Lefter, "how you going to arrange that?"

"I'm going to go find out right now," said Nissing.

"Well, I'm going to take a nap and dream about dinner," said Lefter.

They got up and went their separate ways. Lefter looked back at the

Japanese attendant who saw him and bowed slightly. Lefter thought about asking for a transfer also but quickly dismissed it. It would be great duty for a while but then it would get boring. He would rather be up on the MLR with the action. Additionally, and probably the biggest reason, was that the troops in Japan only got one point per month toward rotating home. Up on the MLR he was getting four points and combat pay. *Besides*, he thought with a big grin, *Mewman would call me a 'number fucking one candy-ass,' and he'd be right.*

"Lefter, Lefter. Wake up. It's time for dinner," called Nissing while tugging on Lefter's feet.

Lefter quickly pulled both knees up in a fetal position and threw both arms up in front of his face. His pulse raced and he broke out in a sweat. He opened his eyes, looked past his arms and saw Nissing.

"What's going on?" said Nissing.

Swinging around and sitting on the edge of the bed, Lefter rubbed his eyes and said, "Just a scary dream, a gook was about to bayonet me." He shook his head to clear away the bad dream, stood up, stretched and said, "Let's go get some of that fancy chow."

Nissing nodded agreement and led the way to the dining room. "Oh damn," said Lefter pointing toward a small cafeteria facility, "we have to pick up our own food." They fell in behind a few men and proceeded to fill their own plate from containers of food placed under an overhanging glass area.

The Japanese attendant who served them the sandwiches stood behind the food line and bowed every time someone looked at him. "What is this for?" said Lefter to Nissing as he tapped the overhanging glass area.

"Sleez bal," said the attendant while bowing slightly.

"What?" said Lefter and Nissing together.

"Sleez bal," said the attendant as he pretended to sneeze.

"Oh, sneeze bar," said Lefter.

"Hai," said the attendant.

"Fancy," said Nissing.

Lefter nodded agreement.

As soon as they placed their plates on a table and sat down, a Japanese woman appeared and said, "Cofa, Yuice, or Melk?"

"Melk, I mean milk," said Lefter.

"Me too," said Nissing.

She hurried off and came back with a quart bottle of milk, poured them each a full glass then set the remaining quart of milk on the table.

Just as they finished eating she once again appeared, picked up the empty plates and said, "Lew likee apule plie ah le modee?"

Lefter and Nissing nodded yes. "Can this really be the Army?" said Lefter.

"I hope so," said Nissing, "because I put in a request for transfer to here this afternoon."

"How the hell did you get that done so quickly?" asked Lefter.

"Never reveal my sources," said Nissing and laughed.

After they finished the apple pie with ice cream and turned down an offer for seconds, Lefter picked up the white cloth napkin, unfolded it and raised it toward his mouth. Stopping just before reaching his mouth he refolded the napkin and placed it back on the table. "Can't do it," he said as he took out his olive drab handkerchief and wiped his mouth.

"Well I'm going to use it," said Nissing as he wiped his mouth with the cloth napkin the laid the crumbled up napkin on the table. "There!" said Nissing proudly.

"That's a damn waste," said Lefter, "now some mama san will need to wash it.

"Yew flew," said the Japanese woman.

As Lefter and Nissing nodded agreement she laid the folded up napkin in Lefter's dirty plate and put the two items on a carrying tray along with the dirty silverware. Lefter stared at the tray and then at the woman. Then she did the same with the dirty plate and unfolded napkin of Nissing. Lefter stared at the woman and she became self-conscious and bowed gracefully. "What a waste!" said Lefter. "But that's the Army."

"Let's go to town," said Nissing.

"OK, how do we do that?" asked Lefter.

"Train," replied Nissing. "I got the directions while you were snoozing." They walked a few blocks to the train station, bought tickets and boarded a passenger train going south to downtown Tokyo.

CHAPTER SIXTEEN

"Where do we get off at?" asked Lefter.

"Tokyo Station," said Nissing, "then we can walk to the Ginza Strip, at least that's what it says on our crib sheet they gave us. Says here a conductor calls out the name of each station before reaching it."

Soon, a Japanese man in a uniform walked past them yelling something in Japanese.

"What is he saying?" said Lefter.

"Sounds like Toy-oh," said Nissing, "that must be it."

"Glad you can understand it," replied Lefter; "sounded like toe-dee-ho to me."

Nissing read from the crib sheet, "It says here to hang onto your wallet, camera and other valuables as you get on and off the train."

The train stopped and they stood up and headed for the door. So did forty or fifty other people who crowded together closely at the door. Then the door opened and the crowd flowed through the door onto the platform outside.

"Holy crap, I don't like that close contact," said Lefter as they walked through the Tokyo Station and out onto the street.

"Their culture, get used to it," replied Nissing.

"Live with it my ass, it's only been seven or eight years since we whipped their butt and they surrendered unconditionally — remember?"

"What's your point?" said Nissing.

"I don't know," said Lefter, "guess I just impulsively responded like Mewman might."

"How does Mewman fit into this?" asked Nissing.

"Oh, I was just thinking about him on the train ride," said Lefter. "We're over here in Tokyo for a week of R&R and his big rest and recuperation is a couple of days behind the MLR at battalion headquarters."

"What about it?" said Nissing.

"Makes me feel guilty," said Lefter. "On the other hand, it don't much matter where Mewman is cause he just gets blind-ass drunk and starts shooting off his filthy mouth to everyone around."

"Right on," said Nissing. "He'd be in the jail after the first night in Tokyo anyway."

"You're probably right," agreed Lefter as the guilt eased out of his mind. "OK, let's find the famous Ginza Strip and check it out."

"There's a cop, let's ask him," said Nissing as he walked over to a Tokyo policeman. "Ginza?" said Nissing. The policeman bowed and pointed down the street. "Arigatou," said Nissing as he bowed slightly. The policeman bowed back.

"What?" said Lefter.

"I said thank you," replied Nissing.

"How do you spell it?" said Lefter.

"Beats the hell out of me," said Nissing. "I learned to speak and understand some Japanese but I can't write it or read it."

"How do you remember all this stuff?" asked Lefter.

"Association. Ah-rhee-got-toe. Think of Sigmon Rhee thanking us for saving his sorry ass in Korea. Rhee bows and points to his toe. Ah, rhee, got, toe; arigatou — get it?"

"Yeah, I get it but it sure is complicated," said Lefter.

"Maybe, but you won't forget it now," said Nissing.

"Forget what?" said Lefter as he smiled and playfully hit Nissing on his shoulder.

They walked around the Ginza area for a couple of hours just taking in the variety of sights and sounds. "Hey, there's a place named R&R Club; let's get a beer," said Lefter.

Standing just inside the entrance door, Lefter and Nissing waited for their eyes to adjust to the dim lighting. The room was small with a U-shaped bar that seated eight to ten people. Seven or eight small tables were crowded into the room's remaining space. Four Japanese "hostess" girls were seated at one of the tables. Two young Marines and two other hostess girls were seated at another table. Nobody was seated at the remaining tables. Nobody was seated at the bar.

Lefter and Nissing took a side seat at the bar and ordered Asahi beer. The two young Marines left their table and took a seat on bar stools opposite Lefter and Nissing. It was obvious they had just arrived from boot camp in the U.S. The only decoration they had was a sharpshooter badge pinned on their uniform. No Army or Marine with combat experience wore the marksmanship badges issued for good scores on the shooting range in boot camp. It was considered amateurish.

"Look at that, a couple of them fucking doggies," said one of the Marines pointing toward Lefter and Nissing. "You doggies want to go a round or two," he added and laughed. The other young Marine laughed and put up his fists in a fighting position.

"Not interested in getting into a fight," said Lefter.

"Me neither," said Nissing. "I don't want to spend any of my R&R in jail."

"Chicken shit," called out both Marines in near unison. They laughed and mocked Lefter and Nissing with clenched fists.

Lefter and Nissing just motioned back with the open palms toward the Marines.

An Army soldier in uniform walked up and took the stool on the left of Lefter and Nissing. He ordered whiskey with a water chaser and didn't look at either the Marines or Lefter and Nissing. He was about five foot six and probably weighted 145 pounds or so. He had three rows of ribbons on his shirt but no rank emblem on his sleeve. He had a shoulder patch that identified him as a Ranger. Highly trained in every aspect of ground combat, Lefter and Nissing knew that Army Rangers were highly-skilled killers.

The Marines stared at the Ranger then started shooting off their mouth. "Look at that, there's one of them fucking Army Rangers."

"I hear they're real tough hombres."

The Ranger ignored the Marines and continued to look straight ahead as the bartender delivered his drink.

One of the Marines walked over and started to put his right hand on the Ranger's shoulder. In a flash the Ranger whirled and grabbed the Marine's arm, twisted the arm violently throwing the Marine to the floor. He lay on the floor groaning with his broken arm twisted grotesquely. The other Marine leaped toward the Ranger and was met by a powerful kick to the privates causing him to bend and grab his crotch with both hands. The Ranger quickly delivered a hand blow to the back of his neck knocking him to the floor in a daze. Then the Ranger kicked him in the rib area.

Lefter and Nissing sat open mouthed, both stunned and impressed by the Ranger's ability. Then, just like in a John Wayne cowboy movie, the Ranger picked up his drink, downed it in one gulp and followed with a swallow of beer. He put down the glass of beer and walked calmly out of the bar. The two greenhorn Marines lay on the floor squirming in agony.

The bartender called someone on the telephone behind the bar. In a few minutes, two military MPs entered the bar. The Marines were still on the floor. "Who started this fight?" asked one MP. Lefter, Nissing and the bartender pointed to the Marines on the floor. "Can you walk?" said an MP to the Marines. "Come with us, we'll sort this out down at the brig," said the other MP. They helped the Marines to their feet and took them away.

Lefter busted out laughing.

"What's so funny?" said Nissing.

"It just occurred to me that the MPs thought the Marines were fighting each other. That's why one said, 'we'll sort this out down at the brig.'"

"You're right," said Nissing and busted out laughing also.

"Well, we handled that real good, buddy," said Lefter brushing his hands together. "Maybe we should follow that Ranger around from bar to bar so he will attract the gung-ho greenhorn Marines instead of us."

"Yeah, well maybe they aren't all as stupid as those two," replied Nissing.

"Eh GI, lew lakee gill?" asked one of the Japanese girls who had walked up next to Lefter and Nissing.

"Not me," said Lefter motioning no.

"Iie," said Nissing.

"Lew buyl me dlink?" asked the girl.

"Nope," said Lefter again motioning no.

"Iie," said Nissing, as he also motioned no.

The girl went back and rejoined the other three girls at the table.

Another of the girls at the table came up to Lefter and said, "Lew buyl me dlink?"

"No," said Lefter.

"Iie," said Nissing.

She went back to her table and a third girl came up and said, "Lew buyl me dlink?"

Motioning no, Lefter stepped down from the barstool and said to Nissing, "Let's move on."

Also smiling and signaling no to the girl, Nissing followed Lefter out of the bar and said, "What now?"

"Let's go find the Ernie Pyle Service Club that the guys come back talking about."

Deciding to take a taxi, they spent several minutes negotiated a deal to pay 500 yen for the trip. Proud of getting the driver to cut in half his opening quote of 1000 yen, they climbed in and rode three blocks to their destination.

"Well, we outsmarted ourselves on that negotiation," said Lefter.

"Yeah, we could have walked here in the time spent negotiating," said Nissing.

"I'm hungry, let's get something to eat," said Lefter.

They were impressed with the dining room of the Ernie Pyle building. "This place is fancier than the ASAPAC dining room," said Nissing. "Did I mention that I'm transferring to Japan?"

"No, and don't mention it a sixth time!" said Lefter. "I have a powerful hankering for sliced tomatoes, fresh cold milk and fresh warm bread," said Lefter to the waitress.

The waitress spoke good English except, of course, pronouncing the r sound. "You want sliced tomatoes, cold milk and walm blead," she asked back while making notes in Japanese.

"Yes, a large bowl of sliced tomatoes," said Lefter.

"OK," she said.

"I'll have a toasted cheese sandwich and a glass of milk," said Nissing.

"OK," said the waitress and scurried off.

The bowl of sliced ripe tomatoes was indeed large. It contained the slices of five or six large red tomatoes. Lefter salted each slice and savored the fresh ripe taste. He ate all the tomatoes along with a small loaf of warm and wonderful smelling French bread. For a beverage, he had two large glasses of soothing cold milk.

Nissing ate his sandwich with one glass of milk. "Let's go find a bar and get a drink," said Nissing.

Lefter took a deep breath and let it out with a whooshing sound. "I am stuffed. That is absolutely the best meal I ever ate. I couldn't eat or drink another thing tonight. I'm ready to go back to ASAPAC and call it a night."

"OK," said Nissing, "I'd probably get carried away and spend a thousand yen for a night with one of them hostesses. That would be way too expensive."

"What!" said Lefter. "At three hundred sixty yen to the dollar, that's less than three dollars."

"Well, that's expensive to me," said Nissing. "Over in Seoul it only costs me an average of thirty-seven cents per screw."

"Thirty-seven cents! How the hell would you know that?" asked Lefter.

"I keep track of it," said Nissing as he pulled out a small pocket notepad. "I never pay cash. I get them little gifts from the PX and keep track of what the gifts cost me."

"And it averages out to be thirty-seven cents per piece?" asked Lefter again in amazement.

"So far," said Nissing.

"You are one cunning fellow, Charlie. Somebody ought to write a song about you. It could be called Trinkets for Ass Instead of Cash." Lefter laughed and Nissing smiled proudly.

Back at ASAPAC they found the Day Room and played pool for an hour or so before returning to the sleeping area. For some odd reason, Lefter felt a little guilty lying down on the white sheets. Hoping to stave off any nightmares, he forced himself to think of pleasant things. Tomorrow he planned to go see the Imperial Palace and maybe get one of those Japanese baths the guys came back talking about. Also, he wanted to get presents for his wife and his father. He kept thinking of pleasant things and soon drifted off to sleep.

Lefter woke up with the white sheet and blanket wrapped tightly around him. Although his arms were being held tightly by the covers, he felt warm and cozy. Then a smothering feeling started and he could feel the moisture beginning to ooze out of the sweat glands in his skin. It's was getting way too warm and he decided to take off the blanket.

He tried to pull his arms out but the sheet and blanket begin wrapping even tighter and he couldn't move his arms. He began to kick his feet frantically. The sheet and blanket cinched up tightly around his feet and legs. Now he was sweating profusely. "Oh crap, oh crap!" He pushed hard against the restraining covers to no avail. He could barely wiggle his fingers and toes.

Suddenly the room was illuminated brightly by the eerie light of a phosphorous flare. "Oh no! No!" A Chinese soldier walked up to his bedside, smiled down at Lefter and removed a bayonet from the sheath on his belt. He waved the bayonet in front of Lefter's face and said, "Solong Maline."

"You son-of-a-bitch!" yelled Lefter and then he spit in the face of the Chinese soldier. The now sneering Chinese soldier raised the bayonet and stabbed downward into Lefter's tightly-wrapped chest and withdrew the bayonet with a twisting motion. Blood began to ooze through the stab hole in the blanket and Lefter felt it soaking his skin inside the covers.

"Ahhhhhhhhh! Ahhhhhhhhhh!" Lefter screamed at the top of his lungs as his mouth began working like a flame-thrower to sear the Chinese soldier's face. Lefter began hissing and blowing flames of fire as hard as he could. Then suddenly he had a carbine pointed at the sneering Chinese soldier with the burnt face. Click! Lefter thought, *Oh crap, crap, crap — a misfire.* The burnt enemy raised the bayonet to a stabbing position again. In a flash, Lefter manually ejects the misfired round, slams the mechanism closed on a new round and pulls the trigger. Click! "Ahhhhhhhhhhh!"

The room lights go on. Nissing was standing by the door dressed only in his underwear. He had one hand on the light switch. "What the hell happened?"

Lefter was now awake, wide-eyed and panting heavily. Every muscle was tense and ready for action. His head swung quickly back and forth as he swept the room with his eyes. He took deep breaths and slowly relaxed. The panic faded from his eyes and he waved faintly at Nissing.

"What the hell happened?" repeated Nissing.

"Just another stupid nightmare," said Lefter. "Sorry, go back to bed." Lefter was sitting up in the bed with the sheet and blanket fitted snugly around him. As with previous nightmares, he was sweating profusely and his pulse was racing wildly. He threw off the sheet and blanket and sat on the side of the bed taking long deep breaths and blowing each out forcefully. "On second thought, leave the light on until I get to the shower room," said Lefter. He took the towel from the hook by his bed and headed for the shower.

Lefter soaked in the soothing spray of cool water falling on his body. He kept his head under the spray and slowly closed the warm water control. The water slowly turned icy cold and Lefter began to shiver. It worked. His mind cleared of the nightmare visions. He quickly turned off the cold water, walked to the drying area and started toweling off. *Might as well get dressed*, he thought, *I'm not getting back in bed with those damn demons again tonight.*

The time was 0545. He walked to the dining room, sat down at a table and held his head in both hands.

"Lew likee cofa?" asks the Japanese waiter.

With startled eyes that flashed panic, Lefter quickly looked up at the Asian man. For just an instant, Lefter saw the face of the Chinese soldier of his nightmare. Then his mind snapped back to the reality of the moment.

"No blekfless yet but cofah OK," said the waiter.

"Hai, coffee," replied Lefter, surprised that he answered yes in Japanese.

When his coffee was delivered Lefter said, "Thank you." A smile crossed his face as he thought of the association for remembering the Japanese word for thank you. "Arigatou," Lefter added with a slight bow of his head. The waiter smiled, bowed slightly and replied, "dou itashi-mashite."

Lefter correctly surmised that expression meant 'you're welcome.'

Lefter had three cups of coffee. Each time he practiced using the word hai and arigatou with the waiter.

"Blekfless ledy, lew ete now?" asked the waiter.

"Hai, arigatou," said Lefter confidentially.

After breakfast, Lefter wrote a note to Nissing on a piece of typing paper, folded it to business envelope size and put it half-in/half-out the shirt pocket of Nissing: *Going shopping at Ginza. Will telephone by 1100 and leave message on where to meet for lunch. Lefter*

Lefter took the train to Tokyo Station and found his way to the Ginza Strip. He wandered into a large department store and noticed a picture of an elephant by the elevator door. An arrow on the photo pointed up so he got in the open elevator. The elevator operator looked at Lefter, bowed and said, "Ohayo-gozaimasu."

Lefter didn't recognize the Japanese expression for 'good morning' so he replied, "Elephant."

"Hai," said the operator with a bow.

The elevator stopped at the top floor and the operator opened the door and pointed outward. "Elephant," said the operator.

"Hai, arigatou," replied Lefter with confidence.

"Sayounara," said the smiling operator with a bow.

Lefter bowed and stepped out of the elevator into a small landing room. Exiting the small landing area, he found himself on the roof of the building. Ahead of him, in a low fenced area stood an elephant. It wasn't a full-grown elephant but it was much bigger than a horse. He wondered how they got the elephant onto the roof. *It looks too big to fit in the elevator. Maybe they brought it up to the roof years ago when it was much smaller and it has grown to this size. Now what? How will they get it down?* Lefter jumped backwards as the elephant unloaded a pile of dung the size of a jeep wheel. It had a terrible stink and lay in a big steaming glob. Lefter was reminded of an Ernest Hemingway book, *Green Hills of Africa*. Hemingway described elephant dung in detail. He described the feel, smell, height, width, look, texture, and so on. Lefter smiled broadly as he thought of one sense that was left out of the dung description — taste. "Yuck! Time to move on."

Back inside the store, Lefter purchased a large set of dishes for his wife and a fishing kit for his father. He prepaid for the packing and shipping. Now he could eat and drink merrily with his remaining money before returning to the MLR in Korea.

Back down on the street, Lefter wandered around looking in store windows. As 1100 hours approached, he started looking for a place to meet Nissing. Spotting a neon sign across the street that read in English, *Tokyo*

Café, he decided that would be a good place to wait for Nissing. He called ASAPAC and left a message for Nissing to meet him at the Tokyo Café at noon.

After wandering the streets until nearly noon Lefter entered the Tokyo Café and was greeted by a Japanese woman dressed in a kimono. The woman bowed deeply and said, "Ohayo-gozaimasu."

Lefter replied confidently, "Ohayo-gozaimasu," and followed her to a table.

She said something in Japanese. It sounded like a question but Lefter had no idea what she said. His confidence slipping a little, he decided to drink a beer while waiting for Nissing to show up. "Beer," he said.

She looked at him blankly so he repeated, "Beer." Still she didn't respond. Feeling lost, Lefter's mind raced around until he finally recalled the name of a beer. "Ah-sa-he," he announced proudly.

Again, she looked at him with a blank expression.

"Ah-sa-he," he repeated.

Still she didn't understand.

Lefter pointed toward a bottle of beer on the table next to him and said, "Beer. Ah-sa-he."

"Ah," she said, "Ah-sa-ee."

"Yes. I mean, hai," said Lefter.

"Hai," she repeated, bowed and scurried away.

Lefter looked around the room. All the tables were occupied with what appeared to be Japanese businessmen.

Lefter nursed his beer for twenty minutes or so and then ordered another by just pointing at the empty bottle. By now, he was sure that nobody in the restaurant spoke English and that made him uncomfortable. Why the neon sign said Tokyo Café in English was baffling to him. Another twenty minutes passed and he ordered a third beer and decided to eat lunch by himself. Nissing must not have got his message but just in case, he better wait awhile longer at the Tokyo Café.

Surely, she will understand hamburger, thought Lefter. He motioned the waitress over to his table and said, "Hamburger."

She stared at him blankly.

"Hamburger," he repeated while pretending to chew something.

"Peanuts?" she responded.

"No, no," he shook his head. "Hamburger." He formed his hands in a circle about the size of a hamburger bun then pretended to hold it to his mouth and take a bite. "Hamburger."

"Ambulger," she said, then shook her head back and forth and said, "Iie." She motioned Lefter to come with her and led him to the front of the restaurant and pointed to items displayed on plates in a glass case. They all appeared to be uncooked seafood concoctions of some sort.

Lefter shook his head no, smiled and said, "Peanuts."

"Hai," said the waitress, who scurried off and soon returned with a small bowl of shelled and salted peanuts.

By the time Nissing came in, it was nearly 1300 hours and Lefter had finished his third beer and half a bowl of peanuts.

"Where the hell have you been?" asked Lefter. "The only English anyone in this place speaks is 'peanuts' and the food is raw fish."

"You ate raw fish?" asked Nissing.

"Hell no, but I'm damn tired of peanuts," responded Lefter with an irritating voice.

"A raw fish meal sounds good to me," said Nissing as he kidded Lefter.

"No way. Let's head for the Ernie Pyle," said Lefter. "I'm starving for a big juicy hamburger."

Lefter put 500 yen on the table and the waitress brought him back 225 yen. The total bill for three beers and a bowl of peanuts was only 275 yen. With the money exchange rate of 360 yen to the dollar, that was less than one dollar. He handed her 100 yen as a tip and she smiled and bowed deeply while shuffling backwards with tiny steps.

"You made her day," said Nissing. "By the way, I checked on Quigley. They say he checked in by phone but they haven't seen him since we came in. He must have stayed in a hotel."

"How about the midnight curfew for military people?" asked Lefter.

"Asked about that," said Nissing. "Just means we can't be on the streets between midnight and 0600. It's OK to stay in a hotel room."

"Ah ha," said Lefter, "a loophole in the rule. OK to be in a hotel room but not in the lobby of the hotel, right?"

"Yeah," said Nissing with a sly grin, "probably deliberate to keep the guys from sneaking hostesses onto the military bases."

"Makes sense," said Lefter. "If they can bed down with them in a nearby hotel, why haul them back to the base?"

Nissing nodded agreement.

Lefter continued with a second thought, "Pisses me off that the brass is always herding us around, even with reverse psychology."

Nissing nodded agreement.

Now Lefter was on a roll. "Jump in, jump over, go forward, back up, piss in the tube, and the worst one — hurry up and wait!"

Nissing nodded agreement.

"Now I'm really getting pissed," said Lefter.

Nissing nodded agreement and made a slashing motion across his throat. "Let's find one and cut his fucking throat."

Lefter looked at him, paused and then said, "Yeah!" Then after another pause in which Nissing just kept nodding agreement and slashing at his throat, Lefter smiled and said, "On second thought, let's go get a big juicy burger."

They both laughed and continued walking toward the Ernie Pyle Club.

At the Ernie Pyle Club they each had a hamburger and shared a quart of fresh, cold milk.

"OK, now I'm ready for a few beers," said Lefter.

Nissing nodded agreement and off they went to find a bar.

CHAPTER SEVENTEEN

"We're creatures of habit, buddy," said Lefter as they sat on the same bar stools at the R&R Club. "Dozens of bars in the Ginza and here we are at the same place."

"Who cares," said Nissing. "The beer's cold, the prices are right, the bartender is friendly, and the girls are pretty."

"Let's hope those greenhorn Marines don't come in here again," said Nissing.

"They're probably still in the brig," said Lefter.

"Oh shit," said Nissing as he nodded toward the entrance door.

Lefter turned and looked toward the door half expecting to see the two young Marines. Instead, it was the battle-savvy Army Ranger. "Isn't that…"

Nissing interrupted, "It sure the hell is — Ranger John Wayne."

"Don't smart off," said Lefter. "You just might get your ass kicked."

The Ranger sat on the same bar stool as the previous day. He ordered a drink and kept looking straight ahead. Lefter and Nissing sneaked glances toward the Ranger. The bartender recognized the Ranger and delivered his drink without comment. Then he retreated to a safe distance at the back of the bar.

Turning toward Lefter and Nissing, the Ranger raised his drink and said somberly, "Nice seeing you again." Lefter and Nissing each raised their beer in a toasting position and mumbled a nervous, "Same here, how you doing." Then they took a drink of their beer.

The Ranger downed his whiskey and took a gulp of his beer chaser. "Another," he said to the bartender.

"I'm buying his drink," said Lefter, "and bring us two more beers, please."

"Thanks," said the Ranger.

"My pleasure," said Lefter. "You probably saved my buddy and me from getting a couple of black eyes. Those greenhorn Marines yesterday were trying to egg us into a fight before you came in."

"I hate that," said the Ranger.

"Maybe you did them a favor," said Lefter. "Not only did they learn a big lesson, they won't be getting to a combat area as quickly as they might have."

"Yeah, I suppose it will take a few days for them to heal," said the Ranger as he smiled for the first time.

"We're in I-Corps," said Nissing. "I'm at I-Corps headquarters and he's attached to the 1st Marine Division."

Lefter held up both hands and said, "The key word is *attached*. I'm not a Marine myself. I'm in the Army and I *was* attached to the 1st Marine's 5th Bat 7th." Now they're in reserve and I'm attached to the 25th Infantry Division."

"Understand," said the Ranger. "I'm also attached. My Ranger Company is also attached to the 25th Infantry Division."

"Small world," said Lefter.

Nissing stepped down from the barstool and said, "You all will excuse me, please. I'm going to womanize for a while." He went to a table and sat down. Immediately one of the hostesses went to his table and sat down.

"Give us another drink," said the Ranger. "This one is on me."

"Thanks," said Lefter. "My buddy Mewman is a BAR man in the 25th. He was in my outfit but got court-martialed and shipped off to the infantry."

"Mewman, Mewman. That name is familiar," said the Ranger. "What does he look like?"

"Little guy about five-two, maybe a hundred and thirty-five pounds. He uses the f word liberally, extremely gung-ho and always wanting to kill gooks. Just loves going out on combat patrols. Let's see, what else," said Lefter.

"Nothing so far rings a bell," said the Ranger.

"Oh yeah," said Lefter, "maybe this will ring a bell. The first day he was on the MLR he rescued the major that court-martialed him."

"Bingo," said the Ranger. "He must be the guy that rescued the stupid major that was trying to bring a jeep up the front side of a hill on the MLR."

"That's him," replied Lefter as he took a cigarette and offered one to the Ranger. "He's a good guy but sometimes he's a few packs short of a carton, if you know what I mean."

"I know," said the Ranger as he accepted the cigarette and a light from Lefter. "That story about Mewman and the major is getting laughs all over the MLR."

"Well, it's all over the I-Corps headquarters too," replied Lefter with a laugh. "Lot of guys call me Lef," said Lefter as he offered a handshake.

"They call me Shrew," said the Ranger. "Nicknamed after that vicious little mouse that takes on opponents three times its size."

"Well, Shrew, I can attest to that," said Lefter. "Those two Marines last night were each a lot bigger than you."

"Wasn't much of a contest, was it?" said the smiling Ranger. "They are probably nice guys but filled with too much bravado right now."

"Agreed," said Lefter. "As a Marine Sergeant friend of mine said, 'they'll mellow out after going up a hill in No-Man's-Land and old Joe Chink gets on their ass'."

"Amen to that," said the Ranger. "It takes the starch out of the best."

"Mewman doesn't seem to be afraid," said Lefter.

"Well, Lef," said the Ranger, "he probably has a death wish. Wants to be a hero so bad that he's willing to die for it."

"I don't think he actually wants to die," said Lefter, "but he's definitely not afraid that he's going to die."

"Yeah, I know," said the Ranger. "It's all a big game for him right now, but if he survives, he's a prime candidate for severe battle fatigue."

"What is battle fatigue anyway?" asked Lefter.

"Nightmares, night sweats, pounding pulse, that's the typical battle fatigue."

"Crap," said Lefter, "I get that now and all I do is sit on my ass in a bunker on the MLR."

"Right," said the Ranger, "but the guys who get *severe* battle fatigue lose contact with the real world. Their nightmares happen to them when they're wide awake in the middle of the day. Anywhere, anytime."

"Hope this isn't too personal but do you get nightmares?" asked Lefter.

"Oh sure, but I've learned to control them," said the Ranger. "In my dream I somehow know that the nightmare is just a dream. It's rare that one even wakes me up nowadays."

"How did you learn to control them?" asked Lefter.

"Mind over matter, will it that way," said the Ranger. "That's my sermon for the night. How about another drink?"

"My turn to buy," said Lefter.

"Not here, let's cruise a few bars," said the Ranger.

"OK, Shrew," said Lefter. "Do you mind if my buddy Nissing comes along?"

"No problem," said the Ranger.

Lefter went to Nissing and asked him to go along. Nissing declined but said he'd wait there for Lefter and they could catch the eleven-thirty train back to ASAPAC. "Remember, it will cost you a lot more than thirty-seven cents to bed down with this chick," said Lefter as he nodded toward the Japanese girl seated at the table with Nissing.

Nissing laughed, "I'll be here when you get back."

Lefter had too many beers and lost track of time as he and the Ranger visited several bars around the Ginza. "Holy crap," said Lefter, "it's almost midnight and I told Nissing I would meet him at 2330. Look me up back on the MLR if you get a chance."

"Same here," said the Ranger. "One of the MPs on this beat is a buddy from boot camp. I'll call him when this place closes and he'll give me a ride back to my sleeping area. That way I don't have to worry about being on the street after curfew."

"Stay safe, buddy," said Lefter as he hustled out the door and headed back to the R&R Bar. Nissing was not there. The bartender handed Lefter a note that read: *Caved in to the testosterone rush. See you tomorrow. Charlie.*

Lefter looked at his watch. It read 2359. It's too late to try getting back to ASAPAC without violating the curfew and maybe getting hauled in by the MPs. He found out from the bartender that a hotel was just one half block away. He scurried down the street to the hotel and rang the bell on the desk. A Japanese man in traditional dress appeared, bowed and said something in Japanese that Lefter didn't understand.

"Room," said Lefter as he pulled out some yen from his pocket.

The hotel clerk looked confused and obviously didn't understand. Lefter put his hands together, put them up beside his ear and laid his head on them.

"Ah, tsukareta," said the clerk as he mimicked Lefter with his own hands.

"Hai, sleepy," said Lefter. "How much?" He put 500 yen on the counter.

"I-Iie," said the clerk and pointed upward.

Lefter put down another 500 yen.

"I-Iie," said the clerk and pointed upward.

Lefter put down another 500 yen.

"I-Iie," from the clerk again.

"Final offer," said Lefter as he put down another 500 yen.

"I-Iie," again.

Lefter picked up the 2000 yen from the counter and waved his hands to signal that he was through negotiating. For 2000 yen he could ride a cab back to ASAPAC and hope to not get picked up by the MPs.

The clerk reached his hand out toward Lefter and said, "Ho-ka, GI," and held up three fingers. Apparently, he didn't realize that Lefter had already offered 2000 yen.

"Deal," said Lefter and handed him three 500-yen bills.

Lefter followed the clerk up one floor and down a hallway where he was shown a small sparse room. It had no bed. A thin woven pad on the floor had a cloth cover and a blanket folded down. The clerk bowed several times as he backed out of the room.

Lefter lay down on the mat with his clothes on. It was hard and not much different from lying on the floor. It was much harder than lying on a canvas cot. There was no pillow. In spite of all the beer he'd consumed, he couldn't go to sleep. After tossing and turning on the hard mat for over thirty minutes, he decided to find the bathroom.

Down the hall next to the bathroom was a room that contained one of those deep Japanese bathtubs. The tub was full of steaming water. The tub was deep enough to completely cover the lower body when seated in the tub. Deciding that a hot bath would help him go to sleep, Lefter removed his clothes and tested the water with a finger. "Holy crap," he said out loud, "that's scalding hot." He stood there naked pondering the situation.

He noticed a heavy board resting across the tub and decided it must be for sitting on while getting into the hot water gradually. Sitting on the board, he submerged both big toes and clamped his mouth shut tightly as the heat engulfed them. "Oh crap!" he said as he jerked his big toes out of the water. He took a few deep breaths and then tried again. This time he dipped a few more toes into the steaming water for several seconds. "Oh crap!" Out come the toes. More deep breaths then another submersion for another few seconds. "Oh crap, crap, crap!"

Lefter kept trying to get into the tub of hot water but never got submerged any deeper than his ankles and then only for a few seconds. Finally, after saying "Oh crap" a hundred or so times, he gave up on getting submerged and decided to take a sponge bath. He dipped a sponge into the water quickly and started wringing the water out of it. It burned his hands. "Oh crap," he said for the hundred and first time and dropped the steaming sponge back into the tub. After several more "Oh craps" with the sponge he finally gave up, got dressed and returned to the hard woven grass mat.

Fully dressed, Lefter catnapped on the hard mat until his watch finally said 0600. Curfew was over. He hustled down the stairs past a smiling desk clerk that bowed and said, "Ohayo-gozaimasu."

"Sayounara," said Lefter as he rushed out the door and headed for the train station. He got on the train, returned to ASAPAC, went to bed, fell asleep immediately and didn't wake up until mid-afternoon. With a slight headache, but feeling refreshed, Lefter took a shower, shaved, dressed and checked in with the R&R coordinator.

"Nissing left a message for you. He said: 'See you tomorrow — still overcome by testosterone'."

"Yeah, I know what he means," said Lefter. "We're splitting the I&I part of our R&R. I'm doing the intoxication half and Charlie is doing the intercourse half."

The coordinator shrugged his shoulders and said, "Whatever works!"

"What about Quigley?" asked Lefter.

"He called in this morning and said all is well. That's all I know. Maybe he's taking care of both I&I and R&R," said the coordinator with a big grin.

Lefter didn't see either Quigley or Nissing until the last day of R&R when they finally returned to ASAPAC headquarters. Each morning each of them left their "all is well" message with the R&R coordinator. Lefter found lots of non-testosterone things to do such as going to a large musical stage show, visiting the Tokyo Zoo and of course having a few beers at the R&R Bar each day with Shrew, the Army Ranger.

Before each evening drinking session at the R&R Club, Lefter and Shrew met at the Ernie Pyle Club for dinner. On the last night of Lefter's R&R, he was sitting at the bar with Shrew. After several drinks and mundane conversation about this and that, Shrew put his hand on Lefter's leg and said, "You haven't slept with any of these Japanese girls have you?"

"No," said Lefter as he began to get uncomfortable about Shrew's hand still on his leg. Lefter turns around on his swivel barstool and said, "Maybe I'll pick one out for tonight since it's my last chance."

Shrew removed his hand from Lefter's leg and said, "Just wondering, I didn't think you were gay, what with being married and all."

"Hell no," said Lefter. "I just don't think it's the fair thing to do and I don't want to take a chance on getting one of those Oriental pecker-rotting diseases." Lefter took a deep breath, pointed toward the table of hostesses and said, "Think I'll buy one of them a drink. You in?"

"Naw," said the Ranger, "interferes with my drinking but you go ahead."

Lefter called over the bartender and said, "Are any of these girls *just* hostesses?" putting the emphasis on the word just. "I mean, do any of them *not* sleep with GIs?" The Japanese bartender looked confused.

Shrew said, as he pointed toward the table of girls, "Which girl *not* a whore?"

"*Not* whore?" asked the bartender as he shook his head from side to side.

"Hai," said Lefter.

"Naiomi," the bartender replied. "She dancing with sailor, you want to meet?"

"Hai," said Lefter.

The bartender went to the table of girls and whispered something in the ear of the prettiest one at the table. The girl got up from the table, walked to the dance floor and whispered something in the ear of girl dancing with the sailor.

Lefter turned toward Shrew and said, "What's going on?

"You're getting fixed up, buddy," replied the Ranger. They both turned and faced the bartender.

As Lefter took a drink from his beer there was a tap on his shoulder. Turning around he was surprised to see the Japanese girl who had been dancing with the sailor.

"Hi, I Naiomi," she said. "You want to sit at a table?"

"Yeah, sure," replied Lefter. "See you later, Shrew," he said as he got off the barstool and followed the girl to a table.

"Have fun, Lef," said the Ranger.

"Your friend no like girls?" she remarked in a questioning manner.

"Beats me," said Lefter. "Why do you ask?"

"We can tell," she says motioning with her head and eyes toward the table of girls.

"You speak excellent English," said Lefter.

"I am student at Tokyo College," she said. "Major is English language. I plan to be a Diplomat. I pay for college working nights as hostess. I am hostess only. I no sleep with customers."

"Good," said Lefter, "I don't want to sleep around either."

Lefter spent the rest of the evening sipping beer and dancing with Naiomi. He bought her a half dozen or so of the colored water drinks that cost 200 yen each. He had heard that the girl got one half of the money for each drink. At that rate, she would only be making $1.67 for the whole evening. He gave her a tip of 1,000 yen when he left to catch the train back to ASAPAC.

While on the train back to ASAPAC Lefter began thinking about the Ranger. *Is he gay or isn't he? I don't know if the answer is yea or nay*, he thought, *but I'm sure as hell not going to pursue the question.*

Quigley was already at ASAPAC when Lefter arrived around midnight. The three of them had been told to be ready at 0800 to leave ASAPAC for the return to Korea.

"How long you been here?" Lefter asked Quigley.

"Since about noon," responded Quigley in a dejected voice.

"What happened, did you run out of testosterone?" asked Lefter with a big grin.

"No, ran out of money," replied Quigley.

"No money, no nookey, huh?" said Lefter with another big grin.

"Yeah, and I thought she really liked me too," said Quigley. "Dumb, huh?"

"Well," said Lefter grinning, "you know that famous saying — 'never fall in love with a whore unless you have an inexhaustible supply of money.'"

"I never heard that. Who said it?" questioned Quigley.

"OK," said Lefter smiling even broader, "so I just made it up, but it sounds right, doesn't it?"

"Gimme a smoke, professor," said Quigley.

Taking out his cigarette pack and handing it to Quigley, Lefter says, "You didn't save back enough for cigarettes?"

"Hell, I don't even have my lighter anymore," said Quigley as he turned his empty front pockets inside out. "She took everything except my dog tags."

"You better hope she didn't leave you something you don't want," said Lefter. Quigley's quizzical look caused Lefter to add quickly, "You know, one of them pecker-rotting diseases."

Quigley didn't respond so Lefter said, "Keep the cigarettes. I have another pack."

"Thanks, Lef," said Quigley, "I'll give you double back on pay day."

"Naw, forget it," said Lefter, "consider it a charitable contribution."

Lefter went to bed thinking, "No nightmare, no nightmare, no nightmare." It worked. Lefter awoke the next morning refreshed and ready to return to Korea. He and Quigley showered, had breakfast and waited in the sleeping area for the R&R coordinator. Nissing was not there.

"I'm starting to worry about Nissing," said Lefter. "It's nearly time to leave for the airport." In a few minutes the coordinator arrived and said, "OK, let's get you guys to the airport."

"Nissing isn't here yet," said Lefter.

"Sorry, buddy," said the coordinator, "my orders are to leave for the airport at 0800 so you don't miss your scheduled flight out."

As they were loading into the Army automobile a taxi drove up and Nissing stepped out carrying a duffel bag stuffed completely full of something.

"What's in the bag?" asked the coordinator.

"Fabric," replied Nissing.

"They may not let you take it onto the plane. They will think you're going to sell it on the black market. You can try it if you want, it's up to you," said the coordinator.

"It's all gifts," said Nissing.

"OK, load it into the trunk," said the coordinator.

The Air Force Sergeant in charge of loading the airplane asked Nissing about the duffel bag.

"Presents for Korean families I know," replied Nissing. "Here is a list of their names and where they live if you want to check it out."

The sergeant looked at the list, handed it back to Nissing and said, "OK, buddy, take it on board, but you owe me one."

Once onboard the DC-4, Nissing was seated between Lefter and Quigley. Lefter asked Nissing, "What is all this stuff about a list of families you're taking fabric too?"

"Well, it's all true," said Nissing. "Many of the Koreans I know gave me money to buy fabric in Tokyo. They will have a seamstress make clothes from it."

"So you're doing this out of the kindness of your heart?" said Lefter in a questioning tone.

"Some," said Nissing. "However, it does tend to hold down my costs."

"What costs?" questioned Lefter. "Wait a minute. Wait a damn minute. You sly fox, Nissing. You're talking about your cost for sex, aren't you?"

Nissing smiled devilishly and said, "Business and pleasure together is a marvelous combination, isn't it?"

Lefter shook his head slowly back and forth. "You're going to be very successful in life, Charlie. You're devious, cunning, intelligent and slightly to the left of honest."

Nissing raised his eyebrows and extended his palms upward. "Somebody has to clothe these needy Korean girls."

"Is this favor going to lower your average cost per sexual encounter?" asks Lefter. "It will be difficult to beat thirty-seven cents."

"We'll see what happens," said Nissing. "I just lay out a plan, then follow the plan and see what happens."

Quigley was listening in amazement. He pointed to Nissing and said, "Back home we'd call you a 'skunk-in-the-grass' — something smells but it's hard to tell where the stink is coming from."

Lefter and Quigley laughed. Nissing didn't seem to see the humor in it.

The DC-4 accelerated down the runway and lifted slowly into the air. Nobody tried to talk over the roar of the engines until the pilot throttled back the engines.

Lefter said to Quigley and Nissing, "Did you look back into the cockpit when we got on board? It appears the crew has parachutes in there."

"No shit?" said Quigley as he quickly leaned forward and looked toward the cockpit.

Nissing said, "He's just pulling your chain."

Lefter ignored the Nissing comment and said, "Do you guys know the story about the Lufthansa Airlines' plane that crashed into the Atlantic Ocean during the early days of commercial aviation?"

"No, but I'll bet we're going to," said Nissing.

Lefter ignored the Nissing comment and began telling the story. "On one of the first flights across the Atlantic with their two engine passenger plane, one engine quits running. The Lufthansa pilot gets on the intercom and says, 'Ladies and gentlemen, we have lost one of the engines. Do not be alarmed, this aircraft will fly on one engine. However, in case we must make an emergency landing at sea, those who can swim get on the right side of the aircraft and those who cannot swim get on the left side of the aircraft.'

"Soon the remaining engine overheats and fails. Again, the pilot is on the intercom. 'Ladies and gentleman, we are going to make an emergency landing at sea so if you have not already done so, those who can swim get on the right side and those who cannot get on the left side of the aircraft.' The pilot makes a great landing at sea and as the airplane skids to a stop, he is again on the intercom. 'Ladies and gentleman, we have just made an emergency landing at sea. Now, those who can swim, climb out on the right wing and those who cannot swim, climb out on the left wing. Now, those of you on the right wing, jump in the Atlantic and start swimming. Those of you on the left wing, thank you very much for flying with Lufthansa.'"

"I don't get it," said Quigley.

"Precise German organization," said Nissing.

"So what?" said Quigley.

Nissing said nothing but threw out his hands with palms up.

"One more try," said Lefter. "Yesterday, I was lying on my back looking up at hundreds of bright stars and I said to myself, 'where the hell is the ceiling?'"

"Now that's funny," said Nissing.

"I don't get it," said Quigley.

"Forget it," said Lefter.

"This is absolutely my last try," said Lefter. "Two potatoes are standing on a street corner. Which one is the whore?"

Neither man responds so Lefter says, "The one with the sticker that says IDAHO!"

"That's funny," said Nissing.

"I don't get it," said Quigley.

"Forget it," said Lefter. "Dah-dah, dah-dah, that's all folks."

"I get it, Bugs Bunny," said Quigley.

Lefter looked at Nissing and said, "Finally hit on his grade level."

Nissing nodded agreement.

Lefter changed the subject and said to Quigley, "What is the name of that girl you write to back home? You know the good looking one you have the picture of?"

"Her name is Mary Ann Nobley," said Quigley. "She just won the contest as Miss Mississippi in the Miss America contest."

"No kidding," said Lefter. "Is she your girlfriend?"

"Naw, not really. We're just friends from high school," said Quigley.

"Good," replied Lefter, "then you wouldn't mind if Charlie and I write to her, would you?"

"Damn right, you're married," Quigley said to Lefter.

Lefter scratched his head and said, "Oh yeah, but Charlie's single so he could write to her, right?"

Quigley begins to squirm and said, "Well, I don't know about that."

Lefter and Nissing began to laugh.

"What is so damn funny?" asked Quigley.

"You," said Nissing. "Lefter baited you again and you swallowed it hook, line and sinker."

"I don't get it," said Quigley.

"Forget it," said both Lefter and Nissing.

"We love you anyway, buddy," said Lefter.

"Me too," said Nissing.

"What the hell does that mean?" asked Quigley.

"Nothing," said Lefter.

"Me too," said Nissing.

"What the hell does 'me too' mean?" said Quigley to Nissing.

"Nothing," said Nissing with a big smile.

Quigley looked at Lefter for an answer. Lefter just shrugged his shoulders and put both hands out with the palms up.

"I don't get it," said Quigley.

"Me either," said Lefter.

"I get it," said Nissing. "There is a rumor going around that something is being killed, right?"

"Right," said Lefter.

"You guys are nuts," said Quigley.

"Some say the killer is Charlie," said Lefter.

"Some say the killer is Lefter," said Nissing.

"Some even think the killer is Quigley," said Lefter, " but I say the killer is not the important thing here."

"Then what the hell is the important thing?" asked Quigley. "Are we playing Mumblejon?"

"My dear Watson," Lefter said to Quigley, "the important thing here and now is, what is being killed, not who is killing it."

"I don't get it," said Quigley.

"For a guy who doesn't get it, you're doing it rather well," said Nissing.

"What the hell are you guys talking about?" asked Quigley with increasing irritation.

"*Time* will tell, my dear fellow, *time* will tell," answered Lefter.

"Very good," said Nissing to Lefter.

"You'll figure it out, Quig," said Lefter. "*Time* is on your side."

"Very good," said Nissing to Lefter.

"What *time* is it?" said Nissing to Quigley.

Quigley looked at his watch and replied, "Almost ten."

"That's good," said Nissing, "*time* is marching on."

"Tick tock, tick tock," said Lefter.

"What the hell is going on?" said Quigley. "You guys are beginning to piss me off."

"OK, relax," said Lefter, "we're just *killing time*."

"What?" said Quigley.

"*Killing time*, get it, *killing time*," said Nissing.

"No, I don't get it," said Quigley.

"Forget it," said Lefter.

"Me too," said Nissing.

Lefter laughed and slapped Quigley on the leg, "Relax, buddy, we still love you."

"Don't start that shit again," said Quigley.

"Why not," said Nissing, "you got a better plan for *killing time*?"

"Yeah, I'm taking a nap," interjected Lefter.

"Good idea," said Nissing. "You in?" said Nissing to Quigley.

"In for what?" asked Quigley.

"A nap," said Nissing.

"OK," said Quigley. "For a moment I thought you were starting some more of that code talk stuff to piss me off some more."

"We wouldn't do that," said Nissing.

"Agreed," said Lefter.

The flight over the Sea of Japan went smoothly. Lefter and Nissing quit teasing Quigley and soon all three caved in to boredom and fell asleep. The airplane landed hard on the runway at K-2 and Lefter woke up in a panic. He was having another dream in which a Chinese soldier was attacking him with a bayonet. Although his pulse was racing and he was sweating profusely, he was determined to hide the condition from Nissing and Quigley.

"You're sweating like a dog pooping a peach seed," said Quigley. "Are you OK?"

"Yeah, must be going through a change in life," said Lefter with a smile.

"Yeah, right!" said Nissing. "Another nightmare?" he asked.

Lefter nodded yes and quickly changed the subject, "Someone from the 303 should be here to pick us up."

Campbell was waiting at the terminal building and intercepted the three ASA men at the entrance. "Need you back on the MLR right away," Campbell said to Lefter. Then he turned to Quigley and said, "You are wanted back right away also."

"What's up?" asked Lefter as he lit a cigarette with a quivering hand.

Campbell noticed his shaking hand and said to him, "Are you cold?"

"Yeah, it was cold on the airplane," answered Lefter.

Quigley shot a critical look toward Lefter but didn't say anything.

"Lots of voice traffic from the Chinese," said Campbell. "We think they may be getting ready for a big push when the 25th Infantry goes in reserve and is replaced by the 1st Marine Division. Lots of activity in your sector too, Quigley."

"Why now?" asked Quigley. "Word was when I left that them truce talks at Panmunjon were going real good. The fightin' was expected to stop in the near future."

"That is thought to be the reason that the Chinese are planning a big push," said Campbell. "Part of their negotiating strategy. Push us back and influence the final line of separation."

"By the way, Nissing," said Campbell, "Nay told me he is going to expect you to produce more than two pages of typing per day now that you're all rested up."

Lefter and Quigley just smiled. They knew the reputation of Nissing that he typed just one page each morning and one page each afternoon.

"We'll see about that," said Nissing. "If they are going to work my ass off here I just might put in for a transfer to ASAPAC."

"What do you mean, might!" said Lefter. "You already filled out the transfer request papers and turned them in at ASAPAC."

"Shhhh," said Nissing. "ASA movements are confidential, you know."

"Don't start on that double talk shit again," said Quigley.

Campbell gave Quigley a quizzical look but didn't say anything to him.

"I think we can make it to I-Corps headquarters by noon. After a quick lunch there, Lefter and I are driving directly to our detachment."

Lefter gets into the cab of the ¾ ton with Campbell driving. Quigley and Nissing were riding in the rear under the canvas top of the truck where they sat amongst cases of hard liquor that Campbell had already picked up at ASAK. Each cardboard case had the destination written in heavy grease pencil. The truck must have had a load of 50 or so cases of hard liquor.

Later, as they are driving through Seoul, Lefter thought of when he first arrived in Korea and Mewman drove him north to the 303 CRB. "Is this mine?" asked Lefter, holding up a carbine containing a 30-round clip.

"Yeah," said Campbell. "I been hauling it around with me since you left on R&R."

"Thanks, Camp," said Lefter. "I missed that carbine while on R&R. Every now and then, I got the feeling that something was missing. Know what I mean?"

"Yeah, feel the same way about my weapon," said Campbell.

"Whoa, what the hell is that?" asked Lefter.

Campbell stopped the truck in the street. Hundreds of Korean students were milling around in the street about two blocks ahead. They were chanting and carrying signs. Several signs were written in English. "Go home UN," said one sign. Another sign said, "USA Go Home." Yet another read, "Stop the Killing."

Just as Campbell started to turn the truck around, a company size group of American infantry troops in full combat dress came trotting out from a side street. They formed three lines across the entire street and with fixed bayonets began a shuffling side step toward the group of students. With each shuffling step forward they said in unison, "Harump, harump, harump!" The student group broke up, ran in the opposite direction and dispersed into buildings and side streets.

"That was one hell of a display of intimidation," said Lefter.

"That is one of the Army's riot control procedures," said Campbell.

"Well, it sure as hell works good," said Lefter. "Of course I, too, would run like hell in the opposite direction if those guys were coming at me with fixed bayonets."

Within a few minutes the troops broke their formation and sealed off all the side streets. Campbell was motioned to drive on.

"Who are those troops?" asked Lefter.

"MPs," said Campbell. "That compound they came out of is the headquarters area for Eight Army."

"I never noticed that," said Lefter, "and I've driven by there many times."

"Yeah, it is rather inconspicuous," said Campbell. "General Taylor doesn't want to advertise his headquarters location."

"So that's where the head honcho of Eight Army hangs out," said Lefter. "Does he report to Mark Blark in Tokyo?"

"Yeah," said Campbell, "then Blark reports to someone in the Pentagon or maybe he reports directly to the Secretary of Defense. I don't really know. I hope Eisenhower can end this damn Korean War. Ol' 'Give 'em hell Harry' had his chance and flunked. Who'd ever think that a good 'ol country boy from the Show-Me State of Missouri could become President anyway?"

"Hey, watch it, I was born in the Ozark Mountains of Arkansas," said Lefter.

"Right, and you and your family left there, didn't they?" said Campbell.

"Good point," answered Lefter. "My family was there since 1870 and my dad and I left in 1942. My 79-year-old grandmother is still living in Arkansas."

"Does she live alone?" asked Campbell.

"Naw," said Lefter, "she lives with her daughter and son-in-law. She sold the old homestead a couple of years ago. Two hundred seventy-five acres for $2500 dollars."

"Really!" said Campbell. "Unreal, that's less than ten dollars per acre."

"Yeah, I had a lot of fun as a young boy climbing trees and romping around that Arkansas farm. Where is your birthplace?" asked Lefter.

"Similar location to your birthplace," said Campbell. "The backwoods of Minnesota. My folks still own the old Minnesota homestead though."

Campbell stopped the truck at the MP checkpoint located at the turnoff to the 444th Transportation Corps headquarters and storage yards. Dozens of ammo trucks were entering the MSR and raising large plums of red dust as they traveled north in a convoy.

The four ASA guys got out of their truck and stood near the MP motioning the ammo trucks onto the MSR.

"How many trucks in this convoy?" Lefter asked the MP.

"Got me, buddy," replied the MP, "must be a hundred or so and that's just this convoy. Three other convoys have already pulled out today and two of them are back and reloading for another trip. If you guys had got here five minutes ago you wouldn't have to eat all this dust."

"Luck of the draw," replied Lefter.

"What are you hauling?" asked the MP.

"Three guys coming back from R&R and cases of booze," replied Campbell.

"You got a trip ticket to haul booze?" asked the MP.

"All-purpose ticket," answered Campbell as he handed the trip ticket to the MP.

"OK," said the MP, "fall in behind the last ammo truck that comes out."

"Thanks," said Campbell. "Come with me, buddy."

Campbell went to the back of the truck, opened a case and handed the MP a bottle of Canadian Club. "Here, maybe this will cut the dust you're breathing all day."

"Thanks, buddy," said the MP and took the bottle to the plywood guard shack at the side of the road.

"What did you do that for?" asked Lefter. "You're legal to haul the booze."

"True, but they could still seize it all and make me prove that the trip ticket is legitimate or use some other excuse to cause a lot of trouble. Better to share a little of the wealth and avoid any potential complications."

"Good thinking," said Nissing as he spoke up for the first time.

"You gonna tear 'em off a piece of your cloth, Charlie?" asked Quigley with a grin.

"Shhhhh," responded Nissing.

"Loan me twenty bucks until payday and I'll shut my Mississippi mouth," said Quigley.

"You're on," said Nissing. "Now shut the hell up."

"My mouth is sealed," said Quigley.

Finally, after another twenty minutes the last ammo truck pulled onto the

STAY SAFE, BUDDY

MSR and headed north at the end of the convoy.

"Anything else in that truck that I should know about?" said the MP to Campbell.

Lefter could almost hear a sucking sound coming from Nissing.

"Not today," said Campbell, "maybe next time though."

Campbell and the MP both laughed.

"OK, you're free to roll," said the MP.

The ASA guys quickly got back in the truck and Campbell drove slowly ahead into the dust bank.

Under the canvas cover in the back of the truck, Quigley held out a hand with palm up. Nissing pulled out his wallet and handed Quigley twenty dollars in military script.

"You blackmailed me," said Nissing.

Quigley took the bill and said, "It's not blackmail if I pay you back. However, if you're going to call me a blackmailer then I won't pay you back and you'll be right."

"OK, call it a interest free loan," said Nissing.

"Thanks, Charlie," said Quigley. "I'll pay you back on payday."

They reached the 303 CRB in barely enough time to distribute the cases of booze to the awaiting detachment couriers and still get to the mess hall before it closed for lunch. After lunch, Lefter stood up and his carbine pulled over the chair and went crashing to the floor. The mess hall erupted in applause.

Lefter smiled, waved and bowed to the mess hall audience before picking up his carbine. "Guess I need to be retrained after having a week off for R&R," said Lefter to a grinning Campbell.

"Just one of the reasons I carry a forty-five instead of a carbine," responded Campbell.

"What is another reason?" challenged Lefter

"Nobody wants me to stand sniper duty," laughed Campbell.

"Got that right," said Lefter. "At a hundred yards you could catch that forty-five slug with a baseball mitt."

"A slight exaggeration but at twenty yards it outperforms that carbine of yours by a bunch," said Campbell.

"How is it for killing bushes?" asked Lefter with a big smile. "My carbine really tore up that bush out behind our bunker."

Campbell gave Lefter one of those 'poor ignorant bastard' looks and said, "That bush was dead from being shot up long before you hit it with a couple of rounds."

"Couple of rounds, hell, I emptied a whole clip at that bush," said Lefter.

"How many rounds do you supposed actually hit the bush?" asked Campbell.

"Well, you got me there," replied Lefter. "Just one more reason you're the NCO and I'm, as my buddy Mewman would say, just a fucking grunt."

"Speaking of Mewman," said Campbell, "he managed to loose all his money playing poker. He's been waiting for you to get back so he can borrow some money for booze."

Lefter looked surprised. "Didn't he ask you for a booze loan? I'd be amazed if he didn't."

"He asked," said Campbell, "but I said he's your customer and I didn't want to butt in. Truth is that I don't want to be involved with him and liquor. I'm a career man, you know."

"Understood," said Lefter. "I'll take care of him, then you can take care of me if trouble follows."

Campbell didn't respond. Though he and Lefter were good friends, he was still his superior and field commander.

They drove north on the MSR through dust clouds caused by empty ammo trucks headed south. The empty ammo trucks were traveling in twos or threes. They passed by every few minutes. As Campbell and Lefter drove by the artillery emplacement, they could see several ammo trucks being unloaded. Other ammo trucks were waiting their turn to unload.

"Man, it looks like they're really stocking up on artillery shells," said Lefter.

"That's part of it," said Campbell. "The ammo dumps further up are being built up also. The dump near our base camp must have several hundred cases of grenades and mortar rounds. Also, there is a very large stash of machine gun and small arms ammunition. They have doubled the guards on duty at all ammo dumps in the 1st Marine Division."

"When do you expect the Chinese push to begin?" asked Lefter.

"I told the general it could be as early as tonight," replied Campbell. "By the way, I'm sending you up this afternoon to relieve Jobby. Hillman and Jolcomb must have the flu. They're sick and throwing up so Jobby hasn't been relieved for two days."

"OK, Chief, R&R is behind me now for sure," said Lefter with resignation in his voice. "By the way, is one of those cases of booze mine?"

"Yeah," answered Campbell, "we'll stash it all in our sleeping tent for now."

Lefter opened the case. He also gave one bottle to Campbell to replace the one he had borrowed. He put two bottles in his pack along with the usual two packs of cigarettes, toothbrush and toothpaste, writing paper and pencil, two envelopes, and a packet of C-rations. He planned to write his wife and his father and tell them of the presents being mailed to them from Japan. He shoved the remaining partial case of whiskey underneath his cot.

As Lefter climbed into the passenger side of the truck he said to Campbell, "Can we stop by the ammo dump on the way up? I have the feeling that I should have some extra ammo." Then trying to cover up his concern with humor, he added, "That bush may need another good shoot 'em up."

"No need," said Campbell. "I stocked the bunker yesterday with ten fifteen-round clips of carbine ammo, two concussion grenades and a trenching tool."

"Trenching tool?" asked Lefter.

"I'll explain when we get to the bunker," said Campbell.

Neither man spoke on the rest of the ride to the bunker parking area.

"I'll get the water," said Campbell as he picked up the five-gallon can and headed up the backside of the hill.

Carrying only his carbine and the backpack, Lefter followed Campbell up the hill and had to ask for two rest stops along the way. Even with the rest stops he was sweating heavily and panting as they reached the bunker door.

Campbell knocked and identified himself. Jobby opened the door and Lefter could tell instantly that he was exhausted. His eyes were dazed and his posture was like an old man. "Glad to see you, Lef," said Jobby. "I am totally pooped. With all this activity going on, I haven't been able to even take a nap. The worst thing is the anticipation of all hell breaking out and then it doesn't."

"Them gooks probably been waiting for me to get back from R&R," said Lefter. "They know I'm scared shitless of them. What's the latest chatter?"

Jobby turned to Campbell and said, "The constant chit chat is still going on. It still appears they are amassing troops for a big assault."

"They are probably going to attack during the time the Marines are coming back on line," said Campbell, "at least that is what I told the 25th Division and Marine Division two days ago."

"Are we the only place they're going to hit?" asked Lefter.

"Negative," said Campbell. "Nay tells me the massive troop buildup is even bigger in front of the Commonwealth and ROK Division to our east."

"Holy crap!" said Lefter. "Holy crap!"

"If they break through and you think you're in danger of being overrun, do the following two things: first, destroy the radios and second, get the hell out of here and head south. If you have time throw a concussion grenade in the bunker as you leave."

"What is the trenching tool for?" asked Lefter.

"Oh yeah, that's what you use to beat the hell out of the radios," said Campbell.

"What about the DACs?" asked Lefter, anticipating that he wouldn't get a straight answer.

"Play it by ear," said Campbell.

"Oh crap!" said Lefter. "Oh crap!"

"Just keep in mind, Lef," said Campbell, "there are a lot of our troops out in front of you that will fight like hell to hold ground."

"Anything else?" asked Lefter.

"One more thing," said Campbell, "call me on the land-line every hour on the hour or sooner if need be. I'll be standing by."

"You want me to call every hour throughout the night?" asked Lefter.

"Yep, and fill me in on the latest intercepts, OK?" replied Campbell. "Stay safe, buddy."

"OK, Camp," said Lefter weakly as Campbell left the bunker and headed down the backside of the hill.

I have a feeling that this is going to get exciting, thought Lefter. Incoming artillery would be the signal that the Chinese were beginning the softening-up phase of the battle. First, they would pound the outposts with mortar barrages and the MLR with artillery. Then the mortar fire would stop and the trumpets and whistles would signal the ground assault. To light up the battlefield, both sides would probably launch flares. The Chinese would be attacking at close range with burp guns and grenades. Hand to hand combat would no doubt occur in the trenches of the Outposts. It made Lefter feel sick just thinking about it. Additionally, he felt a little guilty for just participating as a frightened observer. It wasn't that he felt like a candy ass stationed many miles behind the MLR, he just somehow felt, well, detached. He felt detached but lucky to not have to be directly involved in the coming battle.

Alone in the bunker Lefter looked at the DACs for the first time since arriving. He was pleased to see that it was Kim Song Lu and Tarcy Fong. Mr. Fong was monitoring the radio and Mr. Lu was lying on his bunk. It dawned on Lefter that this was the first time he thought of calling them Mister.

Previously, he hadn't addressed them by any name for anything. He had always found a way to avoid calling them Mister. At least these two were sociable to him. The other DACs were rather aloof toward him. He didn't know why they acted aloof, maybe because he didn't have a college degree like them. He really had not thought about it until now. To be truthful, he really didn't care what they thought of him. He had followed the advice of Captain Eten who told him, "don't get cozy with the DACs or it could make your job a lot harder to accomplish."

Lefter went to the viewing slit and studied the terrain in front of him. The machine gun nest down by the barbwire looked to be in good condition. He studied it for several minutes but he couldn't see any movement there. He got the field glasses and studied it some more. He still couldn't tell if the nest was occupied. Beyond the barbwire, the unused rice paddies showed no activity even with close inspection through the binoculars. He studied the terrain on the hills where the outposts were located and saw no movement there either. Finally, he focused the binoculars on the barren hills where the Chinese MLR was located and he couldn't see any movement there. *Where the hell are they?* thought Lefter.

Then his heart jumped. What was that? Something flashed through the view in the binoculars. He quit looking through the binoculars just in time to see a Marine Corsair drop a napalm bomb on the Chinese MLR. Several other Corsairs followed immediately in single file and dropped napalm. Anti-aircraft shells started exploding far above the low-flying Corsairs and tracer bullets filled the air around the streaking airplanes.

Lefter went outside the bunker for a better view. He watched in fascination as the Corsairs dove down one by one and attacked the Chinese MLR. A small single engine plane called an L-19 circled slowly high above the attacking Corsairs. The L-19 pilot was telling the Corsair pilots by radio where to target their next run. It was a strange contrast to see the Corsairs screaming through the sky while the L-19 spun slowly in its lazy circle. Lefter's untimely sense of humor kicked as it occurred to him that the L-19 was a real safe plane. *It goes so slow that it can probably just barely kill you.* He briefly wondered why the L-19 wasn't drawing any anti-aircraft fire but quickly decided that the Chinese had all they could handle just trying to defend against the Corsairs. The L-19 was not, in and of itself, doing damage to the Chinese ground troops.

Although the napalm was being dropped a mile or so north of Lefter's bunker it was frightening to watch. Each drop spread a wall of flame that appeared to be a hundred yards or more in length. It made him shiver and shake his head at the horrible sights his imagination was picturing in his brain. The soldiers being hit with the napalm must be screaming while their entire body was afire. "Holy crap," he said out loud. "Holy crap!"

Now the Corsairs were screaming in single file over the hills and firing their machine guns. They made several final passes and then flew southeasterly and crossed the U.S. MLR several hundred yards to the east of Lefter. The L-19 was nowhere in sight. Lefter decided that the L-19 must have retreated south under the cover of the strafing runs by the Corsairs. *Clever tactic*, he thought.

Lefter was still standing beside the bunker when he heard the familiar whistle of incoming artillery. "Oh shit!" he said as he ran back into the bunker. The round went overhead and landed somewhere on the backside of the hill. "You dumb shit," he mumbled to himself, "you dilly dallied around out there until some Chinese spotter called one in on you. You're lucky a sniper didn't pick you off." Then he heard more incoming rounds. The incoming kept increasing in numbers until the air was filled with those eerie whistling sounds. Soon the sound of outgoing artillery rounds combined with the whistles of incoming rounds.

Looking out of the viewing slit, Lefter could see exploding artillery rounds landing down the slope in front of him. Several rounds landed in the barbwire line. The explosions caused gaping holes in the barbwire entanglements. So far, the machine gun nest was intact. Lefter could hear other rounds landing behind the bunker area and along the MLR on both sides of his bunker. A large explosive flash temporarily blinded Lefter. A round had landed directly in front of the bunker. It briefly blinded Lefter but he heard the immediate thumps of shrapnel hitting the sandbags along the bunker. He jumped back and shook his head. As his eyesight came slowly back, he retreated to the wooden table, sat down and buried his head in his hands. Shaking his head in his hands he thought of how lucky he was that a piece of the shrapnel didn't come through the viewing slit and hit him in the head.

"Oh crap," he said out loud as he remembered that he was supposed to call Campbell every hour on the hour. It was ten minutes past the hour so he picked up the field phone and contacted Campbell at the base camp. Trying to remain calm and not show any fear, Lefter blurted out to Campbell, "A flight of Marine Corsairs dropped napalm and strafed the Chinese MLR for a while then the Chinese started pounding our MLR with artillery fire. It is still going on hot and heavy right now. Our guys are sending a lot back."

Then calming down a bit he added, "Lots of whistling, whooshing and booming going on up here."

"Yeah, I can hear it in the background," replied Campbell. "What is being heard over the radio?"

"Haven't checked for a while," said Lefter. "I'll get the latest and call you right back."

"OK," said Campbell.

Lefter laid down the phone and cussed himself for not checking with the DACs before calling Campbell. The DACs told Lefter that the Chinese radio conversations indicated that they were preparing for a ground assault sometime after dark. They didn't know how many Chinese troops would be involved but estimated it could be a regimental-size assault. Lefter asked where the attack would occur but they didn't know.

Lefter called Campbell again and reported that the Chinese were expected to attack with ground forces sometime after dark and that it might be regimental size hitting the 25th Infantry Division. "What is happening east of me?" asked Lefter.

"Same indications that you are getting," said Campbell. "Appears they are going to attack all across the I-Corps Sector."

Losing his cool-acting demeanor for a second, Lefter said, "Holy crap, do you think they are going to try and break through our MLR?"

"Don't know yet," said Campbell, "but it sure appears that way, doesn't it?"

"How long do you want me to man this bunker?" asked Lefter.

"If they start getting through the barbwire line, get yourself and the DACs out of there pronto," answered Campbell. Then he added, "but call me just before you leave and don't forget to destroy the radios."

"OK, Camp," said Lefter.

"Talk to you later. Stay safe, buddy," said Campbell.

"Will do," said Lefter rather unconvincingly.

The artillery bombardment from both the Communist and UN forces continued at a rapid pace and Lefter wondered how they could supply such a massive expenditure of shells. He kept looking at his watch and checking with the DACs for the latest information. The DACs seemed to be getting annoyed. Lefter decided that he was checking with them too often and getting in the way of them doing their job. He sat down at the table, lit a cigarette and tried to look at a magazine. He had no idea what he was looking at as he slowly turned the pages of the magazine. His mind was not on the magazine.

It was just a part of his attempt to appear calm to the DACs.

Every few minutes a round landed close enough to cause the bunker to shake and dirt would sift down from the ceiling. The kerosene lantern hanging from the ceiling would jump causing the flame to flicker. Then the lantern would swing slowly back and forth. Lefter stared at the lantern to see if it would still be swinging when the bunker was again shook by a nearby explosion.

He was startled when one of the DACs tapped him on the shoulder. The DAC handed Lefter a note and pointed at his watch. Lefter nodded agreement. It was time to call Campbell. The note said, "*CCF attack soon after dark.*"

Lefter got Campbell on the land-line and reported that the DACs agreed that the Chinese Communist Forces planned the ground attack to begin soon after dark.

"OK, hang on, buddy," said Campbell.

"Will do," said Lefter and set down the phone.

As the pounding continued, Lefter would report every hour that the DACs still believed that the ground attack would begin soon after dark. Lefter's nerves were frayed. At times, he wished he could be with Mewman in one of the fighting bunkers of the 25th Infantry Division. He smiled as he thought of Mewman. *Mewman is probably eager for the ground fighting to begin. He's probably stroking his BAR and calling it affectionate names.* Lefter smiled wide as, in his mind, he heard Mewman say, "I am gonna kill me some fucking gooks tonight."

"Crap," said Lefter as he jumped when hearing a loud knock on the bunker door.

Just as Lefter grabbed for his carbine, Mewman's raunchy voice yelled, "Open the fucking door — it's Mewman."

Lefter opened the door and said, "Asshole, you scared the hell out of me with that monster knock."

"Hello, buddy, welcome the fucking back," said Mewman as he set down his BAR and hugged Lefter.

Lefter was taken aback. A man had never hugged him before. In fact, he had rarely been hugged at all. He had not grown up in a hugging family environment. The only time he had ever been hugged was by a couple of girlfriends and his wife; in that order, of course. He smiled at the humorous sequential thought.

"What the hell are you doing here?" asked Lefter as he pulled away from Mewman's grasp and held back from tearing up.

Mewman slapped Lefter on the shoulder and said, "Just dawned on me awhile ago that you were due back from that fucking candy ass R&R trip."

"OK, how did you know I would be in the bunker?" said Lefter.

"Didn't, but who gives a fuck. You're here, ain't you?" replied Mewman.

"Come on in and sit down," said Lefter.

"Ain't that against your fucking classified policy orders?" asked Mewman.

"Fuck the orders," answered Lefter, surprised that he had used the f word. "We're not going to stand outside and shoot the shit while this barrage is going on."

Mewman came in and sat down at the table. Lefter closed the bunker door and sat down opposite Mewman. The two men just looked into each other's eyes for about ten seconds. Lefter felt his eyes getting moist so he cleared his throat and said, "So what have you been up to, Mew?"

"Patrols," replied Mewman. "Drives me fucking nuts to just sit around so I volunteer for the patrols. Think I got me another fucking gook while you were sun bathing in Tokyo. The fucker threw a grenade at me and I tossed the fucking thing back before it exploded."

"Holy crap," said Lefter, "it must have had an extra long fuse to allow that much time before it exploded."

"Beats the fuck out of me," said Mewman. "I just grabbed it as it hit the ground and heaved the fucking thing back in his face. You should have seen the horror in his gook ass face as that fucking grenade was headed for him."

"Holy crap, you were close enough to see his face?" said Lefter.

"Yeah, maybe twenty yards," said Mewman, "and it was in that really weird light from the flares."

"You're really something else, buddy," said Lefter, smiling.

"Ain't I," replied Mewman with a wry smile. "Got a feeling I'm gonna get me another fucking gook tonight."

Lefter began to get concerned. He wondered if Mewman knew that the Chinese were going to probably begin a major ground attack soon after dark. He definitely couldn't tell Mewman what he had been reporting to Campbell so he decided to hint around and maybe Mewman would catch on. "Lot of incoming right now," said Lefter. "What do you suppose it means?"

"Means the shit is going to hit the fucking fan on the ground later on after it gets dark," said Mewman. "You should know that, you are in the fucking spy business."

"What makes you think there is going to be a big ground action?" asked Lefter.

"You mean other than what my fucking crystal ball is telling me?" responded Mewman with a question.

"Yeah," said Lefter.

Mewman made a dramatic pause and then said, "That's what them fucking candy asses from Division G-2 told us." Then Mewman let go with a big belly laugh.

Lefter smiled. It was good to hear Mewman's belly laugh again. Artillery exploded nearby and sprayed the bunker with shrapnel. "By the way, how did you dodge all this incoming crap on the way over here?"

"Ran along all fucking bent over in the trench most of the way," said Mewman. "Crawled through a few places where a direct hit had caved in the trench."

"When do you have to be back?" asked Lefter.

"Told Happy I'd be back before it gets dark so I gotta be going pretty fucking soon," answered Mewman.

There was a long pause while neither of them said anything. Then Mewman said, "Sure did miss you while you were on R&R, Lef."

"Well, I missed you too," said Lefter as he fought back tears. "Be extra careful out there tonight."

"Fuck, Lef, that's when guys get it. They get too fucking careful. Know what I mean?"

"No, I don't," said Lefter. "How would I know? I just sit here in the bunker while you go out and duel with the Chinese."

"Ain't no fucking dueling," replied Mewman seriously. "Ain't no fucking gentlemen out there in No-Man's-Land. It's real fucking simple — kill or be killed."

Mewman didn't laugh. He stood up and Lefter saw a furrow form in Mewman's brow. Lefter stood up also. The two men stood staring at each other then Mewman reached out and hugged Lefter. Mewman turned loose of Lefter, stepped back and said, "I got a bad fucking feeling about tonight, Lef. If I don't make it, remember to have that $100 party on me back in the States." He made a half-hearted belly laugh.

"You're going to make it, buddy," said Lefter as tears formed in his eyes. "You'll make it."

CHAPTER EIGHTEEN

After Mewman left, Lefter went over to his bunk and buried his face in the sleeping bag. Tears rolled out of his eyes and he sobbed softly. At that point, he didn't give a crap if the DACs saw him. He didn't give a damn what the DACs thought. They damn well better be good to him. They were unarmed civilians and he was the only one in the bunker with weapons. He rolled over on his back and stared at the ceiling of the bunker. He took out his olive drab handkerchief, blew his nose, took a deep breath and blew the breath out slowly. He continued taking deep breaths and then blowing them out slowly.

"What?" said Lefter as he awoke. The Korean DAC was shaking his feet. "Holy crap, what happened?" said Lefter to the DAC.

"You fall asleep. Time to call in report," said the DAC.

"Thank you," said Lefter, "anything new to report?"

"Same, same," said the DAC.

"OK," said Lefter as he went to the field phone and called Campbell. "Nothing has changed," said Lefter, then he added, "except Mewman was over here."

"What did he have to say?" asked Campbell.

"I think he believes he's going to get killed tonight," replied Lefter.

"Why do you say that?" asked Campbell.

"He hugged me when he got here and then again when he left," replied Lefter, fighting back tears.

"Did you tell him about our predictions for tonight?" asked Campbell.

"No, he said the candy asses in Division G-2 were predicting a big ground assault by the Chinese after it gets dark."

"Wouldn't you know, those yo-yos in Division G-2 would try to grab all the glory and not mention us," replied Campbell.

"Oh well," said Lefter, "the important thing is that our troops know what is coming and have time to get prepared."

"OK, we'll chat later," said Campbell. "Stay safe, buddy, and keep in touch with me."

"OK, Camp, I'm out," said Lefter and put down the phone.

Lefter went over to the Korean DAC and said, "Thanks for waking me up. I don't know how I could have fallen asleep with all this incoming hitting all around us."

"I see," said the DAC, "you have lot of pressure. I have important question for you."

"What's that?" said Lefter.

The DAC looked Lefter directly in the eyes and said in a questioning manner, "You kill me if we overrun?"

Lefter was stunned by the direct question. His mind raced as he quickly imagined being overrun. Should he kill the DACs? Would he kill the DACs? Was he supposed to kill the DACs? He knew he couldn't ask Campbell. It had to be a personal decision. His mind flashed back to the indoctrination talk by Captain Eten. The captain had stressed several times the horror of tortures inflicted by the enemy on those civilians they captured that had been working for the UN. He had said over, and over, "They would be better off dead." Lefter tried to avoid the question by saying, "I'm not sure I could kill you even if I wanted too."

"If we overrun, I die before capture," said the Korean DAC. He pointed toward the Chinese DAC manning the radio and said, "He want same thing." Then pointing to himself and then the Chinese DAC, "We not want to be captured, OK?"

Lefter just kept looking at the DAC and didn't respond. Thinking that the shells exploding outside prevented Lefter from hearing him, the DAC moved up close to Lefter's face and repeated, "No let us be captured, OK?"

Lefter felt trapped. He continued to stare into the eyes of the Korean DAC. The DAC stared back in silence. Finally, Lefter said, "OK, I will try to see that you are not captured."

The Korean DAC took a cigarette package from his pocket and offered one to Lefter. Lefter took one from the pack and noticed that his hands were quivering a little bit. The DAC lit Lefter's cigarette and then his own. *Yuck,* Lefter thought. The cigarette tasted awful to him. Trying not to show his displeasure with the cigarette, Lefter asked, "What brand of cigarettes are these?"

"Doumo," answered the Korean DAC, "they Japanese cigarette."

Lefter took small social puffs off the cigarette and didn't inhale the smoke. It tasted so awful that he wanted to immediately light up one of his Chesterfield cigarettes.

Trying to make small talk Lefter said, "Mr. Lu, how did you happen to go to work for the Department of Defense?" As he finished speaking, Lefter realized that he should not ask about the background of any of the DACs. *Too late now*, he thought.

"I senior at Stanford University when recruiter offer me job to help my country. I want to help South Korea. Also pay very good so I take job after graduation."

Lefter wanted to end the conversation for fear that it was going to get personal. He didn't want to know about the personal life of Mr. Lu. He wasn't sure he could comply with Mr. Lu's request to kill him rather than let him be captured by the enemy. Getting to know him better would make it even harder. "That's definitely a double whammy," said Lefter with finality in his voice.

"What is double whammy?" asked the DAC.

"Double whammy," repeated Lefter. "That's an American expression for, for, ah, killing two birds with one stone."

"What is killing two birds with one stone?" asked the DAC.

Lefter grinned broadly as he realized the difficulty of a foreigner understanding these two American expressions. He thought of a humorous way of demonstrating the two birds saying. Lefter raised a forefinger and said, "chicken." Then he added his middle finger and said, "second chicken." Wiggling both finger he said, "two chickens." The DAC kept nodding his understanding. Lefter held up his other hand in a fist and said, "rock." Then he placed his two fingers on the table and pretended to smash them with his fist. "Double whammy, killed two birds with one stone," said Lefter, smiling proudly and sure the DAC would now understand the expressions.

The DAC looked puzzled. Lefter's confidence in his explanation began to wane. "Make believe fingers are chickens and smash with rock is double whammy?" said the DAC in a questioning manner.

Lefter smashed out the ugly Japanese cigarette and removed his pack of Chesterfield from his pocket, "Have one of my cigarettes."

The DAC took a cigarette. Lefter struck a match and held the flame to the cigarette of the DAC then to his own cigarette.

The DAC took a deep drag, inhaled and blew the smoke out slowly. "Good," he said holding up the cigarette toward Lefter.

"You like Doumo?" asked Lefter, pointing to the pocket containing nearly a full package of Japanese cigarettes.

"Yes," said the DAC smiling.

"I show you magic with Doumo," said Lefter as he held out his hand toward the DAC.

"OK," said the DAC as he removed the pack of cigarettes and handed it to Lefter.

Lefter set the pack of cigarettes on the table with the open end up. He removed one of the cigarettes and balanced it horizontally and crosswise on top of the pack. Then he made a chopping motion toward the cigarette and said, "I bet you I can hit this cigarette on the end and it will fly in the air spinning around and come back down inside the package."

Shaking his head no the DAC said, "No way, Jose."

Lefter laughed and said, "What does 'No way, Jose' mean?"

The DAC laughed and said, "Show me."

"I bet you one hundred dollars I can do it," said Lefter.

"No, no, you have trick," replied the DAC.

"OK," said Lefter, "make the bet five cents.

"OK," said the DAC, "I bet you five cents you not do it."

Lefter took out five cents in military script and put it on the table. As the DAC started digging in his pocket, Lefter said, "That's OK, I'll trust you for the nickel."

"OK, show me," said the DAC as he pointed at the cigarette balanced on package.

"Are you sure you don't want to bet one hundred dollars?" asked Lefter.

"No, no, bet is nickel," said the DAC.

"OK," said Lefter as he raised his hand high and brought it down hard and completely flattened the package of cigarettes. "Oh shit, missed again," said Lefter as he handed the script nickel to the DAC. "You win," said Lefter with a big smile.

The face of the Korean DAC showed shock, then anger, and then he smiled and pointed to the smashed package of cigarettes. He picked up the smashed package, removed several broken cigarettes and dropped them on the table. He started to laugh and Lefter laughed with him. The DAC pointed at the broken cigarettes and laughed harder. Lefter laughed harder also. Soon they were near hysterical with laughter.

The Chinese DAC, Mr. Fong, could hear the laughter even though he had on the earphones. He turned around, removed the earphones and watched Lefter and Mr. Lu rocking with laughter at the table. Mr. Fong probably thought they had cracked up under the stress of the heavy and prolonged artillery shelling which was still going on. Mr. Fong shook his head, put the earphones back on, turned toward the radio and continued slowly turning the frequency selection knob. The Chinese had changed their main communication frequency and he was trying to find their new frequency.

"No tell Mr. Fong," said the Chinese DAC between bouts of laughter. "I show him later."

"OK," said Lefter, working in the reply through his own bouts of laughter.

A loud explosion occurred nearby. It was followed instantly by the whistling and thumping sounds of flak flying through the air and hitting the bunker. It shook the bunker hard and air inside the bunker filled with dust falling from the ceiling. Lefter and Mr. Lu quit laughing instantly. The Chinese DAC whirled around and looked at them with fear on his face. He removed the earphones and said, "I find them, they assembling for ground assault."

Lefter picked up the field phone and discovered that the line was dead. That last round probably cut the communication wire he thought. No way he was going out in that barrage now to find and repair the break. *Hell*, he thought, *Campbell already knows the full skinny anyway. The bastards are going to make a big ground assault.*

The artillery pounding continued without letup throughout the rest of the daylight hours and into the darkness. Shortly after dark the incoming shelling eased up and finally stopped. Lefter ran outside the bunker carrying with him the tools to repair the break in the communication wire. He quickly found the break, repaired it and ran back inside the bunker. Although it only took a few minutes to find and repair the break, Lefter felt like it would never end. His heart was pounding in his chest and he was covered with sweat. He picked up the phone and called Campbell.

"The shelling has stopped and it's spooky silent up here," Lefter told Campbell. "Mr. Fong says they are assembling for a ground assault right now."

"Does he have any idea what time the assault will begin?" asked Campbell.

"Oh crap," said Lefter, "I haven't talked to him for ten minutes or so. The damn communication wire got hit and I had to go out and repair the break. I called you as soon as I came back from repairing it."

"You went out in all that shelling and repaired the wire?" questioned Campbell.

"No, no, I waited until the shelling stopped and then went out," replied Lefter. "No rounds came in while I was out there but I think I got a hangnail from it. Is that good for a Purple Heart?"

"After I get the Medal of Honor," said Campbell. "Check out the latest and call me back right away."

"Hang on," said Lefter, "Mr. Fong is taking a short break right now. Do you want to talk to him?"

"OK," said Campbell, "put him on."

Lefter had the Chinese DAC get on the phone with Campbell. To Lefter's surprise, the DAC was speaking in both English and Chinese. Then he remembered that Campbell spoke the Chinese language. The DAC turned and handed the phone back to Lefter.

"It's Lefter, I'm back on the phone," said Lefter nervously. Then Lefter heard the sound of mortar fire in the distance followed by machine gun fire. "I think it just started," said Lefter into the phone. "I hear mortars and machine guns firing in the distance."

"If they break through, get the hell out of there pronto," said Campbell.

"OK," said Lefter, "I'll keep you informed."

"Stay safe, buddy," said Campbell.

"Will do," replied Lefter.

Lefter went to the viewing slit and looked out toward the outposts. It appeared to him that the action was in the vicinity of Outpost Reno and Carson. The Chinese had held Outpost Reno for some time so they were probably using it as an assembly area to launch the attack on Outpost Carson. Outpost Carson was about one half mile from Lefter's position. There were rapid flashes of light and the accompanying thumps from the mortar shelling. Lefter tried to estimate the number of explosions occurring in one second. He concluded that it was four to six mortar rounds per second. "Holy crap," he said out loud, "that's around three hundred per minute."

Lefter ran to the phone and called Campbell. "I don't know if this has it any value but I estimate the Chinese are pouring in somewhere around three hundred mortar rounds per minute on Outpost Carson."

"That should help a lot," replied Campbell. "I'll pass it on to the Division G-2 although they may already have that info from their men. They may be able to estimate the size of the attacking force."

"How will they do that?" asked Lefter.

"Maximum rate of fire per single mortar. Number of mortars per organizational unit, and so on," replied Campbell. "They will compare it to the reports they're getting from the troops on the ground."

"Makes sense," said Lefter.

"Keep me informed," said Campbell. "I'm out."

"Clear," said Lefter. Lefter thought back to the first big battle he sat through in the bunker. He didn't do anything except sit at the table and shake. "Scared shitless," he said softly. Of course, Campbell hadn't told him to report in at short intervals as he had this night. He decided to quit kidding himself and admit that he didn't contribute anything at all during that first night of passive battle participation.

As Lefter returned to the firing slit, he wondered if Mewman had left on his patrol. Patrol, hell. They would probably be rushing out replacements for all the guys getting killed and wounded at Outpost Carson. Mewman was probably on his way right now or maybe he was already there. Lefter watched the mortar pounding for another couple of minutes before it quit abruptly. For a few seconds it was quiet. No noise anywhere. Then flares lit up the terrain in the vicinity of Outpost Carson. Lefter could clearly hear trumpets and whistles in the distance. Defensive machine gun firing commenced and Lefter could see tracers penetrating through the eerie light of the flares. Muzzle blasts from small arms appeared all around the area of OP Carson.

Horrible pictures of close combat filled Lefter's imagination. He continued to watch the madness. Mesmerized by the massive firepower being unleashed by both sides Lefter lost track of time. He didn't know how much time had passed when the Korean DAC tapped him on the shoulder. Startled, Lefter whirled around and faced him.

Looking scared, the Korean DAC said, "Mr. Fong think attack will build to at least regimental size and maybe division size."

"Holy crap," replied Lefter, "that's a couple of thousand men or maybe seven or eight thousand. Oh hell, I don't remember how many men are in a division."

The DAC nodded agreement. Lefter ran to the phone and reported the latest information to Campbell. Campbell again told him to continue monitoring but leave in a hurry if the barbwire line was penetrated. Lefter heard the familiar sound of outgoing artillery overhead. Again, he knew it was a massive firing because the air was filled with chugging sounds. He hurried to the viewing slit and waited. In a few seconds the rounds started landing in the area of OP Carson. "Holy Crap, they're shelling our own OP," he said softly. Then it dawned on him why that was occurring. The 25th Division troops were abandoning the OP and the shelling was covering their retreat.

Then all hell broke loose across his entire field of vision. Artillery and mortar explosions started occurring in the area of Outposts Berlin, Vegas and Elko. Then it progressed even farther right to Outposts Detroit and East

Berlin. It appeared to Lefter that the Chinese were attacking all along the 25th Division front. Lefter heard the telltale whistling sounds as the Chinese artillery pounded the 25th Division's MLR. Lefter ducked away from the viewing slit as some rounds started landing nearby. Again the bunker would shake and dirt would sift down from the ceiling. Lefter retreated to the table, called Campbell and reported his latest observations. Again, Campbell ended their conversation by telling him to get out if the barbwire line was penetrated.

Lefter sat at the table and smoked several cigarettes while the artillery and mortar battle raged on outside. The Chinese DAC was monitoring the radio and the Korean DAC was sitting on his bunk smoking those foul Japanese cigarettes. Lefter became aware that, although he could still hear outgoing, he couldn't hear any incoming.

He hurried to the viewing slit and looked across toward the outposts. The outposts east of OP Carson were still under heavy artillery and mortar attack from the Chinese. He couldn't see any activity near the location of OP Carson. Flares lit up the area around OP Elko and tracers from machine gun fire could be seen traveling toward the OP Carson area. Lefter thought the Chinese, having taken OP Carson, was now using it to stage an attack on OP Elko. Taking OP Elko would cut off reinforcements to OP Vegas and OP Berlin because they were located north from OP Elko. *Clever bastards.*

Suddenly Lefter heard loud trumpets and whistles. Then flares burst forth their eerie light high above the general area of the barbwire line. Mortar rounds started coming in immediately down the hill in front of Lefter. "Oh shit," yelled Lefter as he scrambled toward the radios. He pulled the Chinese DAC away and said, "get ready to get the hell out of here." Lefter grabbed the trenching tool and started beating on the radios with it.

There was a loud pounding on the bunker door and someone yelled, "OPEN THE FUCKING DOOR. OPEN THE FUCKING DOOR."

Lefter threw down the trenching tool and sprinted to the door. He opened the door knowing it was Mewman.

"GET THE FUCK OUT OF THERE," yelled Mewman. "THE FUCKING GOOKS HAVE BROKE THROUGH THE WIRE AND THEY'RE COMING UP THE HILL."

Lefter motioned to the DACs to move out. They ran out the door. Lefter grabbed his pack and carbine, and ran out the bunker door with Mewman.

"MY TRUCK IS AT THE BOTTOM OF THE HILL," yelled Lefter to Mewman.

"OK," said Mewman as he pulled the pin on a grenade and threw it through the open door of the bunker. "RUN FOR THE FUCKING TRUCK," he yelled.

They all ran along the entrance trench and out onto the backside of the hill. The trail down toward the truck was easy to see under the light of the flares. They scrambled down the trail toward the truck. As they neared the truck a burp gun started firing toward them from over a little knoll in the dirt road along the base of the hill.

"Run for the truck and get it started," yelled Mewman as he dropped down in a prone position and started firing back with his BAR.

Lefter and the DACs sprinted to the truck. Lefter jumped in and started the truck. The DACs jumped into the back. Fortunately, it was backed into the parking area so he didn't need to turn it around before driving away. Lefter looked back and saw Mewman still firing his BAR. Lefter started honking the horn. "Beep-beep-beep." Mewman motioned him to drive off but Lefter was having none of that and kept honking. Finally, Mewman jumped up and started running toward the truck. Lefter looked through the back glass and saw Mewman scramble into the truck just as bullets from the burp gun started hitting the truck. Lefter gunned the truck and sped down the rough dirt road. Soon he was having difficulty seeing the road as they drove out of the area lighted by the flares. He slowed down, and felt his way along the road back to the ASA base camp.

Campbell came running out as Lefter drove in. "Sure happy to see you, buddy," said Campbell, "I was afraid that you'd been overrun."

"We damn near were," said Lefter excitedly. "Them tricky gooks were attacking the outposts east of Carson as a diversion. Then suddenly they came storming right up our throat. We'd be dead meat if it wasn't for Mewman saving our ass."

"Mewman?" said Campbell quizzically.

"Yeah Mewman," answered Lefter, "he's in the back with the DACs."

Campbell turned and headed for the back of the truck. Lefter jumped out and joined him. Campbell aimed his flashlight beam into the truck bed. Mewman and the two DACs were crumbled over in a pool of blood.

Lefter jumped into the back of the truck and pulled Mewman's head into his lap. Mewman was breathing but bleeding from his mouth. "You're gonna be OK, buddy. You're gonna be OK, hang in there, you're going to be OK," Lefter kept repeating as he stroked Mewman on the head.

"Let's get them over to Battalion Aid," yelled Campbell as he ran around and got in the driver's seat and drove the two hundred yards to the Battalion Aid Station. Campbell drove up to the Aid tent and started honking the truck's horn and yelling, "Medic, medic, medic."

A corporal came out and said to Campbell, "What the fuck you making all the noise for?"

"Got three wounded men in the back of the truck," said Campbell.

"Get in line, buddy," replied the corporal, "we've got wounded coming in by the gross."

Campbell jumped out of the truck, grabbed the corporal by the shirt and pulled him up close. "See these First Sergeant stripes, don't be a smart ass with me or I'll have your fucking cock cut off and put in a kimchi barrel."

"OK, Sarg," said the corporal, "we'll do what we can." He walked around behind the truck and aimed his flashlight in on Lefter, Mewman and the DACs. "I'll get a medic out here as soon as I can," said the corporal as he turned and headed back inside the Medical Aid Station.

Campbell climbed into the back of the truck and aimed his flashlight at Mewman's face. Mewman was bleeding from the mouth but still breathing. Lefter was still saying, "Hang in there, buddy. You're going to be OK. You're going to be OK. You're going to be OK, buddy." Campbell aimed the light on the Chinese DAC and discovered that the back of his head was missing. Turning to the Korean DAC, he saw him blink his eyes. "Hang in there, Mr. Lu. You're going to be OK," said Campbell.

The corporal appeared at the back of the truck with a stretcher and said, "Let's get them into the prep tent." He dropped the tailgate of the truck and reached toward Lefter.

Lefter pulled Mewman toward the awaiting arms of the corporal then got out and helped lift Mewman onto the stretcher. They carried him into the Aid Tent where a medic took Lefter's end of the stretcher.

"We'll take it from here," said the medic.

"I'm not leaving him now," said Lefter as he followed them back into the prep area of the huge tent.

Back in the prep area another medic examined Mewman briefly, shook his head and then cut off his fatigue shirt. Mewman was bleeding from a hole in his chest. Blood was also seeping out of his mouth.

"So, what's the deal?" asked Lefter.

"We'll send him out to a MASH unit by helicopter," answered the medic.

"What the hell is MASH?" asked Lefter.

"Mobile Army Surgical Hospital," replied the medic.

Campbell came in and said to Lefter, "They think Mr. Lu is near death also."

Pointing at the Medic, Lefter said, "Mewman is going by helicopter to a MASH unit."

Shortly, they heard the sound of an incoming helicopter. "Let's get him out there," said Lefter as he picked up one end of the stretcher.

Campbell picked up the other end and they carried Mewman outside.

"Wait a minute," protested the medic, "he hasn't been prioritized."

"Prioritized my ass," said Lefter.

"Oh what the hell," said the medic, "take him out to the helicopter."

The medic went with them and secured the stretcher to the helicopter transport cradle. Another wounded man was brought out and secured on the other transport cradle. The H-13D bubble helicopter rose slowly, turned and headed south into the night.

The medic said to Campbell and Lefter, "He's probably not going to make it, guys. We may not have sent him out to MASH if you guys hadn't been here."

"What's his chances, Doc?" asked Campbell.

"Maybe one in ten thousand," said the medic, "and that's optimistic."

"Thanks for the quick aid," said Lefter to the medic.

"You're welcome. I hope your buddy makes it, but I haven't seen one survive those kind of wounds yet."

"Always the first time," said Lefter with a quiver in his voice. He was trying to be optimistic but, in his heart, he thought Mewman would die.

"Yeah, maybe he will beat the odds," said the medic as he extended his hand and said, "Gotta go."

Campbell and Lefter shook the medic's hand. "Rotten fucking war," said Lefter with disgust.

"Got that right," said the medic as he turned and went back inside the tent.

CHAPTER NINETEEN

Campbell and Lefter returned to the ASA base camp. It had began to get light but a fog was forming. They were barely inside the tent when the familiar sound of an incoming mortar round penetrated the air. Immediately after it exploded nearby with a big thud, shrapnel came whistling into the tent. Campbell yelled, "Is anyone hit? Pack up quick, we're getting the hell out of here." No one had been hit but there was a large tear in the top of the tent.

Jobby, Hillman, and Jolcomb woke up instantly, leaped out of their sleeping bags, scrambled into their clothes, then jerked on their boots without tying the laces.

Campbell made a sweeping motion around the tent and said, "Throw all your personal gear and our booze into the back of the deuce-and-a-half, we're leaving in three minutes. I'll get the DACs."

As they scrambled in and out of the tent throwing things into the deuce-and-a-half, other incoming rounds landed over toward the battalion headquarters area. The DACs scrambled out of their tent with their personal effects and climbed into the back of the three-quarter ton truck.

Campbell yelled, "Get your weapons and let's hit the road right now."

Campbell quickly assigned a driver for each vehicle. He jumped in his jeep and said, "Follow me." Lefter was driving the three-quarter ton and Hillman was driving the deuce-and-a-half. Jolcomb was riding with Lefter, and Jobby was driving the other jeep with Hillman in the passenger seat.

With mortar rounds starting to come in nearby, they drove swiftly down the one-lane road and out onto the Main Supply Route. As they passed the artillery emplacement, the men there were scrambling to hitch the big guns to deuce-and-a-half trucks. It was obvious to Lefter and the others that the Chinese had broken through the MLR and were advancing southerly. As the Marine expression goes: "We're not retreating, we're just advancing in a different direction."

Several miles further south they met a long convoy of deuce-and-a-half trucks headed north. Each truck had a squad of Marines dressed in full combat gear. They were coming out of reserve to join in the battle. They were scheduled to replace the 25th Infantry but now it appeared that both divisions might be needed to repel the Communist attack.

The little ASA convoy continued south until Campbell led his group through the guard gate at I-Corps headquarters and into the 303 CRB Compound. They parked in front of the headquarters hut. Campbell went to each vehicle and told them to wait outside for him.

Lefter stepped down from the truck running board and collapsed to his knees. His legs were weak and he started shaking. He lit up a Chesterfield cigarette and inhaled a deep puff of the nicotine-rich smoke. Jobby, Hillman and Jolcomb soon joined him with their own cigarettes. Then the DACs unloaded from the three-quarter ton truck and joined the smoking group with their cigarettes. They were all sucking in the nicotine-rich smoke and inhaling it deeply.

They heard yelling coming from inside the headquarters hut. It was Major Soss. They couldn't hear what was being said but Lefter was sure it was Major Soss doing the yelling. He had heard him yelling in anger before. In a few minutes, Campbell came out the door. His face was red with embarrassment and anger. He said, "The major wants us all to line up and stand at attention. He wants to talk to us as a group.

They lined up in a military formation while the DACs stood aside and continued to smoke. Major Soss came storming out the door. Campbell said, "Ten-hut," and saluted. The other four ASA men saluted also.

Major Soss did his cocky striding back in forth in front of the scraggy ASA enlisted men while he tried to stare down each one. Finally, he said, "I have been in my office awaiting a call from you. You men have all abandoned your post in time of war." The DACs started talking among themselves. He paused and glared at the DACs. Then he again started striding back and forth trying to stare down each man. He didn't recognize it but now he was seeing hatred in their eyes. "Do you hear me!" he demanded. "You have abandoned your post in time of war."

"Bullshit," said one of the DACs.

"What was that?" said the major as he whirled around and looked toward the group of DACs.

"I said bullshit," said the offending DAC.

"Me too," said another DAC, "you bullshit."

"Me also," said another DAC, "bullshit, you big plick."

"Fluck you," said another of the DACs.

"You son-a-bitch," said yet another DAC.

"We le-polt you to Depaltment of Defense," said the first DAC who had spoken up. "You numbe-one fucking big plick." He stepped out in front of the group of his fellow DACs, raised his hands and led them in saying, in unison, "big plick, big plick, big plick." The DACs kept repeating the phrase in unison until the major whirled around and went back in the hut. He quickly came back out, shook his finger vigorously and said, "You men are not dismissed yet."

Campbell and his men remained standing at attention. In a couple of minutes, the major reappeared. He was dressed in his flack jacket and hard hat. He carried the steel helmet under his arm. "DISMISSED," he yelled as he strode past the ASA men. He walked directly to the DAC who had lead the demonstration against him and said, "My apologies to you, sir, and to your associates." Then he strode off swiftly toward the motor pool.

"He may be crazy but he's not stupid," said Lefter. "He knows those DACs can ruin his career. He can't court-martial a Department of the Army Civilian."

"You got that right, Lef," said Campbell. "If all the DACs gang up on him, he's a gone gosling."

The five ASA guys walked over to the DACs and began shaking their hands. The DACs each bowed, smiled and said, "You welcome."

Major Soss came driving slowly by the group expecting a salute and all five ASA men ignored him. He stepped down on the jeep's accelerator and sped off leaving a cloud of red dust.

Campbell went back into the headquarters hut. After about five minutes he came back out and said, "The executive officer says he will arrange for the DACs to stay in I-Corps temporary officers quarters for as long as necessary. We are to stay in I-Corps temporary EM quarters."

"Why don't we just camp out here?" asked Hillman.

"He wants us far removed from the major," said Campbell. "Don't that make sense?"

They each nodded agreement.

In a few minutes the EO, Lieutenant Landa, came out and said to the men, "You all are doing a really good job." Then pointing to the DACs he said, "and that includes you guys." Then he said to Campbell, "I made the temporary living arrangements. You are all relieved of any duty until further notice." Turning to the DACs, he added, "and that includes you men also — with full pay, of course."

"Thank you, sir," said Campbell who was sincerely grateful.

Pointing to Campbell, Lieutenant Landa said, "You'll be staying at the NCO temporary quarters but first come on in and give me and Sergeant Nay a full report." Campbell followed him into the hut.

"Did you hear that?" said Lefter.

"Hear what?" said Jolcomb.

"He said *Sergeant* Nay," said Lefter. "How the hell did he make Sergeant so soon?"

"Who cares," said Jobby, "I need a drink. Did anyone throw in some booze?"

"There's a bottle in my pack that I took up to on the hill for Mewman's Sergeant Happy," said Lefter. "Let's get situated then I'll bring it out."

It was getting light as they gathered their personal gear and Lefter drove them all to the temporary quarters. First he took the DACs to the temporary officers quarters then parked the three-quarter ton truck outside the temporary enlisted men's quarters. Inside they each claimed an empty cot. Lefter took out the bottle of Canadian Club. They passed it around taking sips followed by a low throat clearing sound.

"Good stuff," said Lefter.

They each nodded agreement.

"Another round?" asked Lefter.

They each nodded affirmative.

Another round of gulps and low throat clearing sounds.

"One more?" asked Lefter.

They each nodded affirmative.

More gulps and throat clearing.

"Fuck it, let's kill it," said Lefter and took a final gulp and cleared his throat.

Jolcomb drained the remainder of the bottle with one big gulp followed by a shiver above the waist. Jobby and Hillman started moaning and commented in turn, "Asshole, you drank it all. Prick, you took more than your share."

Jolcomb laughed and said slowly, "Treat me good, boys. I been holding back. I got a bottle in my pack and a gun in my pants." He grabbed his crouch and laughed.

"You a real fucking poet," slurred Hillman.

"Fuck it, fuck it," said Jobby then he yelled, "FUCKKKKK ITTTTTT!"

"Fuck what?" asked Lefter.

"Fuck the whole fucking world. Fuck you. Fuck him. Fuck all of you. Fuck everybody. Fuck this fucking war. FUCKKKK IT ALLLLLL!" Then Jobby broke down and started sobbing softly.

Each of the other men got tears in their eyes and didn't say anything. Jolcomb wiped his eyes with the back of his hand then went into his pack and removed a bottle of Old Crow. He opened the bottle and took it to Jobby. "Here, buddy, you have the first drink."

Jobby gathered himself, took a big gulp and coughed. Holding out the bottle to Lefter, he said, "This shit is going to kill us if the fucking war doesn't get us first."

"Got that fucking right, buddy," said Lefter, "but I'd rather go this way."

Jolcomb and Hillman nodded agreement.

By the time they finished the bottle of Old Crow they were each, in GI lingo, "shit faced." Each man collapsed on his cot, fell asleep immediately and started snoring.

"OH NO!" yelled Lefter as he woke up with a headache and feeling sick. He jumped off the cot, tripped on his pack and fell into Jolcomb's cot. "DAMN IT!" he yelled and ran for the door. He ran about twenty feet outside past the door, bent over at the waist and started throwing up.

Jolcomb came running out of the door and over near Lefter. "Damn you L... Rahhhhhrafffff." He didn't finish the sentence before starting to throw up.

Soon, Jobby and Hillman were also standing nearby gagging and throwing up. For several minutes all four men gagged, cleared their throats and spit up the awful-tasting regurgitated whiskey. Then, heads hanging, they walked slowly back inside, collapsed on their cots and started moaning.

After several minutes Lefter raised up, sat on his cot and, with his head cupped in his hands, said, "Whose stupid idea was it to drink all that fucking whiskey?"

"Yours, asshole," said Jolcomb from a prone position on his cot.

"Well, that explains it," said Lefter as he laughed causing his head to hurt more. "Oh fuck, I never learn, do I?" Then he added, "Of course, I am in good fucking company here."

"Fuck you," said Jolcomb.

"Up yours," said Lefter.

Both men tried to laugh but ended up just holding their heads and moaning.

Why didn't I think of it before? Lefter thought to himself. *Lefter, you*

STAY SAFE, BUDDY

dumb shit. He dug around in his pack, took out the small bottle of Kisoto, removed the lid and started taking whiffs. He felt a little better almost immediately. After a few minutes, he felt like he might live. After a few more minutes of deep inhalations, he felt like he actually wanted to live.

Lefter went over to Jolcomb and said, "Sit up and smell this."

"Fuck you," said Jolcomb.

"No, no," said Lefter, "I absolutely guarantee that it will cure your fucking headache."

"Fuck you," said Jolcomb again.

"Tell you what," said Lefter, "if this doesn't help your headache I'll kiss your ass in the fucking Company Square at high noon."

"Are you shitting me?" asked Jolcomb.

"No, my headache is almost gone," replied Lefter.

Jobby sat up and took a whiff of the bottle Lefter was holding out to him. "It is kind of soothing," he said.

"Here," said Lefter as he handed the bottle to Jolcomb, "keep taking a whiff every now and then until your head feels better."

Jolcomb followed the advice of Lefter and after a few minutes began to smile. "This stuff really works," he said to Lefter.

"Told you," said Lefter with a laugh. "Too bad though, I was kind of looking forward to you kissing my ass in the Company Square."

"You asshole," replied Jolcomb, excited and talking fast, "you said you'd kiss *my* ass in the Company Square if this stuff didn't work. I never said I'd kiss your ass. I never said that. I'm not kissing your ass for nothing."

"Fucking ingrate," replied Lefter with another laugh.

Jolcomb smiled and said, "Fuck you."

"Ingrate," repeated Lefter.

Jolcomb finally figured out that Lefter was "pulling his chain" so he quit talking. Lefter shut up also. Just like fishing, it was no fun if they quit biting.

Lefter tried to get Jobby and Hillman to whiff the Kisoto but they wouldn't have anything to do with it. They just lay on their cots moaning and whining. They also couldn't be convinced to get up and go to dinner at the mess hall.

Lefter had another brilliant humorous idea while sitting at a table in the mess hall. He said to Jolcomb, "Look at us. Dirty and crumpled fatigues, dirty boots, dirty weapons, dirty hands and dirty faces with scraggly beards. We definitely don't look like newbies, do we?"

"Absolutely not. What's your point?" asked Jolcomb.

"Let's give these candy asses in here a thrill," said Lefter. Then he explained his plan to Jolcomb.

"You have a weird mind, Lefter," said Jolcomb.

"No, no, no," laughed Lefter, "warped sense of humor, but not a weird mind."

"Ready, go," said Lefter and both men raised up out of their chairs without removing their carbines from the back of the chairs. The carbines crashed to the floor along with the chairs.

The fifty or so guys seated at the other tables looked at Lefter and Jolcomb and most looked confused. They were not laughing or applauding. They were confused because these two men didn't look like newbies.

Lefter and Jolcomb stood scanning the room. The carbines and turned over chairs lay in a heap at their feet. Then laughter and sporadic applause broke out.

"Now," whispered Lefter. They bent down, picked up their carbines and again scanned the room while holding their carbines in the ready position.

"Load," whispered Lefter. Both men jacked a cartridge into the chamber of their carbines and continued to scan the room.

The applause stopped abruptly and the men at the tables got real still. All had startled looks on their faces.

"Shoulder up and bow," whispered Lefter.

Both men slung their carbine on their shoulder and bowed several times. The room broke out in laughter and then lots of loud applause. Lefter and Jolcomb smiled and waved as they walked to the door.

Outside, Jolcomb said to Lefter, "I shouldn't have let you talk me into that. We could have got our asses shot."

"Yeah, guess so," replied Lefter, "but wasn't it fuuuuuunnn?"

"Yeah," said Jolcomb, "it was fun, up to the point that it occurred to me that there may be some guys in there crazier than us, and they just might have shot our ass off."

Thinking of Mewman, Lefter said, "Loosen up, Jolc, we may not get out of this fucking kimchi bowl alive anyway."

Lefter led Jolcomb over to the EM Club. It had already opened for business so they went to the bar and each bought a beer. Looking around the room, he noticed Mighty Joe motioning them to his table. Nay and Crovelli were also at the table.

"I got the first round," said Mighty Joe.

"Well, ain't you a generous son-of-a-bitch," said Lefter staring him in the eyes. "I'm not buying any fucking beer for you tonight."

"Well then," answered Might Joe, "you're *dead* at *my* table."

Lefter leaned on the table, got close to Mighty Joe's face and said, "How 'bout I stick this fucking table up you smart ass?"

"Hey, hey, hold it," said Nay as he stood up, "calm down, buddy, we're all friends here." He pointed to Mighty Joe and said, "We can get another table if this asshole here wants to drink alone."

Mighty Joe stuck out his hand and said, "Sorry, Lefter. Guess I am being insensitive. Please sit down. Hear you guys had a bad time today."

Lefter shook his hand and sat down at the table. Jolcomb, who hadn't said a word since entering the EM Club, sat down and said, "Lefter fucking near bought the farm twice this morning. Once up on the hill and then again down at the base camp with the rest of us."

"Bad fucking news," said Lefter as he started to choke up a little, "Mewman got hit real bad." He paused and gathered himself. "They hauled him off to a MASH unit in a helicopter. The medic said he'd never seem anyone survive with a wound like that."

Nay reached over and put his hand on Lefter's wrist. "What happened?" asked Nay.

"Mewman got it in the chest with a fucking burp gun," replied Lefter. "Two of the DACs were killed, one outright and the other was dying at the Battalion Aid Station."

Nay already knew what had happened but he wanted to have Lefter talk about it and let out his emotions. Nay knew from some of his college studies that the worst thing for Lefter to do was hold it all inside.

Lefter wiped his eyes on his dirty fatigue shirtsleeve, picked up the beer and emptied the can in several big gulps. Jolcomb also drank the remaining beer in his can.

"You two guys aren't allowed to buy tonight," said Mighty Joe as he pointed to Lefter and Jolcomb.

Lefter's first impulse was a Mewman type of response, "I'll buy if I fucking want too," but he quickly decided to hold his tongue and let Mighty Joe get away with the controlling statement.

Mighty Joe got up, went to the bar and returned with five cans of beer.

Crovelli had also had some college psychology classes and he, too, already knew what had happened that day. Mighty Joe was the only one at the table that hadn't known that the Chinese Peoples Army had overrun the ASA Detachment #1. Crovelli said, "Tell us what happened, guys."

Lefter didn't say anything. He just picked up his beer and drank it slowly.

After a long silence Jolcomb finally said, "Lef was in the middle of it up on the hill," said Jolcomb.

"What happened?" asked Nay as he again put his hand on Lefter's wrist.

All of them stared at Lefter who finally put his beer down, lit a cigarette and said, "They pounded the shit out of us all day and night with artillery. During the night the fuckers overran OP Carson and attacked all the other outposts in the Nevada Complex. They were also hitting Berlin, East Berlin and Detroit. The fuckers started attacking OP Elko from Carson but it was a goddamn diversion. Before we knew it the fuckers were across the barbwire line and pounding the hell out of us with mortar fire."

Lefter didn't realize it, nor did anyone else at the table, but his uncharacteristic use of filthy language was part of his grieving for Mewman. He just knew that Mewman was dead and that was seething deep inside him. He felt responsible for Mewman's death.

"Go on," said Nay.

Lefter gathered himself, took another drink of beer and continued. "I was beating the shit out of the fucking radios with a trenching tool when Mewman pounded on the door and yelled, "GET THE FUCK OUT OF THERE," so the DACs and me ran out of the bunker and down the trail to the truck. Mewman was coming behind us. Those fucking eerie flares made it seem like some sort of weird daylight. Just as we got near the truck some fucking gooks started firing at us with burp guns. Mewman sprayed the fucking area with his BAR and pinned the fuckers down while we got in the truck."

Lefter broke down and sobbed a few times. Nay again put his hand on Lefter's arm and said, "Take a break, buddy. I'll get us another beer."

Lefter lit another Chesterfield cigarette and picked up the new beer that Nay delivered.

"Then what happened?" asked Mighty Joe who had also remembered some fundamentals from his psychology classes. Nay and Crovelli nodded to Mighty Joe. They knew he had caught on. Everyone waited.

"Well," said Lefter as he started to choke up again, "Mewman kept motioning for me to take off but I kept honking the fucking horn until he finally ran and jumped into the back of the truck with the DACs. He was firing the BAR from the back of the truck as I took off down the road. The fucking gooks were still firing the burp guns and I could hear a lot of slugs hitting the truck. They hit the fucking back window and it shattered."

Lefter swallowed hard and sobbed a couple of times. He drank from his beer, looked over at Jolcomb and said with a sobbing chuckle, "Maybe we can get shit faced again and make this fucking war go away twice in one day."

Jolcomb held out his beer can toward Lefter and said, "Cheers, buddy, tell them the rest of it."

Lefter tapped his beer can on Jolcomb's can and said, "OK, I'll try to finish the fucking story." Then he drained his beer and said, "The beer is starting to help now."

"Hang on for a minute while I get us another beer," said Crovelli. Everyone stared at the table until Crovelli returned with more beer and said, "OK, I'm ready."

"Go ahead, buddy," said Jolcomb.

Lefter sobbed once, took a drink from his beer and said, "I drove to our base camp and then discovered that Mewman and the DACs had been shot. Campbell and I took them to the Battalion Aid Station." He looked down at his hands and then at his shirt and pants. "I've still got Mewman's blood all over me." Lefter started sobbing again.

Nay put his hand on Lefter's wrist and said, "We're here for you, buddy."

"Fucking gooks," sobbed Lefter. "Fucking war. Why the fuck are we here anyway?"

"Good fucking question," answered Nay. The other men at the table nodded agreement.

Lefter wiped the tears from his eyes with the sleeve of his fatigue shirt, smiled and laughed half heartily, "Guess we just gotta always be shoving it up somebody's ass somewhere in the world."

"Right on," said Nay. "Let me offer the first toast tonight, Fuck the world!"

They all took a big drink from their beer.

"OK," said Crovelli. "Fuck the galaxy!"

They all laughed and drank from their beer.

Mighty Joe left and came back with a large tray holding 20 cans of beer. "Fuck the universe!" said Mighty Joe.

They all laughed and drank more beer.

Jolcomb raised his beer and said, "Fuck all the big and little fishes in the sea."

They all laughed and drank more beer. Now they were really getting into some serious drinking.

Lefter raised a beer and said, "Fuck all the fuckers that fuck with us." The old Lefter and his sense of humor had returned briefly. They each laughed and saluted him with their can of beer before gulping more down.

They drank beer and made toasts until the EM Club closed at midnight. Lefter and Jolcomb staggered back to the transit area and passed out on their cots.

Lefter woke up fully dressed and lying on top of the sleeping bag. His head throbbed and something smelled rotten. He sat up slowly and looked down at his shirt and pants. They were covered with dried blood and caked with dirt. He immediately thought of Mewman and his lower lip began to quiver.

Lefter walked to the ASA Compound and asked Sergeant Thomas for a new set of fatigues.

"You bet, buddy," said Thomas and got him a new set of fatigues from the shelves. "Here's a couple of pair of socks too. Stay right here for a minute." Thomas knew what had happened to Lefter and he wanted to help him in any possible way.

The supply sergeant left the supply tent and returned in a couple of minutes. He handed Lefter two tee shirts and two pair of underwear. "I'm all out of new underclothes but take these. I just got them back from the laundry. They should fit you, we're about the same size."

Lefter just nodded and said, "Thanks, Sarg."

At the shower dressing area, Lefter took off the soiled clothes and dropped them in the garbage can. He stood looking into the garbage can for a few seconds then said, "So long, buddy." Lefter stood in the shower, sobbing occasionally, while the warm water poured over his head and torso. Over, and over, he kept soaping up and rinsing off his entire body.

"Hey, buddy, save some hot water for the other guys," said the shower attendant.

"Fuck you," said Lefter as he turned off the shower and went into the dressing area.

The attendant didn't respond and returned to the desk area at the entrance.

Back at the sleeping area, Lefter smelled the sleeping bag on his cot. "Phew!" he said out loud. He picked it up, carried it down the room and exchanged it for the clean bag on another cot.

Jolcomb, Hillman and Jobby were gone. Lefter looked at his watch. It was nearly noon. They were probably over at the mess hall waiting in line for the door to open for lunch. "Fuck it, I'm not hungry," he said out loud while lying down on his cot. The last thing he remembered before falling asleep was how good the clean sleeping bag smelled.

Someone yelling startled Lefter awake. Lefter sat up on his cot and looked toward the yelling. It was a newbie, a rookie straight from the states with his starched fatigues and polished boots. Newbie said to Lefter, "Do you know anything about this?"

"Know anything about what fucking thing?" asked Lefter.

"Somebody switched sleeping bags with me," said the Newbie. "Left me this one that smells like shit."

"Oh that," said Lefter, "I saw the guy do it."

"The son-of-a-bitch is in big trouble with me," said the Newbie. "I'm gonna have his ass."

"I'll tell you what the fucker looks like so you'll know 'em when you see 'em," said Lefter. Lefter stood up and reached up toward the ceiling, "He's a big black ugly fucker about six foot six. He's carrying a fucking British tommy gun. He must be one of those fucking Special Forces guys in the Commonwealth Division. I think they are from Ethiopia. You can't miss him, mean-looking fucker. His teeth are black; hear they chew some kind of fucking narcotic that does that and makes 'em crazy and meaner than a fucking alligator. He hasn't been gone all that long; want me to help you find the fucker?"

The newbie had a shocked look on his face. "That's OK," he said, "I'll just keep an eye out for him."

"OK," said Lefter. "If I see the fucker, do you want me to tell him you're looking for 'em?"

"Naw, I'll just keep an eye out for him," said the Newbie.

"Don't blame you," said Lefter. "I wouldn't want that big ugly mean fucker to know I was after him either. Best to surprise a big ugly mean fucker like that, ain't it?"

"Well, thanks," said the Newbie weakly.

"Anytime," said Lefter and lay back down on his cot. He could hardly hold back the laughter. He decided he better get outside because he could feel a belly laugh coming. He jumped up, grabbed his dirty carbine and said, "Oh shit, I'm late for lunch," then sprinted out the door and trotted toward the mess hall, laughing all the way.

Lefter got a cup of coffee and looked around the mess hall. Nay and Campbell were sitting at a table. "Mind if I join you?" asked Lefter as he approached their table.

"Sit down, Lef, and we'll tell you what's going on up front," said Campbell.

"I was hoping you would," said Lefter as he hooked the shoulder strap of his carbine on the chair and sat down.

"The gooks pushed us back across the Imjin River. Then the Marine Division got into the act and helped the 25th Division stop them. A heavy fog came in but now it's lifted and we're hitting them right now with massive air strikes. The objective is to drive them back to their former locations."

"What a fucking waste," said Lefter.

"Agree," said Nay. "It's like a horizontal yo-yo that collapses and then springs back to the original position."

"And this last fucking yo-yo got Mewman," replied Lefter.

"Take it easy, Lef," said Campbell. "Remember, Mewman was doing what he loved doing."

"You got that right," said Lefter, "he sure liked killing them fucking gooks and I think he nailed a couple of them while he was saving my sorry ass."

Lefter took a long deep breath and let it out slowly. Neither of the three said anything. Finally, Lefter said, "When can we go back and set up the detachment again?"

"Now you're talking, Lef," said Campbell. "Keep on looking forward."

"Yeah, I know," said Lefter, "don't look back cause some fucking thing may be gaining on you."

"Well not exactly," chuckled Campbell. "I think the expression doesn't usually include the f word."

"Sounds better that way though," said Lefter. "It puts the right fucking em-pha-sis on the correct fucking syl-lab-le."

"Anyway," said Campbell, "to answer your question, I don't know. Probably as soon as the MLR is stabilized again."

"Can't be soon enough for me," said Lefter. "I'm getting too fucking old to handle getting drunk twice in the same day."

"Yeah, you're an old fart, OK. How old are you?" asked Campbell.

"I'm turning twenty-fucking-one this month," said Lefter, "and it ain't going to be nearly as much fucking fun drinking after I'm legal."

Nay, who had been listening quietly, said, "Maybe you can come down to the EM Club here on your birthday and we'll help you celebrate."

"Good fucking plan," said Lefter as he turned to Campbell. "Can I have my birthday off, Boss?"

"Maybe, if you clean up your act by then," replied Campbell.

Lefter guessed that Campbell was referring to his generous use of the f word. Somehow, using the f word liberally seemed like the thing to do right now. It felt good.

Campbell waited but Lefter didn't respond so he said, "Just when is your birthday?"

"July the *fucking* fourteenth," replied Lefter, putting emphasis on the f word.

"See them First Sergeant stripes?" asked Campbell as he pointed to his shirtsleeve. "Don't toy with me, I'm still in charge, OK?"

The blunt statement shocked Lefter back to the fundamental reality of their relationship. "OK, Camp, sorry for the smart ass em-pha-sis."

Nay jumped in and said, "I've got a better idea. Maybe we can set up a private party. I hear there is a Chinese restaurant that just opened up in Seoul."

"That's a good plan," said Lefter. "Major Soss couldn't bother us down there."

"Best you stay clear of him for a while," said Nay. "He was real upset about the DACs coming down on him and then you guys *forgetting* to salute as he drove by."

"I hear your em-pha-sis, Nay," said Lefter. "I'd like to stuff a salute up that fucker's asshole."

"Get in line," said Nay. "At least you don't have to work with the asshole all the time."

"Thank somebody for that," said Lefter.

"Amen," said Campbell.

"By the way, "said Nay, "Soss is still hot about the bunker you decorated for his inspection trip."

"Yeah," said Campbell, "he's no doubt gonna have my ass if General Stoney rotates before I do."

"Got that right," said Nay. "He's laying for you guys for sure."

Lefter unwittingly kept speaking more and more as Mewman spoke. "Wish the fucker wouda been up there when we got overrun. I wouda left the fucker in the bunker. Fun for me just to imagine that cocky fucker getting his ass tortured." Lefter let out a big belly roar.

"That is an entertaining thought," said Nay. "Can't you just see him sticking out his chest and saying, 'Now listen men, I am a West Point officer so salute me.'"

Lefter jumped in, "And the Chinese soldier would say, 'So solly I salutee wiff big funckee laugh aff I pull out youl fingelnails.'" Lefter gave a big belly laugh. Nay and Campbell laughed also.

Nay looked at his watch and said, "It's after one and the EM Club is open, how about a beer?"

"Didn't think the fucking club opened till six," said Lefter.

"Nowadays, it's thirteen hundred on Saturday," replied Nay.

"Oh, I never know what fucking day it is. I just know it's July."

"Do you know the year?" said Campbell jokingly.

"Just barely," smiled Lefter. "What day is it anyway?"

"Serious?" asked Nay.

"Fucking A," replied Lefter.

"Well, it's Saturday the *fucking* sixth of *fucking* July of the *fucking* year nineteen *fucking* fifty-three," said Nay as he mocked and emphasized Lefter's constant use of the f word.

"I get your fucking point," smiled Lefter. "Let's get a beer."

"I may see you guys later," said Campbell. "I have a few things to do today."

Mighty Joe, of course, had already staked out his usual table. Nissing was seated with him. As Lefter and Nay approached Nissing rose from his chair and said, "Sit down, guys, I'll get you a beer."

While Nissing was getting the beers Lefter said, "What the fuck's up?"

"He's treating us tonight," said Mighty Joe pointing toward Nissing.

"Why?" asked Lefter.

"I know but I'll let him tell you," said Nay.

Nissing returned with the beer and Lefter said, "What the fuck is going on, Charlie? Why the fucking celebration?"

"My transfer came through," said Nissing.

"No shit!" said Lefter.

"Yep, leaving Monday for Tokyo."

"Gotta give it to you, Charlie, you are one fucking smooth operator," said Lefter as he raised his beer in a toast. "Here's to Charlie, he's one fucking smooth operator."

"Here, here," said the others and they all drank some beer.

Nay raised his beer and said, "Here's to Charlie, may you get laid every night in Tokyo."

"Here, here," said the others and everyone drank some beer.

Mighty Joe raised his beer and said, "Here's to Charlie, may you remember your buddies in this asshole land of Korea."

"Here, here," said the others and drank from their beer.

"Here's to Charlie," said Lefter. "Hey, my fucking beer is empty!"

Everyone laughed and Nissing said, "I'll get ten more."

Nissing returned with the beer and Lefter picked up the toasting again, "Here's to Charlie, makes me jealous, he gets to sit on flush toilets while I piss in a fucking tube in the ground."

They all laughed and said, "Here, here," followed by guzzles of beer.

The toasts and here, here responses went on and on, interspersed with Lefter saying occasionally, "Hey, my fucking beer is empty."

"Mine too," Nissing would say. "I'll go get another ten."

Now, Lefter and Nissing were definitely drunk and slurring their speech.

"Hey bu — bu — bud-dee," said Lefter to Nissing. "You — you — you're sh — sh shit fa — fa faced."

"Fu — fu fuck — ling A," said Nissing.

"Hey," yelled Lefter, "ain't, ain't, ain't that som 'em fuck'em Turks." He stood up and pointed toward a nearby table.

"Time to go," said Nay. "Follow me, Lef."

"Fu — fu — fuck no," said the drunken Lefter. "I wa — wa — want a piece — piece — piece 'o them fuck'em Tu — Tu — Turks." Then he slumped to the floor and passed out.

Nay and Mighty Joe got Lefter on his feet. "Wait here, Charlie," said Nay, "we'll be back after we take Lefter back to his cot."

Nissing nodded yes then leaned forward, put his head on the table and passed out.

CHAPTER TWENTY

Lefter slept the remainder of the day. He woke up after dark with a terrible headache. He bummed an aspirin tablet from Newbie. The newbie was still complaining about the sleeping bag switch.

"Thanks for the fucking APC," said Lefter.

Even with a headache and upset stomach, Lefter couldn't shut down his bizarre sense of humor. "Were you over at the EM Club this afternoon?"

"No, why?" asked Newbie.

"I saw that big, black, mean-looking fucker over there this afternoon," said Lefter. "He was arm wrestling anybody in the house for beers. Nobody could beat the big fucker. Think he might have broke one guy's arm."

"Maybe I'll go over there later and see if he's still there," said Newbie hesitantly. Then he added, "I ship out tomorrow morning though."

"Where the fuck you headed?" asked Lefter.

"Twenty-fifth Division."

"Fucking tough outfit. Well, good luck," said Lefter as he decided not to pick on the newbie anymore.

Lefter lay around on his cot napping and finally went to sleep for the night. The next morning he was awake but still on his cot staring at the ceiling when Jolcomb came up to him and said, "How's your head, Lef?"

"Good," said Lefter. "Getting in some fucking thinking time. I been lying here trying to figure out why them fucking Kamikaze pilots wore helmets."

"Whaaaat?" said Jolcomb with a raised brow.

"Why did them Kamikaze pilots wear helmets?" asked Lefter indignantly.

"Who gives a shit!" replied Jolcomb.

"Well," said Lefter, "a man's gotta think of something when he's just fucking off."

"You got a weird mind, Lef."

"Hey, Jolc, did I ever tell you about this fucking weird woman that came up to me back in the States and complained about the suede jacket I was wearing?"

"No, why did she do that?"

Lefter looked real serious as he said, "She pointed at my suede jacket and said, 'Don't you know a cow was murdered for that jacket?'"

"No shit, she really said that?" asked Jolcomb skeptically.

"Yeah, no shit."

Now Jolcomb was losing his skepticism, "What did you do?"

"Well, I was just fucking stunned," said Lefter, "so I just said, 'Huh?'"

"Go on," said Jolcomb.

"So she said again, 'don't you know a cow was murdered for that jacket?' So I gave her a real mean fucking look and said, 'I didn't know there were any fucking witnesses. Now I'll have to kill you also.'"

Jolcomb looked surprised. Lefter wasn't laughing. He wasn't even smiling. "You're screwing with my mind, Lefter."

Lefter smiled and said, "I wouldn't do that, Jolc, you're a fucking good buddy. Let's go have a fucking beer 'ol buddy."

"Naw, skip me today," said Jolcomb. "We gotta go build back the detachment tomorrow."

"No shit?" said Lefter.

"Yeah," said Jolcomb, "I guess you been too busy drinking beer and sleeping off hangovers to get the word."

"Got that fucking right," said Lefter.

Lefter was at the EM Club door long before it opened up. In fact, he was there waiting when Mighty Joe showed up at about fifteen minutes before opening time. Mighty Joe looked shocked and confused. He couldn't remember the last time that he had not been the first one in line when they unlocked the door for business.

"How's it feel to be the second fucking one in line, candy ass?" asked Lefter.

"Weird," answered Mighty Joe, "and why did you call me candy ass?"

Lefter ignored his question and said, "Tell you what, candy ass, I'll switch places in this fucking line with you if you buy the first three rounds."

"Hell no," replied Mighty Joe.

Lefter just turned around and faced the locked door of the EM Club.

In a few minutes, others started to arrive and stand in the line. Lefter continued to ignore Mighty Joe behind him in line. With just a couple of minutes before the scheduling opening of the door, Mighty Joe tapped Lefter on the shoulder and said, "OK, you win this one, let me in front of you."

"Good fucking decision," answered Lefter and stepped aside.

Now at the head of the line, Mighty Joe's confidence returned and he said to Lefter, "You took advantage of me this time but now I'm gonna be after your ass."

Anger crossed Lefter's face as he reached out and grabbed Mighty Joe by the shirt and shoved him hard against the door. Holding him firmly against the door Lefter said, "Don't you threaten me, you fucking candy ass hustler. I'll cut off your fucking balls and throw 'em in a kimchi barrel."

"Easy," said Mighty Joe, "it wasn't meant as a threat. I apologize."

Lefter turned loose of Mighty Joe's shirt and said, "Sorry, I seem to be real fucking edgy nowadays."

Lefter proceeded to get so drunk that he again had to be helped back to his cot. He awakened the next morning with Jolcomb shaking his feet. Lefter had the usual headache and sick-feeling stomach. "Rise and shine, Lef, we're heading north at nine. You've got time for a shower and breakfast if you hurry."

"Good fucking deal," said Lefter as he jerked his feet up in a fetal position, turned over on his side and closed his eyes. He lay there asking himself why he was being such an asshole lately. He decided that the stay in Korea must have been getting to him. He resolved to try and be more civil and quit the wise guy stuff.

"OK, buddy, thanks for waking me," said Lefter as he got up and headed for the shower. The warm water pounding on him helped improve his disposition but the headache and sick stomach remained. He toweled off and dressed. Newbie was already gone so he couldn't borrow an APC from him. Thinking that some food might help him feel better, he headed for the mess hall.

Jolcomb, Hillman and Jobby got up and left soon after he sat down at their table "See you out by the motor pool at nine," said Jolcomb as they departed. Lefter sensed that they were avoiding him. He didn't know that they had discussed his recent behavior and labeled him as a "loose cannon."

Lefter ate breakfast and felt better for a while, then threw up while walking back to the 303 CRB headquarters. Campbell met him at the entrance to the 303 CRB Compound and said, "Wait here, Lef, they are going to pick us up on the way out."

"What the fuck is going on?" asked Lefter.

"Frankly," said Campbell, "we're trying to avoid any contact with Major Soss."

"I suppose the fucker's still hot under the collar," said Lefter with a little laugh.

"Hot! Hell," said Campbell, "he'd burn us at a stake in the Battalion Square if he got the chance. We're not giving him the chance, got it!"

Lefter felt an instant anger but controlled himself and replied, "Got it, Sarg."

Engines started over in the motor pool area and detachment convoy pulled out and drove through the 303 Compound. Jolcomb was driving the deuce-and-a-half that was loaded with their salvaged gear and also new radio equipment and a new tent. The other four guys had done all the prep work the previous day while making an excuse that Lefter was ill with a fever.

Just as the big truck reached Lefter and Campbell, Major Soss came out of the headquarters and yelled, "HOLD IT RIGHT THERE!"

Lefter was instantly furious. "I'm going to kill that f—" Thump! Lefter never got to finish the f word. Campbell hit him hard in the stomach causing him to bend over, gag and start throwing up. Campbell opened the door and shoved the gagging Lefter up into the cab of the big truck. "Get him the hell out of here," he said to Jolcomb.

Jolcomb drove off while Major Soss yelled, "STOP RIGHT NOW!"

The other two vehicles stopped and the red-faced Major Soss stomped up to Campbell and said, "I ordered you to stop and you let that truck keep going. I'm going to..."

Campbell interrupted the major and said, "I thought you were talking to me, sir. The big truck is hurrying back to set up the detachment for your inspection, sir."

Major Soss calmed down, his face formed a smug look and he said, "Good plan, Sergeant, carry on."

"Yes, sir," said Campbell and saluted. The major saluted briskly, spun around and strutted back to the headquarters.

Jobby, who was listening from the driver's seat of the three-quarter ton truck said, "You're one quick thinking Jose, Camp."

"Years of experience in dealing with assholes," said Campbell. He climbed in beside Jobby and said, "Let's get the hell out of here."

As they drove north, Jobby said to Campbell, "What about Lefter?"

"He's grieving over the loss of Mewman," replied Campbell. "I had a talk with a doctor down at I-Corps and he gave me this sheet explaining the stages of grief." Campbell took a paper from his fatigue pocket, unfolded it and read, *"the stages of grief are as follows: Denial and Shock, Anger,*

Bargaining, Guilt and Depression, Acceptance and Hope for the Future. He said it usually takes a year or two to go through all these stages."

"We don't have a year or two to deal with this, Sarg," said Jobby.

"Got that right," said Campbell. "The doc says to be compassionate and understanding. It sounds backwards but the doc said to keep him talking about it."

"OK," said Jobby.

Jolcomb was not having an enjoyable ride north with Lefter. It seemed to Jolcomb that Lefter had complained about everything he could possibly think of. He seemed to be angry with everyone and everything. In addition to his constant complaining and angry outbursts, he held his head out the window several times and threw up. It smelled like a kimchi barrel in the cab of the truck.

"Phew," said Jolcomb, "have you been eating kimchi?"

"What the fuck's it to you!" said Lefter.

Jolcomb didn't respond. Intuitively he knew it was best not to argue with Lefter who just seemed to be asking for a fight.

The detachment site was a big mess. All the tents had been slashed, probably with bayonets. The gear they had left behind was scattered throughout the area.

"Pick up anything we can use," said Campbell. "We're moving a couple of hundred yards westerly."

"What the fuck for?" challenged Lefter.

Campbell raised an eyebrow, "Because the gooks have got the coordinates on this location and we're sitting ducks if we rebuild here."

Jolcomb, Jobby and Hillman nodded agreement.

"You're a bright guy, Lef," said Campbell. "You should know that."

"Don't much give a fuck. Let 'em come. I'd like to rip the heart out of a couple of them fucking gooks."

"I just had a terrible thought," said Campbell, "the gooks might have bobby trapped this location. Don't touch any of this stuff until we can get the area cleared."

The DACs had removed themselves from the three-quarter ton truck and stood around smoking and chatting in their native languages.

"We don't know shit about how to clear an area of bobby traps," protested Hillman.

"Got that right," said Campbell. "Time to call in another chit."

"What do you mean by that?" asked Hillman.

STAY SAFE, BUDDY

"Never mind," said Campbell, "just go on over there a couple of hundred yards and find some tent sites. I'll be back in an hour or so." Campbell took the jeep and drove off.

While waiting for Campbell to return, they took the vehicles westerly about two hundred yards. Jolcomb, Jobby and Hillman were still standing around scratching their heads and had not accomplished anything when Campbell returned.

"Where's Lefter?" asked Campbell.

"In the big truck sleeping," said Jolcomb.

"Good, let him be," said Campbell.

The clanging of a tank and the sound of its powerful engines were heard coming up the road. The tank had a bulldozer blade on its front. In a few minutes, it drove up into the new ASA area. A Marine Sergeant popped his head out of the tank, "Is this the area you want leveled out?"

"Sure is," replied Campbell.

"OK, stand back," said the Marine as he disappeared down into the bowels of the tank.

"You're amazing," said Jolcomb to Campbell. The others nodded agreement. They were all delighted to have Campbell as their leader.

Within an hour, the site was cleared and two tent sites leveled off. The Marine Sergeant popped up in the tank hatch and said, "How's that?"

"Great," said Campbell. He took a bottle of whiskey from his pack, climbed up on the tank and handed it to the Marine Sergeant. They exchanged a few words, then the Marine waved, disappeared down the hatch and the tank rumbled off down the road.

All of them except Lefter worked to erect a new squad tent on one of the sites. They only had one new tent. The other squad tent would have to be one from the old site. They could repair the rips with tent repair kits. But first the old site had to be safe to enter.

A jeep drove up and stopped by their new tent. The Marine Sergeant who had been in the tank was in the passenger seat. The sergeant said to Campbell, "Got those two guys from Engineers I was telling you about. They want you to be at the old site with them while they search for mines and bobby traps."

"OK," said Campbell, "I'll meet you over there in a couple of minutes." Turning to Jolcomb, Jobby and Hillman, he said, "This new tent is for the DACs, help them move in."

Another hour and two bottles of whiskey combined to result in a "clean" pronouncement of the old site by the two guys from the Engineers. They found no mines or booby traps, but Campbell felt it was well worth the whiskey.

They completed erected one of the old tents on the new site before dark. They also salvaged the cots and many other items. Oddly, the GI stoves were missing from the old site. The Chinese must have carried the stoves back north with them as they retreated.

Campbell ran a new communication wire to the splice box at the old site and tested the continuity with a field phone. He was able to establish communication with the 303 CRB headquarters. He deliberately said over the land-line that the detachment has been rebuilt 500 yards west of the old location. If the gooks called in artillery on that location then he would know that they had tapped into their communication wire somewhere. Tomorrow, they would go up the hill and see about reestablishing the bunker operation.

Lefter was still in the truck asleep when everyone else went to bed in the tents. He woke slowly and didn't know where he was until his eyes, and finally focused on the steering wheel of the truck. He raised up and looked out. The moon provided enough light that he could clearly see the two tents and the other vehicles. He looked at his watch. It was nearly 0300 hours.

"Oh shit." Lefter's heart jumped and his pulse raced. A Korean soldier came creeping out of one of the tents. He had a pair of boots in each hand. Lefter felt around slowly until he located his carbine. Then he eased a round into the chamber. He slowly pointed the carbine out through the open window of the truck and yelled, "HALT!"

The intruder started to run and Lefter pulled the trigger and sprayed the dirt with a short burst from the carbine. The intruder stopped immediately, dropped the boots and put his hands in the air. Campbell and the others came running out of the tent with their weapons.

"It's a fucking gook," yelled Lefter.

Campbell hit the intruder in the back of the head with his forty-five pistol. The intruder dropped to his knees. Campbell hit him again and he slumped over on his face.

Lefter got out of the truck, ran over and kicked the intruder in the face twice. "Fucking gook, fucking gook," he yelled. "I hope we killed the fucking gook."

"Easy, buddy," said Jolcomb, "he's out like a light."

The DACs watched from their tent in horror. They didn't like Lefter's behavior. It was scaring them.

"Throw him in the back of the three-quarter ton," said Campbell, "then take him down the road to the MP checkpoint and give him to them."

Lefter, Jolcomb, Jobby, and Hillman each grabbed a leg and arm, then carried him to the truck and threw him over the tailgate. Hillman drove and the other three rode in the back with the intruder.

Each time the intruder would start to gain consciousness, one of them would hit him in the face with their fist. Before they reached the MP checkpoint, the intruder had been hit a dozen times or more. At the CP they dropped the tailgate and kicked the bleeding intruder out onto the road.

"We caught this fucking gook in the tent stealing boots from us," said Lefter to the nearest MP.

"Piss, it looks like you beat the crap out of him," said the MP. "I better call a medic. Wait here," ordered the MP.

"Fuck no," said Lefter, "we're going back to bed. You know where to find us if you end up needing some official statement or some fucking thing."

They got back in their truck, turned around and returned to the new detachment base camp.

Campbell woke them all up before daylight the next morning. Today they would all go inspect the bunker; all that is except Lefter. Campbell wanted to give him a lot of thinking time. Hopefully he would think it all through, accept Mewman's death and get on with his life, and duties in the ASA.

Rather than try to set up a cot in the wee hours, Lefter had just gone back to sleep in the cab of the big truck. He was still sleeping when the others left for the bunker at 0900 hours. Campbell let him sleep but left a note under the windshield wiper instructing him to stay there all next day and protect the compound and the DACs.

Lefter woke up wet with sweat. The sun was bearing down on the truck and it was near one hundred degrees in the cab. At first, he didn't know where he was. His mind flashed to the bunker and quickly rejected that location. His eyes swept around and his brain finally registered the cab of a big truck. Then recent events started slowly falling into place. He found a dirty towel on the dash of the truck and wiped the sweat from his face and neck. He saw the note under the windshield wiper: *"Lef, guard detachment area and the DACs until I return. We are inspecting bunker — Camp."*

"Fuck! They took off and left me here cooking in this fucking truck," he said out loud. He snatched the note from the windshield and looked for a pencil. He intended to write across the note in large capital letters, "FUCK YOU!" He couldn't find a pencil in the truck so he stormed into the tent with the intention of finding a pencil.

The tent was arranged just as the one at the previous location. They had set up Lefter's cot complete with sleeping bag and mosquito netting. His pack was sitting by the head of the cot. Suddenly he wasn't mad anymore. "How could I be such a fucking asshole," he said out loud. Then he sat down on the cot and began to cry.

He was having a flood of thoughts. *Why did Mewman have to die? If anyone had to die, it should have been me. Mewman was saving my sorry ass when he got hit.*

Gunfire erupted outside. "Oh shit," said Lefter as he jumped up and ran to get his carbine from the truck. Outside he realized the gunfire was not nearby. It was probably some Marines sighting in their rifles or just screwing off. He took his carbine from the truck and began walking guard duty around the detachment.

Each time he passed the DAC tent on his sentinel rounds he could hear them chatting. His nose told him they were cooking something. *It can't be kimchi*, he thought, *it don't smell like shit*. In fact, it smelled real good.

One of the DACs came out of the tent and said to Lefter, "Lew hunglee?"

"Yeah, I could eat something," responded Lefter.

The DAC pointed into the tent and bowed. "Thanks, but I have to stay out here," said Lefter with a sweeping motion around the area. "I'm on guard duty."

"Ah ha," said the DAC, "I bling it out hele." He disappeared into the tent and came back with a mess kit full of some kind of mixture.

It smelled great to Lefter. The DAC handed him a spoon and he tasted the food. "Umm, good, what is it called?"

The DAC just shrugged his shoulders, smiled and said, "Chinese stuff. I am Mr. Chung," said the DAC as he offered a handshake.

Lefter shook his hand, bowed and said, "I know your name. We worked together before. My name is Lefter, Private Lefter."

"I know," said the smiling DAC. "Why lew not been flinlee wiff DACs?"

Lefter didn't have a good answer. He certainly couldn't tell him the truth. He was afraid he might have to shoot them if overrun by the enemy. Lefter just shrugged his shoulders, smiled and said, "Thanks for the food, it's delicious."

"Lew welcome," said the DAC and bowed.

Lefter bowed and said, "I better get back to walking guard."

"Lokay," said the DAC and went back inside the tent.

As Lefter returned to walking guard around the detachment area, he thought about Mr. Chung. He had been on bunker duty with Mr. Chung several times, but they had never introduced themselves. Maybe that was the correct thing to do though. Perhaps he would not feel saddened about the death of Mr. Fong and Mr. Lu if he had not socialized with them in the bunker. "Damn it," he said out loud, "now I've screwed up and been friendly with another of the DACs."

Lefter continued to walk guard until Campbell and the other returned in late afternoon. He was dying to have a beer and hoped the Marines would be handing them out with the evening meal at battalion headquarters.

"We stopped by battalion," said Campbell, "they're not set up to serve any meals yet."

"Oh fuck," said Lefter, "back to them fucking C-rations."

"Got that right," said Campbell.

"Thanks for setting up my cot," said Lefter.

"Thank Jolcomb," said Campbell as he pointed to Jolcomb, "he did it."

"Thanks, Jolc," said Lefter. "I'm really fucked up."

"No problem, Lef," said Jolcomb, "you'd do it for me."

They warmed some C-rations on sterno stoves and ate it from the can. Lefter ate a can of beanie weenies. He opened the bottom of the can. He had learned through experience that most of the weenies were at the bottom of the can. He always ate the weenies first and sometimes just discarded the beans. Tonight he ate the entire contents of the can and it tasted good. He thought of Mewman who refused to eat beans because he didn't want to take a chance on farting while on night patrol and therefore giving away his position to the enemy. Lefter smiled and his eyes got moist.

Lefter had been doing more drinking than eating for the last several days. He had a strong craving for a beer but he would settle for some whiskey. "Anybody got a fucking bottle?" he asked the guys sitting on their cots.

Each man responded in near unison, "No, all out."

"Fuck," said Lefter. "I need a fucking drink."

Nobody responded so Lefter said, "OK, we can't drink so let's have a friendly fucking game of poker."

None of them wanted to play poker but Lefter kept at them until finally Jolcomb, Hillman and Jobby gave in and sat down at the table in the center of the tent. Campbell declined by claiming he had paperwork to do.

Lefter seemed to have lost his ability to analyze and make logical decisions in the poker game. In a nutshell, he played stupid poker. He lost every hand. Finally, holding two sevens, he pushed all his money into the center of the table and said, "Gimme three." Amazingly, he drew three kings. Bullying the others into letting him bet 'short,' he won back most of the money he had lost in previous hands.

"That's it for me," said Jolcomb as he stood up.

"I'm out too," said Hillman as he stood up.

"Yeah, I'm tired," said Jobby.

"What's the matter with you fuckers?" asked Lefter. "It's early yet."

None of the three replied as they retreated to their cots. Lefter stood up and stomped out of the tent. In a few minutes, he came back into the tent carrying a bottle of whiskey.

"TIME FOR A FUCKING PARTY," yelled Lefter as he held the bottle up toward the others.

"No partying tonight," said Campbell. "Tomorrow is a duty day and I don't want anymore hangovers."

"Fuck you," said Lefter as he sat down at the table.

"Lefter, this is an order, do not drink tonight. OK?" said Campbell.

"Fuck you," said Lefter.

Campbell didn't respond. He went outside the tent, got in his jeep and drove away. Jolcomb, Jobby and Hillman ignored Lefter.

Lefter opened the bottle, took a large swallow of the whiskey and shivered. "Fuck you all, I'll just drink by myself."

Ten minutes later Campbell drove back into the detachment area. He was followed by another jeep occupied by two military policemen.

Campbell looked inside the tent, turned to the MPs and said, "He's sitting at the table."

The MPs entered the tent, went immediately to Lefter and one MP said, "You are under arrest."

"Fuck you, Copper," said Lefter and took a drink from the whiskey bottle.

"Take your hands off the bottle and put them behind your back," ordered the other MP.

"Fuck you," said Lefter as he started raise the bottle.

One MP grabbed the hand with the bottle and the other MP grabbed the other arm and twisted it behind Lefter's back.

"Ouch, OK, OK," said Lefter and didn't resist.

The MPs handcuffed Lefter, put him in their jeep and drove away.

"Where are they taking him?" asked Jolcomb.

"To have a psychological evaluation," answered Campbell. "He will probably be evaluated by a medic to start with. If the medic agrees with what

I told the MPs, they'll send him to the psych ward at the big hospital near Seoul."

"It's nice of you to do that rather than have him court-martialed," said Jolcomb.

"He's a good man, just all screwed up because of what happened to him, Mewman and the DACs when the Chinese overran their position."

"Is he all through in our detachment?" asked Jobby.

"That depends on how he responds to treatment," said Campbell. "I'll try to get him back with us if he recovers."

"I sure as hell hope he makes it," said Hillman. "Ordinarily, he's a real good man."

As Lefter was being driven to the medical facility for evaluation, he began to get on the nerves of the MPs with his filthy mouth and constant chatter.

"What the fuck do you guys think you're doing?"

"Shut up!" said an MP.

"I didn't do anything wrong."

"Just shut up," said the MP.

Again ignoring the MP order, Lefter said, "What did that fucking Campbell tell you anyway?"

"Shut up!" ordered an MP again.

Still ignoring the order to shut up, Lefter said, "Where the fuck are we going anyway?"

"Let me put this in your language, buddy," said the MP. "Shut the fuck up and don't open your fucking filthy mouth again or I'll shut it for you." The MP shook his nightstick at Lefter and said loudly, "Understand, asshole?"

"Fuck you," said Lefter.

The MP didn't hesitate. He hit Lefter at the base of his skull with his nightstick. Lefter went limp.

"Why don't some of them learn to shut up when they're told to?" said one MP.

"Well," said the other MP in a southern accent, "used to be an old boy back home named Will Rogers. He said, 'some folks learn by reading and listening, others by observation, but a lot of 'em just gotta piss on the electric fence for themselves.'"

The other MP laughed and said, "That's a good explanation."

Lefter was just getting conscious as they carried him upright into the medic station and sat him down in a chair in front of the admittance area.

"What happened to this guy?" asked the admittance clerk.

"His first sergeant wants him to have a psychological evaluation. Here's the paper request."

"I heard that," said Lefter loudly, "I don't need no fucking psychological evaluation. I'm not nuts. What the fuck is the matter with all of you? You're all a bunch of fucking jerks."

Lefter started pointing his finger at each of the men and saying, "Fuck you, fuck him, fuck him." Then he pointed to an army doctor sitting at a nearby desk and said, "Oh yeah, fuck that asshole over there too." Proud of himself Lefter let out a big belly laugh.

"I've heard enough," said the army doctor, "transport him to the hospital in Seoul for a full psychological evaluation."

The doctor checked off a couple of items on a sheet of paper, signed it and handed it to the MP.

"OK, Doc, we'll get him there."

Meanwhile, Lefter kept on running off at the mouth with near-constant jabber. As they led him back outside the MP showed Lefter his nightstick and said, "I'm not going to put up with your diarrhea of the mouth all the way to Seoul."

Lefter finally got the message and shut up.

CHAPTER TWENTY-ONE

As the jeep bounced along the dusty road toward Seoul, Lefter began to cry. He sobbed continuously until they delivered him to the admittance area of the hospital. Then he began making the same comments as before.

"I'm not nuts. You fuckers are the nutty ones. Fuck you all." Then he began yelling and pointing around, "FUCK YOU. FUCK YOU. FUCK ALL OF YOU."

Lefter was still yelling obscenities while two orderlies led him away to the psychological treatment ward.

"Take this pill right now," said the medic in a stern voice.

"What the fuck for?" replied Lefter.

"Because if you don't, we will hold you down while I shove the same sedative in your ass with a big hypodermic needle. What's your choice, buddy?"

Lefter grabbed the pill and glass of water, then swallowed the pill. "Now what the fuck are you going to force on me?" asked Lefter.

"Not a thing," said the medic. "Take him to Room 8 and lock him down," said the medic to the orderlies.

"You assholes, you're locking me up. Fuck you, I didn't do anything."

As the orderlies led Lefter to his room, he was already getting drowsy. In the room he lay down on the bed and fell asleep almost instantly.

An orderly shook Lefter by the feet, "Hey, buddy, time for breakfast, here's a food tray for you." He pointed to a tray sitting on a small table. Then he left the room.

Still groggy, Lefter yawned and looked around the small room. He walked to the door and tried turning the knob. The door was locked. "Fuck!" He went back to the table, sat down and began to eat the breakfast items on the tray. "Fuck, this is good chow," he said out loud. He ate all the food on the tray then noticed for the first time that he had been sleeping on an actual bed. He lay back down on the bed and felt its comfort. "This is right comforting," he said trying to mimic Jolcomb's southern accent. Just as he was about to doze off, the door opened and an orderly came in and said, "Are you ready to meet the doctor?"

"What the fuck for?" replied Lefter.

"Guess not," said the orderly as he left and closed the door.

"What the fuck was that all about?" Lefter asked himself.

Lefter tried the door several times before he became convinced it was locked. Finally, he looked around the room frantically. He had to urinate. Behind a screen, in one corner of the room, he found a toilet bowl and sink. "Holy crap, this place is modern," he said out loud.

Shortly after noon, the door opened and the orderly came in with a lunch tray. "How do you like the food here?" said the orderly as he set down the lunch tray and picked up the breakfast tray.

"Breakfast was real fucking good," replied Lefter. "I'm getting kind of fucking claustrophobic being locked in this room though."

"From what I hear you're lucky you're not in the brig," said the orderly.

"Where the fuck would you hear that?" asked Lefter. "Seems to me that I am in the fucking brig. I'm locked in this room."

"After lunch you can see the doctor if you promise to behave," said the orderly.

"What the fuck do you mean by behave?" asked Lefter.

"First," said the orderly, "clean up your language. Second, be honest with the doctor. Third, if you can't do the first two then just eat your lunch and enjoy this room cause it's going to be your home until you shape up."

"Fuck you," said Lefter.

"Have a nice lunch," said the orderly as he went out and closed the door.

There was nothing to do in the room; no magazines, no radio, no cards, nothing. It was getting boring. Other than a couple of short naps, there was nothing to do but try to think of something pleasant. He thought about the R&R in Japan and smiled. Then tears would form as his brain switched to the memory of Mewman, the DACs and himself fleeing from the Chinese assault.

Finally he thought about the Mumblejon beer drinking sessions and smiled. Then more tears would form, as the last scene with Mewman would again unfold in his mind. He would think of his wife back home and smile. Then tears. Smiles to tears, back and forth, it continued like that until the orderly came back hours later with a dinner tray.

"How you doing, buddy?" ask the orderly.

"Getting real fucking bored," replied Lefter.

"Well, brace yourself, it could get worse," said the orderly.

"What the fuck do you mean, it could get worse?" asked Lefter.

"Cooperation or lonely meditation, your choice," said the orderly.

"Fuck! Cooperate on what?" asked Lefter in frustration.

"I'll say it once more, listen carefully," said the orderly. "First, clean up your language. Second, be honest with the doctor. Third, if you can't do the first two then just eat your lunch and enjoy this room cause it's going to be your home until you shape up."

"So when do I get to see the fu...the doctor?" asked Lefter.

"Not tonight, doctor don't work nights," said the orderly with a smile.

"Why the fu...why not?" asked Lefter. "Everybody else in this fu...this kimchi bowl does."

"Doctor is afraid of the dark," said the orderly with a big laugh.

Lefter laughed back.

"I can get you an appointment right after breakfast tomorrow if you want," said the orderly.

"OK," said Lefter. "What is your name?"

"Tell you later," said the orderly. "Gotta go, see you tomorrow."

"OK," said Lefter.

Lefter finished his dinner, reclined on the bed and started the same seesaw of thoughts and emotions. Smiles and laughing then tears and sobs.

Over, and over, and over, the happy and sad thoughts and emotions continued until he finally fell asleep.

"AheeeeeeEEE!" yelled Lefter as he sat up in bed and started frantically grabbing around the head of the bed looking for his carbine. An eerie sliver of light beamed through a small high window and dimly lit the room. At first his mind thought it was light from a flares outside the bunker. He thought the bunker was being overrun and he was frantic because he couldn't find his carbine that was supposed to be leaning against the head of his bunk. His thoughts raced, *Something is really screwed up here. This doesn't smell like my bunker. Where the hell am I? Am I in a Chinese prison camp? Where the hell am I?* He began to tremble all over his body. He put his head in his hands and slowly the present came into focus. Then he whispered, "I'm in the hospital. Lefter, you dumb shit, you're in the hospital."

After he used the toilet, and returned to the bed, the trembling had subsided, and he was getting cold. The bed was wet with sweat and uncomfortable but he finally calmed down and went back to sleep. Lefter awoke several times before dawn. Finally he dressed and sat on the side of his bed until dawn started showing through the high window. The light was beautiful and he wished he could be outside smelling the fresh, crisp, early morning air. Time passed slowly as he awaited the arrival of the orderly and breakfast. He kept pushing thoughts of the past out of his head and concentrating on the light coming in the window. He yearned to be outside in this Land of the Morning Calm. Early morning was the only time of day that Lefter liked being in Korea.

Finally, Lefter heard the door open and in walked the orderly with two breakfast trays.

"Mind if I have breakfast with you?" asked the orderly.

"OK with me," answered Lefter. "It's pretty fu…it's pretty boring in here with nothing to do but pick my nose and think."

The orderly laughed and handed Lefter one of the trays. They sat down across from each other at the small table in the center of the room. Both began eating and didn't speak for a few minutes.

Finally, Lefter said, "You said I could meet the doctor today, right?"

"Sure did," said the orderly as he smiled and held out his right hand. "I'm Doctor John Teele, glad to meet you John Lefter."

"Well, I'll be fu…I'm really surprised," said Lefter.

"Don't get too impressed," said the orderly. "With ten years of higher education, almost anyone can do what I do."

"Treating psychos, right?" replied Lefter.

"Nope, just helping guys find their way out of a desperate situation," said Teele. "You can call me Doc. What do you want me to call you?"

"OK, Doc," said Lefter, "some call me Lefter and a few buddies call me Lef." Then he smiled and said, "Nowadays some of them are probably calling me shithead."

"Well, shit happens, we can't avoid that," said Doc.

"Where did you hear that expression, shit happens?" asked Lefter.

"It's a favorite expression of one of my outpatients," said Doc. "I started using it and now the hospital staff is starting to use the expression a lot too. It expresses a lot in just two words. Why do you ask?"

"I thought I was the originator of that fu…that statement," said Lefter. "I wrote it on a sign and hung it up in the supply tent when I was in I-Corps headquarters."

"Maybe this guy saw your sign," said Doc. "I think he is from that area."

"What's his name?" asked Lefter.

"Can't say," said Doc, "doctor and patient confidentially you know. But if you originated that statement you've got my vote to a medal for helping hold up morale."

"Oh yeah, thanks," said Lefter and laughed. "Any chance of getting out in this fresh morning air?"

"Good idea," said Doc. "Let's return these trays to the kitchen along the way." He picked up one of the trays, unlocked the door and held it open while Lefter walked out with the other tray.

After returning the trays to the kitchen, Doc led Lefter out into a central patio area. The area had picnic tables with large umbrellas projecting from a holder in the center of the table. An ashtray in the center of the table reminded Lefter that he hadn't smoked since leaving the detachment. That amazed him since he usually smoked a pack or more per day. He hadn't even thought about smoking but now he was thinking of it.

"Got a smoke?" asked Lefter.

Doc pulled out a pack of cigarettes and handed it to Lefter.

"Good, this is my brand," said Lefter as he took out one of the Chesterfield cigarettes and searched his pockets for matches.

"Here," said Doc, as he handed Lefter a package of matches. "I don't smoke. The cigarettes and matches were in your pocket when they brought you in."

"Well, I'll be fu...I'm surprised," said Lefter. "Thanks, Doc."

"No problem," replied Doc, "now tell me, how long have you been in Korea and what have you been doing?"

Lefter lit up a cigarette, took a hard puff and inhaled deeply. "Well, Doc, I've been here since early January. Been on the MLR now for a couple of months."

"What do you do on the MLR?" asked Doc.

"Just sit in a fucking bunker; oh sorry, just sit in a bunker and worry."

"That's your job, to worry?" replied Doc.

"Well, not exactly," said Lefter, "but I'm not allowed to participate in combat."

"You're on the front line but you're not allowed to participate in combat, why not?" asked Doc.

"I can't say," replied Lefter, "it's all classified shit, ugh, I mean classified stuff."

"How close have you been to the enemy?" asked Doc.

Lefter puffed on his cigarette and his hands began to tremble. He stubbed out the cigarette in the ashtray on the table. "We got overrun and my buddy was killed," he blurted out, then buried his head in his hands and sobbed gently.

Doc reached across the table, laid his hand on Lefter's shoulder and said, "How did it happen?"

"He was saving my sorry ass life," said Lefter, "and he lost his life doing it." Now Lefter broke out crying loudly. He was embarrassed although there didn't appear to be anyone else in the patio with them.

Lefter cried for several minutes while Doc patted him on the shoulder occasionally. Finally, Lefter gained control, wiped his eyes and said, "Sorry for the outburst."

"Understandable," said Doc. "Well, we'll have to continue this conversation later, I've got a couple of appointments now. I'll meet you in the dining room for lunch, OK?"

"You mean I don't get locked up in my room again?" asked Lefter.

"Here," said Doc as he rose and handed the room key to Lefter. "You're free to roam around the hospital area anywhere there isn't a sign that says Quarantined Area, Restricted Area or Off Limits to Patients. See you at lunch."

"You're trusting me to stay here?" asked Lefter.

"Why not, where else would you go?" replied Doc with a laugh.

"Right," said Lefter as he laughed also. "I'm in a real big hurry to get back to my bunker and eat C-rations," he said sarcastically.

"See you at lunch," said Doc as he walked away.

Lefter looked at his watch. It was only nine o'clock. He had no idea of what to do with three hours before lunch. *Weird*, he thought as he walked into the building and started wandering down the hallways. *This building seemed to go on for blocks*. Large rooms off the main hallway had typical military names over the wide entrance doors. Ward B, Ward C, Ward D; and so on. He decided to go back to his room and take a nap but he couldn't find the room. Finally, he asked an orderly walking down the hallway.

"You say you have an individual room?" asked the orderly.

"Yeah," said Lefter.

"Gotta be Ward P, that way," said the orderly as he pointed ahead and scurried off.

Lefter finally found Ward P and entered through the big doors. He didn't remember coming out through big doors but there were rooms along each side of the Ward just inside the entrance. He looked at the key. It was engraved with R8. "There it is!" he said triumphantly as he spotted R8 on a room door.

He lay on the bed and started thinking about recent events. He was embarrassed by his behavior since the day on the MLR when the bunker was overrun. "What the hell happened to me?" he said as he shook his head in disgust. "My personality seems to have changed radically. Well, at least I'm getting some semblance of control over using the f word." He still had a strong almost overpowering urge to use the f word liberally. "Why?"

Lefter had a relaxing nap then walked out into the wide hallway of Ward P. The sign on a closed door across from his room said, *Do Not Disturb - Session in Progress*. Lefter walked over by the door, stopped and listened. Inside the room, he could hear men talking. He recognized one of the voices as that of Doc Teele. Then a familiar voice penetrated the wooden door and sent chills up the spine of Lefter. It was Major Soss. Immediately, his pulse raced and he felt his face flushing. Anger flared up in his chest and he had the urge to kick open the door and yell out, "Fuck you, Soss!"

Trembling, he quickly walked away from Ward P and headed for the patio. In the patio he sat down at a table and smoked a cigarette. After a few minutes, the trembling subsided and he began to think rationally again. "Holy crap, Lef, you damned near fucked up royally back there," he whispered. It was a shock to hear Major Soss' voice in that completely unexpected situation. Soss was the only person on earth that Lefter actually hated, and hated with a teeth-grinding passion.

Lefter walked slowly around the patio area, hands behind his back, head down and thinking about the present situation. After each stroll around the patio he would sit down at the table and smoke a cigarette. Finally, at 1145 hours he started walking slowly toward the dining room area. He stopped, turned around and started walking fast back toward Ward P.

He went over by the door across from his room. Voices were still coming from the room. He moved quickly across the hall and into his room. Pulse racing, he stood by the door and waited. In a few minutes, he heard the door across the hall open followed by voices in the hallway. He cracked open his door and peeked out. *Oh shit!* he thought. *It really is Asshole Soss.* Lefter waited until the hallway was completely quiet, then went out and walked slowly to the dining room.

Just as he entered the dining room Doc Teele called out, "Over here, Lef." Major Soss was sitting at the table with Doc Teele. *Oh crap, oh crap,* thought Lefter. *Keep your cool, keep your cool.*

Major Soss had a stunned look on his face but didn't say anything as Lefter approached the table. Lefter noticed that he was not wearing his shoulder clusters or any other officer identifications.

"Lefter, this is Soss. Soss, this is Lefter," said Doc Teele.

Lefter nodded. Soss nodded. Lefter didn't offer a salute. Neither man offered a handshake.

Doc Teele looked at the expression of the two men's faces and said, "Do you two know each other?"

Lefter nodded in the affirmative.

"He's an enlisted man in my command," said Soss. "I'm the major in charge of the battalion he belongs to."

"I may be *assigned* to your battalion but I don't *belong* to no fucking battalion," replied Lefter. "Nobody *owns* me!"

"Hang on guys, guess I forgot to mention that we don't use any rank stuff around the hospital, especially in Ward P. The Army has known for a couple of hundred years that rank can be a deterrent to any hospital treatment program, either physical or psychological."

Neither Lefter nor Major Soss responded.

"Our objective here is to heal," said Doc Teele. "We don't favor either officers or enlisted men for healing."

"Lefter is just a peon in my battalion," said Major Soss with a sneer. "He's a bunker rat whose job is to be the servant of a couple of other people."

Lefter flushed beet red but before he could say anything, Doc Teele said, "Don't say anything back, Lefter, it will only lead to more conflict."

Lefter kept his mouth shut but glared at Soss.

Doc Teele said, "You guys get your lunch trays and I'll meet you back here at the table in a few minutes. OK?"

Soss and Lefter nodded agreement and got up from the table. Doc walked out of the dining room as he said, "I'll be right back."

A few minutes later Doc walked up to the table and sat down. He was wearing bird colonel emblems on his shoulders. Soss stared at the silver bird emblems on his shoulders. Lefter felt amused and grinned at Doc Teele.

"I see you're both surprised that I have suddenly become a bird colonel."

Major Soss and Lefter nodded agreement.

"Our policy in this hospital is that the staff can assume any rank necessary to accelerate the healing process," said Doc with a smile. He looked directly at Soss and said, "Unfortunately, you don't know if I'm a real colonel or a pretend colonel. However, I assure you the policy has the full blessing of the Eight Army Commanding General — so don't test me. OK?"

Major Soss and Lefter nodded.

"OK, from now on, it's Soss, Lefter and Doc. That is how we address each other. OK?"

Neither Soss nor Lefter responded.

"OK, back to healing, as soon as I get my lunch tray that is," Doc said with a big smile.

Back at the table with his lunch tray, Doc said, "Where were you born, Soss? Do you have brothers and sisters? Are you married? Do you have a family of your own? In other words, tell me about your life outside the military. I don't want to hear anything about the military."

Soss picked at his food and stalled.

Lefter was thinking to himself, *That son-of-a-bitch wasn't born, he was hatched — the chicken shit asshole.*

Soss took a deep breath, looked at Lefter then at Doc and said, "OK. I was born in Iowa. I have no brothers or sisters. I'm not married, so I have no family of my own."

"OK, Lefter," said Doc, "it's your turn."

Lefter looked at Soss and Doc and then, after a long pause said, "I was born in Arkansas. I have no brothers or sisters. I am married but we do not yet have any children."

"Are your parents living?" asked Doc of Lefter.

Lefter sighed, "My mother died when I was five years old. My father is still alive."

"How about you, Soss, are your parents still alive?"

"No!" said Soss bluntly.

"OK," said Doc, "Let's eat and think for a few minutes."

Soss and Lefter remained silent while they finished eating their lunch. Then they sat quietly and awaited directions from Doc. While they were sitting at the table several people walked by and said with a smile, "Good afternoon, Colonel." Lefter took that to mean that Doc was getting a bit of a razz from the other hospital staff folks that he knew. *Or maybe he is a real colonel.*

"What say we retire to the patio for some more socializing?" said Doc.

Soss and Lefter followed Doc to the patio and all three sat down at one of the tables.

"OK if I smoke?" asked Lefter of Doc.

"Dirty habit but go ahead," replied Soss.

"I didn't ask you," shot back Lefter.

Soss glared but didn't reply.

"It's OK with me if it's OK with Soss," said Doc.

"OK," said Soss sharply.

"Now that you two know a few things about each other outside the military," said Doc, "I want you to ask each other a question. You go first, Soss."

"Oh what the hell for?" asked Soss indignantly.

Doc didn't say anything. He just pointed to the eagle emblems on his shoulders.

Lefter was thinking that Soss wouldn't remember a damn thing about what Lefter had said a few minutes ago.

"What caused your mother's death?" asked Soss.

Lefter was surprised. The bastard was listening. "She had a heart attack while recovering from pneumonia," answered Lefter.

"Your turn, Lefter," said Doc.

Lefter thought for a few seconds then said, "What about your parents' deaths?"

"They each died of pneumonia just a couple of months apart," replied Soss.

"Stay on the same subject and ask him a follow-up question," instructed Doc to Lefter.

Lefter didn't hesitate. He was already thinking of a follow-up question but would have never asked on his own. "How old were you at the time of your parents' deaths?" asked Lefter.

Soss paused then replied softly, "Five."

Lefter was stunned. He knew how difficult it was to grow up without the love of his mother. What would it have been like to grow up without either parent? Suddenly, he felt some compassion for Soss. Then he quickly thought, *What the hell is the matter with me? I know from personal experience that Soss is a number fucking one asshole.*

"Your turn, Soss," said Doc.

Soss didn't hesitate, "What happened to you after your mother died?"

Lefter opened up and told him that he and his dad lived with his dad's parents for a couple of years on a farm in Arkansas. "My grandmother took care of me while my father worked for the WPA during the late 1930s. I romped barefoot in the woods during the summer and enjoyed being a young boy in the country." Lefter caught himself and quit talking. He wasn't sure he wanted Soss to know about this part of his life.

"Interesting," said Doc. "What about your early childhood, Soss?"

STAY SAFE, BUDDY

The face of Soss took on a hardened look. His lips were tight. He took a deep breath, let it out slowly and said, "I, too, lived on a farm in my early youth, a farm for orphans. I didn't get to do any romping. From the day I arrived, which was just a few days after my parents died, I started milking cows and doing other farm chores. Other than going to school, it was all work and no play."

Lefter was confused. Although he didn't want to, he couldn't help it, at that moment he felt sorry for Soss. He blurted out a question to Soss, "When did you leave the orphan farm?"

"The farm was owned by a church," replied Soss. "A staff member there helped me get into a military boarding school in Minnesota."

"Then what?" asked Lefter.

"Pretty boring stuff," said Soss. "I was the poor kid at military school with little money so I had lots of time to study. Graduated top of my class and got an appointment to West Point. What about you, Lefter, as I recall you entered the Army from Washington state. When did you leave Arkansas?"

Lefter felt strange. He was starting to relax around Soss. He was beginning to see him as a human being. *Fascinating*, he thought, *that Soss could have two distinctly different personalities.* It hadn't dawned on Lefter yet that he was also displaying two distinctly different personalities. Musing the personality issue around in his mind, Lefter just stared out across the patio area.

Doc touched Soss on the wrist and said softly, "Ask him again."

"When did you leave Arkansas?" asked Soss again.

Lefter leaned back, breathed deeply and looked up into the clear blue sky. "The sky is so damn blue here. Early morning can be so peaceful and quiet." He paused and tears formed in his eyes. "Right now it's hard to believe that a lot of men are fighting and dying thirty-five miles north of here." Lefter put his elbows on the table, cupped his head in his hands and sobbed softly.

Soss reached over and squeezed Lefter's arm. "I understand," said Soss.

Lefter didn't respond but he felt a little comfort from hearing Soss make the comment. Maybe the man was a tiny bit human after all.

"Well, I've got to go do some work," said Doc as he stood up from the table. "You guys continue your discussion and I'll be back for a mid-afternoon coffee break." He turned and walked away.

Lefter had himself under control now. He wiped his eyes, looked at Soss and laughed softly.

"What the hell is so humorous?" asked Soss with a half grin.

"This quirk of fate. The whole damn thing here," replied Lefter. "You and I talking like equals."

"Yeah, it does feel strange, but it feels good also," replied Soss.

"Can I ask you a real personal question?" said Lefter.

"You can always ask. You may not get an answer, but you can always ask," said Soss.

"Why are you such an untrusting, aggressive hard ass?" said Lefter with a smile.

At first, Soss tensed up and his face showed surprise followed by an angry expression. Then, while Lefter stared at him, he slowly relaxed. He grinned and said to Lefter, "Can I bum a cigarette from you? Been trying to give up the damn things, but get an overwhelming urge every now and then."

"Sure," said Lefter as he tossed his pack of cigarettes and matches on the table. He wasn't about to light the match for Soss. He still didn't trust him, although he was beginning to understand him just a little.

Soss lit a cigarette, looked deep into Lefter's eyes and said, "If I tell you, will it be in the strictest confidence?"

Lefter was taken aback. He had never been asked by an officer to keep a confidence, except for the official duty to protect classified materials of course. This was personal. His mind flashed to a future Mumblejon session. Could he refrain from saying anything about meeting Soss at the hospital? Could he refrain from revealing anything he had learned about the background of Soss to any of his Army buddies? "Holy crap, you've really put me on the spot," said Lefter.

Soss just waited.

"OK," said Lefter in an uneasy voice, "you have my word that I won't tell anyone."

"I grew up as an orphan," said Soss. "Like you, I had no mother to nurture me but I also had no father to guide me. In the orphanage we were all fairly equal in social status but we were far from equal in other ways. Some of us got bullied, by both staff and other orphans. The farm orphanage just fed us, worked us and gave us some basic education. When I got into the military high school, it was a big adjustment. The other students were not from orphanages. Most were from nice middle class families and a few from the upper crust of society. I didn't fit in with any of them. It seemed to me that they had every advantage over me and I wouldn't be able to compete with them in any way. Is this boring you?"

"No, no," said Lefter. "I find it very interesting." In fact, Lefter was finding it similar to his own youth. He was also the poor boy in amongst others from mostly middle income and a few higher income families.

"Are you sure this isn't boring you?" asked Soss.

"No, no, like I said, I find it interesting," replied Lefter.

"Why do you find it interesting?" challenged Soss. He stared unblinking at Lefter and waited for a reply.

Lefter hesitated for a few seconds and nervously lit a cigarette. He offered a cigarette to Soss who declined with a shake of his head. Lefter gulped and said softly, "I have a somewhat similar background. I was from a very poor family."

"OK," said Soss, "as I said, it didn't seem that I would be able to compete with my fellow students in military high school. Then one day I went for a run on a trail along the shore of a lake. After running for a couple of miles I sat down on the bank and thought about my competitive situation, not only at school, but also in life itself. Then I made a decision that changed my life."

Lefter waited but Soss didn't continue speaking. He was just staring deep into Lefter's eyes. Lefter had not yet seen this penetrating look on the face of Soss. Of course, until now, he hadn't really looked at Soss for long because he had detested the man. Soss continued to stare intently at Lefter. Feeling uncomfortable, Lefter said, "Well, what the fu…I mean what did you decide?"

"I decided to be successful," answered Soss.

"That's it! That's all!" replied Lefter.

Soss ignored Lefter's remarks. "Having decided to be successful, I then had only one thing more to figure out." Again, Soss paused and stared deep into Lefter's eyes. "Think I will have that cigarette now if you don't mind."

Lefter tossed the pack of cigarettes and matches on the table. Soss lit one and took a deep drag, looked at the cigarette and said, "I never smoked or drank alcohol until a couple of years ago. It was not in my plan for success."

Lefter was getting annoyed with all the dramatic pauses. "So what the fu…what was the one thing more that you had to figure out?" asked Lefter.

"How!" replied Soss, "*how* to be successful. It all fell into place for me. I felt that I'd discovered the key to a wonderful life. Just make two decisions, decide to be successful and then decide how to do it."

"What did you decide to do in order to become successful?" asked Lefter who was now intently interested.

"It didn't come to me right away," replied Soss.

Oh crap, he's going to drag this out all afternoon, thought Lefter but didn't say anything out loud. Lefter was eager to hear the "how" part of his formula for success.

"Every time I had some spare time I would go out and run along that trail by the lake and think about success. My desire to be successful was overwhelming and I couldn't seem to concentrate on figuring out *how* to be successful. I'd stop running, sit down and think about it, but nothing came to mind about *how* to be successful. Frustrated, I'd get up and run some more. Is this getting boring to you?"

"No, no," said Lefter.

Just then, Doc Teele appeared. "How about a coffee break?" asked Doc.

Terrible timing, thought Lefter but didn't say anything. They went to the dining room, drank several cups of coffee and discussed sports back home. It was obvious that Doc was a big sports fan. He said that the great Boston Red Sox baseball star, Ted Williams, was a Marine fighter pilot in World War II and the Korean War. Lefter and Soss both knew that Williams was a great baseball star but didn't know that he had been in both World War II and the Korean War. Doc knew all about what was happening in professional sports back home and a lot about the college sports programs. He was an encyclopedia of sports trivia. Finally, Doc said, "Let's call it a day and get together again tomorrow morning for breakfast, OK?"

Lefter wanted to say, *No fucking way, I want to hear the rest of Soss' story right now*. However, he restrained himself and nodded agreement.

"See you tomorrow morning then," said Doc.

"OK," said Soss.

"OK," said Lefter.

They each went their own way.

Lefter went back to his room, lay on the bed and thought about the long conversation with Soss. Soss was becoming human to him and he wasn't sure he liked that. He would prefer to think of Soss as a subhuman species of some sort. However, it was becoming clear to Lefter that Soss was no dummy. "He may be nuts but he's definitely not stupid," Lefter said to himself.

CHAPTER TWENTY-TWO

"I think it is beginning to have an effect," said Doc Teele. "If the Patient to Patient Program works, we will have reduced the grieving recovery period by an astounding multiplier."

Doc Teele was sitting at the table in the hospital's main conference room. A dozen medical doctors from all branches of the military were seated at the table.

"Doctor Teele," said one of those at the table, "how much compression of the grieving period do you think is possible?"

"I don't know," said Doc Teele. "I think it depends on each individual patient, but I am betting my position as head physician of the psychiatric unit that it is substantial."

Another doctor raised his hand and said, "In this initial test case, which you are calling 'Lefter and Soss,' what is your treatment plan?"

"The Patient to Patient Program, call it PAPA Program, got under way as soon as Lefter and Soss were left alone to talk about their situation on equal terms," said Doc Teele. "Another day of them talking together may change their view of each other dramatically. In other words, they are in the process of humanizing each other."

"Do they know you are taping some of their private conversations?" asked another doctor.

"No, and it is not important that they do," said Doc Teele. "We eavesdrop on them only to monitor progress and develop an effective treatment plan."

"Even if you are successful with this test case," said another doctor, "isn't is too individualized to be cost effective for treating combat shock generally?"

"It takes somewhere between five and nine months for a man entering the military to be trained and enter a combat area," said Doc Teele. "Even then, they are inexperienced 'newbies' as they are called by the combat veterans. We can afford to give a lot of individual attention to getting an experienced and physically able combat man back in action. If it works, we will find a way to staff it appropriately."

"Thank you for the report, Dr. Teele," said the general sitting at the head of the table. "As Commander of the Eighth Army in Korea, I am eager to see the final results of your experiment. I hope you find a way to quickly treat combat shock and return the men to their front line assignments."

"Thank you, sir," said Doc Teele.

"Have a good day," said the general as he rose and left the room.

Back in his room at Ward P, Lefter tried to take a nap but he couldn't fall asleep. He kept thinking about the conversation with Soss. It was all so confusing. It seemed unreal. On the one hand, he absolutely detested Soss. On the other hand, he was now seeing him as a human being. *How could this be? What was Soss thinking about me now?* He felt that Soss was out to get him in any way possible and was just waiting for the opportunity. After all, Soss had experienced several humiliating situations involving Lefter. He hated to admit it but he could understand how Soss might feel. However, all things considered, Lefter still believed that Soss deserved all the grief he had been given by everyone in the past.

Lefter was sitting on his bed whistling softly when he heard a knock on the door. He hadn't realized he was whistling until the knock interrupted his rendition of 'Oh Suzanna, don't you cry for me.'" Without thinking, Lefter got up, walked to the door and had his hand on the handle before it dawned on him that the door would not open from the inside. To his surprise, the door did open when he turned the handle. Soss was standing outside.

"Hello, Lefter," said Soss. "Hope you don't mind but I decided to stay over and go to dinner with you. Is that acceptable to you?"

"Yeah, why not," replied Lefter. He looked at his watch and said, "It's a couple hours yet till dinner, come on in and sit down."

Soss sat down at the small table in the middle of the room and Lefter sat down on the bed. Neither man said anything for a while. Soss was looking at his interlocked fingers and Lefter was looking at his shoes.

"I was going to return to the 303 CRB this afternoon," said Soss, "but Doc Teele offered a dinner discussion if I wanted to stay. I stopped by the dining room on the way here. Swordfish is on the menu tonight. It is one of my favorite meals. Do you like swordfish?"

"Yeah," replied Lefter, "I used to have it at the I-Corps mess hall. Nowadays, I eat mostly C-rations though."

"Say, Lefter, do you want to continue the conversation we were having earlier?" asked Soss.

"Yeah, sure," replied Lefter. He was eager to continue the conversation but didn't want Soss to hear any enthusiasm in his voice.

"Let's see, where were we?" asked Soss.

"I think you said you had an overwhelming desire to be successful but didn't know how to do it, or something like that," said Lefter.

"Oh yes, I remember. I told you I would run awhile then stop and try to figure it out. Then, getting no result, I'd run some more. Stop again, then run some more."

"Did you figure it out?" asked Lefter.

"Sure did," replied Soss. "It took a lot of days of running, stopping and thinking, then running again before I finally figured it out." Soss paused and stared at Lefter.

"So, what's the answer?" asked Lefter.

"It is going to sound so simple that you may think it's stupid," replied Soss.

"Try me," replied Lefter.

"I decided that success in life is like running a marathon race," said Soss. "Now here's my answer: The race is not always to the swiftest of foot, but to the one that slows the least."

Lefter looked puzzled. "Did you say the one who wins the race is the one who slows the least?"

"Yeah," replied Soss.

"What about the one who runs the fastest?" asked Lefter.

"He might win one leg of the race of life," said Soss, "but there are thousands and thousands of legs in the race of life. Nobody can run full out for life, so the one who slows the least will win the race of life. Get it?"

"Yeah, I get it now," said Lefter, "but how did this help you at the time?"

"I applied that philosophy to my academics in high school," replied Soss. "Additionally, I kept on running, and running, and running. I quickly became the school's best marathon runner. Those two things were the key ingredients for my appointment to West Point.

"So, in a nutshell," said Lefter, "the one who slows the least wins the race of life. Is that right?"

"You got it, Lefter," laughed Soss, "it's the old *Tortoise and the Hare* story."

Lefter started laughing. Soss started laughing again.

"Oh crap," said Lefter with tears in his eyes, "that's classic, isn't it? Are you making all of this up?"

"Absolutely not," said Soss. "It's all the gospel truth."

"Whatever works, huh?" said Lefter.

"Got that right, Lefter," replied Soss, "but everyone has to figure it out for themselves."

"Can I ask you a question again?" asked Lefter.

"Sure," replied Soss.

"Why are you such an untrusting, aggressive hardass?" asked Lefter.

"Overreaction," said Soss seriously. "Overreaction!"

"What do you mean?" asked Lefter.

"Blinded by ambition," replied Soss. "Too much drive to succeed that has led to stupid decisions that I later regretted but couldn't bear to reverse."

Lefter was temporarily speechless. He just stared at Soss.

"Do you know what I mean, Lefter?" asked Soss.

"Was the court-martial you threatened me with one of those decisions you regret?" asked Lefter.

"Yes, definitely an overreaction on my part," replied Soss.

Lefter didn't know where to go with the conversation now. Clearly, Soss was apologizing for his past behavior, but Lefter didn't want to accept it, at least not yet.

Lefter stumbled a bit, then said, "Would you have gone through with the court-martial if Captain Eten hadn't intervened?"

"I don't think so," replied Soss. "I probably would have dropped it in favor of a couple of weeks restriction to our compound, just to save face."

"That's still real chicken shit," said Lefter.

"Sorry," said Soss, "just being truthful, for what I hope is helpful to both of us."

"Do you know that your fellow officers don't like you?" asked Lefter.

"Yeah, most of them don't care for me," said Soss.

"Do you know why?" asked Lefter.

"I have an idea," replied Soss, "that my Combat Infantryman's Badge is a big sore point, another overreaction on my part."

"Then why the hell do you continue to wear it on your uniform?" asked Lefter.

"Good question," replied Soss. "Are you suggesting that I don't wear the medal?"

"Does a bear shit in the woods? Of course, don't wear it. Isn't that obvious?" replied Lefter. "If you can't figure that out, I'd say you need to be watered twice a week." Lefter laughed. *Damn*, he thought, *this is turning into fun.*

Soss grinned slightly.

"Anything else?" asked Soss.

"Yeah," said Lefter, who was getting on a roll now. "Quit strutting around like a rooster in the hen house, it looks stupid!"

"What else?" asked Soss in a tone that was starting to become unfriendly.

"Eliminate that John Wayne flying salute," said Lefter. "That really looks stupid. Why the hell do you insist on the enlisted men saluting you here in Korea anyway? Don't you see the other officers deliberately looking the other way when they pass by enlisted men?"

Soss didn't respond but he was beginning to show signs of crumbling emotionally.

Lefter had fire in his eyes now. He was enjoying this tirade against Soss. "Another of your dumb ideas was to have a formal inspection of the Detachment #1 bunker. Now that was number one fucking stupid. You dumb ass, don't you know that pissing off guys on the front lines can get you killed by *accidental* friendly fire?"

The bottom lip of Soss began to quiver. His eyebrows were lowered and a furrow formed in his brow.

"And taking the guys on a camping trip in the middle of a war zone has to be your *really* big number one fucking stupid idea. Think about that. Stupid, stupid, stupid — right?"

Soss was looking distraught now. His shoulders were slumped forward and his head was sagging down. He was wringing his hands in his lap.

"And, and, that humiliating thing you did to Captain Eten was especially a crock of shit. Oh yeah, you didn't know we knew about that did you? Treating him like a houseboy and ordering him to clean out your stove in the middle of the night was brutal. How could you do that to a dedicated career officer?"

Lefter was letting it all out but he didn't realize that, at the same time, he was breaking down Soss. He only knew that it felt especially good to unload on him. "You're hated, detested, and ostracized," he said to Soss.

Wrinkles formed in the brow of Soss and his lower lip quivered.

Lefter continued on his outburst, "If you hadn't shipped my buddy Mewman off to the Infantry, he would still be with us." Then, with fire in his eyes, Lefter yelled, "I HATE YOUR FUCKING GUTS, SOSS!"

Lefter was breathing hard, but started to settle down as he slowly realized the explosion of hatred he had just hurled at Soss. Now, Lefter noticed that

Soss was sobbing softly and tears were running slowly down his face. Lefter hesitated, then took out his olive drab handkerchief and handed it to Soss.

Soss quickly got himself under control, wiped his eyes and handed the handkerchief back to Lefter.

Lefter was feeling a little sheepish, but he didn't regret tearing into Soss. He thought to himself, *The bastard deserves it.*

Lefter looked at his watch and said softly, "Let's head for the dining room, it's almost dinner time."

Soss stood up without speaking, followed Lefter out of the room and down the hallway toward the dining room.

Lefter and Soss were eating their dinner when Doc Teele walked up and said, "Lefter, I see on your records that tomorrow is your birthday, is that right?"

"If tomorrow is July 14, then it's my birthday," replied Lefter.

"That's the date," said Doc Teele.

"Holy crap," said Lefter, " tomorrow I can vote and legally drink." Lefter looked across the table and said, "How old are you, Soss?"

Soss laughed and said, "Way too young for my age."

"Tell you what," said Doc Teele, "go ahead and sleep in tomorrow then meet me in the patio at ten for coffee and birthday cake."

"OK, it's a deal," replied Lefter.

Doc Teele waved as he turned to leave, "See you then."

"I gotta hit the road too," said Soss. "Oh yeah, here's a pack of cigarettes I picked up for you."

"Thanks, my brand too," said Lefter.

To Lefter's surprise, he awakened early the next morning without having had a nightmare or even a bad dream. He felt refreshed for the first time in weeks. The sun was just coming up as he sat down at his table in the patio and lit his first cigarette. Two small birds resembling sparrows fluttered to a landing on the adjacent table and began pecking at some crumbs. "It is so peaceful in the early morning here," Lefter said to himself.

Then he heard the whirring and thumping of helicopter blades. Louder and louder, until suddenly the helicopter flew slowly over the hospital building and began its hovering decent to a landing pad near the end of the patio.

The two birds leaped into the air and flew away. One of the birds squirted a stream of excreta from its rear as it fled in panic. *Figures*, thought Lefter, *the shitty war is back.*

The helicopter landed and throttled back. Four hospital orderlies ran out, removed wounded men on stretchers and carried them swiftly through a nearby doorway. Then the helicopter lifted off and flew easterly. Soon another helicopter landed and again, hospital orderlies carried away stretchers containing wounded soldiers. A third helicopter brought in two more wounded soldiers, making a total of six.

"They're being brought in from a MASH unit," said Doc Teele, who was standing behind Lefter.

"You startled me, Doc," said Lefter. "Do you know what division they're coming from?"

"Marines," said Doc Teele.

"Oh shit!" said Lefter, "that's my outfit. Wonder what the hell is going on up there?"

"We never know," said Doc Teele, "we just repair 'em and send 'em back, or send 'em home. See you for coffee and cake at ten."

"Yeah, OK," said Lefter half heartily. He was thinking of the day that he put Mewman on the helicopter at the Battalion Aid Station. "Rotten fucking war," he said as he lit up a cigarette.

Lefter had lost his appetite so he skipped breakfast, went back to his room and napped until almost ten o'clock. *Crap,* he thought, *wish I hadn't told Doc I'd do that birthday thing.* Reluctantly, he walked to the patio and sat down at the usual table. He was sitting at the table gazing into the clear sunny sky when he heard singing. Looking toward the door, he saw several men walking toward him. Major Soss was leading them in singing the happy birthday song. Others in the group were Campbell, Crovelli, Nay, and Mighty Joe.

"What the hell is going on?" said Lefter as the group approached him and finished the birthday song.

"We have a present for you," said Campbell who turned toward the door and motioned to someone. Doc Teele came in pushing a wheelchair containing a man dressed in hospital patient garb.

Lefter started to feel faint. The patient looked like Mewman. He shook his head as his heart began to race. "It can't possibly be!" said Lefter. "Holy crap! Holy crap! *Holy crap,* it is, it's Mewman!"

"How the fuck are ya, Lef?" asked Mewman with a big grin followed by a belly laugh.

Tears welled up in Lefter's eyes. "You're alive, how the hell did that happen?" asked Lefter.

"I'm too fucking mean to die," said Mewman. "I'm a mean, gook-killing machine." Then he belly laughed again.

Dr. Teele rolled the wheelchair up and stopped it beside Lefter. Lefter reached out and patted Mewman's hand. "Sure good to see you, you ugly little gook killer," said Lefter with a smile as tears rolled down his face.

Mewman's eyes welled up. He cleared his throat and shook his head affirmatively. "Looks like we may be fucking bunker buddies, Lef."

"That's right," said Major Soss. "I got Mewman's court-martial set aside, his security clearance reinstated, and he's being transferred back to the 303."

"They wanted to send me back to the States," said Mewman. "I wanted to go back up on the MLR and kill some more fucking gooks. My second choice was to get back in ASA."

"I'm trying to make up for my past overreactions," said Soss. "I have apologized to the entire 303 and promised them a compassionate commander in the future."

"How about a cool one?" asked Nay. He winked as he said, "We got permission to bring a few beers to your birthday celebration."

"I'm looking the other way," said Doc Teele.

"Me too," said Major Soss.

Crovelli set a paper bag on the table, took out a beer, opened it and held it out to Lefter. Then he gave one to everyone else except Major Soss, who declined. Doc Teele accepted a beer though.

"Tell them the good news about yourself," said Mighty Joe to Crovelli.

"No big deal," said Crovelli, "I just got a transfer to the 501st in Seoul."

"It is a big deal, he's the new manager of the EM Club there," said Nay.

"Sounds like this conversation is headed places I shouldn't hear about," said Doc Teele. "I'll see you later."

"Me too," said Major Soss. "I'm leaving also."

"Oh yeah, one more thing, Lefter," said Doc Teele, "you're free to check out of the hospital and go back to your outfit immediately."

"What about me?" asked Mewman.

"Can you walk?" asked Doc Teele.

"Fuck yes," replied Mewman as he rose from the wheelchair and took a couple of cautious steps.

"Well then, get the *fuck* out of my hospital," said Doc Teele with a laugh as he turned and walked away.

After checking out of the hospital, Lefter and Mewman rode with Campbell in his ¾ ton truck. They stopped at the 501st and loaded up the covered bed of the truck with twenty-eight cases of whiskey. All this whiskey was already sold to soldiers of the 1st Marine Division and the 25th Infantry Division. Campbell also placed the order for the next shipment. Lefter and Mewman found enough cash to order three cases each.

"We should be back in the detachment before dark," said Campbell as they drove through the streets of Seoul.

"Before you ask, little buddy," said Lefter, "we don't want to stop at Madam Dong's place."

"No problem, Lef," said Mewman, "right now a good fuck would put me back in the hospital."

A few minutes later, Campbell honked the truck's horn and all three men laughed and waved as they drove past Madam Dong's place.

"Of course, one fuck passed up is one lost forever," said Mewman followed by his belly laugh.

"You are really crude," replied Lefter.

"Yeah," replied Mewman. "I'm a crude and mean, fucking gook-killing machine." Then another belly laugh.

"I give up," said Lefter with a laugh. "You're hopeless."

"Yeah, that's right, I'm a hopeless, crude, and…"

Campbell interrupted, "Will you two shut the hell up for a while, you're driving me nuts with your constant chatter."

Lefter and Mewman fell silent and cat napped for the rest of the trip. At the detachment, Campbell made up a new duty schedule and assigned Lefter as Mewman's trainer.

"Hey, little buddy," taunted Lefter, "do you think you can figure out how to fill a five-gallon can on the water run?"

"Fuck you," replied Mewman.

"Look, it's not easy," said Lefter with a laugh. "The water cans are white, the gas cans are red and the kerosene cans are gray. Of course, the contents is written on the can but you can't read, can you?"

"Fuck you," replied Mewman.

"OK, smart ass," said Lefter, "what color is the kerosene can?"

"Fuck you," replied Mewman.

"See, you don't know, do you?" said Lefter.

"Fuck you," replied Mewman.

"Will you two shut the hell up or get out of here?" said Campbell. "Again, you're driving me nuts with the constant chatter."

"Well, I'm deep fucking hurt," said Mewman with a belly laugh.

"Me too," said Lefter.

"Get the hell out of here!" yelled Campbell. "I have reports to fill out."

"Come on, little buddy," said Lefter, "we can take a hint, can't we?"

"Fucking A," replied Mewman.

"Out, out, OUT!" yelled Campbell as he pointed toward the tent entrance.

Deliberately grumbling to further annoy Campbell, Lefter and Mewman walked slowly toward the tent entrance. They paused at the entrance, looked back and smiled devilishly. Campbell was still watching them, pointed toward the outside and said, "Out, out, OUT!" As Lefter and Mewman disappeared through the door, Campbell shook his head and smiled.

The next several days passed routinely. Lefter taught Mewman the detachment chores and the bunker duty. No actions of any consequence were occurring on the MLR. Only the occasional artillery rounds and a machine-gun man firing off a burst here and there to relieve boredom. But the boredom would soon end with a flourish.

CHAPTER TWENTY-THREE

UN forces were passing the word around that the peace talks at Panmunjon were accelerating and the fighting would soon stop. While Lefter was in the hospital during mid July, five Chinese armies had launched a major attack on the central sector of the UN defenses. Advancing as much as six miles into the UN positions defended by five divisions of ROK IX Corps, they were finally driven back by counter attacks of a reinforced IX Corps. Many of the UN intelligence people believed that it was the Communists final offensive, designed to show the world the strength of their resolve.

Campbell was not convinced that the fighting was over. His DACs were intercepting conversations indicating that the Chinese were assembling a large number of troops and supplies in the area opposite the Marine Division sector. He reported this to General Stoney who confirmed with night patrols and other intelligence that the Chinese were mobilizing for some sort of major action.

Then during the night of July 24, it happened. The Chinese launched a heavy attack in the area held by the 1st Battalion and the 7th Regiment of the 1st Marine Division. Division Intelligence estimated that around 3,000 Chinese ground troops were in the attack force.

Upon hearing of the attack, Mewman wanted to immediately go to the bunker although he had just came off bunker duty. "Send me back up there so I can kill some fucking gooks," he said to Campbell.

"Your job nowadays is not to kill gooks," replied Campbell, "at least not directly. We're the ears of the 303; we don't fight, we listen."

Mewman was showing obvious frustration. "I am going to go fucking nuts just sitting here in the detachment area while all that action is going on up on the MLR."

Lefter, who was sitting on his cot reading a magazine, said to Campbell, "I've got the bunker duty on the 26th, maybe he can go up with me for a little more training. Meanwhile, is it OK if Mew and me go visit his old outfit at the 25th Division?"

"Good plan," said Campbell. "Go, take the jeep. Just be back by dark." Campbell didn't want another round of constant chatter from Mewman and Lefter regarding the duty roster.

"Come on, little buddy," said Lefter to Mewman, "let's get the hell out of here and go visit Happy."

Grumbling, Mewman followed Lefter to the jeep. Lefter drove a few miles south on the MSR to the location of the division reserve area. After several inquiries, they were finally directed to the area occupied by Charlie Company. As they drove into the company area Mewman yelled, "There he is. HEY, HAPPY. HAPPY!"

The entire company of over one hundred men was standing at attention for an inspection. Sergeant Happy was standing at attention in front of his squad of men. Happy glanced sideways and smiled.

Lefter stopped the jeep and Mewman jumped out and ran toward Happy. "Don't you know who the fuck I am?" said Mewman as he ran up and stopped in front of Happy. Happy smiled broadly and shook his head while the entire company of men broke out in laughter.

"You dumb shit," said Happy, "can't you see we're in an inspection formation?"

Lefter sat in the jeep shaking his head in disbelief. Mewman's occasional stupid actions still amazed him.

"Who is this man?" asked a greenhorn lieutenant.

"He was one of my BAR men," replied Happy. "He's been listed as MIA since we got overrun on the MLR."

"Fuck, I'm not missing in action," replied Mewman, "I was damn near KIA, but never fucking MIA." Mewman belly laughed and the entire company started breaking up with laughter.

"COMPANY DISMISSED," yelled the lieutenant to the formation of laughing men. Then, turning to Mewman, he said, "Soldier, report to the headquarters tent, I'll deal with you there."

Lefter yelled out as he jumped from the jeep and trotted toward Mewman and the lieutenant, "DON'T SAY ANYTHING, MEW, JUST DO AS HE SAYS." Lefter ran up and grabbed Mewman by the arm, then turned to the lieutenant, saluted and said, "I'll see that he reports there immediately, sir."

Mewman started to say something just as Lefter spun him around and said, "Shut up, let's go to headquarters right now and explain the situation." He pulled and half dragged Mewman toward the jeep as he kept saying,

"Shut up, shut up, keep your mouth shut."

The lieutenant followed them to the jeep and said, "The bumper says you're with the 303 CRB, what is that outfit?"

"It's the 303 Communication Reconnaissance Battalion, sir," replied Lefter. "We're in the Army Security Agency and we man a bunker in this sector of the MLR."

Sergeant Happy was standing near the lieutenant and said, "Sir, I know that to be a fact." Pointing to Lefter, he continued, "I know this man, Lefter, to be one of the men from the ASA bunker. The ASA bunker was just west of my position on the MLR." He pointed to Mewman and said, "Mewman here was transferred to us from the ASA and he was my BAR man. I reported him MIA after we were overrun."

"I wasn't MIA, I was in the fucking hospital down by Seoul," said Mewman.

"Well nobody told me that," responded Happy, "so I reported you MIA." Then he said to Lefter, "So you're just giving him a ride back to his outfit?"

"Oh crap, I can see this is going to get confusing," said Lefter. "He's been transferred back to the ASA." Turning to the lieutenant, Lefter continued, "If you will contact Major Soss at the 303 Communication Reconnaissance Battalion in I-Corps headquarters, he will explain it all to you."

"Do you have a copy of your transfer orders?" asked the lieutenant to Mewman.

Mewman pulled his shirt tail out of his pants, lifted the shirt high and said, "Are these fucking scars from a burp gun blast proof enough? They're just barely healed. The fucking gooks shot me and I was in the hospital; I wasn't MIA."

"For all I know, you may have abandoned your post during the battle," said the lieutenant.

"That's a fucking lie," snarled Mewman.

"Shut the hell up, Mew," said Lefter. "Let me handle this."

"Sergeant," said the lieutenant as he pointed at Mewman, "put this man in custody until I get to the bottom of this. You come with me and we'll contact your Major Soss right now," said the lieutenant as he pointed at Lefter.

"What the fu…"

Lefter interrupted Mewman and said, "Shut up, Mew, and go have a visit with Happy while I straighten this thing out."

Lefter followed the lieutenant to the company headquarters tent where he called for Major Soss on their field phone. Unfortunately, Major Soss was not in his office nor was the executive officer. Lefter handed the phone to the lieutenant and said, "Major Soss is not available right now, please tell them how the major can contact you, sir."

The lieutenant took the phone and coldly left the information on how to contact him in the company reserve area. Just as he finished speaking on the phone a corporal came up and said, "Sir, here is a message from battalion; they want us to leave immediately to reinforce the 1st Marines on the MLR."

"OK, Corporal," said the lieutenant, "assemble the men immediately with their combat gear."

The corporal said, "Yes, sir," saluted and left the area.

In a few seconds, the corporal's voice came over loudspeakers in the area. "ATTENTION ALL PERSONNEL. ATTENTION ALL PERSONNEL. REPORT TO YOUR ASSEMBLY AREA IN TEN MINUTES WITH FULL COMBAT GEAR. REPORT TO YOUR ASSEMBLY AREA IN TEN MINUTES WITH FULL COMBAT GEAR."

"Oh crap," said Lefter as he sprinted out of the tent and toward the jeep. "Which one of these damn tents is Mewman in? Calm down, calm down," he kept saying to himself. He decided to sit in the jeep and wait for Sergeant Happy to come to the assembly area. Mewman would be coming along too and they could get the hell out of here.

Lefter smoked a cigarette and fidgeted. Then he smoked another cigarette and fidgeted some more. Finally, men started assembling in the area in front of the jeep. Sergeant Happy finally appeared with Mewman at his side. Mewman had a full combat pack and was carrying a BAR and a bandoleer of ammunition. Lefter yelled out, "Mewman, what the hell are you up to?"

"Doing my duty, Lef, just doing my duty," said Mewman with a big grin. "Looks like I get another chance to kill some fucking gooks."

"That's right," said a smiling Happy. "Until I have an official notice, he's still my BAR man."

"Oh crap," said Lefter as the men began loading into trucks for the trip north to the MLR. "Mewman, I ought to kick your little ass right here in front of everybody."

"Careful, Lef," said Mewman, "you don't want to match your fucking little carbine against Barrie here." He patted his BAR. "Tell Campbell I got drafted into the 25th Infantry again." He let out his belly laugh as he climbed into a transport truck with Happy.

Lefter was furious. He climbed into the jeep, started the engine and spun the jeep around kicking up dirt and dust as he sped off toward the ASA detachment. As he drove along he kept saying, "That stupid little shit. That stupid little shit."

Back at the detachment base camp, Lefter explained the whole sorrowful tale to Campbell. He started by saying, "You're going to find this hard to believe but it's the gospel truth."

Campbell listened in amazement then said just one word, "Bizarre!"

"Yeah, weird, ain't it?" responded Lefter. "What are we going to do about it?"

"Nothing," said Campbell.

"Nothing! We have to do something," said Lefter.

"No, we don't," said Campbell. "Sometimes it's best to not interfere with the natural course of things. Mewman is doing what he wants to do so let's see how it plays out. OK?"

"OK, Mew, I defer to your superior judgment," said Lefter.

"Are you being a smart ass?" asked Campbell.

"No, you're absolutely right, I just get caught up in my own emotions sometimes," said Lefter.

Lefter was surprised that he quit worrying about Mewman. After all, Lefter reasoned, *Mewman was doing what he wanted to do — trying to kill gooks.* That made sense to Mewman and Lefter had no right to interfere with his wishes. He thought of the saying, "Que Sera, Sera" or "What will be, will be."

The heavy fighting on the front lines accelerated each night and Lefter was nervous when he reported on the morning of July 26. "They pounded the hell out of us last night," said Jolcomb, "but we pounded the hell out of them right back."

"Mostly artillery exchanges?" asked Lefter.

"Naw, everything," answered Jolcomb. "It's like they're trying to use up all their ammunition. Scared the hell out of me."

"Maybe they used all their ammo last night," said Lefter with a grin.

"Yeah, right," said Jolcomb cynically, "and bears won't shit in the woods today cause they used it all up last night."

"OK, you can leave now," said Lefter, "you have dutifully scared the crap out of me already."

"Well, anyway, stay safe, buddy," said Jolcomb.

"Will do, you too," replied Lefter.

Mid-morning, Lefter answered a call on the land-line from Campbell. "We're having a party down here, Lef. I just got the word that a cease-fire has been agreed to at Panmunjon. The fighting stops tomorrow morning at ten. Keep your head down and don't take any chances at all. I'll be up there at ten tomorrow morning."

"Great news," replied Lefter, "I'm not even going outside to take a piss from now on. Hang on, Camp, a DAC just handed me a message he intercepted and it reads: 'War end tomorrow at ten.'"

"The gooks damn near got the news to you first," replied Campbell. "Anyway, stay safe, buddy, and go ahead and piss in your steel helmet if necessary. After tonight, you won't need it anymore."

Both men laughed and hung up the land-line phone.

Lefter heard explosions in the distance. He went to the viewing slit and looked out across No-Man's-Land. Mortar rounds were exploding out near each of the outposts and flares were being launched into the sky. He had never seen flares in the daytime. Then he heard the telltale sound of incoming artillery rounds. "What the hell is going on?" he whispered. "Are the gooks going to attack in the daylight?" They always fought at night to avoid the American air power.

Lefter jumped as he sensed someone behind him. He turned around quickly and the Korean DAC was standing there. "What happening? Radio say war ending."

"Take a look for yourself," said Lefter as he stepped back and pointed to the viewing slit. Before the DAC could step up to the viewing slit a round of artillery exploded nearby. Some dirt and a small piece of shrapnel came flying through the viewing slit. The piece of shrapnel hit the inside of the bunker wall with a thud.

"No, no, I go stay by radio," said the Korean DAC.

Lefter laughed and pretended not to be affected by the close call with the shrapnel. In reality, Lefter was experiencing a queasy stomach from the incident. He swallowed hard and suppressed the urge to throw up. The DAC returned to the radio area and Lefter sat down at the table and lit a cigarette.

"What to do? What to do," he kept asking himself. He took a pad of paper and pencil from his nearby pack and poised his hand in the writing position on the paper. Nothing came to mind. Outside, the incoming artillery and outgoing artillery seemed to be passing overhead every second. He watched the second hand on his watch and counted twelve whistles going overhead in ten seconds. Then he counted eight explosions in ten seconds occurring forward of the bunker. Then he counted the outgoing artillery at twenty in ten seconds.

He decided to call Campbell and report the massive barrage.

The phone was dead. One of the Chinese artillery rounds must have cut the land-line. Lefter knew the communication wire was lying on top of the ground and he could probably find and repair the break. However, it would be dangerous, even stupid, to go out in this barrage. He decided to wait until it stopped.

The barrage continued at the accelerated pace for another half-hour then tapered off to almost nothing. Lefter went to the viewing slit and looked out across No-Man's-Land to the Chinese positions. A dozen or more American and British fighter planes were bombing and dropping napalm on the Chinese positions. Each napalm drop would hit and spread flame a hundred yards or more along the terrain. Lefter cringed as he visualized the Chinese soldiers that were being set afire with the napalm. He felt sorry for them.

Lefter returned to the table and wrote on the paper, *What the hell are we doing this for? The war is ending tomorrow at ten so why the hell try and kill each other now?* Then he tried to think of answers to the questions. *Macho image*, he wrote. *Last chance for each side to shove it up the other's ass.* In the distance, he could hear the warplanes still diving and pounding the Chinese lines. Lefter figured that the Chinese would start the barrage again as soon as the planes left. That would be their way of saying with action that the air attack didn't scare them one damn bit.

Lefter was right. As soon as the planes left, the Chinese resumed the artillery barrage. Of course, the US responded with a massive artillery barrage. "Insane!" said Lefter as he threw his hands into the air. The barrages continued for another half-hour and then tapered down to nothing again. More warplanes must be attacking again, he thought, as he heard explosions coming from the north. He went to the viewing slit and confirmed his suspicions. American fighter planes were attacking the Chinese lines again. These were prop-driven Marine Corsairs. The previous planes had been jet fighters. The jets would probably return after refueling and taking on a fresh supply of bombs and ammunition.

Lefter decided to calculate the time that the jets would return. He brushed the ceiling dirt from his pad of paper and began to calculate. "Let's see, 50 miles divided by 200 miles per hour equals .25 hours, and .25 hours times 60 minutes equals 15 minutes." His mind raced on, "Landing, refueling and taking on more bombs and ammunition might take another fifteen to twenty minutes. Another twenty minutes for takeoff and return to the MLR. Twenty plus twenty plus twenty equals one hour. They should be back in about one hour," he concluded. "Bet them college boys couldn't figure it out any better," said Lefter proudly. He looked at his watch. It was almost noon. Time for some chow.

Lefter looked through the supply of C-rations, selected a can of beans and wieners and opened it from the bottom with his GI can opener. Using the fork from his kit, he ate the wieners and about half of the beans from the can. He quit eating when the artillery barrage started and dirt again started sifting from the ceiling of the bunker. As he lit a cigarette, it occurred to Lefter that he was sitting through the worst barrage of his experience and for some reason, he wasn't afraid. He smiled as he thought of his paralyzing fear when sitting through the first artillery barrage. "Que Sera, Sera."

Lefter shook the dirt from the pad of paper, picked up the pencil and began to write. For some odd reason, he felt poetic. He got lost in thought and his mind blanked out the pounding going on outside the bunker. Without thinking about it, he kept wiping off the dirt sifting down from the ceiling of the bunker. He was concentrating so hard that he forgot to smoke a cigarette. Ordinarily, during one of these artillery barrages, he would be smoking one Chesterfield after another. Finally, he completed the first five lines. With a feeling of satisfaction, he lit a cigarette and reread his creation:

Greetings Dumbshit, said the official looking letter
Your friends and neighbors have selected you
To take a little training on how to kill, then go for a long sail
Take a ship to Korea and risk your tender young ass
While back home, your friends and neighbors BBQ on the grass

Lefter looked at his watch and was amazed that it had been almost an hour since he began writing. The attack planes should be returning soon. As if on his clue, the incoming and outgoing artillery barrages began to die down. Lefter went to the viewing slit and saw the first of the fighters as it dived down and dropped napalm. Then others followed in single file and dropped bombs and napalm. Then they each took turns strafing the target area. Lefter shivered as he again thought of the terror the Chinese must experience when being attacked with the napalm bombs. "Why?" It didn't make sense to him. "Why kill some more people when the war would be over tomorrow morning?" Of course, the whole Korean War didn't make sense to Lefter.

After the air attack was over both sides started firing artillery again. Lefter returned to the desk, dusted off the paper and reread his first poetry writings. Smiling, he poised the pencil and began thinking about the next "stanza, paragraph, passage, or whatever the hell poets call it." He got completely lost in the poetry writing effort. He didn't notice the hourly lulls in artillery when the attack aircraft would return for another round of bombing and strafing.

Finally, he started getting tired. He looked at his watch and couldn't believe it. The watch said it was nine o'clock. He jumped up and hurried to the viewing slit. It was getting dark outside. Now he could see the flashes of the exploding artillery along the Chinese positions. Tracers filled the air as they raced northerly from the machine guns along the MLR. Incoming artillery rounds landed on the front slope, back slope and along the MLR. Tomorrow his ears would be ringing from all the noise here tonight.

Lefter wondered if Mewman was firing one of the machine guns. Surely, he would be firing something somewhere. Mewman was probably belly laughing, yelling obscenities and having good time. *He's weird but he's my little buddy*, thought Lefter. *Stay safe, buddy.*

Lefter returned to the table and reread his poetic creation to date:

Eat C-Rations and drink an occasional warm beer
Shower every other week or maybe a month
Heat water in your steel helmet for a shave now and then
Piss in a tube outside of your bunker and shiver in the cold
While back home, your friends and neighbors BBQ on the grass

Lock and load one clip of ball ammunition
Then crawl on your belly through the mud and the cold
Hugging the ground while scared shitless
Looking for Gooks that you hope you don't encounter
While back home, your friends and neighbors BBQ on the grass

Firefights at night under the flare's eerie light
Mortar and artillery rounds landing all around
BARs and burp guns squaring off in the night
Fix bayonets; throw some grenades, then charge into the dark
While back home, your friends and neighbors BBQ on the grass

Struggle back to the MLR still in the black of night
Caked with dirt and the blood of a buddy
Exhausted but relieved to get back to relative safety
Crawl into a dirty sleeping bag in a bunker with the rats
While your friends and neighbors BBQ on the grass

What is that you smell as you lie in your bag?
It resembles kimchi but stinks much worse
Blow into your hands and recoil in horror
Your breath smells like your nose is stuck up your ass
While your friends and neighbors BBQ on the grass

Lefter chuckled and decided to take a nap. He lay down on top of his sleeping bag and relaxed. Outside the barrage continued. *Oh crap*, he thought. The urge to urinate became strong. Unwilling to go outside and use the piss tube, he started thinking of where he could relieve himself. He smiled as he remembered Campbell saying, "Piss in your helmet if you have too." Then it occurred to him that a partial bottle of whiskey was hidden under the bunk. He could pour out the whiskey and urinate in the empty bottle. He rolled off the bunk onto his hands and knees and started reaching back under the bunk area.

Snap! A͟H͟H͟H͟E͟E͟E͟E͟E͟! Lefter let out a cry of pain and jerked his hand out quickly. "What the hell!" He raised his hand while continuing to moan in pain. Someone had set a rat trap and placed it under the bunk. It was now clamped on Lefter's fingers. Both DACs came scrambling over to Lefter as he continued to yell in pain. Lefter held out the trapped hand and said, "Get this damn thing off of me." One DAC held the trap while the other opened the trap far enough for Lefter to pull out his fingers.

"Do you have an open bottle of booze?" said Lefter to the DACs.

"Booze not allowed in bunker," responded the Korean DAC.

"Agleed," said the Chinese DAC.

"Don't bullshit me," said Lefter shaking his aching hand. "I know we all have a bottle hidden away somewhere."

"Ho-K, ho-k," said the Chinese DAC who then went to his pack and retrieved a partial bottle of whiskey.

Lefter took the bottle to the table and poured the contents into his canteen cup. The canteen cup was full to the brim and still some whiskey was left in the bottle. Lefter tipped up the bottle and took a large swig, then handed the bottle to the Chinese DAC. "Drink up," said Lefter in a commanding voice.

The Chinese DAC hesitated. Lefter gave the drink up sign with his aching hand. The Chinese DAC looked at the Korean DAC who was shaking his head affirmatively. He handed the bottle to the Korean DAC who immediately took a large drink. "Lew now," he said as he handed the bottle back to the Chinese DAC.

The Chinese DAC took a large drink and handed the bottle to Lefter. Lefter took a large gulp and drained the bottle dry. He turned the bottle upside down to show the DACs that it was empty. Then Lefter turned his back, took out his penis and urinated into the whiskey bottle.

The DACs stood in stunned silence.

"Thank you," said Lefter to the DACs as he set the partially-filled bottle on the table and buttoned his pants.

Both DACs started laughing and Lefter joined in. The Korean DAC picked up the bottle turned his back and urinated in the bottle. He held up the bottle, which was now nearly full and said, "To plece."

"Yeah," said Lefter, "a toast to peace."

The Korean DAC pretended that he was going to take a drink from the bottle of urine. Lefter held out his hand with the aching fingers and said, "No, no, wait." He held up the canteen cup of whiskey.

The DACs came to the table and each took a drink from the canteen cup. Then Lefter took a drink. They took turns until the cup was empty.

The Chinese DAC picked up the canteen cup. He held it above his mouth and let the last bit of whiskey drip into his mouth. Then he turned his back, undid his pants and urinated into the canteen cup. He turned around, set the cup on the table and said, "We all done now." All three men laughed heartily.

Outside the artillery barrage continued but Lefter and the DACs didn't really notice. They were feeling real loose. Lefter's hand still throbbed but he didn't feel any pain.

"Before we get too shit faced," said Lefter, "do either of you have an Kisoto?"

"Have-a-yes," answered the Korean DAC who went to his pack and set a bottle of Kisoto on the table.

"OK, now all we need is some more booze. I hid a partial bottle under my bunk there. Go get it," said Lefter as he motioned toward his bunk with his swollen fingers.

"No way, GI," said the Chinese DAC, "maybe nuther lat tap."

"No, only one trap and it got me," replied Lefter.

"I do," said the Korean DAC. He retrieved a flashlight from the radio area and shined it under Lefter's bunk. He reached under and retrieved the bottle of whiskey.

Lefter popped himself on the forehead with an open hand, laughed and said, "Check it out first with a flashlight. Why didn't I think of that? One more reason why you college guys are paid the big bucks."

They opened some C-rations and ate as they shared the remaining whiskey. They remained oblivious to the artillery barrage outside except when one hit close by. A nearby hit would cause the ground to shake and an extra amount of dirt to would sift from the ceiling of the bunker. They sat with one hand covering the open C-ration can to keep the falling dirt from the food. With the other hand, they passed around the bottle of whiskey.

Lefter's head was spinning. He felt as though he was about to pass out. Something in the back of his mind said, "Whiff the Kisoto." He got the Kisoto from his pack and began to breathe deeply of its fumes. The dizziness went away and he was left only with a tired and sleepy feeling. "I've had it," said Lefter as he went to his bunk.

Each of the DACs took several deep inhalations from the Kisoto bottle then went to their bunks. Within a few minutes, the outside battle sounds were mingled with the heavy snoring of the three intoxicated men.

Lefter awoke to heavy pounding on the bunker door. Then a voice yelled, "OPEN THE FUCKING DOOR, LEF."

Lefter smiled as he went and opened the door. It was daylight. He looked at his watch. It was nearly nine-thirty. "Mewman, you dumb shit. What are you doing here?"

"The fly boys are attacking the gooks again," said Mewman, "so I decided to hustle over here to see how you're doing." He let out a big belly laugh, slapped Lefter on the shoulder and said, "So how the fuck are you doing?" He picked up the whiskey bottle on the table and said, "Looks like you had a party without me."

Then before Lefter could say anything, Mewman took a big mouthful. Spitting it out, he said, "What the fuck is this? It smells like piss."

Although it hurt his head a little, Lefter started laughing. "You dumb shit, Mew, it is piss. We wouldn't go out in the barrage last night so we just pissed in whatever."

"Ahhhhhh," said Mewman, "I ought to slit your fucking throat and gargle with your blood."

"What a real buddy you are," said Lefter with a big grin. "Think of it as a learning experience, now you know what piss tastes like. That's more piss knowledge than I have."

The DACs were awake and listening to Lefter and Mewman's conversation. They couldn't hold their laughter any longer and began to snicker.

Mewman pointed his BAR up toward the ceiling and let a few rounds fire on automatic. "What's so fucking funny?" said Mewman to the DACs. The expression on the faces of the DACs instantly changed from amusement to fear.

"Easy, buddy," said Lefter, "these guys are on our side." He lit a cigarette and handed it to Mewman.

Mewman took a deep drag on the cigarette and inhaled the smoke. "Yeah, sorry, guys," he said as he waved toward the DACs.

Remembering a conversation at the hospital with Major Soss, Lefter paraphrased, "Think fast, act slowly and live longer."

"Yeah," said Mewman, "I get that fucking backwards, don't I? I won't live long because I act fast, then think slowly." He let out a belly laugh. "Just don't forget to have a big fucking party with that hundred bucks I gave you."

"OK," said Lefter, "but try and be there, will you?"

"Fucking A," replied Mewman.

"Another thing, buddy," said Lefter, "back home you're going to have to clean up your language cause I'm going to introduce you to some nice girls."

Mewman raised his right hand with the little finger extended beyond the other curled up fingers. "Are you going to teach me how to drink tea from them little tiny fucking cups?" He let out a big belly laugh.

"Just start out by eliminating the f word from your speech," said Lefter.

"OK," said Mewman, "how's this? Hey baby, I'll give you ten bucks for some sex."

"Wrong, wrong, wrong," said Lefter shaking his head.

"What the f…I mean what the hell — ah, ah — what the heck is wrong with what I said?" replied Mewman.

"Because," said Lefter, "nice girls are going to be insulted with that offer." He couldn't resist the chance for a punch line and followed with, "You're going to have to offer at least twenty bucks."

Outside the artillery barrage was starting again. The fighter planes must be through with this attack. Lefter looked at his watch. It was five minutes before ten. The cease-fire was supposed to take effect at ten but outside it sounded like a thousand Fourth of July celebrations. He kept watching the time as it approached ten o'clock.

Lefter didn't notice Mewman slip out the door with his BAR. Mewman crawled up on top of the bunker and started firing his BAR from a sitting position.

Lefter went to the viewing slit and looked out into the air filled with thousands of tracer bullets flying northward. Puffs of smoke, dust and dirt flying all around were the telltale signs of exploding artillery and mortar shells.

At a couple of minutes before ten, the explosions and machine gun firing started slacking off quickly. Soon all activity stopped, except now Lefter could hear the BAR firing from the top of the bunker. He turned around quickly and looked for Mewman. "You dumb shit," he said as he ran out the bunker door.

Lefter scrambled to the top of the bunker and yelled into Mewman's ear, "Stop firing, the fucking war is over. The fucking war is over."

Mewman quit firing the BAR and turned toward Lefter. Mewman had a disappointed look on his face. Lefter was crying. "It's all over, buddy, it's all over," said Lefter happily through his tears. "You made it."

"Yeah," said Mewman in a disappointed voice.

Without any further words, they sat on top of the bunker and looked out across No-Man's-Land. The hills occupied by the Chinese were soon swarming with thousands of men. Lefter was amazed. He wondered how they could have survived the massive artillery and air assaults. He wondered what the Chinese were seeing as they looked southward to the Marine sector of the MLR.

Whooping and hollering broke out along the MLR and Lefter and Mewman joined in the yelling. Soon the DACs were standing on top of the bunker and participating in the hollering. Then they began to faintly hear the Chinese hollering from their positions across No-Man's-Land.

Lefter, Mewman and the two DACs sat atop the bunker, smoked their cigarettes and gazed across No-Man's-Land. Each man was engulfed in his own thoughts about the end of the Korean War.

Lefter was glad the war was over. It meant he would probably live to return home to his wife and family. On the other hand, he wouldn't get the four points per month toward rotation so he would have to stay longer than if the war was still on. Also, he wouldn't be getting the extra fifty dollars per month for combat pay.

Lefter heard a thump. Mewman gasped and slumped sideways into Lefter's lap. Blood was gushing from his head and soaking Lefter's clothing.

"OH SHIT," yelled Lefter. "A SNIPER JUST SHOT HIM."

The DACs scrambled off the top of the bunker. Lefter dragged Mewman off the top of the bunker and into the access trench. There, he sat with Mewman's head in his hands. He knew that Mewman was already dead. This time it was a certainty. The bullet had made a small hole in his forehead and a large exit hole in the back of his head. Soon, Lefter knew that Mewman's heart had quit because the flow of blood had stopped.

Lefter felt someone pulling on his arm. It was Campbell. "Come on, Lef, we can't do anything for him now."

Lefter lowered Mewman's head gently onto the ground. He leaned over and said softly into Mewman ear, "So long, good buddy, I'll never forget you." Then he followed Campbell into the bunker and they both sat down at the table. Lefter's eyes were moist but he wasn't crying.

"Here, have a drink," said Campbell as he took a bottle from his pack and offered it to Lefter.

"I don't really want one," said Lefter, "but I'll have one for Mewman." He took the bottle in both of his blood-covered hands, pointed it toward the top of the bunk and said, "Here's to you, good buddy." He took two big gulps, shivered and handed the bottle back to Campbell. Then he started sobbing softly into his blood-caked hands.

Campbell picked up the bottle, took a big gulp and said, "Fucking war! I'll arrange for picking up his body. Do you want to stay here with him, Lef?"

Lefter nodded his head affirmatively.

"Your relief should be here anytime," said Campbell. "It's Jolcomb's turn and he's moving a little slow this morning. Too much partying last night."

"Yeah," said Lefter softly.

Lefter sat at the table for a long time. He would get himself together for a minute or so then the sadness would return and he would tear up. Finally, he took an army blanket from his bunk and went outside. He covered Mewman's body with the blanket, sat down beside him and lit a Chesterfield. "This is our last smoke together, little buddy. Rest in peace."

Campbell returned with Hillman and the two relief DACs. "The body recovery guys are here," said Campbell as he turned and pointed to three men just then coming into the entrance trench.

A corporal, carrying a clipboard, came up and lifted the blanket from Mewman's body. He removed one of the dog tags from the chain around

Mewman's neck. He took the contents of Mewman's pockets and put them in a small cloth bag. "OK, load him up and take him down the hill," he said to the two Korean civilians. They lifted Mewman onto a stretcher and carried him away.

Turning to Campbell and Lefter, the corporal said, "Who can tell me about him?"

Lefter spent several minutes telling the corporal about Mewman then summarized, "In a nutshell, Mewman grew up in an orphanage and has no family. As far as I know, I'm the closest thing to family that he had."

"OK," said the Marine Corporal, "I'm listing you as next of kin. Here is the stuff that was in his pockets. What do you want done with the body?"

Lefter's head started to spin. The corporal waited patiently while Lefter thought about it. "Can he be buried in a National Cemetery, like Arlington?"

"Yes, for certain in a National Cemetery, but I don't know if it will be Arlington. I'll put it down as your preference and someone will be in touch with you in the next twenty-four hours. I already got the contact information from your sergeant."

"Thanks," said Lefter.

"No sweat, buddy," said the corporal as he shook Lefter's hand.

He handed Lefter a business-size card and said, "Here's how to contact my outfit if you don't hear from us tomorrow." Then turned and left.

The next day, Lefter was contacted and told that Mewman had been buried at the UN Cemetery near Pusan. It was standard Army procedure, no exceptions. However, upon request of the next of kin, his remains could be exhumed later and transported for burial in the United States. Also, Lefter was told that he was officially appointed Mewman's next of kin, as the Army records did not list any next of kin or person to contact. Lefter vowed to himself that he would someday have Mewman's remains buried at a National Cemetery in the United States.

CHAPTER TWENTY-FOUR

Now that the cease-fire was in effect, life in the detachment became boring. Bunker duty was especially boring for Lefter. It was strange but he missed the feeling of impending danger and the heightened sense of awareness that came from knowing that combat could erupt at any time. Radio communication by the Chinese fell to almost nothing. However, the higher command didn't trust the Chinese to maintain the cease-fire and insisted that the ASA listening bunkers continue to operate.

Lefter didn't see much reason to stay in the detachment, and live in a tent with a dirt floor when not on duty in the bunker. Also, the Army stopped paying combat pay and reduced the rotation points from four per month to two per month.

In the bunker, the food was, of course, still C-rations. Lefter just ate the wieners from the beans and wieners, or the crackers and canned fruit. Now, by comparison, the duty back at 303 headquarters seemed like a plush assignment. Lefter spread the word around that he would like to be transferred back to 303 headquarters as soon as possible.

It was a hot day in August when Lefter and Jolcomb decided to break the boredom by going fishing with hand grenades. They drove to the Marine ammo dump and picked up a case of concussion grenades. From there they drove to the Imjin River and parked near a ferry operated by Korean civilians. They opened the case of grenades and set it on the ground about ten feet from the riverbank. Lefter and Jolcomb took turns throwing grenades into the water. The explosion would result in two or three fish floating to the top. Two Korean ferry workers swam out and got the fish before more grenades were thrown.

Perhaps half of the case of grenades had been used when Lefter pulled the pin on a grenade and swung his arm back to throw it underhand over the five-foot bank. His hand hit Jolcomb who had walked up behind him. The grenade handle sprung off as the deadly explosive dropped at Lefter's feet.

In three or four seconds, it would go off and they both of them would be killed or maimed for life. Fortunately, Jolcomb immediately kicked the grenade into the river before it exploded.

"We damn near bit the dust," said Jolcomb.

"Got that right," replied Lefter. "This is a stupid game isn't it? No, correction, it's not the game that's stupid, it's us that's stupid for playing games with grenades."

"How 'bout we go pheasant hunting?" asked Jolcomb with a big grin.

"Yeah right!" replied Lefter. "Why don't we just cut right to the chase and go tiptoe through a minefield."

Both men laughed. They loaded up the remaining grenades and returned them to the ammo dump. "Now let's go for a swim," said Jolcomb. "It's a whole bunch safer."

They drove the three-quarter ton truck back to the Imjin River at a location where the bottom was composed of gently sloping solid rock. Jolcomb drove the snorkel-equipped truck out over the rock until the water was just below seat level. They swam off the truck while it set idling in the water.

Finally, Lefter said, "I'm thinking maybe we're doing something stupid again."

"How's that?" replied Jolcomb.

"What if this truck dies out here, ain't we in deep kimchi?"

"I don't think so," said Jolcomb, "not if we drove it out here to wash the vehicle."

"Good plan," said Lefter, "let's wash it."

"What?" replied Jolcomb.

"Really," said Lefter as he took his army towel and began to wash the dirt off the truck.

Jolcomb reluctantly joined in and helped wash the dirt and grime off of the truck. For the next couple of hours, they alternated between swimming to cool off and washing the truck.

"This thing looks right spiffy," said Jolcomb with his big southern smile.

They parked the truck on the bank and let it dry before returning to the detachment base camp.

The summer of 1953 was hot with daily temperatures reaching into the high nineties. When not on bunker duty, the men of Detachment One spent a lot of time cooling off in the Imjin River.

In early October, Lefter was transferred back to 303 headquarters and put in charge of the mail room and message center. When he was first assigned to the 303 headquarters, it seemed like rustic living. Now, after living at the detachment and in the bunker, he felt like he had moved into luxurious facilities. The tents had plywood floors and electric lights. Of course, there was the Day Room Tent for relaxing, reading and writing letters. Major Soss had lifted the restriction regarding alcohol, and beer was again kept in the cooler.

Major Soss had done a complete flip-flop. Previously he had been hated and feared. Now he was overly lenient. Generally, both the enlisted men and officers of the 303 ignored him. He spent a lot of time escorting the horde of politicians that "suddenly" decided to visit the war zone. Most of the politicians carried a copy of their special invitation that had been printed in the Stars and Stripes Newspaper.

Lefter fell back into the routine of duty at the 303 headquarters. Now that the war was over, nobody showed much enthusiasm for doing his job and that included Lefter. Most of the men just floated lazily through the workday in a lax environment. They read magazines, wrote letters home, and shot the bull.

Crovelli and Nay organized a big party at the Chinese restaurant in Seoul. Many enlisted men of the 303 got drunk but Lefter sipped beer and stayed sober. The photo being passing around showing him, Nissing and Smoky throwing up embarrassed him.

The lax attitude was not restricted to the men of the 303. It was widespread and obvious to all observers, including the I-Corps Commander. General Blark decided to "shape up the troops" and ordered a general inspection of the whole of I-Corp. He gave a week notice and made it clear that all the men, their living quarters, their weapons and vehicles better be in spotless condition.

Grudgingly, the men of the 303 and the rest of the troops in I-Corps cleaned and organized living areas and work areas. Motor pool personnel spent days cleaning and polishing the vehicles. The men made sure they had clean and pressed uniforms.

On the big day, the men of the 303 were up early and ready for the visit from the general. Lefter was waiting at his duty station in the cage at 0800. The door opened and in walked a greenhorn lieutenant that had just recently been assigned as the ASA detachment leader in the British Commonwealth Division. He had on a dusty and wrinkled fatigue uniform. He waved at Lefter and walked straight into the office of Major Soss.

Soon Lefter heard Major Soss revert briefly to his old personality as he yelled, "Get the hell out of here and don't come back until after lunch, and hide your dirty jeep somewhere."

"Where should I hide the jeep?" asked the greenhorn lieutenant.

"Just get out of here and hide it somewhere until our inspection is over," said Major Soss. "Hurry, the general is due here any minute."

The lieutenant ran out the door, started the jeep and drove off. Unfortunately, the lieutenant assumed that the inspection included only the 303rd CRB. He hid the jeep in amongst several vehicles parked across the road from 303 headquarters.

Ten minutes later, Lefter answered a loud knock at the door. It was an Army Sergeant. "The general is chewing my ass up and down about a filthy jeep parked in his motor pool area. He's really pissed off. I finally showed him the 303 CRB on the bumper and he calmed down long enough to send me over here to get your CO."

From his office, Major Soss had overhead the loud talk of the excited sergeant. The major came out of his office and accompanied the sergeant to the general's motor pool parking area.

Lefter went out the door and watched as the major approached the general and saluted. Major Soss stood at rigid attention while the red-faced general chewed on him. After several minutes, Soss saluted briskly, did a snappy turn and trotted back to the 303 headquarters. Lefter had not been able to hear what the general said but it impacted Soss considerably. He was pale faced. He went immediately into his office and closed the door.

General Blark never inspected the 303 headquarters building. Instead, he went immediately to the AG Office. Mighty Joe was in the outer office and saw the general storm in. He walked directly to the office of the colonel in charge. He slammed the door and demanded that Major Soss be court-martialed. The colonel calmly reminded the general that Major Soss was a fellow West Point man and suggested that a transfer might be a more appropriate punishment.

"Look, Fred," said the general, "we both know that Soss is a space case and a piss-poor leader. Here's our chance to get rid of him."

"I agree," said the colonel, "but maybe he just needs to be sent to a hospital for some more psychological treatment."

"OK, Fred," replied the general, "but I'm betting that he won't cut the mustard."

"You're on for ten bucks," said the colonel. "I think he will come out of it and be a good officer."

"Deal," said the general as he shook the hand of his best friend and West Point roommate.

The next day, Major Soss received his orders to leave Korea immediately and report to Walter Reed Hospital in Washington, DC. The men of the 303 were indifferent about his transfer. Although they didn't hate Soss anymore, they still didn't respect him.

Major Soss was replaced by a stern, no-nonsense, spit-and-polish captain. Captain Harrah was about six foot three inches tall and he dressed immaculately. He began his army service at the start of WWII as a private and received combat promotions through the ranks. By the end of WWII, he was a company commander. He had a huge scar running from his right ear to his chin. The scar was from a bayonet wound he suffered during hand to hand combat.

At first, the men of the 303 complained and bitched as Captain Harrah performed the inspections that General Blark had promised. Cleaning the latrine was the standard punishment handed out by the captain for anyone who failed an inspection.

Several guys got to know Shit House Charlie well before they finally shaped up. Shit House Charlie would stand by, smile and watch them cleaning his domain. Then after they finished the cleanup and were leaving, Shit House Charlie would smile and say, "Tank yew, GI."

However, as the captain knew would happen, after several weeks the men began to take pride in their personal appearance, their clean weapons, clean clothes, and clean living areas. Then Captain Harrah eased up somewhat and even drank a beer with them occasionally in the Day Room Tent. The men of the 303 both respected and admired Captain Harrah. Although they were mostly a bunch of desk jockeys with no actual combat experience, they would have followed him into battle. He had proved his leadership ability to them.

Lefter drank less and less. He quit drinking hard liquor completely. While he still went to the EM Club for a beer now and then, he didn't get drunk. He would sip a couple of beers and shoot the bull with the guys. He didn't care much anymore for the Mumblejon game and rarely participated. Usually, he would make some excuse and leave when a game was being organized.

Lefter started using his off duty time to tour the area and take photos. I-Corps opened a photo shop where soldiers could learn to develop and print their own photos. He learned how to develop and print his own film.

Lefter spent more time writing letters to his wife and father. While on CQ duty one night, Lefter spent hours carefully typing a letter on toilet paper.

The letter to his wife was twenty sections long and ended with, "If you think it's tacky to write this letter on toilet paper, you know what you can do with it!" Lefter had changed a lot but he still had his sense of humor.

Months passed and Lefter was again eligible for another R&R. He and Nay went to Tokyo for a week. They went sightseeing, went shopping, sipped beer on the Ginza Strip, and ate like kings. At one of the small Japanese restaurants, Lefter had the tenderest steak he had ever tasted. It was said that, two weeks before slaughtering a steer, the Japanese fed it nothing but grain, and gave it daily massages.

In April of 1954, Lefter rotated back to the States. He had a year left to serve on his three-year enlistment. He was assigned to duty at the National Security Agency in Washington, DC. Again his travel and transfer orders specified "first available transportation" but unfortunately, the first available transportation was a troop ship sailing direct to Seattle, Washington. The trip was boring and uneventful. Lefter was not assigned any duty aboard so he spent the time reading, sleeping and walking around the deck of the ship. Finally, after what seemed like months, the ship reached Seattle.

Lefter and his wife bought a car, and had a second honeymoon as they drove cross-country to his new assignment with the National Security Agency in Washington, DC. Lefter soon found out that he was back in the chicken-shit army he had known before his tour of duty in Korea.

Just before he left Korea, Lefter was recommended for promotion to Sergeant. After giving him a promotion quiz, Lefter's new CO at Arlington Station denied him the promotion the first month of his assignment there. Reason: "baggy socks." Real reason, "new boy on the block must get in line behind the old boys on the block." Lefter got the sergeant promotion without comment the following month.

The NSA was a super secret agency that had just been formed in the last couple of years. Its headquarters in northwest Washington, DC was called a Naval Station. Hundreds of civilians were already employed at the NSA. However, NSA was headed by a high-ranking military man. Lefter was assigned to the mailroom.

The mailroom supervisor, Vera, was a thirty-something-year-old swinging single woman. She wore heavy makeup and, as the troops in Korea would say, was "stacked like a brick shithouse." She didn't say much and seemed to spend most of her time in the office chatting on the telephone. Lefter had the feeling that she had got the job by "political appointment." Eleven other civilian women worked in the mailroom with Lefter.

Joany, whose job was to sort incoming mail, trained Lefter in his mailroom job. Joany trained Lefter by saying, "I will either check off a box on this general routing slip or make a handwritten note on it and attach it to each piece of mail. Your job is to replace it with an original typewritten routing slip."

"That's all, that's my whole job?" replied Lefter.

"That's it," said Joany as she winked at Lefter. Lefter would later find that Joany, a cute little shapely blonde, was barely eighteen years old but lived alone in her own apartment. Periodically, Joany would invite Lefter to stop by her apartment for an after work drink. At Vera's Christmas party, Joany had the gall to ask Lefter's wife, "Can I borrow your man for a weekend sometime?" Lefter began to think of her as "Horny Joany."

Desks in the mailroom were arranged in pods of four, touching back to back and side to side. Joany was directly across from Lefter. Norma, a devoted Christian, sat at the desk next to Lefter and wanted to talk religion with him at every opportunity. She was as persistent toward recruiting Lefter to Christianity as Joany was toward getting Lefter to bed down with her.

Betty sat at the desk across from Norma. Married with two young children, Betty was soon treating Lefter like "one of the girls" and freely telling him of her marital problems. Her husband didn't understand her, especially sexually. "No romance, no foreplay, just wham-bam," said Betty to Lefter.

"Excuse me," replied Lefter as he got up from his chair, "I'm going out for a Coke."

The fundamental problem in the mailroom was that nobody had more than an hour or so of work to accomplish in each eight-hour workday. Lefter's job of typing routing slips could be done in less than an hour per workday. Not only was Lefter's job humiliating and boring, it created a lot of pressure on him because of the work environment.

Several times each day, Horny Joany would wink and purse her lips at him. Bitchy Betty would corner him for a session of complaints about her husband. Preaching Norma would want to have a prayer session with him. Each time one of the "girls" would put the squeeze on him, Lefter would excuse himself and go out for a Coke.

Not only did Lefter have to put up with "the girls," he was having nightmares about the Korean War. Nearly every night he would dream that he was back on the MLR and being overrun by the Chinese. He would wake up shaking and in a cold sweat.

When Lefter became nervous and shaky during waking hours, his wife convinced him to see a doctor. The regular Army physician couldn't find anything to explain Lefter's nervousness so he sent him to an Army psychiatrist.

The psychiatrist told Lefter the nightmares were common for soldiers who had been in a combat area. Time would heal the nightmares but the nervousness and outward shakes were caused by something else. Asking a lot of questions about Lefter's daily life, the doctor found that Lefter was drinking up to a dozen Cokes each day to "escape from the girls."

"One Coke upsets the body's nervous system like having three beers," said the doctor. Lefter substituted the drinking fountain for the Coke machine and the shakes and nervousness went away.

Except for wearing the uniform, contact with the Army was almost non existent. Lefter checked the bulletin board at the Army base once each week on his way home from the NSA. One Saturday morning each month was scheduled for Army training. That Saturday morning was wasted. Show up and sit around for a couple of hours then go home; that was the training.

A couple of months before the end of the budget year, Vera told Lefter that he was to receive a new electric typewriter.

"Don't want one," said Lefter, "I like this manual that I can pound on. The electric typewriters are too sensitive for me."

"OK," said Vera but two months later, over Lefter's protest, a new expensive IBM electric typewriter replaced his manual typewriter.

"Couldn't help it," was her explanation, "the procurement office overrode us. They wanted to use up this year's budget."

Lefter's three-year enlistment was ending soon and he could hardly wait to leave the mailroom malady at the NSA.

"Would you believe it?" asked Lefter to his wife. "They offered me that damn routing slip typing job as a civilian. They promised me a GS-5 pay grade to start and GS-7 in six months."

"What did you tell them?" asked his wife.

"Well," replied Lefter, "I thought about it for a half second then told them to go suck a radish."

"What does that mean?" asked his wife.

"Translated, it means kiss my ass," said Lefter laughing.

A few days later, with his Army discharge in hand, Lefter drove away from the guarded gate of NSA for the last time. He thought of Mewman and yelled at the top of his voice, "FUCK YOU, NSA. FUCK YOU, ARMY."

CHAPTER TWENTY-FIVE

Forty-five years later, in 1990, Lefter retired early as a mid-level manager of a major US corporation. He started researching the Korean War and found a few of his Korean War buddies. More and more, Lefter was thinking about his MLR buddy Mewman and the hundred dollars he gave Lefter for a future drinking party.

Finally, after procrastinating for years, he decided that it was time to bring Mewman home from the UN graveyard at Pusan and have the drinking party. Since Mewman loved to gamble, Lefter selected as a burial place the Southern Nevada Veterans Memorial Cemetery, located at Boulder City, Nevada. Boulder City is just 23 miles south of world's biggest gambling area, Las Vegas.

In December 2002, Lefter mailed a letter or e-mail to the Korean War buddies he had located.

> *Dear Korean War Buddy:*
>
> *Remember the 303CRB and the men we served with? One of our buddies, Mewman, is still in Korea. He is buried at the UN Cemetery at Pusan. I have arranged with the US government to bring Mewman's remains home to be buried at the Veterans Cemetery in Boulder City, Nevada.*
>
> *As you probably remember, Mewman loved to gamble and usually lost his entire month's pay within a few days after each payday. An exception occurred one month when I tried to entice him into starting a savings account in the States. He wouldn't start a savings account because he had a strong feeling that he would never return alive. Instead, he gave me $100 and asked me to have a party on him when I got back in the States. That was over 50 years ago. Now it's time for the party!*
>
> *The Department of Defense has agreed to have the remains*

available for burial at the VA Cemetery at 1p.m. on May 19, 2003. Arrangements have been made with the cemetery for burial at that time and date. The ceremony is intended to take less than 20 minutes. Afterwards, we will meet for drinks in the Mumblejon Room of Mighty Joe's Hotel & Casino in Las Vegas. The first $100 for drinks is on Mewman. Then I'll cover the next $100 of drinks.

    No reservations are necessary. Just show up a little early at the cemetery and we'll get reacquainted prior to the burial and then we'll meet for drinks and a bull session in the Mumblejon Room in Vegas. Please feel free to bring a wife, friend or significant other.

    Hope to see you there,
    John Lefter

PS: On second thought, please let me know if you plan to attend and give me your phone number and/or e-mail address so I can let you know if plans change.

Lefter added the PS statement because it dawned on him that the Army of today might be as good at screwing things up as they were fifty years ago. If they didn't, then maybe this really was the NEW Army that lived up to their slogan, "Be All You Can Be."

Lefter and his wife arrived an hour early at the cemetery office. He was surprised to find Jolcomb, Campbell and Nissing were already there. In the next few minutes, Mighty Joe, Nay and Crovelli arrived with their wives. They made small talk until it was time to leave for the burial site. The cemetery folks were very attentive and gave them each a map with directions to the burial site.

The remains were already at the burial site in a casket suspended above an open grave. A man in Army uniform was standing nearby. He was holding a trumpet. Lefter kept an eye on his watch and at precisely one o'clock he spoke up.

"Thanks for coming. As you all know, Mewman was a unique individual. He was a gross little fellow but very likable. He used filthy language. He had a ready smile. He was a sponge for trouble. He got drunk and did stupid things. But he never meant to hurt anyone except the enemy. He hated the gooks. Some of you may not know that Mewman was an orphan who never knew his parents. He lived in an orphanage until he ran away, lied about his age and joined the Army. At the time of his death he was 27 years old and had been in the Army for twelve years. He was a weird little fellow but he was very likable, and he was our buddy. As you know, he was wounded while saving my life. He recovered from those wounds only to be killed later by a sniper just a few minutes after the cease-fire took effect. Welcome home, little buddy. Rest in peace."

Lefter nodded to the trumpeter and he started playing "Taps." By the time the trumpeter finished handkerchiefs were out and wiping wet eyes.

"I hope to see you all back at the Mumblejon Room in Las Vegas in an hour," said Lefter with a quivering voice. "As I said in my letter, the first $100 of drinks are on Mewman then the next $100 is on me."

"You're not paying for the drinks at this session," said Mighty Joe. "The cost of the whole bull session is on the house."

"What am I going to do with Mewman's $100?" protested Lefter.

"Give it to a charity in Mewman's name. Maybe an orphanage."

"Good plan, I'll do just that, along with my own $100," replied a satisfied Lefter.

The Mumblejon Room bull session was enjoyable, informative and reserved. It didn't have the zest and zeal of the sessions at the EM Club in Korea. *Maybe*, thought Lefter with a smile, *it has something to do with our age. In 1953, we were a bunch of energetic young men looking forward to living a long life. Now, in 2003, we're just a bunch of grizzled old men thankful for one more day of independent living.*

They reminisced for a couple of hours. Then the session broke up and everyone thanked Lefter for organizing the mini-reunion.

"Glad to do it," said Lefter as he shook hands with each one of them and said, "Stay safe, buddy."

"You stay safe, too, buddy," said each of them as they shook Lefter's hand. As they turned and walked away, Lefter knew he would never see them again.

Lefter sat at the table engulfed in a multitude of thoughts for several minutes. Then he turned to his ever-patient wife, took her hand in his and said, "Let's go home sweetheart. It's all over."

BIOGRAPHIES

Sergeant Campbell became a successful illustrator, art director and humor writer for a national greeting card company. After retiring, he wrote three novels. He died November 27, 2002.

****

Crovelli started and operated several successful businesses in the wine country of California. He became Chairman of the Board of a large bank in the Napa Valley. He is now retired and spends a lot of time enjoying fishing and hunting trips in the Western states, Alaska and Canada.

****

Captain Eten reverted to the rank of Master Sergeant although his superiors in ASAP tried to convince him to withdraw his resignation as an officer. He retired after 40 years of Army service. His last assignment was the Sergeant Major of the Army, the highest possible rank that an enlisted man can attain.

****

Jolcomb spent his last year in the Army assigned to Arlington Hall near Washington, DC working at the National Security Agency. He is a retired widower living in North Carolina. It comes as no surprise by anyone who knows him that he is a caring and doting grandfather.

****

General Stoney spent forty years in the Marine Corps. His last assignment was Commander of the Marine Corps. As the highest ranking Marine Corps

Officer, he still spent most of his days talking face to face with the enlisted men of the U.S. Marine Corps. General Stoney retired to Florida and wrote an autobiography called *Once a Jarhead, Always a Jarhead*. He was killed in an auto accident while driving to a Marine Corps Reunion in Atlanta, Georgia.

****

Major Soss spent several weeks in the psychiatry ward of an Army hospital. He made a complete recovery, and finished 25 years of Army service working in staff positions. He retired as a Lieutenant Colonel. He is now deceased.

****

Nay went to Harvard Law School and graduated with honors, then joined a large New York City law firm. He rose to the top position in the law firm before retiring. He now resides in Florida during the winters and on a farm in Ohio during the summers.

****

Nissing was discharged from the Army in Tokyo and became a diplomatic courier making regular round trip flying runs to San Francisco and other locations around the world. He is now retired and lives on his own ranch in New Mexico.

****

Sergeant Noitra, after many months of red tape, finally got Smoky transferred to his base in South Carolina. Later, Noitra was KIA in the Vietnam War. He received two Silver Star Medals for heroism in the jungle battles of Vietnam. Smoky lived out his days as a pampered and happy alcoholic mascot.

****

Quigley received an honorable discharge from the Army and returned to his home state of Mississippi. No further information is available.

****

Sergeant Thomas transferred to the Army Special Services Branch in Tokyo and became the Club Manager of the famous Ernie Pyle Club in Tokyo. Named for the famous WWII war correspondent Ernie Pyle, who was KIA during the invasion of Okinawa, this six-story building was a central focus for men on R&R from the Korean War. After 25 years of Army service he retired and bought two nightclubs in Tokyo. When last seen, he was riding back and forth to work in a chauffeur-driven limousine.

****

Mighty Joe never went back to law school. He got into the commercial real estate business in Las Vegas, Nevada and made a fortune. He had a large casino built and called it Mighty Joe's Place.

In the center of the casino's enormous gaming floor is a unique slot machine. Ten feet tall, it is named Mighty Joe's Mumblejon. Instead of cherries, bells and the other typical symbols, it has beer cans with a variety of labels. The machine has five wheels. In addition to the beer cans, one wheel of the machine has a PFC stripe, the next wheel a CPL stripe, and the third wheel a SGT stripe. The fourth wheel has a devilish-looking character with a rye smile labeled Mumblejon and the fifth wheel has a wide, friendly-smiling character dressed as a priest and labeled Mighty Joe. If all three of these stripes plus Mumblejon and Mighty Joe line up after a spin, the payoff is $1,000,000.

Another unique thing about the machine is that it has no means of accepting money itself. The machine is attended by a real live human being 24 hours per day. Mighty Joe himself attends the machine personally when veterans are holding reunions at his casino hotel. It costs ten dollars per spin with one exception; any military man or woman in uniform or any military veteran gets one free spin and a beer on the house.

****

Lefter earned a degree in Civil Engineering from Washington State University. He spent 30 years working for a large, private, electric utility company. He is now retired and lives near Portland, Oregon with his wife of 50 years. During retirement, he wrote a novel based on his experiences in the Korean War.